KIN & KIND

The Shard of Elan, Book 4

Laura VanArendonk Baugh

ÆClipse Press
Indianapolis, IN

Cover design by Damonza

ISBN 978-1-63165-030-7
www.Aeclipse.com

To Luca, who never once made it onto the cover. I'm sorry.
For that, and for a lot of other things.

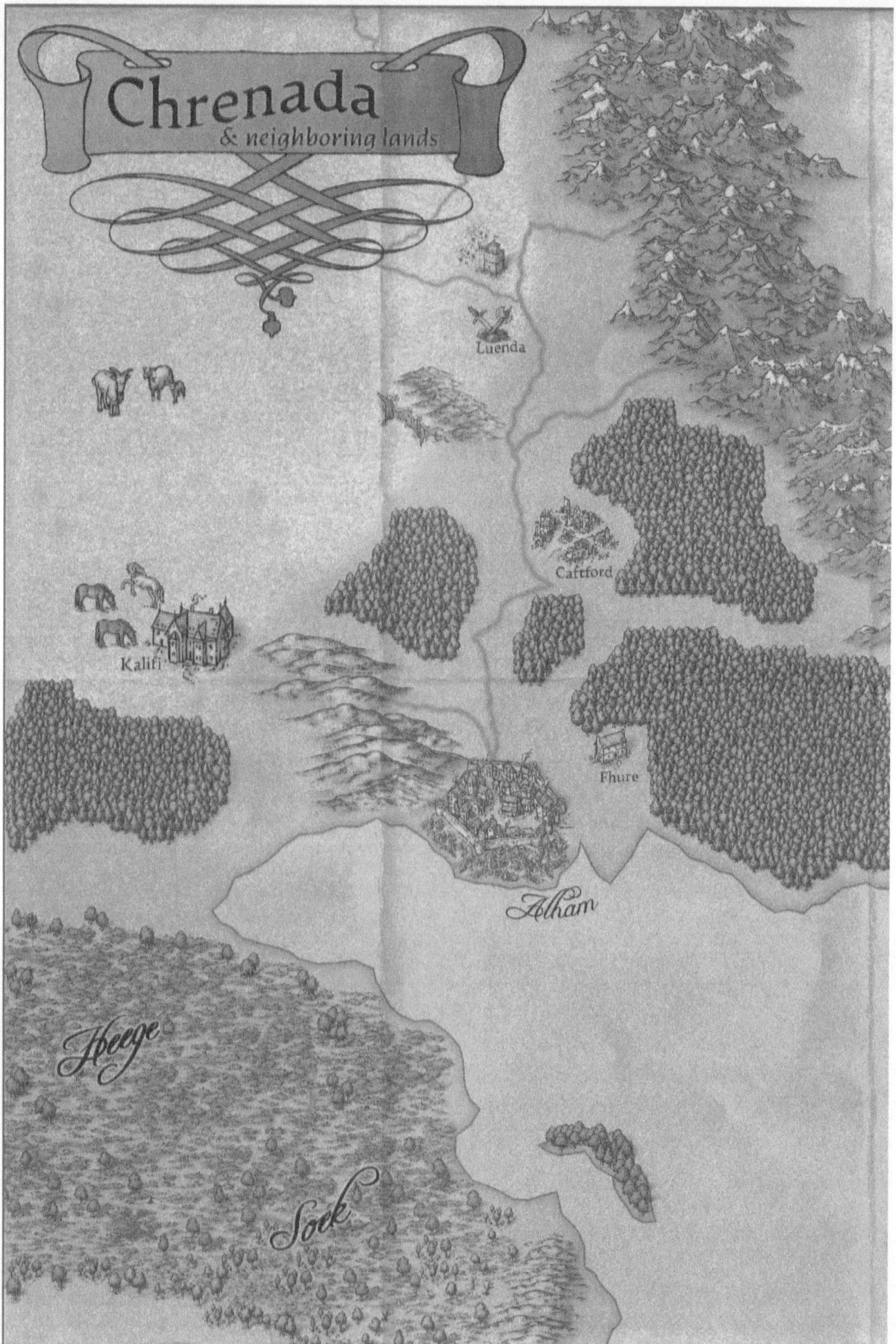
Chrenada
& neighboring lands
Luenda
Caftford
Kalifi
Fhure
Alham
Heege
Soek

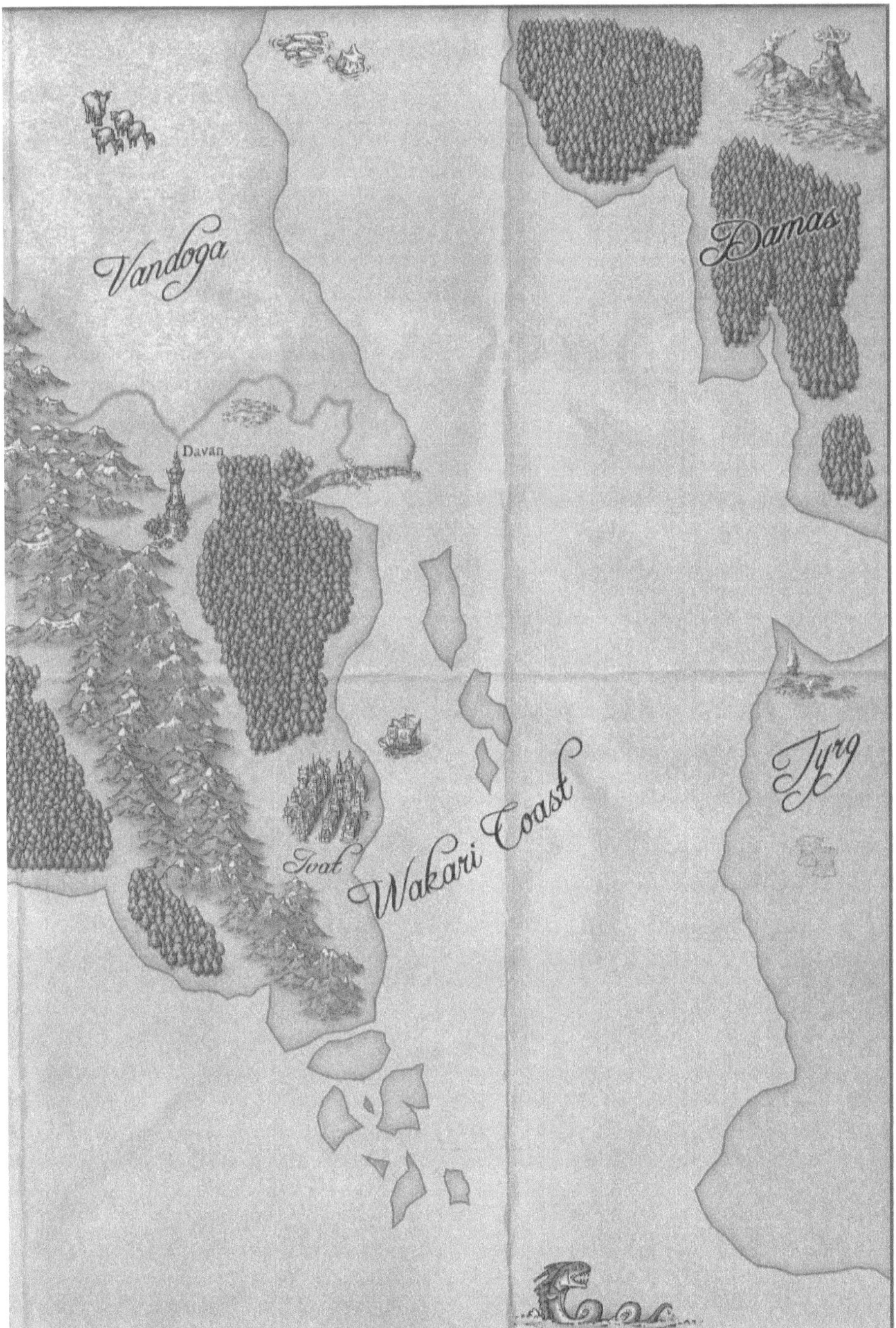
Vandoga
Davan
Damas
Tyrg
Ivat
Wakari Coast

CHAPTER 1

Shianan did not like being married.

He had not seen his wife—what a strange word—since the moment of their handfasting and vows, and the not-knowing was a new kind of torment.

He sank lower in the bath, so the warm water lapped his ears. Around him, other soldiers made quiet jokes or reached for towels as they emerged steaming into the chilly air.

Shianan was accustomed to not knowing the situation of other military units in separate campaigns; he had learned long ago to focus on his own command and not waste strength elsewhere. But that was before Ariana was assigned to other commands, and against a new enemy with unfamiliar tactics.

He rose from the pool and squeezed water from his long hair. Strictly speaking, Marshal Vanguilder's deployment was not even late. It was foolish to worry. He dressed and tied back his hair, hating how he hesitated to extend his sore arm. No need to worry before they were due back. He went out of the bathhouse.

The man who accosted Shianan in the street was not one he had intended to speak with ever again, nor even see. But Flamen Ande stepped forward as Shianan rounded the corner, moving into his path with one hand stretched as if to catch his arm if necessary. "Commander Becknam."

Shianan stared at him. No suitable greeting managed to work past the sudden jam of questions and resentments that crowded his mind.

Ande smiled, a spider's greeting. "I expect you did not anticipate seeing me again."

"That is a fair statement." Shianan took a breath and summoned his best practice of saying neutral things while withdrawing his reactions to a place where they could not be touched. "You have been released by the court."

"I have." Ande straightened his blue flamen's robes, flaring them though they had not been crooked. "In the end, they finally saw that I was an innocent man falsely accused."

Not innocent, Shianan thought savagely. Ande had not plotted to destroy the protective shield, but he was anything but innocent.

Words fought in his head. *We are none of us innocent.*

"I wonder if we might sit and speak," Ande was saying.

Shianan's stomach tensed. "I cannot imagine we have so much to say to one another. I performed my duty in negotiating with you, and you performed your task in Alham. Surely after all this, you are anxious to return home."

"Oh, I am. But we should have a drink together first." Ande smiled, an amiable monster. "You have something I want."

Shianan's blood went frigid in his veins, and for a moment he could not move. He had stolen Luca, from the prison where he had been taken with his master Ande. After that, Luca had been given to Jarrick—but would that stand under law if he had not been Shianan's to give? And if Jarrick could not legally take him from Chrenada, then perhaps Luca had not been truly freed, and then—

It was too much, too complicated, and too dangerous. For one wild moment Shianan wanted to knife Flamen Ande in the gut, a quick upward stab to ensure a long bleed, and end the possibility of what he was saying.

But they were standing in the market, with men and women passing around them, and it was possible Ande had chosen this place precisely to avoid such a reaction. The king's bastard could not murder an exonerated prisoner in the street.

His face had betrayed him, for Ande was smiling.

The key to surviving an ambush was to avoid going still with shock. Shianan rallied himself and entered battle. "I suppose we can talk." The key was to react, to force the fighting to the ground of your choosing. But Shianan would not bring him to his own office—he would not risk Luca entering to find Ande at the desk. "There's a little public room near here, the Rollicking Wyvern."

"I don't know the place, but I trust your judgment when it comes to drinks," Ande said. "Please, lead the way."

Shianan gestured ahead on the street. Next he should signal for reinforcements. He scanned the crowd until he saw one of the children who earned coins for messages, and he whistled her over. "Go to the White Mage and ask him please to join Bailaha in the Rollicking Wyvern. If you don't find him in his office, look elsewhere. Someone in the Wheel will know his home, but try the Wheel first. And speed matters."

The girl looked at the two coins he put in her hand, and her eyes popped wide. "I can fly like a Ryuven," she promised, and she took off.

Shianan avoided Ande's smirk. Let the man think what he would. Shianan was not prepared for this fight, and he needed someone who knew the law—knew it, knew how to protest it, and knew how to break it.

They entered the Rollicking Wyvern and took a small table in the corner, where the coming argument would be less visible from the street. If Shianan were going to kill this man later, he did not want their conflict to be widely known. A servant came to ask their preference, pushing sleeves back over dull cuffs, and Shianan fought down his frantic impulse and instead asked for watered ale. He would need his head for this.

Ande asked for wine, and the look he gave Shianan suggested he wouldn't be paying for it.

Shianan set his forearms on the table, flat and uncompromised, and took a steadying breath. This was battle, for high stakes, but he had fought many battles. He fixed his eyes on Flamen Ande. "Perhaps you should say plainly what it is you want."

The flamen was gaunt and showed the wear of prison, but already he had reclaimed his old air of expectant authority. Perhaps the exoneration had given him confidence. Perhaps he now felt himself untouchable. "When I was falsely arrested for your shield's collapse, I had some property with me, and it was stolen. I am told you were the one who took that property, and so I have come to ask its return."

Shianan opened his hands. "If you mean the slave you had with you, as it happens, I have a bill of sale for him. I bought him from two merchants coming out of Cascais. They purchased him at a regular market, after he left Alham."

Ande sniffed. "Your forged papers will not—"

"The papers are perfectly valid. It may take some time to find the merchants, but Alham is on their usual route and it could be done, and they can testify to the sale." They could also testify that Luca had told them he was stolen, Shianan realized with horror, but he rushed over that. "You won't find it so easy to ignore a legal bill of sale."

"It is not legal if I can demonstrate that the purchased property was stolen property."

He was probably right. Shianan did not know. He was unarmed for this conflict. Sweet Holy One, what if at last he lost Luca, and to Ande again?

What if Luca had freed Ande only to be bound to him once more?

"Surely he cannot be of so much use to a Gehrn priest. Why do you want him back?"

Ande looked at him flatly. "I had Luca for a long time. You could say I had gotten used to him. It wouldn't be the same going back without him."

Shianan stared. "You owe him a debt. You owe him for speaking the words that saved your life."

"And perhaps for waiting so long to speak them." Ande gazed back unflinchingly.

"Luca saved your life."

"And he neglected to save me from arrest." Ande sat back in his chair. "If he saw the blood on the desk, then he knew at the time I was falsely accused. He knew all that time, and he said nothing. I have spent months in prison, under hardship and torment and false accusations, while he collaborated with the enemies who accused me."

"If you believe he was collaborating with your enemies, then why would he have spoken at the end to save you?"

"Because in the end, training carries true. Strict discipline means that at last he was compelled to tell the truth obediently. Strict discipline made him truthful, and so it is for his own good that he must return with me."

Shianan felt his jaw drop. "Do you think that he spoke to save you because of what you did to him?"

The high priest did not answer, for the White Mage came in the door. He was not alone; Mage Elysia Parma was with him. They spotted Shianan, and he saw their expressions shift when they recognized Flamen Ande. They came stiffly to the table and seated themselves.

"Well, I suppose we're all here now." Ande looked around at them. "And what is it that you all must be together to say to me?"

"There is nothing to say yet," began Mage Hazelrig. "We've only just arrived, and we don't know the question."

"Well, that's easy enough. I've come to request the return of my property. No more, no less." He looked at Mage Parma with a cynical eye. "I am told the Silver Mage has made a point of studying the sacred aspects of our order, so I am certain she can speak to the legitimacy of my request. By our rules, and by the laws of this land, I am due my stolen property."

Mage Hazelrig's face darkened. "Did you so recently receive your freedom in so narrow an escape, and your first thought is for possession of a slave?"

"I only want my own property."

The drinks came, and Shianan seized his with unseemly haste. He had meant to ration the watered alcohol slowly, but Mage Hazelrig's discomfiture rattled him, and he drank half in one draught.

Mage Parma caught the servant's eye. "Two more wines, please." Her tone was frosty.

The servant left, and the four of them stared at one another.

Flamen Ande sat forward in his chair. "The truth of it is, I have a valid legal claim, and every person at this table knows it. You can argue it in court, but ultimately you know my claim will stand. Now, I have no idea why one ordinary and mediocre slave should be so important to two mages of the Circle and a military commander, but that is not my concern. My concern is my property, and my rights."

"If you mean to take this to a court of law," said Ewan Hazelrig, "then why ask first in a public room?"

"There is no reason this could not be done simply." Flamen Ande sat back comfortably and looked around at them. "As my claim is legitimate, you could simply do the right and expedient thing by handing him over to me. There would be no need to waste our time in court."

Shianan sat rigid in his chair. He thought he might break the cup in his hand.

"But, as it seems the right and simple thing is not your interest, then I suppose we could come to another path. That could be going to court and working through the legal ramifications of his original theft and subsequent illegal sales. Or, it's possible that we could come to another arrangement."

Mage Parma's mouth twisted. "There it is."

"What do you mean by that? I am trying to be accommodating, since this property is clearly so important to some."

"I am only noting that arrangements seem to be a common solution for the Gehrn."

Shianan felt useless, sitting still in his chair, but he was happy to cede the field to the mages. He was a soldier of action, while they were more accustomed to bureaucratic arguments.

"I am told that two of my order visited you, Mage Parma," said Flamen Ande. "They reported that you seemed rather resistant to arrangements, and indeed to the idea of negotiation in general."

"Negotiation is not what was offered. They asked me to go outside the law as a particular favor to the Gehrn. As you already know."

Ande raised an eyebrow. "I can assure you, this matter of my slave is entirely inside the law. Again, as we each of us already know."

Shianan's mind was reeling. He thought of Prince Soren, but the prince could not counter the law of the land. Even the king could not simply countermand a law. If Ande's claim was valid, and it seemed it would be, then there was nothing even Soren could do.

Mage Hazelrig's face was set in deep lines of concern. Looking at him made Shianan despair. If the White Mage could see no way out, then there was none.

He had utterly failed Luca. Ande had come for him, and Shianan could do nothing.

Mage Parma looked from Shianan to Hazelrig, and her eyes rested on the White Mage for a long time. At last she stood. "Then I suppose there is only one thing to do," she said, "and that is to accept the inevitable." She turned and called across the room, "Never mind the wine." She looked back at all of them. "Come please. I have something to show that might make this easier to accept."

There was nothing to make this easier to accept. Shianan set down coins for his drink and the high priest's, and he rose to follow the Silver Mage out. He kept his eyes from Ande's smug face, lest he be tempted to strike it.

Could he? If he found the high priest alone at night and beat him, could he drive him from Alham without Luca?

Dare he do more?

Mage Parma stopped in the street and turned to face them. "What I have to share is not for you, commander. I am sorry, but I must ask you to leave us."

Shianan didn't understand. "But if this is about—"

"I know the slave is important to you, and I am sorry to ask you to trust me on this. But I must ask you to trust me. As Flamen Ande says, our only remaining option is negotiation, and what I have to offer is not something that is yours to give."

Shianan did not understand her at all, but the idea that she would barter for Luca was a thin line in a stormy sea. He jerked his head once in a nod, and then he made himself turn and walk away without looking back, imagining Ande's smug smile and recalling

Hazelrig's look of deep distress.

Sweet Holy One, let them find a way. Let Luca stay. His heart burned in him, and his fingers twitched, and he wished he had finished even the watered ale.

CHAPTER 2

Ewan Hazelrig stepped aside at the door, putting the Gehrn priest between Elysia and himself. That was good tactics, and it did not feel right to go through a door first, leaving his back to the Gehrn.

Elysia Parma lifted a hand to gesture. "Walk with me please, Flamen Ande."

The three of them passed through Alham, moving away from the Wheel and the Naziar and down beside the market. They passed neat rows of townhouses, and Elysia paused at one street corner. "Which of these is the Gehrn's house?"

Flamen Ande indicated the second from the end, a small but sturdy structure nestled between its siblings. It needed paint and brightening, but it was far from shabby. "That one."

"That is where your priests have been staying during your trial?"

"And where I will stay now, until I return to Davan."

"I see." She picked a strand of hair from her face. "How many Gehrn are here in Alham just now? I believe I have seen three."

Ewan looked from the priest to the mage and said nothing. He did not know Elysia's mind on this errand; best to stay out of her way.

"There were seven of us here," Ande answered. "I know Flamen Mennti and Flamen Gregorio paid you visits."

"Yes, that's right. I suppose it's only polite to ask after them."

"Flamen Mennti is well, thank you. I have not seen Flamen Gregorio since my release. He has not been in the townhouse for several days, it seems."

"Oh, I know where he is," Elysia said helpfully. "You had only to ask. I can take you to him now."

Ande looked surprised. "It's not appropriate for any in the order to recreate outside without informing his commanding priests."

"I suppose you can address that when we get there. This way."

They walked on and took a turn toward Elysia's own home. Ewan knew then what Elysia meant, and he walked a little wide in case a flanking position might be required.

The most direct route took a narrower street that fed into an alley. Between tall walls the passage dimmed in the evening light, and when Elysia stopped they no longer cast shadows. "This is where I wanted to bring you, Flamen Ande."

The ground was wet and mucky, mud over stone, and their feet squelched faintly as they faced one another. A few empty crates waited against a shop wall to be refilled.

Ande looked around, and the corners of his mouth turned down. "I don't understand. I thought you were taking me to Flamen Gregorio."

"Yes."

"Well? Where is he?"

Elysia held his eyes, but her voice was soft. "You're standing in him."

Ande stared at her and then looked down, lifting one foot slightly from the mud. "I...I don't understand."

"Oh, and there." Elysia pointed at some flaking grey fragments caught against a crate near the wall, in an eddy of the wind. "That's likely the last of him."

Ande lifted his head and fixed her with a horrified glare. "What happened?"

Elysia kept her hands open as she spoke in a low, clear voice. "First of all, if you send a man to intimidate me, make sure he is capable of doing so. He pushed too sharply and too unwisely, and at last he picked a fight he could not win. He chose this place to press his foolish demand, and so here is where it ended."

"You killed him?" He sounded at once incredulous and furious.

"I defended myself from a fanatical ruffian who repeatedly threatened me and assaulted me. He did not return to the Gehrn townhouse. But that brings us to the question of the Gehrn townhouse."

Ewan took another step back, letting Elysia take the conversation and giving himself space to react if necessary.

"The letters Commander Shianan Becknam carried to Davan—were those given to you, Flamen Ande?"

"What has this to do with Gregorio?"

"I know the content of those letters, Flamen Ande, because I drafted them. I know they verified the identity of our messengers, explained our need of the Shard of Elan, and offered handsome payment for it."

Ande scowled. "Yes, I received them. What of it?"

"When Becknam returned with the Shard, he explained he had

offered his townhouse as a Gehrn site in Alham, since the priests were reluctant to give up their unique possession without compensation." Elysia lifted her chin. "What happened to the offer I wrote, Flamen Ande? You remembered it well enough when you came to collect it before you performed your rituals. Did you think to extort a military officer for the safety of the whole kingdom?"

"You know nothing of how our negotiations progressed," Ande growled.

"Becknam would have delivered sealed letters, or they would have been worthless as attestation of identity, so he did not know what you were offered. I wonder if you also kept their contents from your own priests? Did you neglect to mention the promised payment to them, asking instead for the townhouse for the Gehrn and thinking to keep the royal payment for yourself?"

"No!" he snapped. "No, our order does not permit the keeping of personal property."

"Which is why it is so odd that you had a slave to bring with you."

Ande's face settled into established lines, more comfortable with this defense. "A slave may belong to the order and serve its head. I brought him to fill a necessary role in a ritual."

"And now you will leave him, as you will leave the townhouse." Elysia did not raise her voice, did not harden her tone. She simply spoke as if observing the sky was blue and the ground was beneath them, her words equally incontrovertible. "Whatever ownership you contrived by misleading the commander has been lost, as Bailaha promised you the townhouse for as long as the Great Circle held the Shard. When it was stolen by the Ryuven, your claim to the townhouse ended. And no new contract has been negotiated since the Shard's return."

Ande's eyes blazed.

"You misled an officer into giving up his own property for the good of the kingdom, which says much of both his character and yours. You will leave it and Alham by the morning after tomorrow, which provides you adequate time to pack and find passage. You'll need that time to pack with your own hands, as your Gehrn tenets are quite specific on the merits of personal labor, and it would be poor observance to let a slave cheat you of the practice of physical and mental strength. So the slave will stay with Commander Becknam."

Ande, gaunt and bruised, set his jaw and glared at the Silver

Mage. "You have no authority," he growled. "You have no right to evict me, to keep me from my property. And if you will play at word games, so will I. I will call upon the people and tell them what this bastard has done, how he attempted to bribe the Gehrn to claim credit for bringing the Shard of Elan and how he stole from a man unjustly imprisoned. I will invoke their disdain for a man already disgraced and so recently accused of attacking the prince. What if a witness to that could be found? The prince was unconscious, and a searcher might have come across the attempted murder just in time to see and interrupt. I will raise riots in the streets, I will—"

"Push me," Elysia said shortly. Her eyes were stone, and her voice was no longer as calmly factual. "Push me as Flamen Gregorio did. You want a war, Flamen Ande; you may have one, and it can start here, in this moment, and you may be the glorious first to die."

For a long moment they stood there, eyes locked, and Ewan was not sure how it would end. They could not strike down a man, even a Gehrn priest, for speaking in the street. He had to wait until Ande acted.

But the Gehrn spat on the ground, narrowly missing Elysia. "I will leave this corrupt and weak city behind, and good riddance. I will return to our untarnished rural home, and when the coming wars engulf all of Chrenada and the world, it is my wish that you will be consumed slowly in their fires while the noble warriors of the Gehrn rise to claim your spoils."

"Be careful. You're spitting upon one of your noble warriors."

For an instant Ewan thought Ande would strike her, but the Gehrn preferred weaker victims, and so he turned with a huff of his blue robes and stalked down the street to the wider lanes of the marketplace.

Elysia waited until he had disappeared into the street, and then she let out a long breath, working her jaw to loosen it. "Vile man," she muttered.

Ewan looked at her with an expression of long forbearance. "You enjoyed that, and don't pretend to deny it."

Elysia raised an eyebrow. "The hallmark of a good worker is to take pleasure in a job well done."

"You nearly started a war."

"That would have been kind of me, granting his life's ambition. A pity it would have been over so quickly." She pushed her hair behind her shoulders and adjusted her silver robes, small gestures of control and structure and recovery. For all her calm bravado, she had been uncomfortable, too. "I am sorry for the people of Davan."

"That is another concern for another day," Ewan said. "Let's go and inform the commander. And then you will come to supper, won't you? You don't want to go home alone and remember him all through your evening." And he did not want her home alone, in case the Gehrn took their eviction poorly. Elysia could take care of herself, but a small battle on a city street would do no one good.

She nodded. "I would love supper, thank you."

Shianan sat at his desk, gnawing his lip and his thumb and staring blindly at the papers before him. When he tried not to think of Ande, his mind filled with soldiers falling under ambush, Kuolema thrashing in the water, mages gasping that the Ryuven magic overran theirs.

When Luca entered, moving stiffly but with a cheerful greeting, Shianan cut him off with a curt gesture. "Out," he said gruffly, with a gesture cut short by his aching shoulder. He could not bear to look at Luca, not while everything hung in the awful balance.

Luca hesitated for only a moment, stung, and then he nodded as if nothing were wrong. "Of course. I will be in the quarters. If you should need something, call."

Shianan wanted to apologize, wanted to explain, but he didn't want Luca to know. Shianan didn't want to see his expression when he learned the doom that hung over him. He stared at the reports, their ink blurring into rivers and puddles before his glazed eyes, and wished with all his might.

He could hide Luca—send him away, and then tell Ande that he had run away. But that was hardly safer; a captured fugitive would suffer even before he was turned over to the Gehrn priest.

A knock sounded at the door, and Shianan leapt to his feet. He rushed to it before Luca could come from the other room and opened it to find the two mages. Immediately he held up a hand to prevent their speaking. He stepped outside the office and closed the door behind him.

With Luca safely barred away from any chance of hearing, he faced the two mages and braced himself. "Please, tell me something was arranged. If it's money he wants, I will get money." He would sell Fhure.

They shook their heads in unison. "I don't think it will come to that," said Mage Hazelrig.

Mage Parma's mouth curled in disdain. "I am pleased to tell you, your lordship, Flamen Ande has relinquished his claim. If you should hear from him again, I would appreciate being notified immediately. But it is my belief that he will not trouble you again with his request."

Shianan stared. "What did you do? What did you offer him? If there's something I owe—"

"There is nothing you owe me, your lordship, and it would be beneficial to both of us if you would not offer again. The business I concluded with Flamen Ande was business between himself, myself, and the kingdom of Chrenada, but primarily between the Gehrn and myself. It was not a transaction that involved you, and you want no stock in this trade."

Shianan, confused, looked to Mage Hazelrig, who shook his head tightly. "It was a negotiation initiated by Flamen Ande, and negotiation concluded by the interested parties. That is all you need to know, with the conclusion that Luca will not be returning to Davan with him."

Joy, cautious and slow, began to bubble deep within Shianan. He looked back and forth between them, reading their faces for hedging or under-confidence, but as they gave him steady and reliable looks, the fountain within him began to grow. "Oh thank you, thank you so much. If I can—" He wanted to leap forward and embrace them each in turn, but they were mages of the Circle, the Silver and the White, and they were in full view of the courtyard, and so he did not.

"If there is ever anything I can do," he said to each of them, looking back and forth. "If there is ever anything I can do for you, I owe you a debt, and you have only to ask." There was not much service he could likely render to a mage of the Circle, but he understood his obligation.

Mage Hazelrig shook his head. "The truth is, neither of us wanted to see that man get his way. Whether or not he destroyed the shield intentionally, he did at the least destroy it through omission, and our lives would've been very different for the past year without his actions. I will not say it was a pleasure, but I will say that any debt you think you may owe is probably not as great as you imagine."

"I will not say it was a pleasure," said Mage Parma, "but it was no chore."

Shianan nodded, not fully understanding but understanding enough. "Please, I hope that neither of you will say anything to Luca. If he never knows of this, I will be glad."

They each nodded. "Of course."

Shianan drew a long, deep, clean breath. "Thank you, my lord and lady mage. Thank you very much."

They nodded again. "Oh, and one more thing," Mage Parma said. "The Gehrn have no further need of a townhouse here in Alham. I am not sure of the exact paperwork required, but I think a natural reversion to you should be expected."

Shianan blinked. "What did you say to him?"

Mage Hazelrig coughed. "We have a meeting to attend. There are decisions to be made about the Ryuven raids, after all."

"We must get back to the Wheel," said Mage Parma. "Take care, your lordship."

The two mages turned and started back across the courtyard, and Shianan looked after them with a lighter heart than he'd had in a long time.

CHAPTER 3

Garl Asher took a steadying breath and wished Esar wasn't such a sniveling idiot. It was difficult enough to do this work without having to convince two people instead of one. "Now look, it'll be in and out, easy as walks, safe as locks."

He wondered if *safe as locks* was the wrong choice of idiom, given that this whole endeavor was to get around locks, but he guessed Esar wouldn't be given to questioning his turn of phrase.

Indeed, Esar was busy fretting. "I don't know. It's one thing to cut a purse, or even to cut a throat out on the open road where there's no one much to see. But to walk into one of the biggest trade houses along the whole Wakari Coast—it just feels different. Dangerous."

"Dangerous?" Garl spat into the dust of the road. "Didn't you help to throw over an entire mercantile caravan on the open road, guards and all?"

Esar bristled a little. "I more than helped. I did most of the talking to bring over the guards who were with us."

"All right, then, you did, and look what you did." Garl swallowed his protest that he had been the more charismatic brother, who had talked many of the hired guards into joining their betrayal and looting the caravan. "And what did that net you? Quite a lot of hard coin, from the goods we took and the slaves we sold. And wasn't that dangerous? Of course it was! And that's why it paid so very well. But this—no one is fighting back with this."

Garl Asher had done the role of guard-turned-brigand several times, targeting greater caravans and merchants in succession. He had brought his elder brother, a thief in his own right, into his more recent jobs in the hopes of minimizing risk by appearing to have a more organized contingent of thieves when confronting guards he thought he could turn. It had worked, but it had also meant more arguing with Esar over pointless small tasks that Garl should have been able to dictate, as the more experienced turncoat and the brains of the team, while Esar thought as the elder sibling he should carry some authority.

Their last projects had been their most risky, turning on caravans to not only rob but enslave most of their victims and sell them at a hurried discount in a nearby market. It was a calculated risk;

expensive slaves might be scrutinized, and proof of training and provenance requested, but cheap labor sold fast and without attention to detail.

The first attempt had gone just as well as his best hopes, and they had made thousands of pias in a few days and then left the market town of Cascais far behind, without any hint in the local sales records of where they were going. Even if one of the unfortunate new slaves protested, it was unlikely they would be believed and less likely they would know the names and location of the guards who had turned on them. It had been a simple and profitable scheme, and one they had duplicated twice since.

"It did pay well," Esar agreed. "Which is why we should consider staying to it instead of trying something more. We might be reaching beyond our grasp."

Garl rolled his eyes. "You would ignore such a prize as this?" He took up the thin document wallet and shook it at his brother. "You would let something like this fall into your hand—straight into your hand, not a bit of extra effort—and just leave it by the wayside, without even trying to receive its bounty?"

Esar frowned. "I don't know that it works like you think."

Garl had to admit the possibility. He and Esar did not live in the rarefied world of letters of credit. "Look, I have seen these used before, by men I was guarding, even legitimately. I know how they work. It's dangerous for rich men to carry their riches with them"—he grinned knowingly—"and it's difficult to walk around with a whole crate of coins and jewels on your back. So they carry their wealth in the form of a letter, which they present to a house of exchange, who makes gold available to them as they will."

Esar did not seem convinced. "Where does the house of exchange get the gold?"

"What?"

"If rich men bring letters of credit to the house, and they all want gold to spend against their rich names, where does the house get the gold for them all? If they've all left their gold in Ivat or Alham or where else they came from?"

"Why, other rich men have put their gold in the house, of course. So they can take their own letters to another branch to exchange."

"But it's just a matter of faith that the letter is any good. So the house of exchange has to send for the gold."

"Er, maybe. I suppose they do, sometimes."

"So then the gold is carried after all."

"Yes. But not by the rich men." Garl was growing annoyed with the explanation. "And to our purposes, it is far simpler to rob the rich men than the caravans with their guards. And it is easier to carry a letter of credit than a chest of gold."

"What advantage is it to the house of exchange?"

Garl was not prepared for this line of questioning. "What?"

"Why should they take the risk and expense of transporting the gold and giving it to the men who have letters?"

This was moving beyond Garl's limited knowledge. "I suppose there is a fee. Maybe a percentage of the credit."

"Will they ask us for the fee? What if it's more than we have?"

"What? No! The fee will be deducted from whatever it is we take from the house of exchange. We won't have to pay anything up front." Garl was pretty sure of this and even more resolved to appear certain before his doubting brother.

Esar frowned, trying to work out the hypothetical math.

Garl waved the wallet again to fix his attention on what mattered. "Stop and listen. We have a letter here that entitles the bearer to a full third of an Ivat merchant house. Do you hear that? A full third of an Ivat merchant house! We can draw more money than you've ever seen in your life, more money than you've dreamed of. We can buy women and serving slaves and a townhouse and live fat and glossy like a couple of contented pigs. Even if they hold back a fee, we'll still have more money than you'd make in two hands' worth of thieving jobs. All for the taking, all for just walking in and asking for it."

Esar wanted to believe, Garl could see it. The greed glistened in his brother's eyes, hazed by a remnant of fear. Esar had always been more inhibited.

Garl would carry him over. "You don't have to say anything. You don't even have to go in if you don't want; I can do it all. You can wait safely outside and I'll come to meet you. There's just one name on the letter, after all."

The greed sparked with fresh energy. "You want to pick it up all by yourself? Without anyone watching?"

"Not like—you can come if you want, of course. I just meant, if you were scared to go into the house of exchange, you didn't—"

"I'm not scared to walk inside," Esar snapped. "I can walk

where I like, like any free man, and I'm not ashamed to enter a house of exchange where the rich men of the city go."

"That's not what I meant."

"And I won't let you carry the key to a treasure in by yourself and take it by yourself and just say with a word that you'll share it out later," Esar continued. "I've seen you promise loyalty and safety to men you planned to murder, and I know what your word is worth."

"Now wait," Garl snapped, his ire piqued. "That's something else altogether. That's not family. What I promise to fat rich pigeons to soothe them has nothing to do with my word to you. You are family, and I will not cut you out."

"Then you won't mind if I come along."

"Then I—you great wool-for-brains, that is exactly what I have been trying to get you to do."

Esar frowned at him suspiciously.

Garl sighed. "Do you have any clothes without stains and with less wear? We don't need to be in fine clothes to pass; younger sons are among caravans often enough, and they take some scuff and wear on the road. The letter is the thing, and we have that."

CHAPTER 4

Soren turned restlessly upon his bed, squeezing his pillow higher or pushing it away, but nothing cleared the persistent images from his mind's eye.

He had known, of course, but he had never *known*.

He'd heard the debates in the council, endlessly repetitive arguments over whether slave rebellions should be suppressed with greater ferocity or quelled with a dangled possibility of earning freedom through diligent work. He'd heard the philosophical platforms, whether slaves were incapable of honor or whether those enslaved through their criminal or irresponsible choices, or through the choices of their criminal or irresponsible parents, could ever aid society as law-abiding and responsible freemen. He'd known abuses happened, as within any large system, and he'd known discipline could be strict.

But he had never realized. He had never understood beyond mere knowledge.

He knew Luca was dear to Shianan. He himself loved Ethan as family and trusted him far beyond his courtier friends. To see what had been done to Luca, to know it was considered normal and even necessary, and not in coercion but with a willing witness...

To know that it was not the worst that had been done...

He wanted to push shut the door newly opened, to dismiss Luca's torture as an excessive aberration in a largely functional system, to pretend what he had heard of Luca's experiences was an outlying example of abuse by a cult that glorified violence, to believe these incidents could not be typical or common. He wanted to believe his life had not been in ignorance, merely untroubled by the occasional but uncommon atrocity.

But that would be dishonest, he knew, just as his ignorance of what the king had done to Shianan had been wrong.

Soren threw back the blankets and let the cold air wash over him, squeezing his eyes against memory.

It was not true that slaves could not have honor. He had heard enough to know Luca hated his former master, feared him, had every reason to rejoice in his arrest and downfall—but Luca had gone to testify at great cost to himself in defense of the man he hated, simply because it was unjust to sentence a man for a crime he had not committed. No one could argue again that a slave could not be honorable or trustworthy.

Soren tried to imagine coming upon someone hurting Ethan in such a way, and he knew he would have been more vengeful than Shianan—but Shianan knew the reality of the world, knew what he could and could not protest, knew he could not protect his friend but needed the prince to do it.

Soren rolled again, shoving his pillow. But the prince could not protect Luca. Even if Soren wanted it to be different, the world rested too heavily on the shoulders of slaves. Slave labor planted crops, cooked meals, cleaned houses, built bridges, laid roads, delivered cargo across kingdoms. Enslaved criminals became profitable instead of harmful. The labor market was as strong as any other in the economy; even a prince, even a king could not strike it away without riotous protest and financial collapse.

And now Soren understood the danger of knowledge, the danger of caring.

He turned once more, tugging at a blanket, and wished for sleep.

Luca lay on his stomach, his face turned to the wall, his arms folded beneath his chest so that the posture did not feel quite like the extractors' table, and he studied the wall's minuscule cracks, and the dust in the slanting morning light, and insects' tracks, and anything that might fill his eyes and his mind.

Flamen Ande had been released. Luca thought he should feel something about that—satisfaction that his testimony had changed the course of the trial, worry that Ande was free in Alham again, anger that Ande would face no further effects of his brutality—but whenever he tried to cup his thoughts together to examine them, they ran through his fingers and left him hollow and numb.

Luca had done the right thing. That was all. He had known the truth, and he had not wanted to see someone punished for what he had not done—no matter what else he had done. He had believed injustice was not corrected by more injustice. How had that been so wrong?

Some stupid, stupid part of him had believed too much in the past few months, in Shianan's friendship and Thir's inheritance and

Marla's kindness, and he had believed things could be different, that now he would be all right if he just did the right thing. He had been afraid, of course—terrified—but some new, credulous part of him had still hoped. He had been willing to testify for Shianan, his friend, and he had not been taken for extraction. Surely if he testified for Flamen Ande, whom he loathed, they would believe him.

Sweet Holy One, he had been so wrong, and the betrayal cut deep.

Sweet Holy One. He was not sure if he meant it as a prayer or a curse.

He wanted to go to the temple and slip into the side nook he preferred, to shout at and plead with the god who had abandoned him, but he was afraid to meet a temple priest who might ask what troubled him. He could not bear to face even a kindly question. He couldn't explain to Shianan; he couldn't even explain to himself. He did not want to try to answer a priest.

Shianan had been right to be angry. Luca had been stupid.

He did not have words for the angry hurt, and it was easier to stare at the flaking wall than to face his worst doubts realized.

The morning dragged on and on. Shianan had told him to let most tasks and chores pass while he recovered, and he had chided Luca gently when he attempted to work anyway, but that left too much space for the enormity of his poor decision to press on him. He had only tried to do the right thing, tried not to be the sort of man Ande himself was. How had it been so wrong?

Not just the beating—he had known, on some level, that might come. But the dull, bruise-green terror that had returned with it to haunt him, to circle his mattress at night or make him catch his breath when he heard Shianan's chair creak in the next room... He had not fully known how freely he walked these days, a different man from when he'd come to Alham, until he had lost that, until his stomach twisted each time a piece of laundry slid on the line.

The bruises would fade in a fortnight, but he did not know when he would breathe freely again. He had been willing to give a few hours to save Ande; he had not known he would give his peace.

He muttered an oath and pushed himself from the mattress. He could not stare at this wall any longer, and he could not silence the protests in his head. He could not speak to Shianan. His master mostly hid his residual anger, but still Luca could not explain his doubts to one who had been furious for their cause. Only, he had nowhere else to go, no one else to speak to.

But he had to go somewhere, or he would go mad. He passed through the office and went out into the courtyard.

He wished he could do more to help Shianan. The new Ryuven raids were devastating, and the creases between the commander's eyebrows rarely faded while he received and sent reports. Shianan had lost the queen's horse, had lost many soldiers, had not seen Lady Ariana for days of fighting. When Luca thought of carrying the burden of soldiers killed in ambush, he was ashamed of his own fear of the dark. He would gladly immerse himself in Shianan's tasks and bury his own worries, if only he had any skills to offer. But the officers did not need a slave's ignorant enthusiasm.

He paused near the temple. Of course he had come here; he had nowhere else to go. Even at the public rooms that were open to slaves, he had no real friends, no one he knew more than by sight or by name. There was no place a slave could linger without drawing suspicion. The only place he could safely go was the temple, and so he did.

It was lively, with a number of worshipers and supplicants moving through the closely decorated space. Luca moved as quietly as possible, avoiding all, until he reached the side prayer nook where he hoped he would not be disturbed.

He sat cross-legged, the posture he had adopted instead of kneeling, and closed his eyes against both the nearby temple traffic and the fierce hurt that boiled in him. *Why? Didn't I try to do what was right? Even though it terrified me?*

And Ande had gone free. Not saved from death, but saved from all punishment, just and unjust. Luca's effort to preserve justice had extended injustice.

Why? He folded his clenched fists against his torso and bent over, silent in his rage. He could not let the people standing nearby hear, could not let the priests know. He could not let the all-knowing Holy One see. It was dangerous to be angry.

I did everything I could. I tried so, so hard. And now he had lost his inheritance and his family, and he had freed his captor, and he ached with welts and bruises.

What was I supposed to do?

Everything Flamen Ande had done to Luca was permitted under Chrenadan law, the same rule of law that forbade Luca's manumission from such a man. And yet when Luca tried to uphold the law, he had been caught in its wheels and crushed.

In Furmelle, slaves had fought against cruelty and subjugation.

Luca braced his whole body against the memories. He had seen terrible things, heard terrible things. He had cowered in a storage room with the children he'd tutored, frantically talking of pirate histories, wishing spirits, anything to distract them, until at last nothing could draw their minds from the screams in the streets.

While early fighting had been waged with fists, feet, teeth, chains, and perhaps the implements of their labor, the rebels soon armed themselves from the buildings they took. Slaves found weapons in the houses they broke into, murdering and ransacking, or continued with rakes, kitchen and butchering tools, grain bale hooks. The family Luca served had not died, but some of their neighbors had. One had been torn apart just paces from the house's gate.

After the first horrifying day, Luca had hidden from all; slaves who did not eagerly join the rebels were killed as if they were freemen. He was newly enslaved, broken with his family's betrayal and the steep shock of his position, but he could not bring himself to kill for it.

And then in the end they had sold him with the others, purging the town as if he too had murdered, as if he were a dog just as rabid, as if he had no humanity.

Cole, the slave he'd bought out of his own caravan line, had been briefly impressed when he learned Luca had been at Furmelle. Cole would have fought with the rebels.

Luca gritted his teeth. He had believed that if he just kept trying, he would prove himself worthy of human respect. *Endure, Luca.* But that had been a lie, too.

He could not simply do what was right and hope, not anymore. That had never been true, not for his treacherous father, not for Ande, not for the heartless adjudicators.

He wondered again where Cole had gone from the slave market in Cascais.

Chapter 5

Ewan Hazelrig went to the deep blue door and steeled himself. This would be difficult, but essential. He knocked and waited.

"Come in," called Taev Callahan from within.

Ewan did.

Mage Callahan raised his eyebrows. "Oh, hello. This is a surprise."

Ewan had not used the crystal communication board to call Callahan because he wanted the extra bit of flattery of going to the Indigo Mage's own office. Holy One knew, flattering Callahan was both critical and challenging. "Good morning. I hope I'm not interrupting."

"Not at all. Would you care to take a seat?"

Ewan did not waste time in small talk neither of them cared for. "I've come to ask if you would take on an essential task in our new peace with the Ryuven."

"Oh?" Taev slid into a neighboring chair.

"They suffer a blight on their crops."

Taev shook his head.

"No one is as knowledgeable in botany and arcane botany as you. You could—"

"I could do what? I cannot go there," Taev said practically. "If I went to the Ryuven world, I would die, like every other mage save one. I may hold one rank higher than your daughter, but I don't pretend to her talent or luck. Even if I were willing, it would be impossible."

"I didn't mean you should go. Samples of their crops could be brought here for—"

"Absolutely not," snapped Taev. "Would you bring the blight to our own crops? Why do you think I was so insistent that the dall sweetbud must be dried? And I'm not entirely comfortable with that. Whatever this devastating blight is that beggared their land, we don't want it in ours."

Ewan felt like an idiot. "Of course," he said. "That's a very practical concern, and your immediate response only demonstrates why you are the best choice to advise the Ai on their crops."

Taev sighed. "And how am I to do that?"

Ewan looked at him. "How would you like to do it?"

Taev frowned. "Haven't we just eliminated both taking me to the blight and bringing the blight to me? What do you think is left?"

"Those aren't the only two options. Someone could go between you and the blight. You could train someone in what to look for, analyze the reports they carry back, send back various approaches to try."

"I suppose you have a troop of educated folk anxious to be carried to the Ryuven world? I doubt anyone is eager for that. Too easy to be trapped there, as you know. And then you have to do all your work looking over your shoulder."

Ewan shook his head. "I was thinking more of someone who could carry himself back and forth, someone who could move about the Ryuven fields without worry."

He had surprised Taev. "You would bring more Ryuven here?"

"They might feel the need to look over their shoulders as well," Ewan conceded, "but at least we already have precedent for Ryuven guests, so they might feel more comfortable."

"King's oats, you're serious." Taev scratched his chin and squinted, stretching his scar. "You want me to take on Ryuven apprentices and train them, then send them to research their own fields and bring back reports so I can formulate a solution to their generations of famine."

Ewan nodded firmly, as if it were a reasonable request.

"Well, with expectations like that, how could I fail to impress?" Taev crossed his arms. "Do you have the Ryuven all picked out, too?"

Ewan had only just learned that Ryuven plants should not be brought into Alham. But some Ryuven apprentices could surely be found—perhaps nim, anxious for employment and less overtly dangerous to the human officials he would have to convince. "I don't. But now that I know you are willing, I will make that my next task."

Taev shook his head. "I haven't said I was willing, but I suspect that will make little difference."

Ewan smiled. "I'm glad we have such an efficient understanding."

Taev sat back and waved a hand. "If you can find me a Ryuven or two who aren't too murderous, I will at least teach them how to bring me a useful field sketch."

"Thank you." Ewan rose from his chair. "Thank you indeed."

The final rise into Alham's gates seemed more like one of the mountains to the east. Ariana's feet hurt, her legs ached, her eyes burned. It was not at all the first time she had walked for days, but it was different this time.

They had not returned from a short, victorious war. Marshal Vanguilder had maneuvered them through perilous situations, and Ariana was proud of her work with the soldiers and grey mages, but they had suffered heavy losses in a pincer trap, rushing after a group of wounded Ryuven who had appeared to be fleeing. Tamaryl had fought with them, but he was only one Ryuven against many, seemingly reluctant in Ariana's view, and he shared no elegant choreography of magic and weaponry with the human soldiers as the mages did; it was too soon to fight alongside a Ryuven, let alone a legendary enemy warlord.

Vanguilder had coaxed and roared and gotten them on the road home, but Ariana could feel the destroyed morale like damp wool hanging over the train. Arakadamia had been too recent to face another such overwhelming opponent.

They had exhausted all the healing amulets the mages had carried, and many wounded rode in the wagons or lagged in the ranks. Ariana kept pulling her thoughts away from the bloody rut of wondering how Shianan's contingent had fared. Marshal Vanguilder had said fighting these Ryuven was different than what they were accustomed to. What if Shianan had been injured by their unfamiliar new tactics?

As a mage, she had fewer duties upon their arrival in the capital, and Vanguilder released them before they even reached the military grounds. She plodded to her townhouse, weary beyond reason, and let herself in.

"Ariana?" Her father's eager voice came from his workroom. "You're home?"

"I'm fine," she answered. "It was a rough expedition, but I'm all right."

He came out and embraced her. "You at least know to head off my questions," he said warmly. "Sit down."

She did. "Have you heard from Shianan?"

He glanced at her. "We've talked, yes."

"Then he's all right." A tension went out of her, and she

recognized its enormity only in the relief it left behind.

Her father frowned. "It was rough, wasn't it?"

"Marshal Vanguilder says they fight differently. Different tactics. Which I suppose makes sense, and it lends credence to Tamaryl's argument that they are a different clan, but...we had losses." She forced herself to say what terrified her most. "Their magic—it's different. Our shields weren't effective enough."

She had his full attention. "They could penetrate the shields?"

"Eventually. It wasn't that their magic simply broke through; it was more like it pressed through. Shoving attacks through a thick jelly. We could slow them, and sometimes stop them, but not often enough."

She knew him well enough to know he was attempting to hide his concern. "I will want to hear more of this."

"Of course. I made some notes, mostly impressions, but I did not want to leap to any conclusions." With the assurance of Shianan's safety, the nagging pressure of her other news surfaced. She was tired, but her father deserved to know. "Could we invite Shianan for supper tonight?"

"Are you sure? You don't look like you'll be awake for supper."

Oh, she would. "I can fit in a bath and nap before."

"I suppose I can send an invitation to the commander and a request to the Merry Goat. Should I invite Elysia as well? Ranne or, er, Princess Calissa?"

Ariana shook her head. "Not tonight, I don't think."

He looked at her for just a moment, and she wondered wildly if he had guessed. But he only nodded. "I'll take care of it."

The ripples of Vanguilder's return reached Shianan in the training yard, and he left Torg to finish the drills so he could go to see their arrival. The bedraggled train was a report as clear as any written on his desk.

His first scan did not find Ariana, and a fist began to tighten about his heart. Nor did he see her on his second. Then he noticed there were no mages at all, and he fought down the irrational conclusion that they had all been killed for the more likely explanation that they had been released from duty already.

That meant he should go to the Hazelrigs' home. But if Ariana was not there, if Shianan encountered Ewan Hazelrig alone and waiting—

King's runny oats, his mind had been more settled when he had been alone and with fewer vulnerabilities.

A strange paralysis seized him, a weird terror of finality. As long as he did not know, then Ariana was alive and unharmed. As long as he waited to learn, she was not dead in a river. He had to ask—but not immediately. He would return to his quarters, change out of his training clothes, allow enough time for Hazelrig to have been informed.

He was pulling on a dry shirt when Luca admitted the messenger into the office. "To join the Mages Hazelrig for supper" was the most gloriously musical phrase, and Shianan sank onto a nearby chair as Luca thanked and tipped the runner.

Luca came into the room. "You've been invited—"

"I heard." Shianan sighed, almost giddy with the rush of air. "That means she's safely home."

Luca stifled a smile.

"Don't give me that," Shianan said, pointing a finger at him. "You laugh at my concern, but I know something you do not."

"And what is that, my lord?"

"Ariana Hazelrig is my wife."

Luca's jaw dropped.

Shianan rubbed at his chin. "That was very odd to say aloud."

"Master Shianan—are you serious?"

"She took my hand on the road, and we swore our vows. That makes us legally wed."

"No wonder you've been distracted," Luca said. "But I am happy for you. What will you do now?"

Shianan looked at him and shook his head. "I haven't the faintest idea."

Chapter 6

Shianan did not go directly to the Hazelrigs' townhouse. He did not go often to the paper market—the supplies for his endless reports were delivered to his office—but he knew what he was looking for, and it did not take him long to find a stall with delicate paper flowers, cut and folded into blooms out of season. He bought seven, trusting the vendor to choose appropriate colors and combinations, and tucked them safely into the crook of his arm. He stopped next to purchase a bottle of wine, of a finer vintage than he usually bought.

He paused beside the little fruit trees in the tiny front yard, braced himself, and then went to the door and knocked. Within a few heartbeats, Ariana opened the door and seized his wrist. She pulled him over the threshold and into her arms.

Shianan only just managed to get the paper flowers and wine out of the way before they came together. He held her tightly, quelling the last of his worry for her, drinking in her presence, breathing in the warmth of her. She was solid in his arms, real, reassuring.

She bent her head against his neck and stayed there. "Was it bad where you were?"

She had worried for him, too. "It was."

"We lost many soldiers."

"We were ambushed. We should have known better, but we believed we'd had an easy victory."

She nodded against his neck. Some flowers slipped from his grasp.

After a moment, Shianan slid his lips across her dark hair and pressed his face down to hers. She turned up and met his lips, and they kissed a long while, explaining much that was unsaid.

At last she pulled back, breathless. "We should go back. Supper's been brought, and Father will be waiting."

"Does he know?"

She shook her head. "Not yet. I wanted you here, too. What's all this?"

He looked down at the remaining flowers, bent in his grip, and the few that had fallen to the tiled floor. "Sunlight on flowers is harder at this time of year, and these were the best I could do. They...looked better before."

"I can fluff them. And you brought wine?"

"To my knowledge, no one has ever bribed the White Mage, but I thought it couldn't hurt."

She laughed, though he didn't.

She led him into the dining room, where a crock of stew steamed on the table beside two loaves of brown bread. At one end of the table, Ewan Hazelrig was reading a book, his hand resting on a stack of notes.

"Shianan's here," Ariana said.

Ewan Hazelrig looked up with an easy smile. "Ah, yes, I know. But you two were occupied, so I thought I'd wait in here. Plenty to keep me busy. Please, sit down, and let's eat."

Shianan felt heat over his face and neck.

The White Mage tore apart a loaf and put a large chunk on Shianan's plate. "There's butter and honey just there. The stew is lamb and root vegetables, from the Merry Goat. One of my staples when Mother Harriet isn't available."

"I brought wine," Shianan said woodenly. "A good vintage, she said."

"Well, then, let's pour it," Ewan Hazelrig said amiably.

"Before you do that," Ariana interrupted, "we have something to tell you." She looked at Shianan and reached to take his hand. "Together."

Shianan wasn't sure if she was urging him to speak. Which would be more appropriate, the bridegroom or the daughter?

The White Mage looked between them and smiled. "Yes?"

Shianan's stomach clenched.

"If it helps, you're not going to surprise me." Ewan Hazelrig sat back in his chair and smiled at them. "I've been waiting for you to work up to a betrothal."

"No betrothal," Shianan said. "We're married."

Hazelrig went still. "Well, then. Perhaps a little surprised."

Shianan's stomach sank, and he squeezed Ariana's fingers.

"You handfasted outside of Alham?"

They nodded. Ariana said, "Just before the units separated. It was like something out of a tale—I reached up to Shianan on Kuolema—his horse! He has a horse to ride now!—and we clasped hands and swore, and I kissed a man on a horse." She grinned giddily.

Shianan's gut twisted further, and he wondered how it was

possible to be so happy and so upset all at once.

But the White Mage nodded and lifted a hand, forestalling anything Shianan might have offered. "I am surprised. But I am happy for you."

The constriction in Shianan's throat eased a bit.

"I cannot deny, I am also a little afraid for you. I don't know the best way through this. But I know each of you, and I know you will face whatever comes with courage." He reached to take a hand from each of them, so that they were linked in a circle. "I want the best for each of you, and I will help you however I can."

"Thank you, Father."

"Thank you, my lord mage."

"Now, that's a bit too formal at this late stage, don't you think?" Ewan Hazelrig sat back and beamed at them. "I should be more worried, I know, but I am just so happy for you both. Now sit down and eat. Ariana, you should have told me at least enough that we could have a more celebratory meal! I feel something of a failure, providing only lamb stew and bread for your marriage." He tipped his head. "Though I suppose it must be better than your road rations. That would have been a poor wedding meal."

"Not even that," Ariana said with a chagrined smile. "We made our vows just before we separated. No meal at all."

"No meal?" Ewan's fingers slowed on the bread he was tearing apart. "You simply pledged your marriage vows and walked away, and you haven't seen each other until now?"

Shianan watched him calculate and conclude.

Ewan cleared his throat. "Well, I suppose I'm flattered that you wanted to take the time to break the news to me over supper."

Ariana laughed, embarrassment coloring its sound. Shianan's neck burned hotter, and he shifted awkwardly under Ewan's knowing gaze.

But—it was different. This was embarrassment. Not shame. He had not thought on the difference before, and it was surprising how much it mattered.

Ewan ladled a surprisingly small serving of stew into his bowl and started on it. "Have you given any thought to how you'll go forward? Will you try to preserve the secret, or will you live openly and hope to blunt the king's response?"

"I had hoped that a successful campaign might influence him in our favor," Ariana admitted. "But after things went as they did..."

"Deeds won't win him," Shianan said quietly. Deeds might earn the king's favor, but not his acceptance. Not what Shianan had wanted. "We'll have to register our marriage, record its legality as soon as possible. After that, he can do as he likes to us, but he cannot undo the marriage."

Ariana held his eyes, suddenly grim and determined, and he regretted his words. This should be their celebration, their joy.

Ewan Hazelrig scraped his bowl and set it down. "I'll think on it. If we can hide a Ryuven for fifteen years, we can handle a marriage." He began to stack his notes on the book. "Well, I have much to review. I'll ask Elysia to go over these with me. I think after twenty years or so, she's finally coming around to an interest in Ryuven history."

"You're leaving?" Shianan asked stupidly. Yes, the White Mage had just said he was happy for them, but to cut short their supper and walk out—was that a sign of some deeper disapproval?

"I'll be out late," he answered, picking up a hunk of bread and balancing it on the stack in his arms. "Very late."

Oh. Heat raced anew through Shianan.

Ariana put her hand to her face, crinkled with a smile.

"Good night," called the White Mage, and he swept out the door.

Shianan sat there in awkward stillness. This, facing one another over lamb stew, was never how he had imagined their first lovemaking.

Ariana looked at him, still smiling, still embarrassed. "He means well."

Shianan shrugged one shoulder, trying for nonchalant. "I don't think he did so poorly."

Ariana laughed. "I suppose I could come around the table." She rose and rounded her father's empty chair, coming to rest on Shianan's knee. She slid an arm around his shoulders.

They had kissed only a handful of times. Now, with all the night before them, Shianan felt as if he stood on a precipice, anxious to fling himself into the inviting pool below but teetering on the edge.

Ariana looked as if she felt the same, nervous but eager. He slid his arm about her and tipped his head back to invite her to him. Her lips were firm and yielding, sweet and hot, all the wild contrasts that made her.

She broke away from the kiss, a little breathless. "My bedroom is upstairs."

"I know. I've been there."

"Oh? Oh, after the Shard. When you were recovering."

Shianan whispered against her jaw, "I'll enjoy it more with you there, too."

She laughed, and she kissed him, and somehow they made their way up the stairs.

CHAPTER 7

Luca was rolling maps after dusting their pigeonholes when the knock came. He tucked the roll into place and opened the door. "How can I—"

The man outside was in Gehrn robes. Luca froze.

It was not Ande. Luca only vaguely remembered this one, one of the younger members, barely Luca's own age. He fixed baleful eyes on Luca. "Deliver this to your new master," he snarled, and he flung a heavy fustian bag into Luca's hands hard enough to sting. Luca's fingers closed by reflex, catching it from falling.

The young Gehrn stepped forward and delivered a heavy open-handed slap, snapping Luca's head to the side.

Luca reeled, caught himself, automatically ducked and cringed backward, shielding himself as he gave way. But the Gehrn did not follow him into the office, and when Luca raised his head, he was gone.

Luca closed and locked the door, and then he retreated to the sleeping quarters. He lowered himself stiffly onto his bed, moving jerkily more from the rigidity of his muscles and the sudden numbness of his limbs than from the bruises, and drew his legs onto the low mattress. He took long breaths, thinking hard of nothing at all.

He had known the Gehrn were in Alham. That had been so for months, since Ande had brought Luca with him to perform the ritual on the Shard. But he had not expected to see them, and not at Shianan's own door, and not striking him as if nothing had changed.

He squeezed his fists so that his nails tore his palms as he clenched his jaw, anger flooding in to replace the ebbing shock and panic. He was furious with himself at freezing at the sight of the blue robes. He was not subject to that any longer; he owed them no allegiance or service or fear. He should stand in his new life, in his new position, safely out of their reach and influence.

His body had forgotten his new life at the sight of his old.

He uncoiled his aching fingers and picked up the fustian bag, two hands-breadths long. He undid the drawstring—it wasn't his place to examine his master's things, but this had come from the Gehrn and he could not stop his hands—to reveal a solid key, weighty in Luca's palm, with a silken tassel dangling from the end.

Luca didn't understand. What meaning could this have for Shianan? Was it a message from the Gehrn? Had it come because of Luca's late testimony in Ande's trial?

And Luca had opened the door to it, opened the door to another Gehrn, who had struck him as if he belonged to the order and not to Shianan, and Holy One knew what it could mean.

Luca returned the key to the bag and got stiffly to his feet. He set the key on Shianan's desk and then, with angry embarrassment, he moved it inside a lockbox where it was less visible, unable to catch his eye as he worked.

With less road dust and more expectation, Garl and Esar set out to the house of exchange. The House of Lombard had a large and highly visible office in the center of Flerinz, prominent and near to all the major markets. Garl judged that it would be foolhardy to present the letter in Ivat, and Flerinz was a prosperous trading city in its own right, well able to fund a deep withdrawal on a merchant letter and busy enough to forget the faces of two men who left soon after their business was done.

How deep should they draw? Garl had been debating the question with equal consideration to both approaches. Drawing lightly meant they might be able to return again and again, shearing the sheep for regular profit instead of slaughtering it with one wild, draining withdrawal that would certainly call the attention of the parent house. The idea of acting so recklessly gave Garl a moment of hesitation, like Esar—and considering himself for a moment like Esar, he resolved to be bold.

The letter was the chance of a lifetime, and not to be wasted with too much caution. Even small repeated draws might alert the parent house and invite eventual capture. Better to strike boldly, profit hugely, and walk away safely.

He straightened, taking the air of a wealthy merchant who had every right to expect respectful service from such an establishment, and he pushed through the door into the offices of the House of Lombard.

The office was impressive, designed to exude confidence and reliability, with floors of expensive grained stone polished to a shine and heavily carved wooden chairs for those waiting to transact business. Rows of benches and counters hosted most of the common interactions, while private offices were available in the rear for extensive negotiations and larger amounts. There was also a set of barred doors in a stone wall, and Garl's eyes were drawn again and again to them against his will. That would be where the chests and coffers of hard money lay, waiting to be withdrawn against family credit. That was where their prize rested.

Only a few moments more.

"Good morning, my lords," called a clerk, his face cheery against their worn travel clothes. "How may I serve you?"

Esar grinned at this boot-licking. Garl ignored him, hoping his brother wouldn't say something stupid, and began, "I have a letter of credit, and I would like to take out a large sum."

"Please, come and have a seat, and I'll be happy to assist you."

Garl had often negotiated for funds, but always at the cheap moneylenders in the lower markets, where the usury was high and the courtesy low. Taking a seat at one of the house benches was like a dream, play-acting at being a mercantile success. He gave a little wriggle on the cushion to rub his common buttocks across it.

Taking this document from the gasping, whining young man who had lost it had been the best choice of his life.

"Thank you, thank you, and now how can I help?"

Garl withdrew the document wallet and passed it over the table. "I'm Luca Roald, and as you can see I have a considerable amount of funds available to me. I have a business deal to arrange, and so I need to pull out some hard currency. Gold coins preferred."

The clerk smiled. "Oh, my lord, there's no need for that. I can write out a letter for you for the exact amount of your business, and you can take that to your arrangement. It will be much simpler than transporting the gold, especially if it is a large amount. It won't take but a moment."

Esar twisted his mouth in suspicion and displeasure.

The clerk noticed, and his tone grew a little placating. "It would be safer, too, as I can make the letter redeemable only by the individual you specify, so that there's no benefit to theft. That protects both you and your business partner."

Garl snorted. That wasn't such a protection.

"And the seal of the House of Lombard is accepted by all, with sterling reputation. There would be no concern."

"I would have concern," Garl said gruffly. "I would have concern that I asked for gold and was offered paper. What sterling reputation, if I can't even get my own money?"

The clerk shrank back. "I'm sorry, my lord. I didn't mean—I was only trying to help. Of course you can have your gold, if you prefer. I only meant to simplify your transactions."

Esar grinned, and Garl preened a little, happy to have displayed his prowess before Esar and to have silenced his doubts.

The clerk looked down at the letter for the first time. "Yes, yes, this is one of ours, and I can just—oh! Luca Roald! Of the Ivat house! I'm sorry, I didn't recognize it when you introduced yourself. But yes, you're in luck, my lord! I'll just step to the back and get things started. How much did you want?"

This was the key question—how much could they carry? They couldn't clear out a third of a merchant house's treasure, no matter how attractive the idea; the Asher brothers were strong, but gold was heavy, and Garl didn't trust anyone outside family to help with a prize so tempting.

But Garl had a plan ready. "Four hundred thousand pias," he answered, trying for a casual tone as if he talked of such amounts all the time.

The clerk, well-trained, betrayed only a second of hesitation. "Of course, my lord," he replied. "And will you be collecting it here? You understand, we cannot deliver such an amount outside of our protected offices—"

"We'll carry it out," Garl said, ignoring Esar's stunned look. "You box it up, we'll get it out."

"Right, my lord," the clerk said. "In the usual case, we would need to complete a few steps to begin such a withdrawal, but as I said, you've come in on the right day. Did your caravan come early? We weren't expecting you."

Garl needed to deflect any questioning. "My business is my business," he growled.

The clerk looked abashed. "I'm sorry if I gave offense," he mewled.

Oh, but how these hired men scraped for the rich. Garl could drink this power like wine.

"I'll just go and get things started. If you'll wait here, my lords?"

"We'll wait for the money," Esar said, and the clerk scurried away.

Esar turned to Garl. "Four hundred thousand? I like your ambition, but even in large coin, that's going to be quite the load. How are we going to manage that?"

"They're going to bring it here in cases," Garl said. "I'll wait here with the money, safe in the office. No one is going to try to rob me of it while I'm still inside. But you will take a handful and go down to the labor market, where you'll pick out a half dozen big brutes. We'll load them down and drive them over the hill to just outside Sienna. Then we kill the slaves—it's a waste not to sell them, but we can afford it for the silence and safety—and hire some porters to carry it all into town, where we'll load everything into a boat like it's grain or pot metal. Then we sail away to wherever we like, and set up to live like princes."

Esar's wide grin showed stained teeth. "I like that. But why should I go down to buy the slaves and leave you here with the money?"

"Don't be a suspicious fool!" snapped Garl. "How am I going to carry it off by myself? I have to stay with it because I am the one who had the letter, and they're not going to believe that I would withdraw such a sum and then leave it here. I've got to stay with it." He harrumphed. "Might be as good to ask if I can trust you to come back with the slaves, once I send you off with a few thousand."

Esar's eyes narrowed and his grin went suddenly false. "I wouldn't leave you, little brother. Not with so much gold at your feet."

They smiled at each other, and Garl wondered if he would have to kill Esar with the slaves.

They settled on the cushioned seats to wait for their new fortune to be counted and packed.

CHAPTER 8

A knock at the door interrupted their comparisons of figures, and the senior accountant called, "What is it then, Rendle?"

Thir Roald sat back in his seat, privately grateful for the reprieve. The sight of confirming figures in reassuring black ink would never grow old, not after what he had known, but the strain of focusing on the tiny, neat handwriting of Lombard's clerks was beginning to tell. If he wanted to continue managing the house's affairs without relying wholly upon the word of others, he would soon need a reading stone or magnifying lenses. He smiled at himself. He wasn't so old, but he supposed years of figures might take their toll.

They hadn't seemed to harm Margaret Lombard's eyes, however.

"I beg your pardon, my lady, my lord, but it's about a guest who has come to make a withdrawal," the interrupting clerk said. He seemed pleased with himself. "He's all travel-worn and seems to have just arrived in town, so I can't imagine that he knew to meet anyone, and so I thought Master Roald would be pleased to hear in advance that his brother has come."

Thir looked up at his name and needed a moment to run back over the words he had been ignoring. Then he had a moment of confusion, as Jarrick was supposed to be managing in Ivat. At last realization opened on him like the dawn. "Luca? Luca is here?"

The clerk smiled and nodded. "He is. He came to make a withdrawal—a large one, for business, he says. I thought you might like to go and greet him. I kept the surprise for you."

"Certainly I would." Thir looked at Margaret, a middle daughter of a side branch of the Lombard family, and gestured to the several open ledgers and logs across the wide desk. "You don't mind if we leave this for a few minutes, do you?"

"Of course not," she said. "Go right ahead."

It was not uncommon for members of merchant families to see each other only rarely, as they were often traveling to different markets to broker new deals, soothe ruffled contracts, discover new goods. Luca's separation had been something else entirely, and while Thir had been unable to mend that in the way it should have been done, caught between protecting his father and his own ashamed fear of facing his brother, he had at least provided for Luca in the best way he could. If he could now also see him, away from home and all the cargo of it, he would not miss this chance.

He paused at the end of the little corridor for the private offices and scanned the main hall, looking for his brother's face. He did not see him, and a little quiver of fresh guilt pricked at him—but no, he would know Luca's face, even changed as it was. Luca must have moved to wait elsewhere. "Rendle, where did you leave my brother to wait?"

The clerk stepped beside him and nodded across the hall. "Just there. He has a friend with him. Together near the statue of the fallen Ryuven, do you see?"

Thir could see two men beside the statue at the end of Rendle's gaze, but neither was Luca. For a moment he was confused, and then a dark suspicion took hold. "Rendle, did he present you with a letter of credit?"

"He did, sir, all sealed just as usual. Signed with your own name."

Thir pressed down a quick stab of fear. "What exactly was this letter?" If it was just a letter of credit, it would be just ordinary fraud, someone trying to pass a counterfeit. There would be a quick arrest and all would be done.

"It was a little unusual in content, my lord," Rendle allowed. "It authorized a third of the House of Roald."

Horror struck Thir like a punch in the gut, and for a moment he couldn't breathe. This was no common fraud; this was someone with the original letter he had given to Luca. Someone who had taken it from Luca. This was, in all probability, Luca's murderer. And now he sat in a gilded hall on a cushioned chair, waiting to collect Luca's inheritance.

"What is it, my lord? You look as if someone had poured snowmelt all down your collar. Is that not your brother?"

Thir took a breath and made an effort to steady his voice. "Rendle, please be so good as to send someone quietly for the city guard. There is an arrest to be made."

Rendle nodded. "There's a post just down the corner, my lord. It won't be but a moment."

"What was the amount they wanted?"

"Four hundred thousand, my lord."

The number should have made no difference—the price of Luca's life had already been set once—but just the same the words ran through Thir like a shock. He nodded, a jerky maneuver he should have managed better. "I will go and make sure they wait comfortably until the guard arrives," he said as levelly as he could. "Thank you for alerting me."

Rendle's face was taut with concern, but he nodded and scurried off down the corridor to find a runner.

Thir flexed his fingers, rolled his shoulders back, and went out into the hall to play the mercantile negotiation of his life.

"Good morning, my lords," he said, sliding behind the counter where the two men waited. "I am so sorry you were kept waiting. Which of you is my lord Roald?"

One man raised his hand slightly. "Luca Roald, that's me."

Thir bit down a stab of dismay and put on an unctuous smile. "Yes, yes, thank you. It's just being counted now. I apologize for the delay, but it's quite a lot to count, you know."

The false Luca turned to his companion, who grinned greedily.

Thir had never been tempted to violence; all his life, problems had been created and solved on paper, and solutions were best directed through a ledger. But now, watching that man who had killed his brother smile, he understood the desire to plunge a sharpened pen into the man's face.

He measured his words out into little cups of poison. "You have been such a valuable client to our house," he said, putting on his most subtly flattering tone. "Where did this last journey take you?"

"We were out near the border," the false Luca said. "Toward Chrenada."

That was vague, but was it true? Would Luca want to return to the kingdom where he had been a slave?

That was a foolish question. Would he want to stay in the land where he had been *made* a slave?

"Ah," Thir said aloud. "Yes, there's quite a lot of good trade coming through Chrenada. We hope to establish a new branch in Alham soon. That would save you some trouble, wouldn't it?"

The false Luca, whoever he was, wasn't from a mercantile background; he hesitated in trying to find the appropriate answer. "Yes," he managed, "yes, it would save carrying these heavy chests across the mountains."

Thir nodded as if this were an astute observation. He was saved from needing to invent more simpering small talk by the arrival of Rendle at the counter's end. "My lords, we're ready for you," the clerk said with a little bob of his head.

Of course the arrest would not be made in the hall of the reputable house of exchange. Thir thanked him and gestured for the two travelers to go ahead. "My lords, if you please? We'll need you to confirm the amount and sign for it."

"Of course," said the false Luca, as if he did this every day, and he rose to follow Rendle.

They passed through the corridor and into a private office, where several chests were stacked in the center of the room. The companion frowned. "Can you fit four hundred thousand into so few?" he asked.

At that moment the city guard closed from the corridor, blocking the door. "It doesn't much matter," Thir said, all flattery fallen from his tone. "You won't be taking any amount with you."

"What is this?" demanded the false Luca as guards stepped to either side of him. He tried to shake them off. "Is this how you treat your best clients?"

The chief guard ignored them. "I need you to formally state a charge, my lord."

Thir struggled for the right words, the words he had to limit himself to. "What we are sure of is that this man presented himself falsely as the legitimate bearer of a letter of credit."

"Counterfeiting?"

"No, the letter itself is authentic. But the man claiming it is false."

"I am Luca Roald!" the man shouted, twisting in the guards' grip. "You have no evidence I'm not and no cause to treat me in this way!"

Thir fixed the man with a glare carrying all the horrified fury he had suppressed. "I am Thir Roald, and Luca Roald is my brother."

The false Luca went still as the enormity of the damning evidence struck him. There could be no recovery from that charge.

The companion began to curse the false Luca in blistering epithets. The guards ignored him as they bound him, but the counterfeit brother began shouting back. With effort, the guards turned them away from each other.

"Sir," Thir said to the chief guard, his fingers clenched, "the charge I have already made is the only one we can be certain of, and that is charge of a crime against the House of Lombard. For myself, I lay a second charge, which is the probability that one or both of these men killed my brother to obtain his letter of credit. I would like to offer a bounty of three hundred pias to the guard who can learn where and how my brother died, so that I might honor his memory properly."

The two men went quiet, subdued by the guards' bonds and Thir's accusation and offer. Then one burst, "We didn't kill all of them! Which one was he? Maybe we didn't kill him!"

"You did enough!" snapped the other. "Trust you to kill the wrong one!"

"I didn't see you holding back!"

The two were dragged apart and shaken to silence. "Thank you for your generosity, my lord," the chief guard said to Thir. "I'm sure we'll have some answers for you in the morning. Will you be remaining in town long?"

"I am staying at the Vandogan's Head."

"We'll know where to find you, then. Bring them along."

As they shoved the men out a rear door, Margaret Lombard stepped in, her hands clasped firmly before her and her face set in concern. "Oh, I am so sorry. I am so sorry—and what a terrible way to learn, and in our offices. Please, go to your rooms and take some time for yourself. We don't need to finish those figures now, or soon. I can take care of things for the moment."

With the departure of the fraudulent men, all the necessity that had held his expression and tone vanished, and the strength of his facade collapsed. He sagged into a chair in the office. "Oh, Luca," he breathed, losing his brother a second time, and it was all he could manage to say.

Margaret sat down opposite him, one hand resting on his forearm, and she simply waited.

Thir's thoughts swam. Luca had been betrayed and sold by their own father. He had come home to find himself rejected again, and their father's viante-eating had grown worse since. That was a set of problems Thir kept tucked locked safely away in a coffer in his mind, the questions and possible answers too dangerous for daily use. Thir had done the only thing he could for Luca, had given him a full share of the house that had failed him and set him to make a new life for himself.

That gift had been Luca's death.

Thir grasped the edge of the burnished wooden desk for

something solid, something stable as the world swung about him. His vision blurred, and he was not certain if he wept; he could feel so little. He would have to tell Jarrick and Sara. He would have to tell his father—tell him Luca was truly dead now, not dead in the lie he maintained to salve his conscience, but truly dead. In a perverse way he wanted to see if his father reacted to that news, if he would show some grief to betray his own awareness of the lie he lived, or if the viante had made the lie so real that he would not even recognize the loss.

The money he had offered the guards should ensure some confession, and he could at least set a memorial marker with the necessary information, as was the custom at Wakari temples. That would solve nothing, but it would give Sara a place to weep, and it would be a permanent and public affirmation that Luca had existed and had been a part of their family.

CHAPTER 9

Everything Flamen Ande had done had been permitted, even supported, by law. It was Chrenadan law that had put the Furmelle collar on the rebel slaves and those taken with them. It was Chrenadan law that forbade releasing a slave except by death-will, a cruel response to revolts and rebellions. It was Chrenadan law that permitted the taking of slaves in the first place, condemning children for their birth or debtors for their debt.

Many slaves were sentenced criminals, yes, but Luca's crime was to be born to a family that had fared poorly in trade and angered a vicious creditor.

Luca was circling the temple, waiting for a worshiper to vacate the side nook he preferred. He recounted his grievances as he circled, passing the contemplative art and the priests in their duties, his eyes forward as he calculated. He had written to the market at Cascais, borrowing his master's name—they would be more likely to check sales records for a commander than for a slave—to ask after Cole. He had promised Cole a chance at freedom, and while Cole had failed him at Cascais, Luca could not wholly blame him, not when Luca himself had quailed into old habits even since. He would give Cole his chance, if he could, and without the bloody path Cole might take.

Luca did not want another revolt—not that, not even now. Furmelle had been too horrible, and in the end it had brought nothing but death and worse conditions for the enslaved survivors. But there had to be *something*. He could not continue like this. He still woke at night, staring breathless into the dark, waiting to hear Shianan's return. He could not face the Gehrn again.

But he was one man, and an enslaved one. He could do nothing.

At last the merchant woman left the prayer alcove, and Luca hurried to it. It had room enough for several to pray at once, but he had grown accustomed to it alone, and the familiar nook was a harbor in a stormy sea.

And he had prayed here before, and those prayers came back to him when he sat here.

Please, Master Shianan is—he's all I have now. Please... have a plan for him. Let him yet breathe, and let him return safely. Please bring him home.

Some prayers were answered. Shianan had returned from Arakadamia, and he had been spared after his clash with the king. Luca was not wholly abandoned, and if he sat here and remembered his desperation then, he could believe for a moment they might be answered again.

The Circle had guests this day, grey mages who had gone with the soldiers to turn back the new Ryuven raids. They were by turns explaining their experiences to the Mages of the Circle, detailing how their magic had failed to disrupt the Ryuven attacks or shield the human soldiers.

Ariana had already presented her observations, neatly arranged and annotated as if enough organization could overrule their underlying message. She had donned her black robes only within the Wheel, having come with her outer robe folded under her arm. She did not feel comfortable risking recognition in the street, being stared at, perhaps resented for the Ryuven's presence or thanked for the dall sweetbud, not when she knew their current danger.

Tamaryl, too, had spoken before he departed for his own world to report to Oniwe'aru. Around her, Ariana recognized subtle signs in the older, more experienced mages as they listened and made notes, their movements growing smaller, their faces less expressive. Ariana understood. She had wrestled with it in the weary hours she had walked silently back to Alham, in the dim hours after Shianan had left her bed, even in the dark hours when he slept beside her and she wondered how long that could last when he would soon be called again to fight this new foe.

She had never known a time when her land, her world, was not under attack. But neither had she ever known a time when her world had lacked defense. Her father was the White Mage—she'd had first a childish faith in his invincibility, then an educated observation of the dedication and efficiency of the Great Circle and the military defense. She had trained her entire life to join them.

But Ariana had seen soldiers fall, had felt her magic fail before this new Ryuven attack, and now she feared in a way she had never feared before. For the first time, she felt a deeper fear: not that the Ryuven might attack, but that they might prevail.

This was futile. She swallowed her rising anxiety and drew a few interlinking circles in the margin of her notes, inking in their overlap. She was only the Black Mage, reporting with grey mages, and the other members of the Circle would, with their greater skill and experience, be more capable of meeting this new threat.

But if they couldn't... Her mind filled with another Arakadamia, another Luenda, thousands of Ryuven advancing through shields and magical defenses. She imagined Shianan, fighting an enemy that could penetrate the shield she threw over him, killing him just as the soldier had died within her shield—just as she had once seen in the cellar of the Wheel...

She closed her eyes, breathed, opened them and drew more interlocking circles in the margins of her pages. A blob of ink swelled dangerously and she drew back, afraid to touch it lest it burst over her sheet. Across the room, the Crimson Mage was asking questions about energy refraction. They had already been answered, but it was easier to pose them again and quibble over the answers. No one wanted to accept the inevitable conclusion, not yet.

"It's not that these new Ryuven are so much stronger," Mage Parma said. "It does not seem they are, by any measure. But we have always, or at least within memory, fought the Ai, and they have their own traditional uses of magic, with certain preferred harmonizations of energies. We practice to counter that approach, and we've become good at it. But that is like a swordsman fighting only one school of opponents."

The generals frowned. "So you need new opponents to practice against."

Mage Parma turned her hands up. "If you know of any Ryuven who would volunteer their services, the Circle would be happy to accept."

Ariana looked about the room. Her father looked stoic, content to let Elysia present this second attempt at explanation after they had balked at his. The generals, already uncomfortable with heavy losses in what should have been simple defensive actions, were clearly displeased to hear the news of the mages' reduced effectiveness. Shianan, sitting out of reach on the far side of General Septime, kept his eyes from her. She knew why—they had to be cautious—but listening to descriptions of why the soldiers were less protected from their magical enemy, she wanted irrationally to be nearer him.

She would find a way to make their marriage safe. To make it real.

There was so much to a marriage that they did not yet have. Even children playing house knew to include the sharing of breakfast, the discussion of the day's efforts and accomplishments, relaxed time together to explore the market or read by the fire, plans for the future. She wanted the marriage she remembered of her parents.

But none of that could happen if these new Ryuven moved on the city.

"What does the Circle need, then?" asked General Kannan. "Do you want us to capture some Ryuven and bring them to you for practice?"

"Well, if you could, that would be very kind." Mage Parma's voice was dry. "Alternately, you could reinforce your patrols and inform your troops that mage support will be less effective until we have had time to study and adapt our techniques."

"If soldiers had to step back and stop fighting every time we met a new combatant," observed Kannan acidly, "we'd have no army left at all."

"No one said anything about ceasing fighting," Mage Parma replied, "and I can assure you we will have both grey mages and mages of the Circle deployed as usual. We anticipate losses will be higher, so be sure your soldiers are aware of the situation and do not spread themselves too thin. Meanwhile, if you would like to lend your apparent expertise in adjustment from shielding against transient polarization to deflecting nonlinear diffraction, I am most open to hearing your suggestions for a reliable technique in the pressure of battle."

Ewan Hazelrig added mildly, "But please be specific, as error will likely instantly kill both the mage and any soldiers being shielded."

General Kannan cleared his throat. "I'm sure you'll inform us when you have something encouraging to report. In the meantime, General Septime and I have our own work, sorting assignments in readiness for more raids."

Ariana smothered a smile. There was not much to smile about in the current raids, but the unflappability of Mage Parma and her father was harbor in a storm.

CHAPTER 10

Tamaryl pressed his wings together and clenched his fists, tensing muscles without moving from where he stood. So much depended on his plea to Oniwe'aru. The King's Council was on the point of re-erecting the shield despite the treaty, and who could blame them? A peace with the Ai was no advantage if they suffered raids by the Ientu. Tamaryl knew his ability to travel between courts hung by a tenuous thread. He needed to convince Oniwe'aru to make a show of good faith, and he needed to convince the council that honoring their treaty with the Ai was worth their risk from the Ientu.

And he needed to choose which world, should the shield be erected once more, he would be trapped in.

"Come, Tamaryl'sho," called one of Oniwe'aru's guards.

Today Oniwe'aru was in the Court of Herbs, lightly shaded by a gilded net which shielded it from eyes above. Tamaryl knelt. "Oniwe'aru."

"Rise, Tamaryl'sho."

There was another sho here—the one with the striking orange hair in a high knot. Ronal'sho, Maru had called him, who had repeatedly maneuvered for the position of Pairvyn while Tamaryl was in prison. Even Oniwe'aru's guards had scoffed at his futile persistence.

And yet he was here with Oniwe'aru.

"I suppose we should be impressed that you were able to return," Oniwe'aru said with studied lightness.

"I pleaded with them to not erect the shield."

It had felt nearer begging. If the shield went up, Tamaryl would be trapped in Chrenada, and all the trade for food would halt, leaving the Ai to starve. If the shield went up, riots would empty the warehouses of their dwindling rations. He had played his most tenuous game piece in the council meeting, pointing out that the prince-heir had been treated with dall sweetbud and leaving the ominous alternative to hang in the air.

But even that would not be enough to prevent the shield if the raids continued. The prince was in no danger now, while the raids were deadly and growing.

Oniwe'aru looked across at Tamaryl, his mouth turning down. "We've found initial efforts at trade more profitable than we anticipated. Human merchants want more than the herb, they want furniture, art, even fabrics. Diversification has been rapid and beneficial. And we carry back enough to blunt the worst of the unrest."

Tamaryl nodded.

"If we lose that trade, however... We can afford to lose the sale of furniture. We cannot afford to lose the grain." Oniwe'aru's jaw tightened. "The imports have helped a great deal, but we are only just keeping up with need. We have not yet begun to replenish the storehouses, and all know it. More riots are only a few days of hunger away."

Ronal'sho snorted. "Things could be put in order if you would allow me to act. I could, with a troop of sho, put down this unrest you refer to. There are laws in this land, and your orders should not be flaunted so shamelessly."

"They act in fear and desperation," Oniwe'aru said sharply. "Making them more fearful and more desperate will not bring peace; it will only suppress the trouble until the next eruption, more forceful for its doubled pressure."

Ronal'sho scowled but did not reply.

"Then you agree that we must do whatever is necessary to preserve this peace," Tamaryl said, ignoring the resentful glare from the sho.

"We have done nothing to endanger it!" snapped Oniwe'aru. "What would you have me do, Tamaryl'sho? Should I apologize for the warriors of another clan, as if their actions are somehow my error?"

Tamaryl shook his head. "Of course not. The actions of the Ientu are their own."

"And you must convince the humans of this."

He was trying. "I will, with time. But they have not known other clans, and while I have explained the situation, they still see all Ryuven as Ryuven, not as Ientu or Ai. For decades the Ai have jealously guarded our raiding grounds, so all the raiders they knew were Ai, and do you recall what you swore in your binding oath to King Jerome?"

Oniwe'aru's mouth flattened. "I know what I swore! I pledged no offensive action, the common pledge of..."

Tamaryl waited.

"Essence and flames," Oniwe'aru bit out.

"Did you swear the common pledge of traveling traders? In its entirety?"

The Ai will raise no offensive action against Chrenada while we are welcome in your lands, permitted to trade freely and openly. We will suffer no other clan to raise offensive action against Chrenada. We will shepherd our own, keeping our traders safe in strange lands and guarding the honor of our oath.

Oniwe'aru closed his eyes. "You have kept me from breaking a binding oath, and yet I do not wish to thank you for it."

"I do not expect thanks. But as you expect me to convince Chrenada that the Ientu do not act as the Ai, I might find it easier if you provided a show of faith and consideration."

Ronal'sho brightened. "Send me, Oniwe'aru. Send me and a troop of sho to challenge the Ientu raiders, and—"

"No!" snapped Oniwe'aru. "Are you trying to open war with the Ientu? I cannot send my warriors against theirs."

He had sent his Pairvyn against them, but he had not realized that. Oniwe'aru had given Tamaryl to aid the Chrenadan troops in a jest, thinking it an insult in his own palace, never to be heard or understood by the King's Council. But Tamaryl had seized that jest and gone out to battle with the military. He had not worn the sash marking him as Pairvyn, however, and he had tried to focus on defensive magics, making as few attacks as possible. At any rate, he had gone with human soldiers, and no one could mistake a human military action as an attempt to conquer a clan in a world they could not reach. Not that Oniwe'aru would see it that way.

"You cannot send your army of conquest against them," Tamaryl agreed aloud. "But you could lend Chrenada your aid."

Ronal'sho went rigid. Oniwe'aru's eyes narrowed. "You don't mean to suggest—"

"Only Edeiya'rika," Tamaryl explained quickly. "And only as another liaison, perhaps to advise the mages on facing the Ientu."

"Do you suggest that we instruct the human mages in how to counter Ryuven magic?" demanded Ronal'sho.

"They already know enough of it," returned Tamaryl, and, unable to resist a thrust at this sho who maneuvered for his place, he added, "as you would know if you had faced them in any real capacity. What I suggest is—"

But Ronal'sho was already flaring his wings with indignation.

"No one may question my courage! I would—"

"No one has questioned your courage," Oniwe'aru interrupted wearily. "Only baited your outrage. Tamaryl'sho, his question has merit."

"As I was saying, the Great Circle are no strangers to fighting Ryuven, and they can be quite effective against Ai magics, as we well know. It is only a matter of time before they are equally proficient against the Ientu. Sending an adept adviser would not significantly change what they will know, but it will lend the appearance of sympathy, a show of support that will cost little but may benefit the Ai."

Ronal'sho thinned his lips in disapproval but watched for Oniwe'aru's judgment. Tamaryl exhaled so that he would not be holding his breath. If Edeiya'rika advised the Circle, it would demonstrate Ai friendship, as he had said. He also harbored a secret hope that the council would not move to erect the shield when it might trap two powerful Ryuven in their court. And if it came to that, Edeiya'rika was strong enough to survive traveling through the shield, as Tamaryl had once done—barely survive, but that would be enough.

Oniwe'aru was skeptical. "And you think the humans could welcome another Ryuven to their court?"

"I have already asked to bring someone. They are anxious for our aid." That was a stretch of the truth, but it was true that Mage Ewan Hazelrig had agreed insight into Ientu magic would be helpful.

Oniwe'aru frowned. "Edeiya'rika is our Tsuraiya, who fights for Ai defense. Would sending her to advise on combat seem to be a claim on Chrenada as our own?"

Tamaryl shook his head. "They do not have separate forces for conquest and defense. And she would not be fighting with them, only advising them before they return to war. I do not think they would take it as an affront."

"Edeiya'rika would," Ronal'sho said gruffly. "The Tsuraiya is not to be sent to soothe human tears."

"Edeiya'rika is likely to be the next silth," Oniwe'aru continued. "If I send her to a human court when, as you have only just said, they are considering erecting a shield to barricade our world, I will be seen as a despot attempting to dispose of a rival. I cannot count upon my Pairvyn stealing the Shard each time the shield is raised."

Tamaryl's heart fell. He could offer no argument to this.

"We will put the question to her and let her decide," Oniwe'aru continued. "She may choose to go to the human world if she believes it will secure our trade—though that is a sacrifice I will not ask her to make."

Ronal'sho crossed his arms, satisfied. Tamaryl made himself nod. "Yes, of course."

Chapter 11

Maru had bottles of philios ready when Tamaryl arrived, and Tamaryl accepted his with surprise. "Philios?"

Maru's jaw clenched and released. "I don't know how often we'll be able to drink it together in days to come."

Struck at his uncharacteristic pessimism, Tamaryl took a drink, feeling the philios burn lightly down his throat. "Why do you say that?"

Maru gave him an impatient look. "You cannot expect me to believe they are not considering raising the shield again. We all know it. We all expect it. And if they raise it with you still in Alham..."

Tamaryl took a long drink to give himself time to choose his words. Maru was concerned for his safety, and Tamaryl could not fault him for that, not even if Maru's worries echoed his own too closely and while Tamaryl needed reassurance. He swallowed and said, "I believe it is possible to preserve the treaty, and keep the shield down."

Maru looked at him over his stoneware cup. "A che died as a trading party was preparing to cross. He went first, and that is how we discovered the shield had been restored." His eyes shifted. "If Sumeh'che had not leapt just a bit ahead of the rest—it would have been eight dead instead of one. And no one would have known what awaited us."

Us. Essence and flames.

If Maru, steadfast Maru, if Maru was losing faith to fear... Tamaryl sat down and tried to look more confident than he felt. "The mages—they believed they were under attack. They *were* under attack, and they believed it was us. They did lower the shield when I said I needed to speak to Oniwe'aru, to confirm that it had not been an Ai raid."

"They made a treaty with us, and then they raised the shield against us and killed us." Maru sat across from him, flattening his wings.

"They made a treaty with us, and then Ryuven killed sixty-eight of them. They were not even aware of the Ientu. They thought we had betrayed them."

Maru's mouth thinned. "I know you have friends there, Ryl. I know you want to believe the best of them."

Tamaryl's heart sank to hear Maru speak so distantly of those whose home he had lived in, whose meals he had shared.

"But you knew, when you came here, that the shield was down. You knew you would make it across, would live. From here... It's not just me, Ryl. We need the trade, we know that, but they erected the shield without any warning while we believed we were at peace."

"They did not understand," Tamaryl answered, but the words were weak even to his own ears. To Maru, killing an Ai che under treaty for an Ientu raid was unconscionable, and Tamaryl could not fault him for that.

"They knew we were desperate, and they killed us."

"Stop," Tamaryl said, and to his relief it did not come out sharply. "I know. I know you're afraid, and between the shield and the empty storehouses, you have good reason. I am sorry about Sumeh'che. But you were the one who reminded me that I could not blame them all and give up my hope of peace."

Maru stared down at his philios. "Maybe I was wrong. Maybe I just prolonged a futile dream."

Tamaryl leaned close. "You weren't wrong," he said in a soft, fierce tone. "You weren't wrong."

Maru met his eyes and smiled weakly. "Then what are you going to do?"

Tamaryl had no idea, and so he took a drink.

Maru's smile faded, and he looked down again.

After a long moment, silver-haired Taro clapped once and came into the room. "Edeiya'rika has come and asks to speak with you, Tamaryl'sho."

The announcement startled Tamaryl; he had not expected such a visit. He had not even been in his home for more than a few minutes. He hoped Fasi'bel and Taro and the others had maintained it according to what Edeiya'rika would expect. "Bring her, of course."

Maru looked at him and set the philios aside, and the clink of stoneware against the polished bench cut Tamaryl. He lifted his own drink and drained it, coughing a little as he ran out of air. Then he looked at Maru.

Maru acknowledged the gesture with a tiny nod, but he stood without his drink and went to the far door as Taro followed Edeiya'rika in.

Tamaryl scrambled for footing, caught between Maru's

lingering distress and his hopes to persuade the Tsuraiya to visit a hostile human world. "Edeiya'rika. I am honored by your visit, and—"

She cut him off with a short wave of her hand. "I apologize for my sudden appearance, but I thought it more efficient if I came directly instead of sending for you when you'd only just returned." She seated herself on the stone bench across from Tamaryl. "I have just come from the Palace of Red Sands."

His stomach tightened. "Where you spoke with Oniwe'aru."

"Yes. And Ronal'sho was there as well, which made things less clear and more difficult." She did not quite roll her eyes, but Tamaryl was relieved to hear the temptation in her voice. That meant, he hoped, that Ronal'sho still lacked a firm foothold.

"Did Oniwe'aru tell you of my suggestion?"

"To send the Tsuraiya to Chrenada? He did." Her eyes fell on the abandoned cup, still half-filled with philios. She looked back at Tamaryl. "I'll be honest; we were not sure what to think of it."

"I would not want you to go in the capacity of Tsuraiya," Tamaryl said.

"Then why ask for me?" She crossed her legs and leaned comfortably on the bench, but her eyes were sharp. "Why bring the Tsuraiya if you are cautious of invoking the Ai defense?"

"It is not the Tsuraiya I wish to introduce to the King's Council and the Circle," Tamaryl said. "It is the next silth."

She arched an eyebrow. "And you claimed to be unskilled in the ways of politics."

"Desperation is an effective tutor." Tamaryl sat forward, willing her to understand. "We need this trade. If we—"

"You don't need to explain that," Edeiya'rika said firmly. "I'm keenly aware of our resources."

"But they do not need our trade as badly as we need theirs. And they know this. Without a compelling reason to honor a treaty that has not protected them, we will lose our trade before you ascend."

"And so you mean to flatter them with a diplomatic visit."

"More, I mean to share knowledge as generously as we hope they will share grain. As I told Oniwe'aru, it is not a question of whether they will adapt to Ientu magics; of course they will. But we can let them do it themselves, or we can help them to do it more quickly and show our commitment to friendship."

"And invoke a sense of obligation, perhaps? To the one who may inherit that treaty?" Edeiya'rika tapped a finger against her chin.

Tamaryl waited. Too much depended upon her evaluation to press her.

"You know that Ronal'sho is maneuvering hard," she said, almost distractedly. "He's called in every favor, large and small, and he's pushing his family. He wants that crimson sash of yours, either under Oniwe'aru or under the next silth or aru. He's certain you cannot survive a second—or third—blunder as Pairvyn."

"I hear he is not the kind of sho who would be an asset in the position. That suggests I have a duty to be successful."

Edeiya gave a tiny, dignified snort. "You already have such a duty, regardless of his candidacy. But I will confide to you that it should press you to greater efforts. I cannot stomach the thought of taking him as my Pairvyn."

"You could simply...not."

She shook her head, her dark emerald hair catching the sun. "I don't know. The North Family has been hinting... Much like the rest of him, his intrigues are not elegant but cannot be ignored. If we want a smooth transfer of rule, there will need to be concessions, and Ronal'sho may be one of them."

"So we must prove him wrong," Tamaryl said firmly. "Let him speak against going to Chrenada and then prove him wrong, weakening his footing. Your position will be stronger as the rika who stabilized a failing treaty."

"I'll be stronger only if I return. How likely do you think this council is to welcome me?"

"I have already suggested it," Tamaryl admitted, "to give them time to consider unhurriedly, though without specifying who it might be who came."

"And you want me to go, to teach magic to those who have only just barely stopped killing us, and then return triumphantly on that act to become silth."

"Yes." Tamaryl tried to make his voice sound more certain.

"And this is important to you."

The words caught Tamaryl unprepared. "Of course."

"And not merely for Ryuven benefit."

He should not have felt ashamed of the answer. "No. I have friends on both sides."

She nodded slowly, her finger on her chin. "Then I will require a favor of you."

His stomach tightened.

"Not yet. But at some point in the future, I will ask my favor."

"I won't harm my friends," he said, keeping his voice low.

She shook her head. "A good silth would not give an order that required disobedience." She reached for the abandoned philios. "Then I'll tell Oniwe'aru that I will go, and we'll have to rise above Ronal'sho's inelegant pressures." She tossed down the philios and set down the empty cup. "Tell me about the human city."

CHAPTER 12

Shianan woke early, as he always did. There was a moment of disorientation—briefer each time—and then he recognized Ariana's room, the strange pillow, the slope of the ceiling in the dim pre-dawn. Ariana was nestled behind him, her softness against his back, her hips cradling him, her skin to his. He reached back and traced the curve of her, just in fresh wonderment that he could.

Ariana, mostly asleep, slid an arm over his ribs and across his chest. Shianan thought he could stay in bed forever.

He should rise and dress, kiss Ariana goodbye and go back to his own quarters. It was too much to expect that no one would notice his evening suppers at the Hazelrig home, and while bakers and servants had little reason to talk of his early morning returns, still at last someone would mention it and someone else would put it together, and word would reach the court. Shianan and Ariana had registered their marriage, legally recorded by a bored clerk who had barely glanced at their names without their distinctive clothing or noteworthy titles to demand attention, and they were as prepared as they could be for when their day of discovery came.

It did not mean they wanted it to come.

With a sigh, Shianan slid from Ariana's embrace into the cool morning air and worked his stiff shoulder into mobility. His clothing was not gathered as neatly as his military training would have normally ensured. He was pulling his shirt over his head when Ariana murmured, "How do you always wake so early?"

"Long practice," he answered.

"The sun's not even up."

"Near enough. I have to go now, if I want to be gone before the delivery teams might see." He leaned over the bed and kissed her.

For being barely awake, she could effectively hold him in place.

At last he pulled back from his wife and finished dressing. He had much to do and under great pressure, trying to plan another defensive mission that would not lose so many soldiers to the Ientu's tactics. They would not fall prey again to feints and traps, but that did not mean they were prepared against an unfamiliar foe.

He both hoped for and feared Ariana's assignment to his

deployment.

He knew the way well enough in the fading dark, though he occasionally kept a hand on a wall to maintain his path. By now he had some sense of his fellow early risers and their usual paths, so he knew to take an extra alley to add a few minutes to his travel but avoid the bakers' boys and girls running bread. He kept a wary eye, though, for those who did not match their usual patterns. He did not carry a light; it was too close to dawn for most cutthroats and thieves, who preferred to hunt those who stayed out late more than those who rose early, but there was no point in inviting trouble or drawing notice.

He let himself into his office and then eased into the living quarters. Luca was still in bed, and Shianan felt a little thrill of victory when the slave did not stir; somehow it seemed that if he could evade the notice of the light-sleeping Luca, he had been successful in his clandestine return. He added fuel to the brazier's embers to start warming the room, and then he went back to his office and the neat stack of fresh paperwork Luca had left him the night before.

Taev Callahan surveyed the Ryuven lined up before him, waiting behind stools like pupils before the start of class. They were pupils, really; apprentices in botany, here to learn the simplest concepts as quickly as possible, so they could bring him useful data on the Ryuven crops.

They were nearly evenly divided, male and female, which had surprised him more than it should have. Of course he was used to seeing Ryuven raiders, and now the Circle understood that their warriors were divided by sex. But this group, being scholarly, was open to any brave enough to take lessons in the human world.

"Well, I suppose we should get started," Taev said. "Take a seat and bring out your drawing materials. The craft of the field sketch is critical to study."

He provided each Ryuven student with a sprig and set them to reproducing it in charcoal. He walked among them, correcting where proportions were misrepresented or insisting upon the addition of fine details. "With the tiny serrated teeth, this leaf is a seedling for a fruit tree. Without them, it's a mildly poisonous herb. Make sure you take down all the details."

At the rear of the room, four human soldiers waited out the lesson. One seemed interested in Taev's instruction for her own curiosity; the other three were bored but pleased their duty was light. There were worse assignments than sitting in a mage's lecture room while less-powerful Ryuven sketched pictures.

The presence of the soldiers reassured the council and gave them footing to assure worried citizens that visiting Ryuven were under guard. Taev did not anticipate trouble in his lessons. He had to grudgingly admit that it was a good group of students; however Mage Hazelrig had done it, he'd found a competent group who could learn quickly. Taev expected that within a week they could start bringing him beginning reports of the Ryuven fields, and soon samples.

"Jen'che," he said, "hold up your sketch for all to see."

The Ryuven held his board close. "Your pardon, Taev'sho, but I am not Jen'che."

"Who are you, then? What's your name?"

"I am Jen, but I am nim."

Taev waved a hand. "We're not here to quibble over adornments. Hold up your sketch. Look, the rest of you, at how he's highlighted the seam of the seed pod to help distinguish it from other similarly shaped pods."

Jen remained still for a moment, and then he slowly lifted his sketch. The rest of the room remained stiff. Taev had trespassed somehow in dismissing the error of the name. Runny Ryuven were as fussy about their honorifics as the council.

But they would get over it. There was too much to do.

"Pressings tomorrow," Taev said. "But from here—no Ryuven plants, not until I'm certain you've learned how to prepare them properly. You'll pick some of the basil or parsley from the garden here and prepare it as a sample. Don't be late."

CHAPTER 13

The council was not at ease. This was evident in the constant quiet creak of chairs, the rustle of papers uselessly checked and rechecked, the brush of fingertips against the table's surface, the glances and avoidance at the circumference of the group. What they discussed today, what they decided, would save the peace or plunge them back into war.

It was up to Tamaryl, sitting by himself at one end of the table, like a child called to account for his ill behavior, to persuade them.

King Jerome, with Prince Soren at his side, entered, and all rose as they took their places at the high end of the table. As they were seated again at the king's gesture, the council began.

Tamaryl looked to the White Mage, sitting in his place of authority, and immediately wished he hadn't. He loved the mage, and he owed him for so much that had made possible this peace they were trying to protect, but he had to sustain this plea on his own. Mage Hazelrig would support him once he had presented his argument, but he had to present it as an envoy of Oniwe'aru and make them hear it.

"Let us begin promptly with the issue most concerning us all," Chancellor Uilleam said. "Tamaryl'sho, you asked us for leave to speak to Oniwe'aru and bring us further explanation. Are you prepared to address us with that answer?"

Tamaryl swallowed. "I do bring you Oniwe'aru's word on the Ientu attacks upon Chrenada and—an offer of aid."

Essence, why had he hesitated on the words? He knew they would be suspicious of them, but by hesitating he made them more suspicious. So much depended on this, and he could not afford to stumble.

All around the table eyes were fixed on him in various expressions of wariness, early affront, or rejection, but Chancellor Uilleam lifted a hand to quiet the swelling response and said, "Let us hear what your aru has said before we hear or say anything else."

Tamaryl nodded. *Don't stay too long on the fact that it was the Ientu. They are not interested in excuses or who is not to blame, they want reassurance. Give them a promise of help.* "Thank you, chancellor. As you recall, I believed it was not the Ai but another clan, the Ientu, who attacked Nalarbor. This was borne out when your soldiers encountered the Ientu directly. Oniwe'aru was deeply upset to hear of the deaths your people suffered when they believed—with reason—there would be no threat. I have requested, and he is willing to consider, the extension of military aid to Chrenada."

"What would this aid cost us?" asked Washe pragmatically.

Tamaryl shook his head. "I am not authorized to discuss a long-term collaboration," he said, "but this immediate assistance would be offered without any expectation or exchange. It is not a mercenary force."

Another asked, "So once Oniwe has sworn friendship with us, then he will fight with us when we are threatened? Against Heege, even? That seems, if you will forgive my skepticism, an unlikely offer."

Tamaryl straightened and took a breath to give himself time to select his words. "While we do honor the friendship of our treaty, the nascent trade with Chrenada is valuable to our people, and whatever threatens that peaceful trade threatens us. It is for our own good, as well as for friendship, that I encouraged this offer."

They paused to think on that, and Tamaryl took a breath. That was good. They would understand self-interest more than they would trust the alliance of so recent an enemy.

"What sort of aid do you propose?" Chancellor Uilleam prompted. "Will you be fighting with us as Pairvyn ni'Ai?"

Good, good, they were at least interested. "My role here is diplomatic, not military." He pushed on before they could decide if they were relieved or disappointed. "I participated in the first excursions against the Ientu, with limited permission from Oniwe'aru, because of the great urgency, but I cannot fight within Chrenadan command. In addition, the role of Pairvyn is inherent to an offensive force, not suitable for a defensive operation."

They frowned and shifted, probably wondering if he meant to withdraw any real offer of aid. Tamaryl was recalling more and more clearly why he had been a warrior and not a courtier. Each time he went before the King's Council, he wondered anew why he had ever thought he could accomplish more by surrendering the active role of a warrior, where nearly any problem could be solved with a concussive blast, and had taken instead the role of a negotiator, requiring caution for every potential misunderstanding, allowance for every recalled slight, consideration for every ego in the room.

"I have already spoken to the Circle and to General Septime," he continued, "about bringing a colleague to observe and report to Oniwe'aru with me, a second voice. A colleague would also be able to advise the Mages of the Circle on the unfamiliar magics your mages encountered, so that they may be better prepared to counter them in their next battles.

"Mage Hazelrig, as White Mage of the Great Circle, was adamant that no Ryuven may leap directly into the palace, so we have arranged for the Silver and Black Mages to provide an escort into the council when you are ready."

"Are we in the habit of inviting yet more Ryuven into the city?" someone muttered.

Mage Hazelrig turned a mild gaze on the speaker. "We are still bound by our word to welcome peaceable Ryuven into our cities for the purposes of commerce and diplomacy. At this moment, the treaty still stands."

Tamaryl spoke as if the gentle rebuke had not happened. "With your permission, my lords, I will ask General Septime to call them in?"

The general waved, and one of the men by the door exited. Tamaryl took a breath. It was started, now, and there was only to wait and see how it ended.

He looked again toward Mage Hazelrig, who gave him a quiet, patient smile in return. Strange how he wanted reassurance from a man who had helped to wage war on his people and who had kept Ryuven prisoners—but who had also sheltered the enemy champion and protected him from death at the hands of his own. Things were complicated.

Things were always complicated.

The door opened, and Edeiya'rika entered, flanked by Lady Ariana and Mage Parma. She looked composed and self-possessed, as she always did, but her gaze slipped around the room to take in the council, the king, the mages, the eyes.

This was her first day to see humans, Tamaryl realized. She had never before crossed the between-worlds. Other than Ariana, ill in the Ryuven court, this was the first time she would have seen them.

"Good morning," she said directly, her voice modulated to perfect regal control.

"This is Edeiya'rika," Tamaryl said, "who is Tsuraiya ni'Ai."

"Like the Pairvyn ni'Ai?" asked Devinne.

"Of a similar rank, but performing a different service."

"I am the champion for defense," Edeiya'rika supplied.

"I'm sorry, but I don't understand. What do you mean by that?" asked General Septime.

Tamaryl turned to him. "Edeiya'rika commands our defensive host—that is, we have two armies, one for conquest and one for defense."

"With respect," began General Kannan gruffly, "your defensive force is commanded by a woman Ryuven?"

Mage Hazelrig winced visibly. Tamaryl caught his breath, unsurprised by the confusion but regretting it all the same, and regretting that he had not thought to prevent it.

Edeiya raised an eyebrow. "I had not heard that humans had such a love of jests, even in the midst of war councils."

"The general only seeks to confirm your rank," Tamaryl said quickly. "Of course he never expected to see rika in the human world, which had been a battleground of conquest."

Edeiya'rika looked at him, aware that there was some cultural angle hanging invisibly in the room and unable to grasp it. "Perhaps later you could explain further," she said carefully. She did not want to jeopardize his venture.

Mage Hazelrig gave a tiny cough to call her attention. "Edeiya'rika, allow me first to introduce myself and give you welcome. I am Mage Ewan Hazelrig, the White Mage of the Great Circle—I believe you have already met my daughter—and it is my great pleasure and greater honor to welcome you into Alham."

"Thank you, Ewan Hazelrig'sho."

"Now, the difficulty is that our army is predominantly male."

She nodded. "I understand that. Our army of conquest is the same."

Mage Hazelrig nodded patiently. "We have just the one army, to serve both needs."

"Ah, I see. I suppose there may be an efficiency in that." Edeiya'rika nodded and then Tamaryl saw her hesitate. She had realized. "So I may assume it is not common to see female warriors in Alham?"

Mage Hazelrig smiled gently. "It is not unheard of, but it is not common."

"I see," she repeated, using the polite phrase to mask her feelings. She was not offended, Tamaryl knew; how could she be offended at such a silly, barbaric practice? She was probably reflecting that it was no wonder that the Ai had been able to continue their raids for so long. But she was at a loss how to proceed, worrying about unwittingly tripping into some other cultural stumbling block. Too much rode on this meeting.

"We are so pleased," Mage Hazelrig said, "that you might bring your expertise and experience to our Circle, to advise our mages and also our military on opposing this new threat."

Beside Edeiya, Ariana said, "I should be particularly honored to have your advice and assistance."

Mage Parma spoke as if the words were piled inside her to spill out. "I hope we can work together not only on this question of security and confirmation of our treaty, but perhaps on questions of arcane research as well."

Edeiya regarded Mage Parma, and Tamaryl could guess that she was working out the Silver Mage's position and sincerity. She knew the concept of the Great Circle well enough, having heard all her life about Chrenada's magic-wielding defenders, and she must be feeling as disoriented as the humans in the room at the thought of working together with their hereditary enemies.

But whether it was because she knew the Silver Mage ranked highly, or because she trusted Tamaryl's assurances, she nodded. "I would be glad to help you to defend your people and goods, to confirm our goodwill and underpin this treaty so critical to us both."

"Hold on just a moment," General Kannan said. "How long will you stay? And where? We haven't given any talk to the idea of inviting more Ryuven into our cities, especially military Ryuven, especially during this period when—"

"If you will excuse me, general," Mage Hazelrig interrupted with an iron smile, "I believe that question has already been answered with the language of the treaty, which allows for such Ryuven as are necessary for the small trading operations to function efficiently and safely and for diplomatic purposes. We have the small contingent of Ryuven who have begun studying with Mage Callahan, to further diplomatic cooperation. Thus far, Edeiya'rika is merely a consultant to our own military, an aide to Tamaryl'sho in his diplomatic role here."

"An aide *with* me, if you please," Tamaryl intervened gently. "Edeiya'rika carries full authority to advise or authorize, without need for my approval."

"What does that mean for our treaty?" asked Kannan. "If she can act without oversight from the authorized Ryuven liaison?"

That was a fair question.

Edeiya answered it herself. "Lord, I have not come to replace Tamaryl'sho nor to subvert him. I am here at his invitation, for my own observation. When Tamaryl'sho says I carry full authority, he refers to my Ai authority, where I hold high position. That position is the reason he asked me to come here; I can order what he cannot."

Kannan seemed placated by this, and he settled into his chair with a quiet harrumph of permission.

"I asked Edeiya'rika to come and see the situation here," Tamaryl said, "so that she can observe and evaluate what I, as liaison, have submitted to her. But with respect, the particulars of Ai court procedure are not the most important issue before us. A third entity is disrupting the peace we both so dearly want and need, and we need agreement to act to preserve our treaty."

There was a moment of uneasy silence, eyes on the table, on interlaced fingers, anywhere but on Tamaryl. They did not like being pressured by a Ryuven, emissary or no. He had spoken too far and invited resistance.

"Perhaps you and Lady Edee-Edeiya would be good enough to let the council discuss this," Chancellor Uilleam said.

Tamaryl nodded. He withdrew, Edeiya following, and wondered how he would explain to her if they failed.

CHAPTER 14

"I am sorry for my limited hospitality," Elysia said, gesturing about the small stone room. "I hope we can be comfortable nonetheless." As comfortable as anyone could be in this task Ewan had pointedly assigned her.

Edeiya'rika, the Tsuraiya ni'Ai, stood in the narrow doorway and surveyed the entire room without turning her head. "It is, perhaps, cozy? In human regard?"

Elysia considered that the Ryuven, as creatures of flight, probably preferred more spacious areas where they could stretch their wings and if necessary find room to launch into the air. It would do little good to explain that the Circle and the King's Council had deliberately chosen a cramped and sturdy room of solid stone for the first meeting with an unknown and powerful Ryuven warrior. "Human preference tends both to small, cozy rooms and to open space. The latter is primarily for display, and the former for comfort."

"So I may assume that you bring me here to suggest comfort and not to impress me with your luxury of space?" Edeiya'rika pressed her mouth into a smile. "Then I will appreciate the sentiment."

Behind her, another Ryuven waited. This one was of a servant caste, and Elysia had already forgotten his name, though Ewan had seemed somewhat familiar with him when he had appeared with the Tsuraiya. He had, it seemed, come to the human world on several occasions, including the negotiation of the treaty and its historic conclusion, as well as trading visits in several markets.

Elysia gestured to a moss-green leather chair, seamed in an artfully disarrayed patchwork. "I hope the back on this will be low enough to be comfortable. I do have some stools, if it will not serve, but I thought to start with the luxury I could offer here in my cozy room."

The Ryuven went to the chair and eased herself into it, adjusting her wings several times and finally settling for folding them to the side.

Elysia watched the male servant too and so noted his quickly suppressed expression of sympathy. "I am so sorry," she said hurriedly. "I did not know how best to choose accommodation for you. Let us move to the stools instead."

"No, this will do," the Tsuraiya said. "I can manage. I'm sure you would find some of our Ryuven furnishings inconvenient."

Elysia looked at the Ryuven servant now standing behind the Tsuraiya's chair, trying to stay out of the way of her wings as he pressed himself to the wall. No doubt bumping the wings of one of the highest-ranking Ryuven was a social offense. "Would you prefer to wait on this side of the room?"

He gave her a wide-eyed look and made a little shake of his head. "No, rika."

"I see you do not have a servant to attend you," Edeiya'rika noted. "In truth, I brought Maru only because Tamaryl'sho suggested that I might be considered differently if I kept a servant with me in the human fashion."

Elysia cocked her head. "That is indeed a habit of many courtiers or those wishing to display wealth, but it is not a universal one. I assure you, I will treat with you quite the same if you have an attendant or if you do not."

"In that case, I will release Maru to his other duties," Edeiya'rika said. She turned and smiled at the servant. "Please inform Tamaryl'sho that I have come safely to Parma'rika's hospitality."

Maru looked simultaneously distressed and relieved. Elysia wondered if he had come to the human world before the trading and treaty visits, as a fighter. That might account for his discomfort; he could not help but view a mage of the Great Circle as an enemy. He had perhaps lost friends to their magic, perhaps to Elysia herself.

Elysia felt much the same way when she regarded Tamaryl in their meetings, despite all assurances that he was a diplomat now. But, somewhat irrationally, she did not feel the same when she looked at Edeiya. There was something to be said for starting afresh, with fewer preconceptions or experiences. Female Ryuven were so foreign and novel that they did not immediately invoke the same defensive feelings.

Maru retreated to the door and, with a final conflicted look, closed it behind him, leaving the two alone.

Elysia was the hostess. "Thank you very much for coming," she offered. "I know this is an unusual situation, to say the least, and we have the great honor of being the first to attempt not only conciliation but collaboration between our peoples, and I am glad you have joined me in this attempt." She hesitated. "Forgive my awkward question, but there are no precedents to follow and protocol stewards to ask. Is

Edeiya'rika the manner in which I should address you? Or would it be more appropriate to call you my lady mage, as we style our mages of the Great Circle?"

The Ryuven nodded with a smile. "Edeiya'rika is the complete address. There is no need for any additional honorific; it is all included. And then is it my lady mage for you, or shall I call you Mage Parma?"

"Mage Parma is simplest," Elysia agreed. "There are a few other options, but there's no need to complicate matters while attempting to focus on the task at hand."

"Indeed." Edeiya'rika shifted in the chair, adjusting her wings. She smiled, faintly uncomfortably. "Well, then, let us begin that task. Has Tamaryl'sho apprised you of his suggestion?"

Elysia shook her head. "I'm afraid he has not. I am here at the order of the Great Circle, and I am told you may explain to us some of the details of Ientu magic. I will not deny that this feels a bit like asking the fox to guard the chickens." Elysia surprised herself with her directness.

A Ryuven, to teach her magics to fight Ryuven. She had not expected this. She had not expected anything like this. Ewan had—had Ewan known?

But for all she knew, this Edeiya'rika might instruct her in inferior techniques, teach her and the other mages to rely upon them, and then set them to fall in battle, leaving Chrenada vulnerable without its Circle.

Edeiya'rika pursed her lips. "I am sorry to have surprised you."

"Surprised," repeated Elysia. "I will say this in the most bluntly respectful way I know how, Edeiya'rika, but I have spent my life fighting Ryuven invaders, and I did not think to hear that the solution to our latest Ryuven invasion is to bring more Ryuven into our land."

Edeiya'rika lifted her chin, and Elysia knew that was the moment she had lost the encounter, the treaty, the peace. She had spoken too rashly in her surprise and defense.

But Edeiya'rika nodded once. "I can see that. The chickens should be wary of inviting a fox into their roost."

Elysia wished she had chosen a different metaphor. "The chickens may have beaks and spurs, but it is easier to fight at one door than many."

"Of course. But let me explain that in this case, the fox should not allow another to choke off the source of its eggs."

"You assume the fox prefers eggs to meat."

"The fox might take meat, but as you say, chickens have beaks. Eggs make a safer and more reliable meal. And he must defend them to enjoy them."

"Until he grows tired of eggs and longs for the meat he once had. Then only his fear of the chickens will save them." Oh, this metaphor was growing tedious and ridiculous.

Edeiya'rika's face was strained. "Mage Parma, I am the Tsuraiya ni'Ai, charged with the defense of my people's welfare. I am no fox. Are you a chicken?"

Elysia looked at the Ryuven, saw the frustration evident in her expression, saw the ill-fitting green chair pushing her wings aside, saw the chance of alliance slipping away.

Her words to Ewan returned to her. *I suppose I should trust your judgment—should trust in my own judgment in placing you here—and obey this order to work with the Ryuven in our midst.*

Elysia met the Ryuven's eyes. "Bawk bawk."

For an eternal heartbeat they stared at one another, the words hanging in the air between them, nothing moving. Then Edeiya'rika broke into merry laughter, her shoulders and wing joints shaking. "Oh, essence, I thought for a moment you were serious," she gasped. "I had no idea how to go forward."

Elysia began to laugh too. "I was feeling so trapped in that figure of speech."

"Bawk, bawk! Oh, I have misunderstood humans."

"I have never seen a Ryuven laugh."

Edeiya'rika sobered at this. "No, I suppose not." She adjusted herself in the chair, shifting her wings as she could. "Do you mind if we try again, but without the foxes and chickens this time? Just as two dutiful rika, each determined to protect their own from harm?"

"I can understand that." Elysia kept her gaze level but open. "But for all my life, protecting from harm has meant barring the Ryuven."

Edeiya'rika nodded. "I do not know if it will help if I explain that I cannot—cannot—participate in a battle of conquest. That is the place of the Pairvyn and his warriors, and I would no more touch that than he would usurp my place to defend the Ai against invasion."

This idea was so strange to Elysia. "Are you saying that if your city were overrun, your men would not fight in its defense?"

"Overrun? Yes, yes they would—but it would be in desperation, and it would be an enormous dishonor, whether we were successful or not."

Elysia shook her head. "I don't quite understand."

"Would you be proud of failing so completely that children were forced to fight in your place?"

"Of course not. But they aren't children—they are experienced fighters who have been raiding for generations."

"But they are the army of conquest, and we are the army of defense, and they would be out of place."

She could not comprehend it. But it did not matter if Elysia understood it, she realized; it mattered that Edeiya'rika did, and that it drove her actions. She sat forward in her chair. "Tell me about Ryuven magics."

CHAPTER 15

Ariana was in her Wheel office, reorganizing her materials closet—because if she could not control the chaotic madness of resentful groups gathering armed in market plazas to murmur against the new Ryuven unbelievably attending the Indigo Mage's botany class, and if she could not guess the moment when King Jerome would learn of her marriage and come for her husband, she could at least put her herbs in order by use and name—when a knock sounded at her door. "Come," she called.

The door swung open to reveal Elysia Parma with a pleased grin, and the Ryuven Edeiya'rika immediately behind her. "Hello, Ariana," Mage Parma said. "Put down your work and come with us. We have important experiments to conduct, and we want company who will appreciate—that is, who will understand and apprehend the nature of our research."

Ariana would have leapt at any chance to break from the poor distraction of sorting and counting basic materials, but especially at the intrigue of arcane research with so exalted a company. "Of course, I should be glad to come. Where are we going, and what do I need to bring?"

"Just your cloak for the weather," Mage Parma said. "I've packed everything else we need."

If there was any surprise at the Silver Mage and the Black Mage walking through the city streets with a female Ryuven, no one expressed it aloud, though Ariana caught multiple wide-eyed stares and noticed more than a few children guided out of their path.

Mage Parma selected progressively less trafficked streets and led them to the north and west, until they finally came to a gate in the city wall. "Where are we going?" Ariana asked, a little belatedly.

"Into the hills," Mage Parma answered. "We will need some space. Unpopulated space."

"I should have brought a pie," Ariana ventured with a grin.

The Silver Mage laughed. "Not to worry. I have pies and drink in my bag." She glanced at the Ryuven. "After all, we have a guest, and we cannot fail in our hospitality."

They nodded to the gate's guards, awakened from their

drowsy duty by the unexpected appearance of a Ryuven and then perplexed by her exit from the city, and took the road to the hilly northwest. There were few travelers on this route, and as the road climbed Ariana wondered if Edeiya'rika kept to the ground out of a sense of politeness for her slower human companions or if walking required less effort than flying. Humans could run, but often it was more efficient to walk. So many questions she still hadn't asked...

After an hour's walk, they came to a wide gap between hills, barren and ugly. "Gravel was collected here," Mage Parma said, "so it's not worth much for anything now but magical experimentation."

Edeiya'rika turned in place, looking at the scoured rock. "I think this should do nicely, since you do not have fup rings."

Ariana pricked her ears at the word. "I remember fup, but I remember it as a punishment."

"It can be that, but it has other uses as well." Edeiya included Mage Parma in the explanation. "Fup is, put most simply, a material that absorbs magic. It can be used to temporarily draw the inherent magic from a Ryuven, which is the punishment you describe. It can also be used to restrain a prisoner. When Tamaryl'sho was bound by Oniwe'aru before the treaty was concluded, he was kept in fup-forged chains."

Ariana nodded, keeping her face perfectly still, and made a note to demand the rest of this story later. Tamaryl in chains? This was what he had kept from her. If he would not tell her, she would have the story from Edeiya'rika, once she'd earned the Ryuven's confidence.

"But it is also useful in non-punitive ways. In training, for example, we often spar in fup rings, enclosed by walls containing lines of fup to bound the magic. It prevents magics from spilling outside the ring, and it damps the effects within, allowing the opponents to practice realistically without limiting themselves."

"That sounds quite useful," Mage Parma observed. "And then is it useful as a defense in battle as well?"

For just an instant Edeiya's face clouded, and there was a moment when no one seemed to breathe, but then her brow smoothed. "No, for it would limit the wearer as much as anyone attacking the wearer. One could not be attacked magically, but neither could one defend oneself."

"That makes sense," Ariana said, and she smiled to reassure the Tsuraiya.

Did fup work on human magic? She didn't know. It clearly

hadn't affected her when used on Maru, but it had been directed at Maru, not affecting Daranai either. It was an interesting question to pose, but she would not ask while it might still sound less like an academic pursuit and more like a furtherance of war.

Edeiya also seemed anxious to leave the potentially unsettling topic behind. "And do we have our material for practice?"

"I've brought it," Mage Parma said. She set her pack on a rock and opened it, first removing a stack of wrapped pies and a jug of ale, true to her word. Then she tugged down the sides of the pack to reveal the tall crystal inside.

The Shard of Elan sat before them, cool and faceted and faintly violet in the sunlight. Edeiya reached a hand to touch it. "So solid," she said, almost a whisper. "So much energy, caught in stillness."

Ariana stared. "Is it—is it all right to bring it out here? Away from the Wheel?"

Then the significance of the scene struck her—Elysia Parma, the Silver Mage, had brought the Shard of Elan out of the Wheel and placed it within the grasp of Edeiya'rika, the Tsuraiya ni'Ai. The only hope of shielding the kingdom from Ryuven attack lay under the hand of a Ryuven, who could leap with it into another world entirely and leave the two mages helpless behind her.

Mage Parma laid a finger to her lips and grinned. "The Circle is charged with protecting the Shard," she said. "I can't protect it if I'm here and it's somewhere else, can I? Besides, it's ever so much more fun to play with it out here."

"Play with it?" Ariana repeated.

Something had happened. Somehow Mage Parma had found a common footing with Edeiya'rika and they had forged enough trust to come together with the Shard.

Mage Parma looked at Edeiya'rika. "We have some very important research to perform on the nature of collaborative energies refracted through crystalline ether. Research that requires certain large-scale experiments, which would be unsafe to host even within the careful construction of the Wheel. The responsible researcher would naturally seek out an empty gravel quarry to safely conduct these experiments."

Edeiya's expression broke into a wide conspiratorial grin.

Ariana gaped. "You're going to blow things up."

Mage Parma gave her a disappointed look. "That is such a mundane way of putting it. And so unscholarly."

Ariana hovered on the blade's edge between affronted shock and eager amazement. "You have brought the legendary and priceless Shard of Elan out to a gravel quarry, simply to destroy things."

"Well, we are supposed to be entertaining our guest of state," the Silver Mage answered. "I thought she might like to play with our best toys."

"Indeed," Edeiya answered with a prim nod of acknowledgment. "I would love to, and I thank you for your kindness."

"And this is why we asked you along, young Mage Hazelrig," Mage Parma said. "You are the only one who has used the Shard to enhance Ryuven energy brought from across the between-worlds."

Ariana gasped. "You want to do that?"

"After we've slagged a few unoffending boulders first, of course. But all jesting and funning aside, that is a very real area of research which has not been pursued, for obvious reasons. It requires a Ryuven to hold open the entry into the between-worlds and draw the energy into the Shard." She nodded toward Edeiya, who nodded in return. "Aside from military application, there are quite a lot of academic questions to be addressed, questions which, if answered, might shed light on everything from the similarities of human and Ryuven magic to the nature of the between-worlds." Mage Parma put a hand on the top of the Shard, wrapping her fingers about the crystalline angles. "And of course, it might be fun."

She extended her other hand toward the wall and released a bolt of energy into the dirty grey wall. Ariana felt it shiver through the air, heard its impact, saw the color in her sight that was not truly seeing.

"Well, that was disappointing," Mage Parma observed. "Merely typical, not enhanced by simple contact with the Shard. I had read as much, of course, but I had never tried it myself."

"But it wasn't a bad effort," Edeiya observed. "A good defense."

"Bawk, bawk," Mage Parma answered, and the two of them laughed over Ariana's confused look.

Edeiya turned to Ariana. "When you and Tamaryl'sho shared power, how did he feed the Shard?"

Ariana shook her head. "We didn't take the time to discuss it. Maru held a shield to protect us from below, Tamaryl kept the between-worlds open to draw power, and I directed it out of the Shard."

"Well, let's see." Edeiya placed two hands on the Shard, for balance, and glanced upward with her eyes half-closed.

Ariana felt the rift, as if the air around her had thinned and the cold black of the between-worlds threatened to burst through into the sunny quarry. She tightened and looked at Mage Parma, who she saw had also sensed it. But the sky did not fade into dark, the sun stayed warm on their skin, and the Shard brightened, both in Ariana's second vision and to the natural eye.

"Try it now," Edeiya said, her eyes still half-closed.

Mage Parma put her hand between Edeiya's and extended the other toward the wall again. Energy crackled out, flashing bright—visibly bright, actually *visible*—and slammed into the wall so that it cracked and powdered at the site of impact, sending a little stream of dust and pebbles toward the ground.

"King's sweet oats," Mage Parma said. "That tingled."

"I could *see* it," Ariana reported breathlessly. "Not in my mind. I could really *see* it."

"So could I," Mage Parma said, a little awed. She stopped to sneeze. "And let me tell you, it smelled quite strongly, too."

Edeiya had opened her eyes and was looking back and forth between them. "What do you mean, see it? Smell it?" Then her eyes widened. "Oh! You don't—magic is not a natural sense for you! Ah, I understand. It's like a snake flying with a bird, and telling the story of how they jumped."

Mage Parma harrumphed. "I am not sure how I feel about this illustration, but you have the general idea. We experience magic backhandedly through different senses, but to see it with one's own natural sight is not usual."

"What does it feel like?" Ariana asked eagerly. "To you? What does magic feel like?"

Edeiya pursed her lips. "It feels like...magic. I don't know how to say it! It's... Well, you know how birds can fly to their nesting places, regardless of where they start? How they always know which direction is north?"

"Yes," Ariana pressed.

"Tell me, what does north feel like, to know which direction it is?"

Ariana screwed up her face. "I see your point. I am not a bird, to have such a sense. Nor am I a Ryuven."

"But you can sense and manipulate magic," Edeiya added

quickly, "even without a natural sense for it. By contrast, you can't fly without wings. That's impressive."

Ariana nodded slowly. "Can others in your world use magic?" she asked suddenly, hardly thinking of the question before speaking.

"Other Ryuven? Of course they can."

"No, not Ryuven—animals. Magic is natural to your world, inherent to your people. Is it inherent to everything? Can animals in your world use magic? Plants?"

Edeiya considered. "We have tried magic to boost our agriculture, but with limited success, so I think it is safe to say that our plants do not inherently use magic. And no, our animals do not, either, other than that which only appears to be magic, like birds knowing how to sense north."

Ariana nodded. "So only Ryuven, and only humans. And we learned to use magic that arguably shouldn't exist in our worlds, because it's not inherent to anything else."

"Now you're sounding like your father again," Mage Parma said. "And I'm sure his questions are valid and useful, but they are far more attractive to contemplate over a plate of cheeses in front of a warm fire, and just now I think I would prefer to try blasting that slide of gravel into a slag pile. Edeiya'rika, if you please?"

Edeiya placed her hands upon the Shard again, and Mage Parma touched the crystal and extended her hand to release another bolt. Ariana flinched away from it—something she had not done since she was a child—and the crackling light slammed into the wall, triggering a small cascade.

"Hold a moment," Ariana said, and she jogged to the targeted area. She squatted and peered at the fallen stone. It had a white powdery coating now. "It's changed?"

"Hmm." Mage Parma frowned as she crouched beside Ariana. "Ah, of course. We've made quicklime. Don't touch it."

Edeiya'rika knelt on Ariana's other side, shifting her wings for balance. "That suggests a very intense bolt of magic, with quite a lot of surplus heat thrown off into the surrounding rock."

"Yes, and I didn't throw anything that should have lent heat. We're seeing an inelastic collision with tremendous kinetic to thermal conversion."

Ariana tried to work the formula, and her mind shrank from the math.

"Hmm." Mage Parma's face was abnormally still.

Ariana began to suspect that she was hiding her true reaction. "What aren't you saying?"

Mage Parma gave her a look that bordered on annoyance. "Nothing against your skills, Mage Hazelrig, but I think you didn't have any particular target when you quelled that battle."

"What? No, I just—I am ashamed to say it, but I just thought of wanting them to stop and I struck out. It was nothing at all like what I had trained for, but then it felt nothing at all like I had trained for, and of course I'd never dreamed to face two armies from the sky." Ariana realized she sounded defensive, but it hurt to admit she had reverted to apprentice-level frantic casting.

Mage Parma nodded. "We were all initially distracted with the excess of perception, but this energy has a certain chaotic quality. Which I suppose is only to be expected, by the time we drag it from another world and channel it through a hardened star, but you see, I had aimed my blast at that vertical crack just there." She pointed a dozen paces to their right.

Edeiya'rika followed the gesture and turned her mouth down. "You don't strike me as one who often misses her target."

"Not to brag, but no."

"Shall we try again?"

They resumed their positions, and Mage Parma jerked her head to urge Ariana further back, next to Edeiya'rika and the Shard. Then she released another crackling bolt.

Dust plumed into the air, but they did not have to wait long to see that the blast spread wide over the wall, this time two dozen paces to the right of the crack.

"You aimed for the same crack?" Ariana asked, more to confirm aloud than in doubt.

"I think," Mage Parma answered dryly, "that I'm successfully hitting the wall only because it's so generously large and not moving too quickly." She dropped her hand from the Shard and placed five rapid bolts tracing the twisting crack in quick succession. "Oh, good, I haven't just gone bad. Ariana, you'll find a book and a graphite pencil in my bag. Be good enough to write this down, please?"

Ariana found the items and began to roughly sketch the wall, marking the crack, Mage Parma's precise bolts along its line, and the two sprawling, smoking blast points.

"It's too charged, coming across and through the Shard." Edeiya'rika grasped the crystal again. "I can't bring over the energy without pouring it into the Shard; it just dissipates without a physical reservoir. But it's so volatile, coming over, and the Shard itself is so...I don't know if it can be gathered like ordinary magic."

"But it could be used as a weapon, right?" Ariana asked. "It's powerful enough."

"Perhaps, if one didn't care too much for one's own front lines," Mage Parma answered. "But if I tried to target an opponent over my soldiers' heads, there's a fair chance of taking off some of those heads as well."

"It's a good thing, then, that we're pursuing academic research and not developing a new weapon," Edeiya'rika observed with a pointedly light tone.

Mage Parma turned back. "Just so." She smiled. "Let's go on then and see what we can learn."

CHAPTER 16

"Do you have a moment?"

"Of course!" Ariana beckoned Calissa inside the townhouse door. "Can I offer you something? I didn't know you were coming, so you'll have to make do with stale spice cake. Very embarrassing; don't speak of my poor hospitality or there will be an international incident."

Calissa smiled, but it didn't reach her eyes. "No princess jokes today, please. That's part of why I'm here."

Ariana stopped and turned back to her. "Are they recalling you home?"

"No. Well, not yet. But they might, when they hear." Calissa shook her head and went to the stuffed chair she preferred. "I'm getting ahead of myself."

"Take a minute to organize your thoughts," Ariana said. "Three minutes, to be precise. I already have the fire up, so that's the time it will take to prepare tea. And stale cake."

When she returned, Calissa had her legs drawn under her and both hands resting on one arm of the chair. "I know you can keep a secret, so I won't insult you by asking, and I'll just leap into the deep: I think I'm falling in love with Prince Soren."

Ariana bit her lip and eased the tray she held onto the table. "Just let me get that out of my hands before you tell me any more. You say you're falling in love?"

"Or, perhaps better said, I already have. We've been seeing quite a lot of each other. Last night we stayed up until moonset discussing tariff reforms."

"My, you certainly lead a charming romance any bard would yearn to tell." Ariana gave her a plate with crumbly cake.

Calissa chuckled. "I know it sounds dreadful, but that's just it—it wasn't. We have good ideas together, testing each other's assumptions and pressing for better answers. I could have talked another three hours, but he had morning meetings. But Ariana, what do I do?"

"What do you mean?"

"I am a princess of the Wakari Coast; I can't just fall in love. My marriage is not for me, but for a country. More, my sister was supposed to marry him and that went awry; that leaves me in a peculiar position." Her voice was strained. "I can't want the prince-heir of Chrenada."

You'd be surprised what you can want, Ariana thought, but aloud she said, "I remember someone teasing me about a forbidden love."

Calissa lobbed a pillow at her. "Curse your accurate memory at this inopportune time."

Ariana pushed the pillow aside and picked up her tea. "Let's start with the foremost question: what does Prince Soren think?"

Calissa folded into the chair and looked down. "That's the worst part of it."

"He's not interested?"

"No—I think he is. Maybe it's presumptuous of me, but...I think he cares for me too."

"Calissa! Why is that worse?"

She covered her face with her hands. "Because we can't want each other. Because if I cannot want the prince-heir, then of course we cannot both want an inappropriate match."

"What if it's not so inappropriate? If they wanted an alignment with your sister, why not with you?"

Calissa uncovered her face and rolled her eyes. "Because I am a younger princess, not suitable for a primary alliance. There are protocols for this sort of thing. Chrenada would be insulted by the offer."

Ariana shrugged one shoulder. "If what you say is true, maybe not all of Chrenada."

Calissa stared. "Don't play coy with me, Ariana. Do you think it's possible?"

"If your advisers want an alliance, and Prince Soren wants an alliance, it seems that something could be worked out, regardless of which princess is the bride in the alliance," Ariana said. "I'm no authority on court politics or international negotiations, you'd want Bethia for that, and certainly I'm not to be heeded on strategic marriages. But Prince Soren is a prince; he should have some say in it, shouldn't he?"

Calissa sucked a long, slow breath. "I should have some tea."

"Oy, Wilkin! Got time for a drink?"

The broad-shouldered farmer turned back. "A respectable man doesn't stop his work for drinking, but I expect getting a couple of pints into a disreputable scoundrel like you is the only way I'll get that money you owe."

"Disreputable scoundrel? That's a terrible way to speak of your new father. Or hasn't your mother told you the news yet?"

The two men growled and embraced affectionately. "How are Pirly and the boys?" asked Wilkin.

"Oh, fine, fine," answered Rian. "And I hope your little one is growing well? Last I saw you, she was just a couple of weeks new."

"Oh, she's wonderful." Wilkin beamed. "Eyes like stars and a grip like a smith. She's crawling into everything; probably driving poor Bree to distraction as we're speaking."

"Glad to hear it. That drink?"

"I meant to head out this afternoon, but I've certainly got time for a pint first."

Wilkin took his own produce to the city markets; it was only a couple of days' travel, and worth it for saving the middle merchants' cut. That might have to change soon, now that the children had started coming, and when the time came to stay home, he would probably entrust his goods to Rian.

They went together into a public room and ordered food and drink. "Good trip?" Rian asked.

Wilkin nodded. "Sold everything within a few hours, and good prices. Some are saying it's the threat of Ryuven raids pushing up prices, and some are saying it's the extra demand from Ryuven buyers, and I don't pretend to know the difference, but I'll take the coin, thank you kindly."

"That's a quick return home, too."

"Yes, and I'll take that as well. Might take it direct through the hills, now that the cart's empty."

"Blessed you. I'll be going out in a few days and sweating the long way around." Rian grinned.

"If you're taking that way... Be careful at Greenwell."

"Bandits?"

"No, just... It's hard to say, but there was something odd about it. You know Mother Katie?"

"Sharpest tongue and the biggest heart."

"Just so, and I'd been honing my opening insult for six miles, figured I finally had one to give her pause. But when I came into the village, she didn't even... She just came out with water and a pie, like usual, but barely said a word. I tried to goad her a bit, and she just told me to be quiet. Just like that, straight, not a breath about my descent from pigs or my nose's resemblance to a plow."

Rian shifted in his seat. "Is she ill?"

"She looked well enough, in that way—but it wasn't her alone, the whole village felt off. I was going to spend the night but, and I'm near ashamed to say it, but I went on and pushed to Lowwall instead. I just...didn't feel right."

"That's so odd. Mother Katie! Did you note anything wrong about the place? You would have seen smoking ruins. Did the plague hit them?"

"I can't imagine they've got sickness, or other travelers wouldn't be there, and there were a couple of priests who came out of the inn after Mother Katie. They weren't leaving, either, just standing around like—" The thought occurred to him for the first time. "Like they were just keeping an eye on things."

Rian gave him a skeptical look. "I suppose priests would have a hard time working her out, caught between the cuts she says and the kindnesses she does."

"Not regular priests," Wilkin added. "These were in blue. I don't know much about priests who wear blue."

Rian shook his head. "I don't—is that the fighting group? Something with a G. Something about secret wars."

"Oh, I know the ones you mean. I suppose it might be them. What would they want in Greenwell? There's no war there, not unless someone spills porridge on Mother Katie's fresh linen."

"Couldn't say. But thanks for the word. I don't know, maybe I'll make a point to stop and see how things are. If there's a chance I can see Mother Katie without her making my father weep in his grave for the shame of siring such a failure, I should take it—and if there's something else in the town, we should know of it."

Ariana stopped mid-stride as the nagging feeling that had tugged at her mind all the last two days suddenly crystallized. With a start, she realized what she had not grasped in the gravel quarry.

Fup absorbed magic. Fup could protect from magic. If she could get fup for Shianan, the Ientu could not strike him down in ambush. It was useless for mages, but it could save Shianan.

She went to her desk, abandoning her other tasks, and drew out a fresh sheet of paper. She began noting down questions nearly as fast as she could think of them. *Where is it obtained? How is it activated? Will it function in the same way if held by someone who does not work magic? Does it expire or see its effect fade? How much magic can it absorb or damp?*

How many soldiers can be equipped?

The price could not matter, not for such a prize as this. This could protect their army, protect their towns, protect Shianan. She would bring her questions to Edeiya'rika.

CHAPTER 17

Shianan let himself into his office and pushed the door behind him. Safely out of sight, he unbuckled his swordbelt and dropped it, left-handed, onto his desk. He held out his right arm tentatively and it trembled midair, no matter how he tried to stabilize it. He lowered it and dug his fingers into the sore muscles of his upper arm, hissing his discomfort.

Well, fussing at it would help nothing. He sat down at his desk and flipped his sheaf of reports. There was too much to do, too much to stay ahead of, and he wanted to lock that door and hide behind it until he had at least crawled out from the pile of work threatening to overwhelm him. Between the fresh attacks and the complication of the Pairvyn and all that was happening, he wasn't sure how he could expect to keep up with his usual workload as well, and that was before considering his new marriage.

Someone knocked at the door, and Shianan groaned to himself.

"I'll come," called Luca, and he passed through to open the door.

But the servant outside was not bringing an additional task. He wore Prince Soren's livery. "If you please, my lord, you are invited to join His Highness for supper."

"Of course. Tell your master I will be there."

"And you are to bring your servant as well, if you please, my lord."

Shianan glanced at Luca. "Of course."

Luca took the details of time and place and then closed the door behind the messenger, his face puzzled. "Surely the prince has enough servants of his own not to need an untrained hand at supper."

"I suppose the prince likes your company as well. And you're not so untrained; you know table manners for Chrenada, the Wakari Coast, and Vandoga."

"But not for royalty in any land." Luca's eyebrows were drawn close; he was beginning to fret.

"As you say, it's not that he doesn't have servants," Shianan added. "He's probably got something else for you while we discuss whatever it is he wants. His sitting room is hardly a traditional dining place, so he must have something private to talk about. Maybe he'll put you to work in Ethan's spy network."

Luca made a face, but his shoulders dropped a fraction. "Ethan doesn't need a spy network. He just knows everything." He turned back to the door. "I'll let the Hazelrigs know you won't be joining them for supper tonight."

The evening air was still warm when they crossed to the Naziar and went to the prince's office door. They were admitted promptly, gestured inside by Ethan. "My master is just coming. Please, may I offer you a drink?"

As he waited, Shianan gently worked his stiff shoulder. He wondered idly whether, after what might be a late evening with the prince, he would go to the Hazelrig house for a later night with Ariana, and whether the elder Mage Hazelrig would be irritated if Shianan knocked at the door so late. Then he wondered at the unimaginable grandeur of parceling his time between the prince-heir and a wife.

"Thank you for waiting for me," Soren said as he entered, as if he were not the prince-heir. "Let's sit. Tell me if your day has been as mad as mine."

They started with bread and oil. Ethan held back, letting Luca refill the oil and herbs—an honor, Shianan understood, and a mark of trust in the other servant. Luca, for his part, seemed nervous and glanced often at Ethan, but he performed the tasks without too much hesitation.

"I hope the defenses against the Ientu raiders are coming along," Soren said. "The council is in quite the stir, what with a Ryuven military adviser. I won't be going out for any fighting, not like I did at Arakadamia, so I'll have to rely on you to manage for me."

Of course he would not go; he was still recovering, and the kingdom would not risk its prince-heir a second time. But Shianan said, "That's good to hear. I'll be better able to concentrate if I don't have to watch for princes falling over cliffs."

Soren huffed in mock offense and took a drink of wine.

When the supper came, Ethan inserted himself once more. The food—vegetables coaxed out of season from the royal enclosed garden, dressed in sauces to disguise their age and spread alongside thin cutlets of pork—was good, and the vegetables a welcome change from the usual and more easily preserved winter fare. But Shianan could not shake the impression that Soren was building up to something.

Ethan moved a coffer to Soren's side, silent and unobtrusive and confirming Shianan's suspicion. "I'll bring another pitcher, my lord," he said, and he went out.

Soren glanced at Shianan, as if sensing his thoughts, and then looked down at his plate. He ran a piece of bread through a spill of sauce. "I'm glad you're here. That you came tonight."

"I'm always glad to answer my prince's invitation."

"Well, I suppose I should admit I invited you here not merely for a meal and pleasant conversation," Soren said. "But I find it's harder to bring up, now that we're here."

Ice crystallized all along Shianan's veins.

"Oh—I don't think—I should have told you, it isn't something upsetting. No, for a change, it's good news."

"What?"

Soren cleared his throat. "Well, I'm not sure how to explain this, to start. I sent to Cascais."

Across the room, Luca stiffened.

"This was after you told me what happened, while I was still recovering in bed. My emissaries checked the ledgers at the slave market, and there were no obvious inaccuracies. But when they interviewed the merchants, they found a certain laxity of process, and under stern questions several admitted that they could not be certain of the origin or legal status of all the slaves passing through their market, that it happened that someone might bring in a group to be cuffed and then sold, sometimes hastily or at a bargain price. That, with the story you related and your assertion that freemen are at risk of abduction and enslavement, did not look well for our citizens.

"Your account had prompted me to think about protections against such traffickers. So I have been in discussions with our lawyers. This was started of course before this fresh Ryuven threat arose, but I have been assured that we can indeed establish a certificate of status, to legally protect freemen from enslavement."

"That is good news," Shianan agreed. "It would have saved Luca." He looked at the slave, but Luca was not smiling.

Soren nodded. "I don't know yet when it will go into effect, especially with all this happening, but I am told it can be done, even with expected protests about regulation raising the cost of labor. It's not good business to be losing our citizens. So please keep that quiet until we can announce it properly, but I wanted you—both of you—to know. And there's more." He opened the coffer and withdrew a folded document, heavy and signed with a royal seal just visible as a corner sagged. "With the evidence of laxity in Cascais, I wrangled an official manumission from illegal enslavement. This is for Luca."

He extended his arm, still an inhibited reach, and set the document on the table. Shianan looked between Soren and Luca, but the slave was frozen in place. Shianan reached to take it, unfolding it. Yes, it was a legal document, thick with complicated language but clearly a statement of free status.

"But the law," Shianan said. "How could you do it?"

"The laws forbid freeing slaves," Soren said, "but one must be legally enslaved before they apply. If Luca was a free man as he entered Alham, he should not have been unjustly enslaved, and so the laws for slaves cannot apply to him."

Shianan looked to Luca, his heart swelling with happiness for his friend. "Luca, isn't that—isn't that wonderful?"

Luca was still standing stiff and silent. At Shianan's words, he seemed to catch his breath. "Yes, my lord," he managed. "Yes, of course. Thank you, my lord."

Soren laughed. "I suppose it might be something of a surprise. Go on, Luca, you don't need to wait upon our talk. Go and find Ethan, get a drink to celebrate."

Luca nodded tightly, squeezed out, "Thank you, my lord," and then slipped out of the room.

Shianan looked after him and then turned back to Soren. "It has to be overwhelming. He's changed hands so many times. But thank you for this—for all of it, the certificate and especially for his freedom."

Soren smiled. "I thought you would be in favor of it. Any man who would send his friend to another country to free him would accept a paper to do it here."

"I'm still grateful for your help. That day, with the courts—"

"It's done. It won't be a danger for Luca again." Soren looked down at his plate. "To change the subject, I hope to have an announcement for myself in the near future."

"Oh?"

"I was intended to marry the Wakari princess, as you know, and that match fell through."

"Because of me." Shianan knew it was not his fault, not really, but that did not mean he would not carry the blame of it. If the royal family had not been distracted with arguing over the bastard, if Soren had not needed to retire from the ball instead of meeting the princess, if Soren had not taken the blow meant for Shianan...

"Because of the king's temper," Soren corrected with an even, detached tone. "And so I was left without a princess to wed, a pitiful figure from a bard's second-best tale. And then you were to escort the princess and her emissaries back to the Wakari Coast, only the Ryuven attacked, and so they remained here until their travel should be less dangerous."

"Yes."

"And all those tragedies worked together, and now I again intend to marry a Wakari princess. Just, not the one who was sent for me."

Shianan stared at him. "Another one?"

"Princess Calissa, the younger sister. Do you know her? She is a friend of Lady Ariana. I met her when I went to apologize for the whole disaster, and I thought she was my intended princess—which was more than a bit humiliating, especially as I was attempting to apologize. But it has turned out for the best, and I mean to ask my father to approve our match and request the renewal of the alliance, but with the younger sister." Soren's expression softened to an affectionate, embarrassed smile. "She's brilliant. And kind, and beautiful. I was fortunate to commit the error."

Shianan grinned at him. "But does she think anything good of you?"

Soren flushed. "She has said as much, yes."

"That's good to hear. I hope they are amenable to the new arrangement."

"I have a force in reserve," Soren confided. "If my father balks, I'll ask my mother. Or I might go to her to start. I suspect she had as much to do with the proposed alliance as any of the council."

The words stung faintly; Soren could simply ask for the woman he wanted, and even after a political embarrassment, he could expect to have her. Shianan could not bring himself to be angry with the prince-heir, but the difference chafed.

But he could not complain. He had wed Ariana despite the countless and steep hurdles. They had made a marriage of their own, and he was grateful.

He could not tell Soren, not even Soren. Not yet. But one day.

Shianan reached for his glass and raised it. "To brilliant women."

When Shianan left Prince Soren, Luca was nowhere to be seen. Shianan did not think much of it; with such a great change in his circumstances, he might have gone to walk with his surprised thoughts, or to buy himself a drink to celebrate. Or maybe—maybe he had gone to the temple where he'd somehow been talked into defending Flamen Ande.

The sudden rush of hot resentment surprised him. He was still angry that Luca had gone to the trial, of course—no matter what Luca said about justice and their own complicity, and no matter that he knew Ande was innocent of that accusation if in nothing else, he could not bear that Ande had been released to threaten Luca yet again.

But this was more—too quick, too hot, too familiar. He knew this anger, fast and bright and protective. He knew if he probed this flare of fury, he would find something else in its shadow.

His step hesitated and then he pushed on through the dark. He knew the way, he feared nothing in the Naziar night, and he did not want to think about what it would mean for Luca to leave again.

But when he reached his quarters, Luca was there, asleep in his bed. Shianan moved quietly, by now practiced in not waking him, and went to bed.

Luca left a candle burning against the dark, near Shianan's bed, and went to his own pallet against the far wall. He put his back to the light and lay motionless when Shianan finally came home. His master must have thought him asleep, for he said nothing and quietly went to bed.

Luca had not gone to find Ethan, but Ethan would have seen to the rest of their masters' evening.

Luca wished he had labored harder, in more difficult chores, so that exhaustion would take him from the thoughts that plagued him in the dark.

The next morning, he followed their usual routine, bringing a light breakfast for Shianan before his master went out for his duties. Luca then attempted his usual chores, but they were not enough to distract him, and at last he dropped into a chair and stared at the thick, official document lying on the table opposite him.

He had sat like this before, his chin resting on his hands, staring at a new and surprising legal document that promised to change his life. His eyes ran over the seal, across the heavy texture of the paper, back to the seal.

That paper was freedom, real and assured. He should be overjoyed. He had wanted change. He should be giddy with happiness.

Cole would not have felt conflicted. Cole would not have hesitated. Cole would have fought for this paper. Why wasn't Luca glad, like he knew he should be?

He was a fraud, wishing for and yet frightened by what he had craved for so many years.

He did not hear Shianan arrive until his master came into the bedroom, and Luca scrabbled up and grabbed for the document.

But he was too slow for Shianan's practiced eyes. "That's not an expression of celebration, I don't think."

Luca did not have an answer.

"Sit down," Shianan said, and Luca obeyed. Shianan drew a chair next to him, shoulder to shoulder. "What's wrong?"

Luca still had no words. He gestured feebly at the document, as if it could explain what he himself did not understand.

Shianan waited. Luca knew he had come into the room for another purpose, knew he had stacks of work waiting in the office, but he waited without speaking.

Luca folded his hands in his lap and squeezed his fingers white. Somehow a sentence pushed through the thick scab of his guilty fear. "I'm terrified."

Shianan tipped his head, surprised, but did not answer. He leaned forward, his forearms on his knees, waiting for Luca to sort through his words.

"I'm terrified. I don't—I can't. All my life... I have never been my own man."

Shianan frowned at the floor. "Weren't you a freeman in Ivat and the Wakari Coast?"

"I was." Luca clenched his hands in frustration. This all sounded so foolish when he tried to explain it. "But at first, I was still—I was free, but..." How weak it sounded, put into fragile words.

But everything had been different then. Shianan's betrayal, Jarrick's appearance, even the negotiations with Cole—he'd had no time to wonder at his new situation. And then everything had been different again, and still it had not been enough; he had reunited with his siblings and received an inheritance and taken another name, and even then Isen had seen what he really was.

Here, there was only a piece of paper to say that his life had changed, and suddenly he was supposed to be someone wholly different, someone who had not lived his life, someone who had not immediately lost his freedom and others'.

He made a frustrated gesture. "For a few days only, I was entirely responsible for myself—and also for someone else, and that ended so badly. I have no idea where he is now. I lost my inheritance. To be free—I should be delighted, I know I should be grateful, and I'm so wretchedly guilty that I don't feel that way, but I don't. I'm afraid. I don't know how to go alone."

"Something else Ande stole from you." Shianan's voice was a soft snarl.

Maybe that was true; Luca didn't know. Maybe it had begun when he was a third son. Maybe he had never been able to stand for himself. "I've had no reply. From my brothers and sister." He was afraid to send another letter, afraid it would not be answered either.

Shianan stared ahead, his eyes on the document. "You won't be alone."

Luca couldn't breathe, couldn't see through the blur in his vision, couldn't speak through the tightening of his throat.

"You're free, Luca," Shianan said softly. "That means you can go anywhere you choose—even if you choose Alham."

Luca crushed his hands together, making his fingers flare with pain and then go numb. "Is that all right? Even if I choose the Naziar?"

Shianan stared at the table. "The Naziar is a palace-fortress, all royals and courtiers, and I don't know if they will offer a position for a freed accountant. But you could find a place among the troops attached to the Naziar."

Luca could not see the paper or the table. He couldn't answer Shianan, and he felt strangely helpless. He was vulnerable in his tender new freedom where his decisions could betray his desires and expose new weaknesses, where he could fail in ways that were impossible when his actions were not his own.

"I would have to pay you," Shianan said. "You should work out what an acceptable rate will be."

Luca laughed, a sound like a sob but not born of grief. He wiped his betraying eyes.

Shianan straightened and stood. "I have work," he said simply.

"I'll be in the next room."

Luca heard the unspoken rest, and he nodded.

CHAPTER 18

Tamaryl knew the way through the Wheel, but he had to pretend to look around to find the right route to the Indigo Mage's office. Beside him, Edeiya'rika looked toward the Silver Mage's door as they passed, as if hoping to see someone.

Shianan Becknam walked a few paces behind them, nominally present as Tamaryl's attached escort but also as a guard, either to defend the Ryuven in case of an angry Chrenadan attacker or to act if the Ryuven guests offered trouble. As if Tamaryl or Edeiya would choose to open battle in the very Wheel of the Great Circle.

Tamaryl glanced toward the cellar stairs. Well, he had done so before.

They came to the office they wanted, and Shianan moved to knock on the dark blue door. An irritated voice grated from inside, "Come in."

Edeiya turned her head and raised her eyebrow slightly. Tamaryl shook his head. Irascibility was only to be expected of Taev Callahan.

They were given proper stools—Mage Callahan had them for his Ryuven students, of course—and Shianan took a position near the door. Mage Callahan wasted little time in introductions. "I've had those Ryuven apprentices all over your fields, bringing notes and sketches and pressings and soils. I hope you understand I'm doing the best I can without ever actually seeing what I'm meant to be diagnosing."

"We understand," Tamaryl said. "We appreciate your efforts."

That seemed to mollify Mage Callahan somewhat. "They've been good apprentices. It's not easy to find worthwhile students." He fanned out a stack of pages across the table between them. "The blight—I believe it's a fungus. It's not one like I've seen here; I am making a few educated guesses as to the particulars. But I think I'm near enough to make recommendations. It's a fungus."

"What does that mean?" Edeiya asked. "That is, I know what a fungus is—but so do our farmers. What does that mean for them? How do they treat it?"

"They don't," Mage Callahan answered. "At least, not at first.

The first step is to stop spreading it so widely."

"Our growers are doing their best to stop its spread," Tamaryl said. "They burn the blighted fields. They often lose an entire harvest in trying to stop it."

"And they're spreading it." Mage Callahan pointed to a sketch of a spotted leaf, as if that should prove his point. "The burning is spreading the spores."

"What?"

"Once the blight is visible, the spores are mature enough to spread, and the burning releases them. The hot winds of the fire will carry them, perhaps for miles, though I can't say for certain."

"So we should not burn?" Edeiya asked.

"Rather, you should not burn too late," Mage Callahan corrected. "You must burn before the blight shows."

"But how to know what to burn?" Tamaryl asked. "If the blight isn't yet visible, there's no way to see what's infected."

"It's all infected." Mage Callahan made a broad gesture. "All of it. I can't test that myself, but if what I'm told is even half right, it's endemic. You've been spreading it too long."

"Then...then what do we do?"

"Burn everything." Mage Callahan swept his arm through the air, encompassing the whole room. "Burn it all. All your crops, all your tilled fields. Everywhere you've planted this findore, assume it's tainted and burn it out."

For a moment, Tamaryl could not answer. He could not even imagine doing as the mage said. The idea was simply too large, too dangerous.

"That is impossible." Edeiya recovered her voice first. "We have so little harvest as it is. We cannot afford to destroy everything at once."

"You cannot afford not to." Mage Callahan fanned the corners of the pages until he found the one he wanted and traced his finger across a graph. "Look at how the lines are dropping in near synchronization. If these harvest logs are right, you experience more and more loss with fewer salvageable fields, on average, each year. You stop it, or you watch it slowly take the rest."

There was a long moment of uncomfortable silence in the room while thoughts whirled in Tamaryl's head. If they burned everything—if they razed the fields and purged the ground—

"We would starve," Edeiya said hoarsely. "We don't have

enough stores to manage a season with no harvest at all."

"You would need supplies," Mage Callahan agreed. "Fortunately, Chrenada has had two excellent years, and there is surplus to sell."

Edeiya's eyes blazed. "You mean to impoverish us and make us wholly dependent upon your human aid. You would beggar us, keep us beholden, and then what? And then cut off our only means of survival?"

Mage Callahan sighed and rolled the graph into a tube. "I don't know why you asked for my opinion if you don't want to hear it."

Edeiya set her jaw. "It is reasonable to question so enormous and so critical a suggestion."

"I suppose that's fair." The Indigo Mage straightened and crossed his arms. "Look, I understand you have no reason to trust me. Even at this moment, we—all skilled fighters and elite among our own peoples—are supervised by a military escort to keep our peace, like squabbling children with a nanny."

Shianan shifted against the wall but said nothing.

"But allow me to illuminate this particular workroom a little further. I am your best choice for an honest recommendation. Not only am I the most skilled arcane botanist you will find, but I have few political alliances. I serve the king because I serve in the Great Circle, but my political duties are limited to defending the kingdom—which is not under threat, as we still have a treaty and as you're here without spells flying about—and to conducting my research, which is currently fixed on your Ryuven fields and which, I confess, I am enjoying very much. Beyond that, I have no alliances, and no one cultivates my favor or invites me to private coalition."

Edeiya skewed her mouth into a doubtful scowl. Tamaryl sniffed. "It may be true," he said. "Everyone does hate him."

Mage Callahan frowned at Tamaryl. "It's not that you're wrong, but how did you know that? Did Mage Hazelrig say so, and so bluntly?"

Tamaryl realized with a start that he had spoken with knowledge the Pairvyn should not have had. He had let his shock and frustration run ahead of his careful speech.

Behind him, he was keenly aware of Shianan Becknam's eyes.

"Mage Hazelrig said nothing of the sort," Tamaryl answered, trying to sound more collected than he felt.

Mage Callahan tipped his head to regard Tamaryl out of his

scarred face, and for one panicked moment Tamaryl thought he knew, thought he could see the slave and famulus Tam in the Pairvyn ni'Ai, thought they were at last discovered.

Mage Callahan screwed his mouth up, twisting the scar. "And yet you assumed so broadly."

Tamaryl turned his palms up, as if the answer were evident. "I am present in the court. Many courtiers assume I am too unfamiliar to understand what I might overhear."

Mage Callahan shrugged. "Most of those idiots have no idea what I do for them."

Tamaryl relaxed slightly.

"With respect," Edeiya said, "that protestation does not bring me comfort or assurance. If your own do not trust you, how can we entrust the lives of our entire clan to your advice?"

"I want this peace as much as you," Mage Callahan answered flatly. "Not for the same reasons, I'll grant—don't look for any great altruistic love for your people. But my plans will bear more fruit if our treaty holds."

"And perhaps you intend to ensure that treaty by beggaring our people." Edeiya's voice was cool.

"We need a reason to trust you." Tamaryl shifted uneasily. "Your reputation is for effectiveness, but without much personal investment. If you—"

"You don't understand! I identified the dall sweetbud—the samur. I urged the king and council to seek a treaty and a trade agreement."

Tamaryl stiffened. "I think Mage Ariana Hazelrig had some contribution."

Mage Callahan waved a hand. "How do you suppose she knew what the herb was? Or had the credibility to speak knowledgeably of a rare herb she'd never studied?"

"So you helped to press for the treaty," Edeiya allowed. "That does not mean we should trust you to the point of sacrificing our people."

Mage Callahan rolled his eyes. "I have already sacrificed mine."

No one spoke. Tamaryl's mind spun, trying to grasp what he might mean.

Assured of their attention, the Indigo Mage regarded them with a sardonic half-smile. "Might I earn your trust with a secret? I have already explained I am trustworthy precisely because no one likes me. Now I think I can trust you for the same reason—the word of two Ryuven cannot unseat me. And the word of Shianan Becknam against a mage of the Circle—no offense, commander, but..."

Shianan raised a weary hand. "It's understood."

"Well, then, I will tell you, I do not ask you to risk anything I have not already done myself. Do you think Chrenada was so desperate for peace at any cost that we would have readily accepted a treaty with our old enemy?" He barked a short, bitter laugh. "When Ariana Hazelrig found the rare dall sweetbud—which does have valuable medicinal properties, that's the truth—I knew that would not be enough to open trade, not when the people were accustomed to doing without it. So I made certain there would be demand for a cure."

They stared at him, not quite sure if they should believe him.

"So you see, I did more than risk danger with a comfy trade treaty to cushion the fall. I sickened or killed some in order to stop the military slaughter of more. In return, I do not ask that you also sacrifice your people—only that you trust our existing treaty to supply them while you do what is necessary to save them."

For a long moment, the room crackled with uneasy silence. At last Edeiya spoke, addressing Tamaryl. "I believe you when you say that no one likes him."

"How dare you?" Shianan Becknam's voice grated low and dangerous, drawing all eyes to him. "I risk my life and my soldiers to protect our people. I thought the Great Circle did the same. And you are killing those I swore to protect?"

Mage Callahan turned on him. "Think for a moment before you accuse me, commander. You consider which unit to send into battle, knowing their losses will win safety for others. How was this different? I calculated, instead of killing so many for so long, we could lose a smaller number. We could sacrifice toward a healthy trade and a thriving economy."

Shianan shook his head. "No, that's—"

Mage Callahan pointed an accusing finger. "Didn't you lie to the Court of the High Star and to the prince-heir himself about the Shard?"

Shianan froze, and Tamaryl caught his breath. Did Callahan know about Shianan's theft? About Ewan Hazelrig's involvement? About the Ryuven he had hidden?

But no, Taev Callahan knew only that Shianan had admitted to lying about the theft of the Shard in order to draw out the real thieves.

Nothing more.

"I risked myself in that," Shianan growled, but the edge was gone from his voice. He, too, had been shaken by the accusation.

Tamaryl drew a breath and spoke to draw Callahan's attention from Shianan's worried expression. "So you say that because you killed your own people, we should be willing to risk starvation for ours."

"It's not exactly an exchange," Mage Callahan answered, turning to the Ryuven. "I only mean that we all must risk something to achieve something. And I believe an end to war is worth achieving. It would have been better achieved through other methods, but since that did not come to pass, I took the opportunity I had." He leaned back against his worktable. "It need not be so drastic as you suggest. You could lay in supplies in advance, and perhaps Chrenada could be convinced to donate some in a display of good will and in exchange for your aid against the Ientu magic. There are possibilities."

Edeiya took a long breath and then shook her head. "This is not a decision Tamaryl'sho and I can make here. Oniwe'aru must be informed."

"Do that, then."

"And if we burn our fields? What then?"

Mage Callahan returned to his notes. "I have my apprentices working outside your fields now, taking samples and examining plants. We hope to find that the blight is largely confined to your crops, which are unfortunately mono-cultural. That likely led to this problem but, if we are fortunate, it may also aid in its solution. If that is the hoped-for case, then we can hope to plant clean fields within one or two seasons of burning."

"And if that is not the case?"

Mage Callahan shrugged. "Then you must have greatly offended whatever gods you worship. It will require hundreds of trained botanists spending years to comb through your meadows and forests and grasslands, picking out each little hold of blight."

The words hung heavy on Tamaryl, lessened just by that glistening thread of hope that the blight might be contained to the findore fields.

"How can we know you're telling the truth about the fungus?" Edeiya'rika asked.

Mage Callahan rolled his eyes. "You could start breeding your own strains of beans at twelve, you could apprentice to a botanist at thirteen even while you also study under a mage, you could find an arcane botanist to train under at sixteen, you could continue your studies through the long war you were called to join and during your recovery from a battle that should have killed you as it did thousands of others, until you become the foremost arcane botanist today. Or, you might believe someone who already did so." He turned up a palm. "Or you pick an answer you like and hope it works out. Those are your choices."

As irritating as it was, he was right. Tamaryl and Edeiya did not have the knowledge to assess the blight on their own, and their Ryuven scholars had not discovered a solution in years of trying. They could take Mage Callahan's word, as he was the master expert among both Ryuven and humans, or they could hope for the best.

Hoping for the best had not been working out well in recent years.

"We will report to Oniwe'aru," Tamaryl said. "Thank you for undertaking this research with our students."

"They are good apprentices," Mage Callahan said gruffly.

Edeiya and Tamaryl rose and went to the door. Shianan Becknam followed, stiffly correct in posture and quiet.

Shianan shook where he stood, trembling with fury and with one hand braced against the workroom wall to steady himself against the nauseating sense of the room spinning away. Mage Callahan had poisoned his own people—had killed Chrenada's own citizens—to spur demand for an imported herb. As Shianan fought in defensive battle after defensive battle, never gaining ground, never able to properly pursue the enemy, losing soldiers to protect civilians from raids, Taev Callahan had quietly killed them for his own political ends.

A white-hot hollow opened within Shianan. Was dall sweetbud even worth anything? Had Ariana risked her life for a useless weed?

He wanted to push Taev Callahan to the wall and crush his throat for the murderer and traitor he was. But aside from the foolishness of directly assaulting a mage of the Circle, there was the chafing fact of his escort duty; he could not kill the mage as he met with the Ryuven, or all the council would burst with terrified indignation and rush into war.

The thought checked him. Was the unsteady peace worth

tolerating Callahan's treachery? Did staying his hand mean Shianan accepted the killings?

Ariana—idealistic, honest, naive Ariana—had not known of Mage Callahan's seeding of the plague, that was certain. She could not have known. The White Mage had a more jaded view of many things, but Shianan could not imagine the elder Mage Hazelrig agreeing to killing his own people.

Surely not...

No! No, surely he wouldn't. Mage Callahan had acted on his own, and without their complicity or knowledge. He had acted on his own to bring about the trade they wanted.

Chrenada had always sacrificed some for others. Callahan was right; Shianan himself had often considered which unit to deploy and where. Was this so different?

How many soldiers had died at Arakadamia? At Luenda? In all the battles and raids and skirmishes in between? How many would die in the next year, or the year after that?

No! This was madness and grasping at straws. Shianan's soldiers knew what they faced and trained to live beyond it, and he strained to give them every chance to survive. Taev Callahan had chosen unknowing victims to sicken and die. It was not the same.

He could not strike the mage where he stood, not with the Ryuven arguing with him and the fate of the treaty hanging by a thread. But he would tell Mage Ewan Hazelrig, and—

His heart convulsed anew in his chest, taking his breath. Ariana, bright, idealistic Ariana, would be horrified, devastated to learn she had been involved, however unknowing, in such a thing. That she had provided the impetus and means for the plague would shred her buoyant heart.

But they had to know. They had to know what Taev Callahan had done, how he had killed innocent civilians for his own end—

Just as Shianan had done, when he had stolen the Shard.

The thought scorched through him, taking his breath and overturning his stomach, and for a moment he wavered against the wall. The deaths in Caftford were on his hands—he of all people knew what dangers the missing shield risked—and he had taken the Shard to save just one life, not to bring about a whole peace treaty. He could not accuse Mage Callahan, not to the man who knew what Shianan himself had done.

He sucked an uneven breath, burning with rage in the

treacherous mage's own office, shaking with fury and self-loathing. He could never regret saving Ariana, but he would never be free of what he had done. But now, he had to bury his anger, as always, and present the appearance of a slightly bored, slightly resentful commander ordered to escort duty.

When at last the two Ryuven left the workroom, Shianan pushed himself away from the wall, his movements stiff with what they might see as irritation, and his terse farewell no more curt than usual.

CHAPTER 19

Oniwe'aru paced the small room as if too large for it, threatening to break through the walls with the next agitated shake of his wings. "Burn? Burn everything? We would be starving in a month."

"Not necessarily everything," Tamaryl repeated. He had come alone to Oniwe'aru, to break the difficult report in private. "He says there are signs, indicators to look for. But the affected crops must be burned before the blight becomes visible, or the disease is only spread."

"So says this human, and not just a human, but a mage of the Great Circle! Why should this mage have the authority to judge our crops?"

"Because he is possibly the best botanist in Chrenada, and almost certainly the only one willing to work with Ryuven students."

"Of course. What mage of the Circle would let slip an opportunity to destroy his enemy without even fighting?" Oniwe raised his hands. "Or what evidence do we have, aside from the word of the human council, that this man is even a botanist, much less an exalted one?"

"He is," Tamaryl said, injecting patience into his tone. "I know him myself."

"Know him?"

"I was famulus to the White Mage, as you recall. I know all the members of the Circle to one extent or another. I can assure you Taev Callahan is well respected for his ability." He crooked his mouth with memory. "That the other mages say he is the most skilled is further testament in his favor, as no one will say so for friendship. He has earned that reputation by skill alone."

"Even so," grudged Oniwe, "I do not trust his reasons to say we should burn our remaining crops."

Tamaryl sighed. "You have seen the reports from those who studied and researched with him. Do you think they misled you?"

"No, of course not. But they may be misled. They are che and nim, and willing to study with a human, so they are anxious to take dramatic chances with no thought to the consequences if they are wrong. I, on the other hand, will bear all the blame if I order the crops burned and then we are left bereft and hungry."

"We are bereft and hungry now," muttered Tamaryl.

"That is not an argument to aid you," snapped Oniwe. "If I burn the crops at the end of my administration, then I have left a legacy of smoking fields and children crying in endless hunger as their parents die at the doors of my storehouses."

"And if the next year's seedlings grow in healthy and bearing good grain?"

"Then the next family to rule will be lauded as saviors, and ours will be left in disgrace, and it will be long, long years before we are chosen to rule again."

The words struck Tamaryl like a blow. "You—you would withhold an action to benefit thousands to avoid giving aid to your successor?"

Oniwe did not answer.

"Isn't your successor almost certainly Edeiya'rika? Don't you have confidence in her?"

"In her, of course," Oniwe said gruffly. "I am also confident the East Family will gladly sing their own praises if the fields come in healthy and miraculous, while we in the South Family will be scapegoats for all that has been wrong."

"I cannot believe I am hearing this." Tamaryl began to pace opposite Oniwe, who now stood still. "Even now, as children are caught up in food riots, you are thinking of political advantage over the relief of suffering."

"That is a cold way to put it. You know I have made every effort—you know I sent you, and against your preference, to bring food for them."

"But this is a chance to address the root cause, the blight itself, and you resist lest it lend an advantage to someone else." Tamaryl shook his head fiercely. "Is your loyalty to your Family or to your people?"

"I serve my people," snapped Oniwe. "I also serve my Family, so that we may serve our people again."

"To serve?" The equivocation only fired Tamaryl's fury. "I have given up my position, I have lived as a human slave, I have sacrificed my own convictions and returned to raiding and stealing from people I have loved, I have done everything I could think of to end war and bring relief from hunger—and now you will not even make the small sacrifice of acclaim."

"That is unfair, Tamaryl'sho. And this is why you will not be a candidate for aru. This is why you found even the office of Pairvyn too uncomfortable. You do not understand the complexities and the necessity of—"

"I have heard enough," snapped Tamaryl. "I have heard more than enough." He straightened and faced the aru. "You have received my reports and answers on Mage Callahan, the young botanists' research, and its reliability. I have discharged my duty, and now I will take my leave."

He made a stiff bow and fled from the room, avoiding Oniwe'aru's surprise and outrage. He was trembling, incandescent with his own outrage, the shock of being helpless to change anything no matter what price he paid, and the overwhelming sense of betrayal.

He went into the garden, but its soothing green could not reach him. He passed out of the palace and went to his own home, waving away the servants who came to welcome him and then stopped short at his demeanor.

Credit. *Credit*. That Oniwe was unwilling to attempt a solution, lest it benefit their rival in a future election.

He threw himself onto a couch and wished he was again a boy in Mage Hazelrig's workshop, collaborating with his friend to change the world for the better, working in blind, optimistic ignorance.

Shianan went around to the rear alley, where he could enter the Hazelrig home through the kitchen instead of the front door. He was not sure if it was really more secretive—surely the neighbors had noticed by now that he came by both ways—but it made him feel as if he tried to hide the frequency of his visits.

And if they did notice? They could say only that he often visited the Hazelrigs for supper, and who could find fault with that?

He resented the lengthening days brought by the spring, laying bare his lingering in the evening and forcing him to leave earlier each illuminating dawn.

As he entered tonight, Ariana rose from her chair, closing a book, and turned her face up to kiss him. "Welcome! Mother Harriet has left us fish tonight, grilled and herbed and smelling wonderful. I had such a time today—but did you forget the knots? What's wrong?"

Shianan remembered belatedly that he had promised to bring a batch of the savory, cheesy dough knots from a favorite market stall. He shook his head. "I forgot them."

"I see. And I see there was probably a reason. Do you want to talk about it?"

Shianan shook his head. Not yet.

"Do you want some grilled fish and lovely early shoots, first of the season?"

Fresh greens after a winter of aging stores did sound tempting. "I think I could take some, yes."

"Come on, then. I'll call Father down."

They sat at the table, serving themselves comfortably as they talked, and once more Shianan found himself distracted by the marvel of simply being there. Never would he have imagined himself a guest in the White Mage's home, much less a regular one, much less a—a relation.

"By family!" Ariana was saying. "He argued all aid distribution should be portioned by family and given directly to the male head of household, and I pointed out that did not allow for all, particularly those who might most need aid, and then the discussion degraded quickly into whether aiding fatherless children perpetuated more births, and what did we endorse if we provided aid to the men who fathered those women's children, and then a debate on whether his lordship meant widowhood was also a moral failure, and that is when I began to doodle in my notes because I knew nothing else would be accomplished today."

Ewan snorted. "And you thought being a member of the Great Circle would be all excitement and heroism."

"I certainly thought it would be mostly magic. The fact that I carried a basket of herbs does not make me a qualified expert to consult with a ministry delegation on emergency aid alongside the new Ryuven trade."

"No one expects you to be that expert," her father said with a wave of his hand. "They want the prestige and credibility of having a mage of the Circle in their number, just as when they ask me as the White Mage to speak to something outside my field. It's an inconvenient price of our position, and if it's any comfort, you probably annoyed them at least as much when you spoke up out of all expectation." He grinned.

Shianan cleared his throat. "I think you must have more expertise than you give yourself credit for," he said, unsteady on bureaucratic ground. "Since you thought to point out the need they overlooked."

Ariana's eyes shone, and her delight at his words delighted him.

"And what has been keeping you busy?" asked Ewan, serving himself another piece of herbed fish.

Shianan's gut twisted, and all the thoughts he'd been struggling to ignore pushed to the fore, fighting to escape. But he bit down on the words, afraid of what they might unleash.

Surely they could not have known about the Indigo Mage's actions. They would be shocked to learn. And if Shianan played the hypocrite and accused Mage Callahan, they would feel compelled to act, and if the mages Hazelrig exposed the poisoning, how would that affect the fragile treaty built upon the need for dall sweetbud?

To undo the treaty would be to make the deaths meaningless, Shianan told himself, with nothing good salvaged from their sacrifice, and so he bit down on the slimy truth and swallowed it again.

But Mage Hazelrig was looking at him expectantly over his plate, and Shianan needed to say something, and so he blurted, "Mage Callahan says the Ryuven are doing well in their studies."

"That's good news, at least," Ewan Hazelrig answered. "I thought I'd have to pull teeth, his or mine, to get him to work with them. But if he can brag on them, he'll be just fine. I suppose you went with Tamaryl'sho and Edeiya'rika?"

Shianan nodded. "They were discussing his research." He kept his voice perfectly flat.

"Well, I haven't heard anything yet, but he isn't one to boast without backing, so he must have something they've found." He gave Shianan a curious look.

Shianan shook his head. "The blight is a fungus, he says. I didn't understand most of it. I'm not sure the Ryuven did, either."

Ewan laughed. "That's Callahan. He'll make sure they see it clearly, but only after they see his brilliance first. Here, have another piece of fish."

Ariana slipped a hand to his; she had not been completely fooled. But she did not press for answers, and he was grateful.

But too much was still unsettled, and the food was hard to swallow. After a few bites he tried, "Luca is freed."

"What?" gasped Ariana, and Shianan felt all his tangled emotions heave at her mingled surprise and joy. Odd, how her reflection cast light on his own thoughts.

"How did that come about?" Mage Ewan Hazelrig asked, with an eagerness beneath the words.

Shianan gestured vaguely to the east. "He was a freeman when he entered Chrenada from the Wakari Coast, and he was sold illegally when his caravan was taken by bandits. They had no legal basis to enslave him, so Prince Soren arranged a writ of manumission."

"That's wonderful," Ariana said, beaming. "You must be so glad for him."

"I am," Shianan said, and he meant it, and he wondered why his voice sounded so hollow as he said it. "But he's—he's not chosen to act on it yet. That is, he's not called himself a freeman in public."

Mage Ewan Hazelrig looked at Shianan, and then he ladled more fresh shoots onto his plate. "Even if you're happy for him," he said, his eyes on the plate, "it's a significant change for the both of you. A happy shift in circumstances can still be a daunting one."

Shianan grasped after the words, desperate for their absolution for this... He had not allowed himself to name the sensation yet, so awful was it to even acknowledge his hesitation, to admit feeling anything but utter joy at his friend's release. He should have been nothing but delighted. But despite the steady shoulder he'd presented when he found Luca brooding, he was unsettled and anxious. What would Luca become now, and what would it mean if—the deepest of questions—if he did not need Shianan any longer?

Guilt lanced him afresh. It was wrong to feel this way, surely.

"But surely Luca will stay," Ariana said, perhaps answering her father and perhaps speaking directly to Shianan's unacknowledged fears. "He came back once already."

"To escape his unjust slavery," Shianan answered, but her words were reassuring. Luca had been on his way to Alham when he'd been taken.

"Luca deserves his freedom and happiness," Ewan Hazelrig said firmly. "I wish him all the best."

Ariana nodded. "I don't know what I could offer to help him, but if there is anything, please do tell me."

Shianan nodded at their enthusiastic joy for his friend, unsurprised. They had always been anxious to help, even to their own inconvenience.

And it was good to finally have an answer to the dark cloud that had sat unnamed at the back of his mind, too frightening to even acknowledge until he could refute it. He had lost nothing, now that

Luca could go wherever he wanted. If anything, their friendship had become more dear for now being a result of choice rather than chance.

The knot in Shianan's stomach loosened slightly, and he took a bite of fish.

CHAPTER 20

Ronal'sho had his arms crossed and a glare ready when Tamaryl entered the room. His nod was scant, barely an inclination of the head.

Tamaryl pretended not to notice and gave Ronal a gracious greeting. Ronal snorted. Tamaryl crossed to the far side and busied himself with the copied notes Mage Callahan had given him.

When Edeiya'rika arrived a silent moment later, Ronal's attitude changed visibly. His greeting to her was just short of obsequious. She too pretended not to notice, greeting them both at once.

"Ah, I see everyone is here," Oniwe'aru said as he came into the room. He took his central great chair and looked around at them.

Tamaryl did not know Ronal'sho's place in this, why he was invited to such an audience, but asking would undoubtedly offend. He waited, hoping the answer would present itself during the discussion.

"Tamaryl'sho has reported already on the human botanist's recommendation," Oniwe'aru began directly. "However, this solution he recommends is no solution. We simply cannot afford to set fire to our crops when our storehouses are nearly empty."

"What?" Ronal'sho flared his wings just enough to show. "What a brazen attempt to deceive us into weakening ourselves!"

"I trust him," Tamaryl said evenly, keeping his voice low so that Ronal had to quiet to hear him. "I have the advantage of knowing him outside of this specific question, so I don't expect any of you to trust his word so readily. But I believe his word on this, at least."

"I do as well," Edeiya'rika said, surprising Tamaryl. She had attended Taev Callahan's words carefully, but he had not suspected she was ready to commit.

Ronal'sho scowled. Oniwe'aru frowned. "And what brought you to his conclusion?"

"I received his explanation myself, though I cannot pretend to evaluate his report on the blight. I am not trained in plant lore, and even our best have not been able to master this blight. But, I have read all the Pairvyns' writings from the last hundred thirty years"—she nodded toward Tamaryl—"and they universally record the human mages' conservative approach to combat. I find such a bold attempt at enormous misdirection out of character for the Great Circle."

Oniwe'aru nodded once, listening.

"More, I trust Tamaryl'sho's judgment."

Tamaryl glanced at her in surprise.

"To be clear, I do not agree with all of Tamaryl'sho's decisions and actions, but ours is a difference of approach, not values. I do not doubt his sincerity. And he has spent much more time in the human world, learning human motivation and character, than I have. If he believes this human, whom he knows better than I do, has made an honest recommendation, then I will accept that."

Ronal'sho stiffened. "You speak of risking all our welfare on the word of a sho who abruptly abandoned his position and hid among the enemy for years."

"I did not abandon my position," Tamaryl started, but Oniwe'aru raised a hand to cut him off. Tamaryl fell silent, irritated.

"He gave me ample warning of his departure," Oniwe'aru said with a wry smile. "Repeatedly. Loudly. I would not call it abandonment."

Ronal'sho tightened his wings. Oniwe'aru's defense of Tamaryl in the position for which he'd passed over Ronal'sho had to chafe.

Then why was Ronal'sho here now?

But Tamaryl was not accustomed to playing long politics as Oniwe and Edeiya did. As Pairvyn, he focused on battlefield tactics and strategies for open conflict. Oniwe'aru, however, planned for years and generations, and he wanted North Family support for his decision as well.

Was Ronal'sho the right choice for that support? He seemed likely to disagree purely out of spite, countering Tamaryl's recommendation without pause. Even now Ronal'sho's expression was taut, full of resentment for Oniwe'aru's absolving of Tamaryl. "It still seems a weighty decision to base on the words of one sho who has been absent for years."

Edeiya'rika's face remained passive, unruffled by the challenge to her reason. "Please argue the other side, so that we may hear the advantages to all options."

Ronal'sho straightened, and for a moment Tamaryl thought he looked discomfited. He had come prepared to offer criticism, not possibilities. "Well, obviously we cannot start by disposing of our remaining crops. We must set more guards on the storehouses, enforce rationing strictly, and plant new fields as quickly as possible. Dissent and other wasted energy must be limited; those protesting for more rations would be better served by harder work in the fields. Perhaps we could try burning one field, if the blight takes hold, to test whether the human's recommendation is valid—but we have already tried that, of course."

"Mage Callahan said that by the time the blight is visible on the plants, burning will only spread it through the air," Edeiya explained. "That is why he suggested burning in advance, to purge the contaminated fields."

"Burn in advance?" Ronal'sho shook his head. "That is clearly an effort to have us sabotage ourselves. Out of the question."

"So your advice is to have us do more of what we have been doing." Edeiya's tone was mild.

"It has worked for us thus far," Ronal'sho said defensively. "There have been cries of disaster for years, but we're still alive."

"Alive, but not well. Look at what is happening."

"That has as much to do with the riots as with the fields. That is why I suggested to increase the guard at the granaries. And more pressure could be put on the nim to sow and tend rather than congregate and complain."

It was not just the potential influence for the North Family that had kept Ronal'sho from the position of Pairvyn, Tamaryl realized. He might be a competent warrior in a direct fight, but in strategy, he had no talent for reading the momentum of a battle, even one so slow and bloodless as a creeping famine. How could he hope that planting as usual would somehow yield more stores? How could he believe that the riots were a cause, not a symptom?

How could he believe that his disparagement would win Edeiya'rika's approval?

"Thank you for your insight," Oniwe'aru said, with just a hint of impatience in his tone. "Thank you all for your statements. I will consider them."

Thus dismissed, they took their leave of the aru and left the audience room. Ronal kept his gaze rigidly away from Tamaryl as they shared the airy corridor.

Edeiya reached out and touched Tamaryl's arm—softly, almost an imaginary brush of skin, but it caught his attention. When he glanced at her, she slowed her pace minutely, and he matched it.

Ahead of them, Ronal'sho turned a corner and hailed another sho.

Edeiya stopped, glancing up and down the corridor, now empty but for the female guards at either end. She spoke in a low tone. "Do you really trust this human mage? Wholly trust him?"

Tamaryl shook his head. "In general? Not at all. He's not liked, as I said, and I don't think the Circle entirely trusts him in personal matters. But do I believe him in this matter? I do."

She twisted her mouth into a thoughtful scowl. "I cannot make a decision without relying upon your judgment, and you have not always shown the best judgment."

The accusation was more than fair. "Still," he answered, "I might have been killed several times over, and yet I keep returning to those who have not killed me, so I must have judged them correctly."

She gave him a flat look, and then she crossed her arms. "Why do you believe a selfish, pragmatic human would advise us for the benefit of our people?"

Tamaryl thought for a moment. "The Circle trusts him with the good of the kingdom, or he would not be one of them. And if he can accomplish what the Circle could not in generations, ending this war, and if he can do it by using his unique ability and insight where no one else could—well, I trust to his own ambition as much as anything else. He will want the credit and the glory of being the linchpin in a new peace. And he is wise enough to know that if we found ourselves at the point of starvation, no treaty could hold us back, and we would wage another Luenda or Arakadamia and more in revenge."

"A Lu-what?"

"I mean the greater battles, the ones that devastated both our peoples. We would have no reason to hold back if we were starved into attack; our choice would be a slow death of starvation or a glorious death on the field, and sacrificing warriors toward eventual victory would only be an advantage with limited food. With nothing to lose, we would be a terrifying and relentless foe, and he is clever enough to know that. So between his natural avoidance of unlimited bloodshed and his own desire for recognition and advancement, I trust his recommendation."

She cocked her head, looking down at him. "You do have political insight."

"I wish I had less," Tamaryl said bitterly. "Then I would not have realized Oniwe'aru is reluctant to accept this advice, lest it benefit the East Family."

Edeiya's hair swished over her shoulder. "What? You mean, if he ordered the crops burned, and if I then reaped a recovered harvest?"

"Yes."

"Hmm." Edeiya pressed her lips together, her hair tail catching on one wing.

"And we need Chrenadan trade," Tamaryl continued. "The fields are failing faster now even than I remember. The records confirm that yields are down more each year. But we won't be able to penetrate the shield again, and if we do anything to prevent it, we'll never have another chance at less bloody acquisition. Chrenada is the breadbasket from which we could feed our starving people, and we should be doing whatever we must to foster that trade."

He paused, realizing he had said too much.

"Or is it political insight at all?" Edeiya'rika asked, looking at him with cocked head. "Or does all this strong feeling spring from a different fountain?"

Tamaryl shook his head tightly. "It is true that I have friends in the human world," he said, "people I love. But I had friends and loved ones here when I said I would fight no more. It is true that I would like to see fighting end between us, but still I brought the fragment of Shard to enable limited raiding through the shield. I will do what I believe is best for the people I am bound to serve and protect, as I swore when I became the Pairvyn ni'Ai."

"And it is with the same heart that brought the fragment to subvert your work on the shield that you now support the burning of our fields."

Tamaryl heard only the echo of his treachery. "I should have spoken to Mage Hazelrig instead of stealing it. But yes, in both cases I believed I was acting to save more lives than would be lost."

She looked down the corridor a moment, frowning, and at last she said, "Come, let's go back to Oniwe'aru."

Tamaryl was unsure why they were returning, though clearly it was to speak privately without Ronal'sho of the North Family.

Oniwe'aru was mildly surprised to see them. "Well, that did not take long. What did you two arrange?"

"We only spoke to confirm Tamaryl's assessment," Edeiya answered, "but it's true I hope you and I may come to an arrangement."

Oniwe'aru raised an eyebrow. "And what is that?"

"There is risk in attempting something so new and so different as burning crops that appear to be healthy, especially in the sight of those who hunger. I would like to share that risk." Edeiya held Oniwe'aru's eyes. "If we meet with the Families and settle the question of succession, I will lend my voice as succeeding silth to this order. It will be a joint command, from the two of us, so that we may share the risk and the reward."

The suggestion took Oniwe by surprise. "A joint command?"

"What do you think?"

"I think you have found a way to secure my vote for you as silth," Oniwe said with a calculating tone. "And to take credit for any success of this approach."

"Shared credit," she answered. "And a shared rebuttal to the forthcoming criticism."

"Ah," Oniwe said, nodding. "An alliance between the East and South Families, while the North Family's voice is weakened."

Tamaryl followed almost as quickly. When Ronal'sho complained of the foolish plan and explained he was opposed to it—as he might be doing even already at this moment—then he distanced the North Family from whatever success the unconventional approach reaped.

Oh, but they were clever, these two. Fit to rule, passing their chips and chancing throwsticks as the gameplay continued apace. He was only a warrior, too direct for political stratagems.

Oniwe was smiling. "Tell me what you might expect in this arrangement."

CHAPTER 21

For a sho considered to be a great warrior, Tamaryl reflected, he spent a ridiculous amount of time facing down long arrangements of dour faces scowling in anticipation of the diplomacy he would lay before them.

Perhaps there was something to be said after all for the use of coercion. It might be simpler if he simply overturned the long table in the King's council's meetings and, lashing the air with lightning, demanded that they release the restrictions on the nascent trade. It would certainly feel better as he did it.

But there was no table in this Ryuven meeting. Oniwe'aru had invited his chosen advisers from among the Four Families, each of whom had a chair in a wide oval. Water sat in a jeweled carafe on a low stool beside each seat, lovely in form but a reminder that even the Palace of Red Sands could no longer offer rich smallmeats to its guests.

Oniwe'aru had debated how the announcement should be made, whether the news should come from Tamaryl, who had little political capital to lose, or whether such a source would further taint already contentious orders and they should be given by the aru. At last it was determined that Oniwe'aru would explain the burning, with Edeiya'rika supporting. But they were all braced for fiery resistance.

Oniwe'aru, sensing there was no way to explain this plan smoothly, made short work of the explanation. "And so, given this insight, Edeiya'rika and I have decided together to burn all the fields, in the hopes of eliminating this blight and planting afresh in two years."

The airy room fairly hummed with astonishment. "Are you mad?" Carynn'rika demanded. "Do you mean to end your rule with the decision to kill hundreds, maybe thousands at the whim of a human mage?"

"Is this some sort of scheme to destroy the Four Families?" This was someone from the West Family, though Tamaryl couldn't recall his name. "Do you think you can put us aside by scorching the earth?"

Oniwe'aru raised his hands and gestured for quiet.

The North Family, informed in advance by Ronal'sho, was less surprised and more ready for battle. "He means to beggar the entire clan and then bring a miracle of supplies from the human world, buying gratitude from the very people he endangered. Then he can leverage popular support to continue his influence, if not his rule."

Edeiya'rika's face hardened. "I'm sure you did not mean to suggest that the East Family may be so easily led."

Tone'sho glanced at Ronal'sho and then back to Edeiya'rika. "I only observe that the East Family appears to be bowing to Oniwe'aru's ridiculous plan."

"To the contrary, it was I who suggested to Oniwe'aru that we attempt it jointly." Edeiya'rika stood tall, looking down the room at Tone'sho. "While Oniwe'aru performed his duties here, I went to the human kingdom of Chrenada myself, and there I heard their foremost botanist explain the spread of the fungus and how if we wait to burn what is visible, we only spread the blight. I have spoken with the che and nim we sent to learn more, who have been studying our own fields and hedgerows. I have been to the storehouses and the findore fields. I am uncomfortably aware of all that rests on this single decision, from my own life in public service to the lives of our entire clan. If you allege that I meekly allow it to be made for me, be prepared to back your argument."

Tone'sho was not prepared to back his argument. "Still, even if you've considered it, the practical answer is that it cannot be done. We cannot burn out all our crops and leave our people to starve."

"We will have supplies," Oniwe'aru said. "We have a treaty already in place. Trade is already growing. And the Chrenadan people have made us a most generous gift, in particular with the discovery of this necessary action."

"And there has been conflict."

"We face one another over generations of war," Oniwe'aru snapped. "There will be residual distrust. But none of you can deny that trade has been profitable and useful. Your own house has benefited already, Tone'sho, or do you think I have not seen your trading parties leaping across as often as your raiding parties ever did? If we can grow more of the samur, there is demand for it; we can continue to expand our exchange for herbs and for other goods."

"We know the Ientu have raided the human kingdom," Edeiya'rika said. "That is a great part of the unrest there. Assuring the humans that our treaty is still valid will help to stabilize the trade."

"And how do you intend to do that?" Carynn'rika asked. "Do you think you can simply blame another clan, and the humans will believe that as easily as you have believed their suggestions?"

The protest was uncomfortably valid. Tamaryl looked at Edeiya'rika and wished he could simply order compliance. But even if he could, that would breed distrust beneath the reluctant obedience. They needed something more to bring about real change.

"What can you offer us?" Carynn'rika asked, pursing her lips.

"Do you mean to ask, what assurance can we offer?" Edeiya'rika responded in a velvety tone laced with steel.

Carynn'rika frowned and sat back in her seat. "Well, of course."

"None of us can see the future clearly," Edeiya'rika said. "But we can see well enough that our crops will continue to fail, and that wishing what we have been doing will suddenly prove more successful is a futile and deceptive wish. Can I be certain this is our best choice? Of course I cannot. But I can be certain that doing nothing more than what we have done is not our best choice. If you have any alternative to offer, we would all be glad to hear and consider it, and this is the time to offer it."

Carynn'rika's frown deepened. "I am no farmer."

"Nor I. But I know my lack of knowledge, and so I choose to listen to those with a lifetime of study."

"You needn't take such airs about it," Tone'sho muttered. "There's no pride to be found in following another's guidance."

Edeiya'rika turned to regard him flatly. "You would rather take pride in your ignorance?"

"We stray from the point," Oniwe'aru interjected, raising a hand. "No reasonable argument can be made that we need do nothing. The question is what to do. Edeiya'rika and I suggest a dramatic and far-reaching attempt that presents genuine risk in the next two years with the reasonable hope of success after that. Without alternatives, that seems to be our best choice as a clan. If you have valid arguments against this plan and practical suggestions to present in its place, by all means, bring them now. I assure you, I would like nothing more. But to simply protest that we should continue as we have—that is foolishness."

"We are not fools—" began Tone'sho.

"Not by nature, no, but by choice, perhaps," snapped Oniwe'aru. "You sit in your fine houses day by day, eating from your private storehouses, protected by walls and nets against the voices of those who do not have the same. It is not your children who are hungry, not yet, so you see only numbers on records, and you think it such a small change—what could a hundredth part matter? But a hundredth part of the whole makes quite a lot of bushels, as you would know if you were in the fields or storehouses instead of in your comfortable houses, and when it grows past a hundredth to a tenth, the difference is already too great to recover. Go and face those who bring their children to beg for rations, Tone'sho, go and tell the weeping that it is such a small thing and it should not affect them so, and then come again to tell me that you are no fool and you have the right of it."

Tamaryl watched in fascination. He had seen the political Oniwe'aru, walking a cautious line between factions, but this was a different tone. Was it the new alliance with Edeiya'rika? The approaching end of his rule, leaving him freer to act without reservation for the future? Or had Tamaryl always watched from a position of protest, always seeing Oniwe behind him but without noting he was on the same road?

Tone'sho huffed. "That is not what I said," he growled, but in a low tone. "I am aware that the che and nim suffer."

Oniwe'aru was not prepared to let him slide away. "And yet you would tell them to continue in more of the same?"

"No one has said that nothing should be done."

"That is not true," Edeiya'rika joined. "For how long have the Four Families discussed this blight? For how long was it argued that it was not a threat, that it was a minor inconvenience to a few fields, that it was a sign of poor management in some farmers, that the reports of lower yields were flawed or influenced by those with an interest in stirring feeling against the holding families? It took generations for even willful denial to become impossible, and we cannot respond by denying that denial as a way to delay acting upon solutions."

They would make a good team, Tamaryl observed. It was nearly a pity that Oniwe'aru's rule was coming to an end; a longer period of pairing with the next aru or silth might be a powerful and effective approach. Perhaps Edeiya'rika—supported now by the South Family as well as her own, and growing in favor with the West Family as she confronted Tone'sho of the North Family—might maintain a partnership with Oniwe'sho in her own rule.

For now, the room was uncomfortably empty of words, though loud with the creaking of chairs, the shuffle of cups, the rustle of fabric as they looked toward or away from one another. Edeiya'rika was right; they had all heard fathers and mothers argue against the perceived severity of the blight, or had even learned their current protests from them. Many of them had repeated those arguments even in recent years, blaming those who managed the fields and setting in charge che and sho who knew more about raiding than farming.

If they repeated those denials, they were even more to blame than their mothers and fathers, whose long inaction had brought them all now to this dire dilemma. Now they had to decide if they would acquiesce to silent, self-deceiving death, or if they would fight as they teetered on the ledge.

Tamaryl clenched his fists and hoped their aru and silth could lead them.

"Will you swear?"

"What?"

"Will you swear to bear the blame in both your houses?" Carynn'rika's tone suggested she knew they would not and she had caught them out in their insincerity.

Oniwe hesitated; he had not been to the human world, had not heard Mage Callahan's explanations. He could rely only upon Edeiya's persuasion. He looked to Edeiya.

Edeiya had heard the mage, but she had no history to trust him or the other humans. She had only Tamaryl's faith and intuition. Her head shifted, but she caught herself before she looked at him.

"I will swear," she said.

Oniwe nodded. "We will so swear."

Essence and flame, if they swore a binding oath together—if this went poorly, the South and East Families would give up political power for decades. Generations.

And they risked it all on Tamaryl's faith in their human allies.

Tamaryl closed his eyes. They could not fail. The stakes were no higher for this—they still gambled the starvation of a clan—but in making it a political bargain, they confirmed the political divide, and once again Tamaryl watched sho and rika barter for power at the expense of all.

Essence and flame, Tamaryl, Oniwe, Edeiya, the East and South Families, and the welfare of the entire Ai clan hung on the reliability of Taev Callahan.

Tamaryl wanted to both retch and weep, but he could only hope and pray.

The room went quiet, silenced by their determination. Even

Carynn'rika only stared, unable to protest further.

Oniwe'aru pressed his palms together at the height of his chest and bit down on his lower lip as his teeth shifted and sharpened. Edeiya'rika did the same. Each lifted a hand to tear their lower lips from the pinching teeth, ripping them.

Tamaryl had made a binding oath to Ewan Hazelrig, on the corpse-strewn field at Luenda. It had been an unequal pledge; Tamaryl could not break his oath without causing magic to revert upon him, while the White Mage's had been bound only by his honor, with no consequence but the knowledge he had lied. It had been an unequal pledge, but Ewan Hazelrig had not failed him.

Mage Ewan Hazelrig would not fail them now. He, and Ariana, and the resentful but dutiful Commander Becknam, and even Mage Callahan, they would not fail Tamaryl now.

"Wait!" Tone'sho held up a hand. "I want a recorder."

Others nodded. "Yes, yes, a recorder. Call a recorder!"

It was only a moment before a che hurried into the room. He looked around the room, saw the aru and the probable future silth standing with bleeding mouths, and straightened to face them. He pressed his palms together and then tore his lip.

Oniwe'aru and Edeiya'rika painted bloody streaks across their foreheads, left to right. "We take upon ourselves and our Families the consequences of this venture," Oniwe'aru said. "We act by the best knowledge we have, with the best of intentions, and upon us and our Families be the blame."

"Or the acclaim," added Edeiya.

Oniwe's mouth twitched. "This I swear, the oath of Oniwe, Altayr ni'Ai cin Celæno, Alcyon ni Pairvyn, Majja to Pleione."

"This I swear, the oath of Edeiya, Altayr ni'Ai, Tsuraiya ni'Ai."

The recorder drew blood across his own forehead. "I swear to bear faithful witness to what has passed here this day, a record of word and deed for all to know."

There was no turning back now. Now they burned the fields, turned back the Ientu, and waited to see if Chrenada believed them and honored their treaty and trade.

CHAPTER 22

"It can't be true!"

"But why would they come here? Why now? It's only spring, and nothing is blighted yet!"

The worried murmurs of the watching che and nim reached Tamaryl across the narrow band of cultivated field. It was bright green with new planting, but the field was one that Mage Callahan's students had identified to be burned. Two days before they had drained the field, exposing the tender seedlings, and while the ground was still damp, Tamaryl hoped the plants themselves were unprotected.

They had come this day to set the first fire.

Incredulous watchers had gathered, first to confirm the impossible rumors, and then to protest. Somewhere behind Tamaryl, the che who owned this field sprawled on the ground, head over his knees as he waited to watch his livelihood burn.

Jen, one of Taev Callahan's apprentices, lit a torch and began sharing the fire around to others. They were to use ordinary fire, no magics, according to the Indigo Mage.

The watching Ryuven began to shout. "What are you doing? You'll kill us all! This field isn't blighted!"

"It is," Tamaryl said, facing them and bracing himself for the coming unpleasantness. "It's not yet fully visible, but there are confirmed signs this field will fail and will infect others. It must be burned if we are to have a healthy harvest in the future."

"We can't wait for the next planting!"

Tamaryl nodded to the botany students, who grimly advanced upon the plants.

"No!"

A group of angry che and nim rushed those with torches. A student's torch went out in the soil as she stumbled beneath the onslaught.

"Stop this!" Edeiya'rika's voice cracked across the field, and her concussive blast rocked the attackers back from the fallen student. "This is done by my authority, for the long-term benefit of all."

"There will be no benefit next year if we starve now!" cried a woman. "What about our children?"

"How can you take this from us?"

"You mean to kill us! You could do it more kindly by doing it more quickly!"

Edeiya'rika's expression was strained. She gestured, and Taev Callahan's students bent to burn the plants, holding the torches in place until the short green stalks began to brown and steam.

"We will not leave you with nothing," Edeiya'rika called, turning to face the wide spread of aghast Ryuven. They hardly looked at her, staring at the smoking plants. "We will bring more grain from the human world, as we have done."

But there were tears on the faces of the watching Ryuven, as their hope for the next season smoldered and finally began to flame, and as the fire grew hotter the nearest plants caught more quickly, until at last the fires about the field began to blaze and creep together.

"Do not worry—we will bring food to distribute. This is necessary to stop the blight. We must burn the contagion before it can spread. This is for the good of all."

They did not believe her. Watching, Tamaryl was not sure they even heard her, caught in their despair.

The guards stayed in place, although no one pressed forward any longer; there was no prayer of saving the burning field.

Tamaryl crossed to where Edeiya'rika watched their hopes and trust burn with the plantings. "I'm sorry. I know it's hard."

"I wish I could make them understand." She blew out a long breath. "But why would they? I don't fully understand it myself." She looked at Tamaryl. "I'm trusting you and your opinion of Mage Callahan."

That weight, of her trust and the combined faith and despair of all those gathered to stare at the rising flames, threatened to crush Tamaryl. He looked away. "Mage Callahan would know better than anyone else. No one could argue that."

She nodded tightly.

Tamaryl slid a thumb beneath the strap of a bag he wore over his shoulder, slipping it free. "I meant what I said about Mage Callahan. But I know you're not comfortable in the human world—understandably. If you ever feel..."

She understood. "If I feel threatened."

"And if you don't want to risk the treaty in defending yourself."

She nodded slowly.

Tamaryl opened the bag. Smoke drifted over them, stinging their eyes, and Edeiya'rika waved a shield into place to deflect it. Tamaryl drew out two dull grey cuffs of metal. "These are what I used to conceal my Ryuven nature, while I was there. The magic is mostly human, but you'll be able to see the workings of it. You would need someone else to seal it, but if you need to hide..."

Edeiya looked at the cuffs, and then at him. "These are what you used to conceal yourself."

"That's right. Mage Hazelrig and I developed them, our first collaboration."

Edeiya looked back at the cuffs. "If I need someone else to seal it, I would also need someone to unseal it again afterward, yes?"

"...Yes." Tamaryl realized what she meant.

"If I am with someone I trust enough to seal and unseal my power, why would I need to hide?" Her mouth crooked upward. "And couldn't I just leap back, anyway?"

Tamaryl felt ridiculous. "I suppose I had not thought it through from your position. I had fewer options."

"And this was the best you could make of them." Edeiya put out a hand as Tamaryl started to close the bag. "No, wait. I will take them, if you don't mind."

"I don't; I offered them. But, as you have pointed out their uselessness, may I ask why?"

"They are not useless," she corrected. "They are merely not useful for my situation. That's not quite the same."

"Still."

"I want them because they are a reminder." She picked up the cuffs and weighed them in her palm. "You gave up fifteen years to this cause. I can brace myself to burn a few fields."

Tamaryl looked at the crowd, sullen or sobbing. "It's not the fields that are hard to face."

"I know." Her voice was sad. "And it's not the cuffs that give me hope."

Tamaryl looked at her and caught her grim smile.

"Most make policies for others to live with. You are willing to live—and die—by yours. I may not approve all your choices, but I admire, and aspire to, your commitment."

Tamaryl shifted his wings uncomfortably. "I have wavered in that commitment. More than a little."

"Good. That gives me more faith that I can hold it, too." She jerked her head, her emerald-black hair tail sliding over one wing. "Come on. Let's go to the next field."

CHAPTER 23

Garl and Esar Asher shuffled with the other slaves up the long, low hill, squinting against the white light. Despite the chill temperature, the light burned, reflecting too brightly from the crystalline crust of the ground.

Wind cut through their clothing, making them shiver. One of the slaves ahead, who had only a ragged shirt and no tunic, moaned with the cold, and the nearest driver laughed. "Not to worry, you'll warm up soon enough. They'll keep you working briskly."

Garl closed his good eye against the light and the particulate carried by the wind, trusting the tug on his wrist to keep him going in the right direction. The other was already swollen mostly shut, a blow from his brother who had not forgiven him for their capture.

Never mind that it had been Esar who had collapsed beneath the guards' questioning, offering a confession and tossing Garl to the hogs as the counterfeit claimant in hopes of securing mercy for himself. But the adjudicator had not seen it that way, judging both Esar and Garl guilty of the theft of the document and the enslavement of its owner.

The guards and adjudicator had not worked out, and even Esar had not offered, that the Asher brothers were responsible for the death or enslavement of an entire caravan. That had kept them alive, a blessing Garl was not sure he was grateful for as they made their way to the salt flats.

They could see the harvest now, in the distance. Slaves picked their way along paths in the salt to break apart the hardened crust and carry it back. It was not only salt for preserving food that was collected here, but potash to enhance the fields, so the harvesting operation here fed thousands in several countries. They could afford the brutally high turnover of slaves to labor on the flats.

Even as Garl watched, one of the distant slaves suddenly dropped—not as if he had fallen, but as if he had fallen through the earth. There was a scream, soul-wrenching even heard from so far, but most of the other slaves only glanced up and then turned back to their own work. An overseer shouted at two working nearby and pointed them toward the cries, now intermittent and muffled.

"It's the mud," said the overseer near Garl, a little viciously. "Mind you work just where they say, because if you try to spare your legs from walking and pick too much where the crust is thin, you'll drop through into the mud beneath, and it can swallow a wagon without so much as a belch after."

Under the overseer's direction, the two slaves were inching onto the treacherous area, linking hands as they spread themselves wide over the broken crust. The overseer shouted, and one lay down to crawl toward the dark hole. He grasped the extended hand of the fallen slave, and the three of them together pulled him from the mud. The two recruited slaves immediately bolted as the overseer began to beat the muddy slave while he still lay gasping on the ground.

"Keep your manners nice here," the train's overseer continued confidentially to Garl. "There's a lot to manage, so they'll take a switch to you for shirking quick as you like. Not much water to spare, so be careful to earn your share or you'll have to do without, and then if you're slow because you're thinking of water, there's the switch again. But stay lively, because if they whip you open, there's nothing but salt for it, and salt in the air, and salt in your clothes, and salt in your bed, and you'd better keep moving through it all or there's more whipping and more salt." He grinned and shook his head. "Whatever you did to come here, you poor dog, you didn't choose well to do it."

Garl was already thirsty with the long walk and the salty wind stinging his face, and the idea that water would be limited—something he had not imagined in all his anticipatory worry—struck him so suddenly and brutally that he stumbled in the line.

They arrived at the labor encampment, consisting of a few buildings for the management and chief overseers and then an array of windblown tents for the slaves. Despite the general lack of timber, there was a solid whipping frame erected in the center of the encampment. Another line of slaves was approaching, each bearing a large barrel on his back: the water train, bringing the daily supply up from the mountain stream to the west.

Garl licked his lips and flinched at the salt rime already there. Suddenly he wanted water, wanted water beyond his need from the climb and the wind, wanted it for his sudden terror that he would not have it soon enough, would not have it ever again, would die in the mud with his arm outstretched for water.

His line stopped, and the drivers began to unchain them. Garl and Esar stood beside one another, hating one another, and waited to be directed into their new labor by the overseers gathering around them.

The slaves at the front of the line were pulled away first, sent to help with the water barrels or to receive their baskets and tools for harvesting salt. Then someone gripped Garl's hair savagely and jerked his face upward. "You!"

Garl squinted into the light and tried to guess at the snarling man regarding him. "What?"

"I would have been free," the overseer growled. "He was going to let me hire out and buy my freedom. He promised to invest my pay for me. And you sold him half-muddled for cheap labor and dumped me at your first chance."

Garl blinked the face into recognition. It was the big slave they had taken with the caravan. His training and skills had helped him to bob to the top of the pool of slaves, and he had ended an overseer instead of a laborer.

Garl's overseer.

Weak with despair and surprise, Garl whispered, "Don't kill me."

Cole's mouth twisted, all his bottled hate finally uncorked on the man who had shattered his life. "Oh, no," he assured Garl. "Not soon."

CHAPTER 24

"What's this?"

Luca turned and saw Shianan with one hand on the lockbox lid and the other lifting out the fustian bag. With a start, Luca realized he had never told Shianan of the delivery. "I—"

Shianan upended the bag and shook out the key.

"I forgot to give that to you. It was brought...a few days ago. Last week. I'm not sure."

Shianan stared at the key. "What is it? Who sent it?"

"It was delivered by a Gehrn priest."

Shianan's eyes snapped to the door. "Here?"

"Only long enough to leave that." Luca wouldn't say more.

Shianan looked back at the key. "I suppose it's mine, then."

"What?"

"The townhouse. The one I bartered for the Shard."

"Then—then the Gehrn have left Alham?"

"I was told they would. I suppose this is the evidence of it."

Luca had not realized how heavily the visit had hung on him. For just an instant he felt unaccountably weak, and he had to resist stretching a hand for the edge of the desk.

"I have a townhouse," Shianan said, and he sounded disoriented as well. "I barely thought of it before the Gehrn—but now..."

"We should go and look at it," Luca said, trying to sound normal. "See what condition they left it in."

Shianan frowned. "I suppose they might have treated it poorly. I don't know exactly what happened, but I doubt they were pleased to leave."

Luca recalled the glare and the slap. That had been more than the usual casual cruelty; there had been something else behind it.

"We should go and see it."

"I could ask Mage Hazelrig to join us," Luca offered. "I'll bring a supper."

Shianan stiffened, and Luca wondered what he had said wrong. But aloud, after a moment, Shianan said, "That would be good."

Shianan waited in the little garden at the front of the Hazelrig house, gazing at the fruit trees' buds. He wondered how many neighbors had noticed his regular visits, and whether his ploy to wait outside would be more noticeable or allay their suspicions, since he didn't enter the house. He wondered if he would ever be able to visit his wife without worrying over such things.

"I'm here," Ariana said, exiting the front door. "Ready."

"I'm not sure what it will be. I haven't seen the place, and the Gehrn had it, what, nearly a year."

"They thought it their own for most of that time," Ariana said. "So any destruction would have happened only just at the end."

"One can do a lot of destroying in a day or two."

"True. Well, let's go and see the worst." She fell in beside him as they went into the street.

"I sent Luca for food and ale," Shianan said. "At least we'll have a meal of it."

Ariana chattered happily as they walked, talk well away from the Gehrn and the Ryuven raids and ineffectual magic, and Shianan let the sound wash over him. Faint unease moved within him like a parasite. He shouldn't have invited Ariana to this first visit. But that made no sense; what advantage was there to checking what the Gehrn had left him before bringing her to see it?

It took Shianan a moment to recognize his property; it had been so long since he had visited it, and he'd rarely come this way. He pointed it out to Ariana, who paused to admire its timber and stucco front, fashionable a few generations before. "I like its roof," she declared after a moment. "It looks happy."

Shianan glanced down at her. "Happy?"

"Don't you think there's a happy line to it?" She gave him a mock frown. "You're no fun at all."

"None?" he asked with an excess of innocence.

She elbowed him. "Let's go in."

He wasn't sure he wanted to. He had seen it before, when he was newly Bailaha and not merely Becknam. He had been overwhelmed with the size—too many rooms to keep, especially for a soldier raised in group bunks—and uncomfortable with his new wealth and title, and the looks they brought him among his fellow soldiers. He had locked the townhouse and left it.

But Ariana was moving ahead, her eyes fixed on the front door, and he was drawn along behind her like filings to a lodestone. She paused at the door—marked with a sparse pattern of nails, stylish yet not too ostentatious—and he fitted the heavy key into the lock.

The townhouse was at first glance not unlike the Hazelrigs' house. There was an entry of tile, enlivened with a small mosaic of a stretching cat, and then a sitting room beyond. It was smaller than Ariana's home, but she prowled forward as if it were a new land to be explored.

The house had been lightly furnished when it became Shianan's. He couldn't be sure, but the furnishings seemed to be left as he dimly recalled.

"Here's the kitchen," called Ariana, as if there would be anything else found after a short protective stone passage. "Oh, and the pantry still has some bread."

"Best to burn that," Shianan said, only half-jesting. Ande's baleful expressions still unsettled him. Whatever Mage Hazelrig and Mage Parma had done to dissuade him, he could not have taken it well.

Ariana came back from the kitchen. "Come on, molasses," she teased, taking his hand in the entryway. "I'll be through the whole house and you'll still be here. Let's see what's upstairs." She tugged him after her. "There should be a bedroom."

Shianan's pulse quickened despite his mood. "Luca is coming..."

"I'm sure Luca suspects what you get up to with your wife." She grinned down the stairs at him and rounded the corner.

There was a small room first, with several floor mattresses. The Gehrn had not taken their supplemental furnishings with them. Mattresses were awkward and heavy, and the Gehrn likely had not found transportation for much cargo in their abrupt departure. The larger room at the end of the corridor stood open, and Ariana led him inside.

A bed held the middle of the room, layered with woolen blankets. The ranking Gehrn who had held this room had slept well. A wardrobe and a short chest of drawers stood on the far wall, subtle wealth, and Shianan could not remember if they had been in the house before.

He could bring Ariana here. Shianan looked about the room, Ariana's warm fingers against his. Someday, maybe, when their marriage did not have to be hidden, he could bring her to a home of her own, and they could live like any other married couple.

There was a sound from below, and Ariana started. "Oh, that's Luca. We didn't leave the latch up, did we? I'll let him in." She released Shianan's hand and went back down the stairs.

Shianan looked about the room, at the three additional low mattresses taking much of the floor. There was a real fireplace in the wall, not a brazier. He was seized with a sudden urge to kindle a fire, coax it to healthy flame, and settle before it with one of the woolen blankets. He could wrap his arms about Ariana, and they could sit together, sharing a blanket, staring into the comforting flames, unafraid, secure in each other and their own home...

He went to the bed, finer than the one in his military quarters. There was the corner of a feather tick showing near the head—that was more luxury than his quarters offered, certainly. He took a handful of blanket and pulled it back, and a white blur surged upward, filling his vision.

Instinctively Shianan stepped back, raising one arm to block a blow and whipping the blanket up as a deflective shield. Down exploded into the air, a silent upwelling of weightless cloud, spreading over Shianan and across the room.

He paused—feathers, not a real threat—and brushed clinging down from his nose and mouth. The feather tick, nearly fully exposed now, had been shredded with long, ragged cuts. Withdrawing the blanket had sucked its contents out into the air, spreading on the invisible currents of Shianan's own motion. Beneath the feather tick, long rents in the mattress spilled chaff over the floor.

He had been wrong: there had been no impending blow, but there had been a threat. Ande could have simply destroyed the room, shredding feather tick and mattress and blankets all, so that Shianan had walked into carnage. Leaving the damage hidden in his bed, to be discovered unexpectedly—that was a message.

He dropped the blanket and stared at the down swirling to fill the room. And he had thought to bring Ariana here, thought to have Luca out of Gehrn reach—thought to ever have a day when he did not have to wonder what was safe, whom he could trust, who would sacrifice him to political advancement, who meant him no harm but would endanger him and those he loved through carelessness...

He would never, never have that.

"Shianan! We've brought—" Ariana froze at the door. Luca, one step behind her, stared in shock at the feather-filled room. Ariana raised a hand to her face, partly in surprise and partly to shield it from the whirling down. "What happened?"

He would never have a safe place for them.

Something rose in his throat, and he couldn't face them now—not either of them. "Get out," he said, fixing his eyes on the bed. The mattress deflated as the stream of chaff slowed and pooled beneath it, spilling outward into little dusty rivulets.

Luca did not move. When Shianan glanced toward them, Luca's eyes were wide and staring, the question plain in his expression: *The Gehrn?*

Shianan could not bear the fresh fear in his friend's face, could not bear to recall how Ande had been so confident in his claim, could not bear that even now he did not know how they had been spared—or if they had been. Could not bear that he did not know and could do nothing. "Get out!" he roared, gesturing savagely. "Out!"

Luca slid back, disappearing down the hall. Ariana retreated a step, but she remained, watching Shianan across the room.

Sweet oats, how was he supposed to shout at her again? Couldn't she see that he couldn't abide her just now, that he was smothered by down and frustration and shame, that she was making it worse by—

"Shianan," she said, her voice low, "what's wrong?"

He turned from her, staggered by her incomprehension. He swung one hand in an abrupt arc to encompass the ruined room.

"That's feathers and chaff," she said, her voice low and steady. "That's not cause to shout at us when we come in with your dumplings."

She was right, and yet she was wrong, so wrong, and she did not understand—

"Luca accepts that treatment because he has been a slave," she said quietly. "But he should not have to. And I do not."

Her words lanced him, pierced his most vulnerable point, bled him. He struck back. "I do not abuse him! And I do not shout at you!"

She stood silent before his raised voice, waiting.

King's sweet oats. He stopped, worked his fingers, fought to breathe through the down whirling on the wind of his words. "I'm sorry. It's not my fault," he tried. "It's only that I am so angry, that you don't—"

It's not my fault.

He stopped so suddenly that the king's words nearly choked him. Horror bubbled up his throat, drowning any other words that might have tried to surface. Revulsion spread through him like a heavy dark oil, coating all his thoughts and efforts. He looked at Ariana, grasping for help—but why would she help, why after he echoed the king—

He turned away, caught in too much for words and afraid he would give in to the anger that seemed the only way to clear them.

"Feathers and chaff," she said again, her voice nearer, but she was not accusing him. "It was a nice feather tick, probably costly. But an hour ago you did not know you owned it, so you've lost little in the end. Still richer for the rest of the house."

That wasn't it, that wasn't it at all, but he could not speak yet. He snapped his hand outward, dismissing the feathers, the bed, the room.

She touched him, and he flinched, and that was worse.

She circled him and looked at him, but not too near. Did she fear he would strike her, like the son he was?

But there was no wariness in her tone. "Will you—"

"Stop," he managed, the word squeezing through his throat. "Please."

She did.

King's sweet oats, he actually wished she had pressed, so that the protective fury he felt could be justified. He wanted to be angry, to feel justification and power instead of this horror and guilt, and he wanted to be angry that she had taken that from him too.

He had never realized what cowardice there was in anger.

He drew a breath, conceded defeat—not to her, but to himself. "I'm sorry."

She held out a hand, but he did not think he could take it.

She closed the distance and embraced him, and he did not have the strength to resist for long. He softened, letting his arms close about her, and he breathed the scent of freedom.

"I'm sorry," he whispered.

"It's all right."

But he wanted her to understand. "I only want to be a husband to you."

"You are my husband."

Frustration rose again. Ariana, who had words for everything, who hid from no shame, she could not understand. He drew back.

Ariana let him go. She hesitated for a moment, and then she

turned and began trying to gather the floating down. Every time her hand neared a curling feather, it slid away, moving on its own as if enchanted or as if her hand was shielded by magic. She tried with both hands, cupping them like catching butterflies, but each time the down eluded her. It slid like water from her oil, an illusion which could not be grasped.

Shianan, perplexed, reached out to snatch a handful and found that it floated out of his fingers without contact. He swung his hand through a cloud and it scattered, swirling about him, dancing above his reach.

"This is quite the mess," Ariana observed, turning in place to chase a cluster of down.

"I'm sorry." Shianan waved away down which threatened to tickle a sneeze from him. His stiff shoulder caught, making him flinch. His foot disturbed the heap of spilled chaff, adding dust to the crowded air. "I did not think..." He had to be brave, he had to speak aloud the thing that frightened him the most, to bare the ragged wound to examination. "A bastard I might be, but it seems in part I am a true son, and—"

She turned, sending spirals of down dancing about her. "You are the choices you make," she cut him off. "Including your choice to hear your own words, and your choice to reject them."

He shook his head. It could not be dismissed that easily. "But what I said..."

She fixed her eyes on him, holding him, binding him. "Then make another choice the next time. And the next."

Shianan writhed in her gaze. "I don't want to be that. Him."

"If I thought you were, I would not be here."

She was right—he trusted her, if nothing else. He found a breath. "If ever I become that, you can leave me."

She snorted and turned to wave away the dancing feathers. "Set you on fire, more likely. Don't you think so lightly of peeved mages."

He smiled, cracking apart the tension in his body. "Perhaps you should burn out this down. I don't know that we'll be able to clean it any other way."

"No!" Ariana softened the word with a nervous smile. "No, not with this much particulate in the air and all the chaff below. I don't know that it would blow the room, but it would be simplest to continue in that ignorance."

Shianan cocked his head. "Really?"

"One of the crueler pranks among some apprentices is to inject a puff of flour while your fellow is practicing sparking a candle. More than a few eyebrows have been lost to the result. I don't know if down will have the same effect, but certainly the chaff will catch."

Shianan sneezed. "It may be worth it," he said, and the last of the tension dissipated with the mild jest.

Ariana turned toward the door and went through the down, leaving a swirling path for him to follow. They descended to the ground floor, where sounds of splashing water and clinking stoneware suggested Luca was washing dishes. They went out to the kitchen and found him at a basin, wiping down plates and cups. "My lady, there's clean plates here," he said, "and I'll carry them in half a moment—"

"Oh, I can get them," Ariana assured him. "Thank you. You were on those quickly enough."

"Some were left used," Luca answered, "and it was not so much trouble to wash the rest in the cupboard as well." *Especially given the sabotage upstairs*, they all understood.

"Thank you. Are the dumplings in the dining room?"

"Yes, my lady."

She gathered plates and cups to carry out. Luca set aside a newly cleaned cup.

Shianan stood at the counter, not facing Luca. "I'm sorry."

Luca turned water out of another cup. "It was—"

"Luca." Shianan raised a hand to cut him off. "I'm sorry."

Luca hesitated, nodded, half-smiled.

Shianan jerked his head in the direction of the door. "Come on. Those will wait."

"But my lady..."

Shianan blew out his breath. "First of all, that's *my lady mage*."

Luca's hands slowed, and he looked at Shianan. "That's a freeman's address."

"It is."

"But—the prince procured my emancipation, yes, but how can that be explained to those who already know me as a servant? No one knows I'm not a slave."

Shianan rolled his eyes. "No one knows she's my wife, either. But you know who she is, and she knows who you are—I told her and her father. If we cannot be open in my own Gehrn-cursed house, where can we?"

Luca looked at the water. "She—won't mind?"

It was a curious way to put the question, but Shianan understood. "Didn't you notice she carried out three settings?"

Luca glanced at the clean dishes. He had not.

Luca had spent a few days in the Hazelrig household, but those days had been anything but usual. He might not have realized. "Let me remind you, Ariana Hazelrig and her father raised Tam, and that boy had a more comfortable childhood than I did even before she knew he was anything other than a human slave boy. I'm ashamed to admit I nearly envied him for a day or two. I'll put fair money that she would have carried three settings even if I hadn't said anything about your manumission."

Luca's mouth quirked. "So you don't think she'll mind."

"The dumplings are cooling!" Ariana called from the other room. "You two, leave the dishes and come eat!"

Shianan jerked his head again. "She may not be your mistress, but she is mine. Let's go."

Chapter 25

Shianan was just rising from his desk when the knock came at the door. He muttered in half-hearted irritation, "I'm coming."

Two men were waiting on the doorstep, with servants a little distance behind them. Shianan needed a moment to recognize one of them. "Jarrick Roald."

Jarrick had his hands up to ward off any angry words. "You told me not to come again—but I have news you must hear."

Had they come for Luca? But that was ridiculous; Luca was a free man.

"I am sorry to disturb you, your lordship," Jarrick continued. "I know you cannot be anxious to see me again. But my brother and I—this is my brother Thir—we need to speak with you."

Shianan's sword hung from a peg an arm's length from the door, and for a wild instant he wanted to seize it and pommel Jarrick's face. These men had sold Luca into slavery to cover their debts—or had known about it, at least, and had neither prevented it nor undone it, and that was near enough to the same. These men, when Luca had been robbed and sold again, had not so much as written a letter to answer that his life was more important than the inheritance he had lost.

But Jarrick looked much as he had the last time Shianan had seen him, his face tightly drawn and his eyes ashamed and wary. If nothing else, he wore his guilt, and Shianan was savagely glad to see that he was still uncomfortable facing Shianan. He stepped back from the door and did not look at the sword. "Come inside."

They stood awkwardly together in the office, where they did not sit. Thir was the eldest, Shianan supposed, but he relied on Jarrick's experience here with Shianan Becknam. Only, that was not a relationship to trade on.

Jarrick twisted the gloves in his hand. "We arrived in Alham today." He glanced at the closed door, as if considering escaping through it.

"I'm sure you had business, thanks to your new influence."

"Indeed. I am grateful for your help." But Shianan knew Jarrick was only filling the air with words to cloud over something else.

Thir at last took a seat and folded his hands together. Apparently tiring of his brother's hesitation, he began to speak. "Your lordship, Jarrick has told me of your connection to our brother. Luca spoke very highly of you."

Shianan nodded once and waited.

Thir drew a breath, struggling beneath the heavy silence. "For this reason, we wanted to tell you ourselves... There's no easy way to say this, I'm afraid. But we wanted to deliver the news—"

The door latch rattled, and Shianan's heart quickened. That would be Luca, come from the market, and he did not deserve to walk in and discover his traitor brothers. "Wait," he called, and he looked back at Thir. "Give me a moment."

But Luca was already coming through the door, balancing a wrapped bundle on one hand. "That door is sticking. I'll get a file and—" He stopped, staring into the office, his face rigid.

"Luca," breathed Jarrick.

"What are you doing here?" Luca asked, his voice quiet but even.

"What are *you* doing here?" Thir half rose from the chair. "You're not dead?"

Shianan looked at him sharply. "Of course he's not dead. Do dead men write letters?"

"We've had no letters," Jarrick answered, still looking at Luca. "Only the letter of credit, come back to be claimed."

"They said they'd killed you," Thir said.

Luca looked slowly back and forth between them. He set the bundle on the empty chair. "It was probably too much to remember what they took and whom they killed and whom they sold," he said at last. "I was robbed and enslaved, but not killed. I made a bargain to come to Alham, where I hoped Master Shianan would redeem me."

Thir and Jarrick looked again at Shianan. "So you had him. Again."

"Someone had to," Shianan said as lightly as he could.

Luca gave a wry smile.

Jarrick crossed the small room and embraced Luca. Shianan stiffened, but he saw Luca's arms rise and close about Jarrick, returning the hug. Thir joined them, throwing his arms about them both. Shianan moved behind the desk and sat stiffly down.

"But what are you doing in Alham?" Luca pressed. "You didn't come all this way for me."

"We did not know you were here," Jarrick repeated. "Though I suppose the next time I think you dead, this will be the first place I look. But let's not play that game for a long, long while."

"We came for trade negotiations," Thir said. "We have contracts here; our trade with the Chrenadan military has given us reputation and access to other partnerships."

"You have Luca to thank for that," Shianan muttered.

"But we thought we should—we thought you would want to know," he finished, turning to Shianan. "We never thought you had him here with you."

"And will for some time, I hope."

But Thir's face darkened as he looked at Luca's cuffs. "Are you—"

"It's not like that," Luca interrupted, looking between them. "I have a special manumission; I'm not a slave here."

"You are cuffed, and you called him your master."

"I was a long time learning to call him Master Shianan, and it's a habit which has stayed," Luca said patiently. "And he'll still be my master when he's paying me for services hired. The cuffs... we've not taken the time for that yet. There has been a war, you know, and enough to keep us busy."

"But you—"

"But my life is much the same with or without them just now," Luca said. "I live in his house, I keep him on task, and I bring meals to be sure he eats when he's too distracted to remember basic necessities." He gestured toward the bundle, steaming faintly. "Speaking of which, the pie I brought would have made a supper and tomorrow's lunch, which means it will feed four nicely."

The oblique invitation was a skillful quelling of Thir's anxiety—no slave would so casually invite his brothers to share his master's meal—and Luca went into the other room to arrange a table, much like Jarrick's first fateful visit. Shianan followed, feeling slightly out of place in his own rooms but unwilling to leave his friend unprotected with his family.

"We'll have to write to Sara," Thir said, still amazed. "She'll be so glad to hear."

"So you never received Luca's letter?" Shianan asked again as they sat around the table.

"Nothing," Jarrick repeated. "It must have gone astray. Remember that bridge had gone, and everything was disrupted for a month or so?" He shook his head. "We would not have assumed the worst, not until the letter of credit came."

"The thieves brought it to the House of Lombard while I was there," Thir said. "The clerks alerted me, thinking I'd want to see you, but of course it was not you."

Luca sat forward. "Two men?"

"Two."

Luca nodded. "They had hired guards, but it was two brothers who were the leaders. Did they have a slave with them? A big man?" He looked at Jarrick. "Cole?"

Thir shook his head. "No, it was just the two of them."

Luca looked a little disappointed. "I suppose you had them arrested."

"I paid for the city guards to learn from them where you'd been killed." Thir looked discomfited. "There's a memorial to you in the temple on Sun Street."

A chuckle bubbled up from Luca. "They say that if the time and place of one's death is not recorded, the spirit may walk. Yet, recorded, here I walk."

Shianan sat back in his chair, blowing out his breath. Luca still did not jest often; if he could joke about his death with his brothers, he was not afraid of them. If the letter had gone wrong, Shianan could hardly blame them for not replying, not assuring Luca of his worth and offering him aid. And they had come to share the news of Luca's death, mistaken as it was, with Shianan himself, despite his final words to Jarrick. That was worth something.

Luca cut up the pie and shared it out. The brazier burned and smoked, occasionally popping, and Shianan let their talk move around him, content in their joy at remaking their family.

Chapter 26

"Luca, stop," Shianan prompted with feigned gruffness. "That's the third time you've dropped that spoon. Leave it 'til morning."

"I'm sorry."

"Leave it," Shianan repeated. Luca's apologies grated, especially when Shianan thought he might have echoed Flamen Ande.

Luca set the dishes down and sighed at them. "I'm sorry."

Shianan toed off his boot. Even if the brothers had been happy to see one another, it could not have been easy on Luca. Now that Thir and Jarrick had gone, their ghosts still hung in the room, a reminder that there were other ties and complications. "What do you think of all of it?" Shianan asked obliquely, letting Luca choose what to answer.

Luca sighed. "I don't know what to think. I've not been a slave with a manumission before. It's confusing."

Shianan tried to soften his tone. "It means you can do what you want. Go where you want."

"I don't want to go." Luca gestured toward the table where they had dined with his brothers. "I was so glad that they—that they only hadn't received my letter. That they came. But I don't want to go back with them."

Jarrick had opened that possibility, obliquely but hopefully, and Shianan had watched Luca struggle to deflect the question. No matter what truce or promise of safe passage, the family terrain was still rough to travel.

"You don't have to," Shianan said as gently as he could. It was strange, talking this way. "What do you want to do? Do you want to open a counter, taking in accounting for merchants or armies?"

Luca dropped into the empty chair and laced his fingers together. "I want to stay here."

For a moment, Shianan did not fully hear the words, too caught up in how Luca had sat down to say it. He remembered too clearly how Luca would only stand or even kneel, and the unthinking intimacy of trust swept over Shianan like the air he hadn't known he needed.

But then he realized what Luca had said. "Then stay."

There was a pause, and then Luca looked at him, his eyebrows lifted and close. "I keep feeling I...because that is my family, but... But I don't—I was glad to see Thir and Jarrick, and of course there's Sara, but I don't know how much there is to go back to." His voice grew hopeful, seeking. "But to stay, that would be all right?"

All the warmth of his earlier observation flooded Shianan, and he leaned forward. "Of course." He rested his forearms on his knees. "They'll understand. They already understood once."

Luca dropped his head, in relief or shame or both. "I'm sorry. I feel a fool for wondering, and I know no right-thinking man would hesitate, but—"

"Most right-thinking men have not been both slave and free quite so often," Shianan said shortly. "And speaking of that." He nodded toward Luca's wrists. "You can have them off at any time. You have the royal manumission."

Luca nodded slowly. "I have thought of it. But I worry—even if I go and present the paper, why should they believe me?"

"They should believe a royal document."

"But how would I have such a thing? What if—what if they disbelieved it, or took it from me?"

As his freedom had been taken before, and his inheritance. "I would go with you and scowl threateningly. That puts off most recruits, so it might work on market slavers." Shianan let his smile fade. "You had only to ask."

"You've had so much to do..." Luca trailed off. Shianan guessed at the rest; Luca was still struggling to work out what freedom meant. In a strange way, suspended awkwardly between slavery and freedom, he was more secure now than he had ever been.

"Let me know when you want me," Shianan said lightly, pulling off the other boot. "For now, leave those dishes where they are, or you'll keep me up all night with your clattering."

Luca pulled a face at him and pushed the plates together, a minor defiance which set them both at ease, and went to his own bed.

Elysia Parma had just settled into a chair with an untasted cup of tea when a knock sounded at her front door. It was evening, and she expected no visitors, and for just a moment she thought of Gehrn waiting outside. She shook away the thought and went to the door, one hand cupping a half-formed scoop of invisible energy.

But it was one of the market messengers on her step, looking up expectantly. “Good evening, my lady mage. I’ve been sent to ask if you are receiving visitors tonight.”

“That might depend upon the visitor,” Elysia answered.

The girl’s eyes widened with excitement. “It’s a Ryuven! I couldn’t—begging your pardon, my lady mage, but it’s my first message to carry for a Ryuven. Even if it’s just across the street.”

“What?” Elysia asked, and she raised her eyes.

In the slanting spring sunset, across the street, Edeiya’rika stood watching. As Elysia’s eyes found her, her wings drooped slightly.

“I see.” Elysia drew a coin from the jar she kept by the door and gave it to the messenger, and then she beckoned Edeiya to come.

“I didn’t want to disturb you,” Edeiya’rika said as she approached. “I thought to ask before I appeared at your door. Tamaryl’sho tells me humans are particular about doors.”

“You’re quite welcome,” Elysia said. “Please come inside, and tell me what brings you here.”

“Escape, mostly,” Edeiya admitted. She followed Elysia into the sitting room and accepted the offered tea. “I confess to a form of cowardice. If I am here, I cannot be reached by those who would explain again what a terrible mistake I have made before I am even named silth.”

Elysia poured a second cup of tea. “I’m sorry I haven’t a more appropriate seat for you, but that stool might be the most comfortable. Is that mistake negotiating with Chrenada instead of pillaging her? Or taking the word of an enemy mage in the matter of your ongoing famine?”

“We burned the first fields.”

“Ah. I am glad and sorry.”

Edeiya nodded and cradled the tea in her hands. “I argued our reasoning again and again, and I insisted upon burning their livelihood and their pride of place, and I stood by and watched while they wept and wailed on the borders of their fields. If they believed me, that this is the way through the famine and this would be to their benefit, it still must have been terrifying and disheartening. If they did not believe me... I must be a monster to them.”

Elysia, as a member of the Great Circle, was known as a champion of the people’s safety and was generally greeted as such. She felt the burden of that trust in each of her decisions as a state mage. To struggle with such hard decisions under that burden while facing distrust and despair...

"I hope you'll forgive my honesty," Edeiya continued quietly, looking into her tea, "but I feel more than a little uneasy coming to a human to unburden my conscience."

"One of the enemy, to probe your weaknesses?"

"Possibly." Edeiya smiled without meeting her eyes. "Or to weigh the effect of your ruse." She shook her head. "I don't think it's a ruse. I don't know Callahan'sho well, but he... He is too proud of his expertise to lie about it. He takes a certain pride in his disassociation with the rest of the Circle—"

"A keen insight so quickly," Elysia murmured.

"—but he takes even more pride in his reputation as a scholar of plants. He would not sacrifice that on a lie, not even a lie to tip a war."

Elysia sat back in her chair and sipped her tea. "Hmm. I had not considered it in that way, but I think you're right. An interesting foundation for your trust, but probably a safe one."

"But there is the chance that I am wrong," Edeiya said. "And yet I cannot waver in the sight of my clan, or they will lose what frail hope and trust they have."

"And so you have come to waver in the sight of the humans, instead."

"It may be better to sit with an understanding enemy than to sit alone."

"That is an interesting philosophical question—but one we must treat as hypothetical, for you do not sit with an enemy. Not now."

Elysia could not have guessed at this, this welcoming a Ryuven into her sitting room, not even a few weeks ago when Ewan had ordered her to quell her uncertainties and meet with the Ryuven liaison. But she and Edeiya had recognized themselves in each other, each striving to protect their people, and it had been easier than expected to identify famine as the truer enemy.

Edeiya relaxed into a smile. "Thank you. And thank you for letting me come into your home, even unexpected and late in the evening."

"You are welcome in my home."

It helped, certainly, that Elysia had never faced Edeiya the Tsuraiya in battle, not like she had the Pairvyn—and that even if things went poorly, she never would. Even if all fell apart and their peoples rejoined in war, it would be the decisions of others, and that made it safer to talk as warriors who understood a common passion and need.

"I agreed to be visible at the first burnings," Edeiya explained, "and Oniwe'aru will preside over the next. I have done days of destruction now, and I have had my fill of smoke and tears. And now there is nothing to do but to hope the growers can get a second planting in time, and then to wait until the autumn to see if ears turn golden or black."

"You will need something to fill your days as you wait. May I suggest collaboration on the countering of Ientu approaches, with further exploration of the influences of condensed ether on conventional Chrenadan technique?"

Edeiya'rika straightened on the stool and brightened. "I have a duty to fill here, assigned by my aru, and I mean to fulfill it. And if that requires pulverizing more cliff faces into gravel, then I suppose I must do what I must."

"I too have an assignment, to develop more effective magics. We can pack for a few days' stay near a safely remote testing area and not lose time in daily travel."

"Then—and I do not know if this is an appropriate beverage for saluting or cheering, but—then to duty and diligence." Edeiya'rika raised her tea.

"It will do," replied Elysia, and she raised her own. "To duty and diligence."

Chapter 27

The council room was nearly empty, but Ariana still felt a little tremor of nerves. "Good morning, my lord," she said to the single member, seated on one long side of the table.

"Good morning, my lady mage," returned Chancellor Uilleam. "Thank you for coming today."

Ariana stood straight at the end of the long table, observing his expression. She was not quite certain what he wanted with her.

"I will come directly to the point," Chancellor Uilleam said. "The Black Mage has visited the Ryuven world not once but twice. You were the first to negotiate for the dall sweetbud. You have been consistently at the forefront of our interactions with the Ryuven."

This seemed to be anything but coming directly to the point, as Ariana was already aware of her dealings with the Ryuven, but she only kept a pleasant, expectant expression.

"As the Ai have been kind enough to send an emissary to our court, we have been considering a similar gesture. It is the considered opinion of this council, and the particular recommendation of His Majesty, that you are the logical choice for this role."

Ariana's heart gave a little leap. She had been especially selected? "An emissary? But how?"

"We have already asked the Pairvyn if it would be possible to bear someone to the Ai court if the need arose, and he has confirmed it would be possible. With your acceptance, we would formalize your position and arrange for official visits to carry our words directly to Lord Oniwe, and perhaps to conduct some research of your own."

Ariana caught her breath. To research magic in the densely magical Ryuven world...! That would be a peerless opportunity. "I would be honored, my lord."

"Good, good. If you're amenable, we can begin the arrangements immediately to confer the position."

Ariana nodded, anxious for a new role that would give her regular access to Tamaryl, Maru, and the fascinating, deadly Ryuven magic. She was the logical choice, as the only mage to have survived the Ryuven atmosphere, but she had not dreamed of being able to travel back and forth and even to conduct research.

"We are making a state gift of foodstuffs, a sign of our trust in the Ai despite continued Ryuven predations. Mage Callahan suggested it would be a helpful gesture and recommended that his Ryuven students help to carry it across after the shipment is officially accepted on behalf of the Ai by the Pairvyn here. We thought you might join that ceremony to help present the aid and perhaps make your first formal visit with its first delivery."

Ariana nodded. "If I can help to ensure the success of the treaty, of course I will do everything within my power."

"We thought you would say so." Chancellor Uilleam gave her an approving gaze. "Thank you, my lady mage, for your persistent dedication and efforts. They are much appreciated."

Shianan rushed through a few tasks and then, deciding he was failing to fool himself, sat back from the desk and put them aside entirely. He could take them up again in the morning, and he needed a break and a walk in the evening air, and by fortunate happenstance it was about the time that Ariana departed from the Wheel.

He still was not fooling himself, but at least he would mock himself gently.

She had already left the Wheel, and he cut across the courtyard to fall in beside her. "Good day?" he asked.

She beamed at him. "I'm glad you've come! It will save me the trouble of finding you. I have news."

"Wonderful news, it seems."

"And you'll have it before my own father—though he may already know it, wretched man, as it's Circle business. But he'll have the grace to pretend surprise for me." She grinned. "I spoke with Chancellor Uilleam today. They've agreed—the Ai and the Circle—that we can benefit from more collaborative research." Ariana's words tumbled over one another in her happy hurry. "And while Edeiya'rika might be glad to come here and continue working with Mage Parma, that allows only for research on magics in our own world's atmosphere."

Shianan nodded.

"And as you can imagine, we don't want to risk sending other mages to the Ryuven world, with the hope that they don't die or don't suffer a loss of magic, and so that means I am the official emissary to the Ai!"

Shianan recognized the moment when he was meant to be happy for her, when he should cheer and congratulate her, but his stomach crawled up toward his heart and made his pulse pound too hard.

"My first official duty is to help deliver a gift of food aid. Only I will not be helping, obviously—I'll be a hindrance, actually, as someone will have to transport me instead of a sack of root vegetables, but that's bureaucracy, and I suppose it's the gesture that matters. But if we've exchanged emissaries, that will mean the treaty is holding, won't it?"

Shianan managed, "You're going—there?"

Her enthusiasm was checked, and for a moment she looked confused. "Yes. To do research no one has ever done, ever. I thought you..." The corners of her mouth twitched down. "I thought you'd be glad for me."

"I—I am."

Her voice grew dry. "That is the most curiously unhappy glad expression."

He clenched his jaw. "I am trying to be happy for you. But..."

"But what?"

But he had given so much to bring her back from that place, which had nearly killed her, and she had been abducted there a second time while Shianan lay helpless on the floor, and... "You lost your magic after going there."

"And regained it. I've learned how to handle it now. I was able to adapt when I went back, and I did not lose my magic when I returned, not like the first time. I'll be all right."

"You'll still be gone." The words slipped out before he could think on them.

She looked at him. "I am a Mage of the Great Circle. You always knew I would be gone, at least at times."

Already he regretted what he had said, or at least how he had said it. "And I am a soldier, and I will be gone, too. You knew that." He had known that, too. Their marriage was always going to be stretched and hidden.

She looked at him, examining him, and approved what she saw. "And we will meet at home."

"Or in the field, if you come to join my campaigns," he said with deliberate lightness. "Or in the Ryuven world, if I go to join you there."

She laughed. "I don't know if that is even... Would you?"

Every fiber revolted from the thought, and he wanted only to snatch her and carry them both away from the possibility. "I don't know. Maybe."

She smiled, and it warmed him. "Maybe?"

"If it ended all this and kept you safe, yes, I would." The words were sharp to his ears, but she brushed her shoulder against him as they walked, and he thought maybe he had meant them.

"I am not afraid to go away from you, if I know you'll be waiting to welcome me home."

He nodded. And he was a soldier, an officer, a leaf boat to be set on whatever stream pleased his superiors and to be reclaimed when his purpose was complete. He could not resent her own work. "You know I will wait and watch for you, just as I hope you will wait for me."

"With a catch in my breath and a quickened heart," she said softly. "Now angle to the right and take a pass behind that hanging tarp, so I may kiss you without waiting until we reach my house."

CHAPTER 28

Ariana didn't even glance up at the knock on the office door. "Yes," she called wearily. "Come."

Her father entered with a sympathetic smile. "A bit overwhelmed, are we?"

She exhaled with relief. "Oh, it's you." She gestured to her desk, cluttered with stacks of notes and several books. "I've been fielding research requests all day. I had no idea so many people had so many active questions about Ryuven magic."

"What did you expect? It's been the Circle's primary interest for centuries."

"But not from the other side of the between-worlds! I never expected so many requests so quickly."

"Quite a workload, especially for a newlywed."

She made a face at him. "No more than, say, a fresh series of battles." She sighed. "And yes, he was concerned, and that only makes sense. But he understands this is my work, just as going out to fight is his. We knew from the start we had duties away from one another." She lifted a stack of pages. "I'll sort it all eventually."

He leaned closer to peer at the stacked notes and bound materials. "What sorts of research do you have so far?"

"A little bit of everything." Ariana indicated the respective piles. "Mage Callahan of course wants botany samples—well, drawings, not samples, he's been very clear that I'm not to bring any plant material, and equally insistent that I launder all my clothing before returning here. Mage Fallat wants to know their birds' migratory patterns—don't ask me why. And Mage Parma... I hope her request makes sense after I read it two or three more times." She gave a reluctantly hopeful grin.

Ewan Hazelrig picked up the topmost sheet of the Silver Mage's packet and pursed his lips. "She obviously has faith in your capabilities."

"That's very flattering, but I'm already half-buried!"

"I'm here to finish the job, I'm afraid." He set a satchel on the desk, shoving a stack perilously aside, and opened it. "I have some questions for you to look into, myself."

"Is this perchance related to your Ryuven history hobby?" Ariana gave him a mock glare. "This had better be interesting, at least."

"Oh, I think you'll find it very much so," he answered with curious intensity. "Go ahead, take a look."

She obligingly took a sheet and began to skim it. After a moment she frowned and began to read more carefully. Then she took another sheet, flipping it to examine the notes on either side. Finally she lifted her head and stared open-mouthed at her father. "Are you serious? You think humans and Ryuven are related? Or not just related but—we're the same creatures?"

"Or were, at least," he amended. "Obviously we're different enough now. But we've known each other a long time; look how far back we have winged men in art and record."

"But the Ryuven aren't winged humans," she protested. "And even if they were, how would they have gotten the wings?" She frowned. "We don't even live in the same world."

"That's part of what I want you to look into." He separated a sheet, and she recognized the rough map she'd sketched the night she first returned. "You drew this for Elysia and me. Look at it again now; does it remind you of anything?"

She looked at it skeptically. "It reminds me of a map I drew, of the Ryuven city."

He flipped the sheet over, so that the ink lines showed through the thin common paper, and rotated it slightly. "What about now?" He drew a line with his finger. "Imagine a river here."

The Palace of Red Sands now sat above the market they had walked through, and the hill from which she'd viewed and recalled the strange place lay to one side of the suggested river. Ariana shook her head, and then she hesitated. No, that was only his suggestion...

From his sheaf of notes, he drew out an onion-skin paper tracing of her sketch and then a map of Alham. He layered one atop the other and slid them into position. "And now?"

"Oh," she breathed. "That's... that's much like Alham."

He nodded. "Allowing that it was drawn by a very inexpert cartographer, who did not have a comprehensive view, it's rather surprisingly like Alham. Either you unconsciously drew your own city, or the two share a similar layout."

"But, how would that happen?"

"How do we share a language?" He looked at her. "Did it never strike you as odd that we can speak as easily with the Ryuven as with the Wakari? Yes, we each have a more or less subtle accent of our own—but there shouldn't be a difference of accents between our worlds, there should be a difference of languages. Or perhaps of communication altogether, using skin color or hand signals or scents instead of speech."

"But...."

"Or consider Tam's form—Tamaryl cannot make himself a duck, or a horse, or a tree, but he can slip into a human shape. Why is that, if we are a wholly separate species as much as the duck or dog?"

Ariana's skin began to prickle. "Then—who are they? Or who are we?"

He shook his head, rolling the map again. "I don't know."

It was a staggering idea, and her head spun as she grasped for clues to make sense of it. "Tamaryl told me there were places where it is easier to cross."

"Yes. The Wakari Coast, for example, suffers almost no Ryuven raids."

Ariana caught her breath, and she leapt up to dash to the bookshelf. "Ranne gave me a book, and I've been so busy—here." She cleared a space at the end of the table and set it down.

"*The Stars of the Firmament and Their Tales: An Accurate Reproduction of an Authentic Ryuven Text on the Astronomy of the Ryuven World*," her father read aloud from the title page. "Lovely binding, of course. What are you thinking of?"

"If the city is similar when reversed, what of the sky?" Ariana shrugged. "It's a ridiculous question, but so is the idea that a Ryuven might be my cousin."

Her father frowned. "Fetch your mother's copy of Balthasar, would you?"

Ariana found the book of sky maps and brought it back to the table. Her father already had Ranne's book open to an illustration of a twisting serpent blowing out fire across the sky. On the opposite page, stars hung in the flaming heavens.

"The Burnings," Ariana recognized. She opened her mother's book and turned pages toward the illustration she sought. "And a dragon in the sky."

Balthasar had imagined the mythical event differently, with warring dragons blasting fire at each other which rained down upon the city, but he too had set stars in the aftermath. And the mapped constellations, the visual tale of the beasts in the sky... Ariana rotated the book a quarter turn, so that the two illustrations seemed to mirror one another.

"We have six and six stars in our two dragons," her father said, "and they have a constellation of twelve. Both set at a curve, where the serpent uncoils, but in opposite directions."

"And slightly off on one plane," Ariana added. "Roughly a quarter-circle. What does that mean?"

"I have no idea," her father said cheerily. "But I'm delighted to find it. I don't have to know what it means yet; we just gather the pieces until they seem to start fitting together."

"Well, these seem to fit together very well," Ariana mused. She turned pages, looking for another constellation to compare. "What do you think the Burnings were, really? I mean, we don't think there were warring sky dragons, do we?"

Her father shook his head. "My instinct is to say no. But then, there are strange beasts still in the mountains, and it's possible that there were others at one time. And there must have been creatures we no longer know; look at horses, so much taller than any of our other animals, and what must have fed on them in their natural state, that they needed such long legs and could run nearly from birth? I think what is left in the mountains is a poor showing of what must have been, once." He crossed his arms. "But for all that, I am not prepared to believe in warring dragons which burned out the sky." He nodded toward the table. "And anyway, the Ryuven show only one dragon."

Ariana smiled. "All right, then. But what do you want me to do with this?"

"Nothing at all, not out loud," her father cautioned. "Just bring me what information you may find on Ryuven biology. I have not even asked Tamaryl some of these questions; they were less urgent when we were entirely at war. But if we can collect more pieces to fit together, I would love to engage his mind and perhaps others'. In the meanwhile, I'd like you to skim their writings on related subjects."

Ariana nodded. "That's history, physiology—"

"Don't forget literature and art; that's where some of our earliest references to them can be found."

"Right. I'll just have to move into one of their libraries. At least I won't have a chance to be homesick." Ariana blew out a tired breath. "All right. I'll add your requests to my growing pile."

"Your pile seems tall enough for tonight. Aren't you going

home?" He crooked one corner of his mouth.

"Shianan knows I had a lot to do tonight; I don't think he's expecting me until late."

"A true Mage of the Circle." He started toward the door. "Don't worry too much about it; I know from long experience, the stacks of paper will still be there in the morning."

She nodded. "I have to get through these. Tomorrow Shianan and I agreed to meet at his townhouse."

"Oh?"

"A sort of homemaking, just to make the place ours before we go our separate directions. Light some candles, smudge away the Gehrn miasma."

He laughed. "I won't expect you tomorrow night, then. But still, you may want to come home yet this evening."

"Thanks. I'll go in a few minutes."

"Good night, then."

CHAPTER 29

"Oh, hello, Mage Parma!" Ariana ran to catch up to the Silver Mage, dodging a barrow full of caged ducks. "Are you out for lunch as well?"

"After years of careful observation, it is my educated opinion," Mage Parma answered, "that it's inefficient to work on an empty stomach. I was going to Mother Ellie's cart near the dye market—do you know the one?"

Ariana shook her head. "Not well."

"Then let me introduce you. I'm thinking today is a day for lamb and greens. Come on." As they walked, Mage Parma eyed Ariana. "Are you no longer the Black Mage today?"

Ariana flushed. "I—I don't like to wear the robes in the market. Not for a quick lunch." She was still proud of her place in the Circle, but... Sometimes women stopped her to thank her for bringing their sons home from battles or bringing medicine for their infants, and sometimes men stared at her as they cradled cudgels near where the Ryuven traders came, even if none were expected that day.

Mage Parma nodded. "I felt that way after Luenda. It'll be all right, but take your time."

The dye market was quiet today, but there was a short line waiting at a wheeled cart. A boy, perhaps ten years old, was selling meat and vegetable pies, dispensing filled pastries and change with practiced efficiency. Ariana and Mage Parma got into line.

"How is the work with Edeiya'rika?" Ariana asked.

A glimmer came into Mage Parma's eye. "We're going to engage in intensive research on supplemental energies," she answered with a sly tone. "We'll be out a few days, where we can destroy things properly."

Ariana felt a rush of some feeling she couldn't quite identify. "That sounds—productive."

Mage Parma chuckled. "I expect it will be. More than I would have guessed if someone had dared to mention Ryuven collaboration a year or so ago."

"Good afternoon, my lady mage," the boy said as they stepped up to the cart. "Oh, my lady mages?" He squeaked a little when he saw

Ariana.

That was silly; Elysia Parma was the greater mage.

"Hello, Rand," Mage Parma said. "How's—"

"I've got your favorite saved just in case you came by," the boy said, his words all in a tumble. "Vegetables and gravy." He ducked down behind the cart to retrieve it.

"That was considerate of you," Mage Parma said, neglecting to mention the lamb and greens. "How's your mother?"

"Still poorly," he answered from behind the cart. "The physicker says she won't be up for a week or two yet, even if her lungs come back strong enough."

"I'm sorry to hear that." As the boy straightened, Mage Parma deposited several coins into his box. "No change," she said when he reached for a jar. "Medicine can be dear."

The boy hesitated, looking at the box, and then he pushed a pie over to the Silver Mage. "Thank you," he said, his voice muted.

"Oh! There's a bench opening up," Mage Parma observed. "I'll go and claim it for us. Come and join me."

"Right," said Ariana. "Could I have a lamb and greens pie, please?" She could trade with Mage Parma, who clearly did not want to reject the boy's thoughtfulness.

"I'm—I'm out," Rand said. "Sorry. Do you want another of vegetables with gravy?"

Ariana accepted, of course, and pulled a handful of coins to find payment, picking through for a little extra as the Silver Mage had done. He passed her a hot pie, and she balanced it in one hand while returning the remaining coins into her purse. Behind her, a man asked for three lamb pies.

Ariana got the money safely away and went to join Mage Parma. "This sun is splendid," she said, sliding onto the bench. She turned her face up and closed her eyes. "I wonder if I could stay out the afternoon."

"I won't tell," Mage Parma replied, "but you won't thank yourself tomorrow when you face your desk."

Ariana sighed. "What a way to spoil a happy mood," she said with mock ferocity. She bit into the pie, nearly burning her mouth on hot gravy.

"Careful," Mage Parma cautioned. "They keep a pot of coals in the base of the cart, and it seems Rand left these directly on it. Mine has more than a bit of burnt taste."

Ariana could taste it, too, though there was little black on the pie's crust. "Vegetables and gravy?"

Mage Parma smiled. "It's not actually my favorite, though I do get one now and again. They're generally better than this; this is bitter, under the burnt. But I wasn't going to disappoint poor Rand if he'd tried to be thoughtful. He's had a hard go of it this spring."

"His mother's ill?"

"Yes. Mother Ellie's his grandmother, and she was ill over the winter, and then it took his mother that much worse. Mother Ellie's been staying with her some days, leaving Rand to manage the cart. I try to stop by once or twice a week, though I'm not sure what I think I'm accomplishing. But at least I can slip an extra few pias into his box."

Ariana forced down a bite. "I wonder if today they left Rand to make the pies himself, too."

Mage Parma grimaced. "They really are usually better than this. I wonder if maybe you're right. Though I suspect Rand should be a fair apprentice at cookery, and maybe this is just an outlying exception. He didn't seem himself today."

"Is there a father or grandfather?"

"I know his father is away at a post to watch against Ryuven raiders. I think Mother Ellie may be widowed, though I've never known for certain." Mage Parma pushed the last of the pie into her mouth and wrinkled her nose. "Poor burnt pie. Those vegetables boiled in vain."

Ariana glanced at her remaining half pie, oozing gravy. "You won't judge me too harshly if I drop the last of this near an alley of cats?"

Mage Parma snorted gently. "I will not. I'll hope our next lunch doesn't undercut my invitation."

They rose and started up the street, and though Rand was busy with a short line at the cart, Ariana made sure to glance back, and she chucked the remaining pie aside only when he had his head down over a tray. "It's so bright," she said, turning ahead again.

The Silver Mage was shielding her eyes. "I'm sure it's gotten brighter in the last few minutes."

Ariana squinted against the sun, her eyes blurring with the light. It was an unusual amount of light for this time of year; the rising road must be at just the perfect angle to catch the spring sunbeams. She stumbled; the sloping street was steeper than she'd realized while distracted with the sun.

Her mouth tasted of ash, and she wanted water. She would get some at—where was she going? The Wheel? She had been working at the Wheel, she was mostly sure.

Mage Parma was walking more slowly, Ariana noticed, but Ariana couldn't catch her in the street. People streamed through the street like fish, splitting around the two mages, but Ariana was always two steps behind the Silver Mage. She thought that was funny, though her breath came more quickly on the hill. She thought she should call to the Silver Mage, but somehow she couldn't quite manage it, and her mouth was too dry to speak.

Two men were walking beside them, one on either side, and Ariana realized they had been there for—how long? Three steps? Thirty? One of them looked at her, and she wanted to ask what he was doing, but her dry mouth did not want to open. He had a brown cloak over his shoulders and a blue tunic visible in front where it gapped. He grinned, and she smiled back. At least he was friendly.

The other man stepped up to the Silver Mage—somehow he could catch her in only a step or two—and put a hand on her arm. Something flared in Ariana; she knew that was dangerous. He shouldn't do that. But Mage Parma did nothing, only walked on, her face half-turned toward him, and Ariana thought perhaps she'd imagined it.

But then he pressed the Silver Mage's arm and guided her across the street, tugging her back from a passing wagon's wheel, and Ariana watched them go and thought distantly that there was something wrong about it. The sun was so bright. She felt unsettled, though she could not say why. She turned her head to look after them, and her feet followed.

"Not you, girl," the second man said, and he gave Ariana a shove with his shoulder. She stumbled and stretched an arm to him to steady herself. She saw his arm move, saw him turn toward her, saw the sweep of his hand, knew he would strike her, and yet in all her clarity she could not move. He slapped her, and her head snapped to the side, and for a moment it was even harder to concentrate. She stood still, and he moved away into the street. She tasted blood, and she couldn't figure out which way to go.

"Say, are you all right?" someone asked. A young man leaned toward Ariana, frowning with concern. "I saw him hit—are you all right? Can you hear me?" He lifted a hand, moved it hesitantly before her eyes.

Ariana wanted to speak to him, wanted to tell him that something was wrong and she couldn't remember what it was. But her tongue couldn't manage the words.

"Do you need help getting home?" he asked. "Is there someone I can find for you?"

She knew the answer to this—she knew this... "Wheel," she managed. "Wheel of the Circle." Her words were thick, like she'd been drinking too much.

"The Wheel of the Circle?" he repeated.

"Mage."

"Are you a mage?" He smiled uncertainly. "Did you get a bit too much magic? Come on, I can walk you to the Naziar, and then we'll see if someone can find the Wheel for us."

Ariana started walking with him, her feet scraping on the sloped pavement. "The other man, he asked for lamb pie." This seemed important, but she didn't know why.

The young man was called Dimi, he told her, and he had just been leaving the dye market with a satchel of madder root for his aunt, who would be peeved that he was late but would understand once he explained. He seemed anxious to talk. Ariana nodded as he spoke, but she was faintly worried that she was forgetting something important. Maybe her father would know, when she spoke to him...

Dimi put his hand in the crook of Ariana's elbow and guided her toward one of the guards at the Naziar's gate. "Er, excuse me, but I'm trying to help her, she is sort of lost, and she says—"

"My lady mage!" The guard looked with concern at Ariana. "Mage Hazelrig, are you all right?"

"You know her?" Dimi sounded relieved. "I thought maybe we were chasing geese. She said she wanted to be taken to the Wheel."

"What's happened to her?" The guard raised a hand, summoning another. "Let's get her to the Wheel, then. Bran, take Mage Hazelrig and this lad up to the Wheel and find the White Mage."

They hurried her across the streets and yards, and Ariana wanted to resist but thought there was probably a reason they were in such a hurry. After all, she had something important to say, or to do, and she would recall it eventually if they only stopped rushing her from place to place.

The guard ran ahead once they were inside the Wheel itself, disappearing from sight in the curving corridor, and a moment later Ariana's father came jogging back with him. "Ariana! What's happened?"

The three of them ushered her into her father's office, and Ariana breathed all the smells of his workroom. He'd been doing something with copper. But it did not smell like the blood she had tasted. Why did people say blood smelled of copper, when it was iron running in their veins?

"Ariana?"

"Lamb pie," she said, and while her insistence made sense in her mind, once her words touched the air she could sense their inanity. "He wanted lamb pies like she did, but Rand didn't tell him no."

Her father's face was unnaturally calm, a mask to hide fear. She knew that, even if she couldn't speak correctly. "What pies were these?" he asked her. He looked at Dimi. "Do you know about the pies?"

Dimi shook his head. Ariana knew that he did not know, no one else knew, it was up to her to say the important thing, if only she could remember it. It had something to do with the pies, though.

"I found her near the dye market," Dimi offered. "There's a pie cart there, but I don't know any more than that."

Ariana worked her ashen mouth. She was so thirsty. "We had pies." That was part of it. There was more, and it was urgent...

"I don't—"

"Silver," she blurted. She licked the roof of her mouth, thinking of silver ash flakes. The Silver Mage had gone somewhere, and what was the rest of it?

Her father was hardly breathing. "Ariana? Were you with Elysia?"

The name prompted Ariana to nod eagerly. "Yes. Silver Mage Parma. We had bad pies. Burnt and bitter. Then—then they came." She needed to explain, and all the words ran from her like gravy over soggy vegetables.

"Who came? Who?"

Ariana looked at Dimi, watching her with tense worry, and she reached out suddenly to point at his chest, where his tunic collar gapped to show a dark blue shirt beneath. She tapped the fabric urgently. "Them. Them."

Her father drew his eyebrows together in confusion. Dimi, eyes wide, held up his hands as if to ward off accusation. But then her father asked, "The Gehrn?"

The word sparked in Ariana's mind, and the fear that had been forgotten with their name rushed up in a sudden wave. "Gehrn. They have her."

Her father swore. He turned to the guard. "Fetch a captain and troop, as quick as you can find them. Tell them to come after me, no time to waste. We need to find the Gehrn and Mage Parma."

Chapter 30

Shianan had a sack of garlicky dough knots in one arm and in the other a bundle of flowers and a bottle of wine. The flowers were small things, mingled pink and violet, but they were the first of the season at market and he thought Ariana would be pleased with the surprise. Not that he thought she particularly loved the flowers for themselves, of course, but that he remembered *sunlight on flowers.*

The wine was not exciting of itself, either, a cheap vintage, but it was the idea of it, of buying a bottle of wine to carry to his wife in his home. It was their first attempt to meet in their own house, and he delighted in the mundane task he had never expected for himself.

He shifted the items in his arms, facing the front door and its latch. He kicked the door, not too hard, and called, "Luca?" But Luca must not have been within hearing, and so Shianan balanced the wine bottle, worked the latch (unlocked, surprising but convenient), and caught the bottle as it slid. He went in and toed the door shut behind him.

"Luca?" He went through the entry and into the sitting room, where he froze mid-step.

The room was full of armed men in blue robes, watching his entrance with eager eyes. In the center, facing Shianan, stood Flamen Manceps Ande, his teeth bared in a savage, triumphant grin. Beside his left leg knelt Luca, on his knees with his hands behind his back, and Flamen Ande's hand wrapped around his neck and under his chin, forcing Luca's head up and back against his hip. In his other hand, Ande loosely held a short knife, well away from Luca's face and throat but near enough to reach him before Shianan could.

Shianan could not stop the little rush of breath which carried Luca's name. But Ande already knew his weakness. It was no accident that he had met Shianan with his prize so prominently and vulnerably displayed.

But he had arranged his display for a reason, and Shianan could buy time and perhaps find footing if he let the man indulge himself. He lowered the sack of garlicky bread to the floor and shoved the wine and flowers at a nearby table. "What do you want?" The words came out a growl.

"Flowers, commander?" Ande's voice was incredulous and amused, and it grated against Shianan's exposed tenderness. Then he wondered if Ande had discovered his marriage, and fresh horror heaved in his gut.

Luca, eyes nearly closed in his up-tipped face, did not move.

"What do you want?" Shianan repeated.

"Take off your swordbelt," Ande ordered.

Shianan hesitated, looked at the fingers wrapped about Luca's jaw and the knife resting against Ande's other leg, pulled the buckle loose and let the sword and belt clatter to the floor.

"Now kick it this way."

Shianan did, but at one end, so that it spun between them—out of Shianan's reach, but neither within Ande's.

"How quickly your hospitality fades," Ande said with a mockery of a chuckle.

"It is not my hospitality on the scale," Shianan answered. "You have made yourself quite at home in my house and seem to have claimed it again for your own."

"And everything in it," Ande rejoined, as if the threat were not already clear enough. "And we have brought some furniture of our own." He gestured.

There was someone else at the far side of the room. Shianan turned his head, just enough, and saw the Silver Mage lying on the floor between two blue-robed priests. She was not dead, despite his first shocked thought, only slumped, limp and useless, her head cocked awkwardly against the base of the wall. Her mouth hung slightly open, and her eyes stared across the room, possibly seeing him but without focus.

Shianan tore his eyes from her and the Gehrn squatting beside her—she was in no more immediate danger than before he had entered—and fixed his gaze on Flamen Ande. "You could have sprung on me as I came through the door, but you meant for me to see all this. Again, I ask you, what do you want?"

Ande sobered. "I want you to understand, commander," he said levelly. "I want you to understand all you have done in your arrogance, and its consequences. I want you to fully grasp what you have lost and ceded to us. You thought to reclaim by force what you had promised, setting the court on me with a contrived story of treason and even bribing my slave against me. You underestimated us."

"Underestimated?" Shianan repeated, incredulous.

"Do you think the word of a slave exonerated me?" Ande burst, and his fingers dug trenches in Luca's skin. "Even your courts know our influence; they waited only for an excuse to release a man they knew was too powerful to keep. Some thought us madmen on the edge of society, but now we retake our place here at the seat of power."

Shianan was caught between trying to make sense of the priest's words and wanting to seize him and shake him free of Luca.

"You thought to take both the Shard of Elan and this house for yourself. You thought to make yourself a hero by discrediting me. But all of that has failed, commander, and now I stand in my house, holding my slave, preparing to take my revenge on this mage before the others."

Shianan made his words slow and deliberate. "You want to lecture me? That's what you have waited for?"

The others? Did he mean the rest of the Circle?

Ande's face tightened, but his answer was still steady. "I want you to beg, commander. I want you to beg for her life. And I want you to think of every disdainful word you used against me when I came for my slave, and I want you to taste them again while I take him back to serve me, as he is meant to do now and for always. Won't you, Luca?"

Luca, eyes closed, did not answer.

Ande's mouth tightened into a scowl. "Did you not hear me?" He tightened his hand, tipping Luca's face higher until he made a small choking sound. Shianan felt ill.

"See what you have done?" Ande chided Shianan, and he gave Luca's neck a little shake. "His discipline will be your doing, too. But he'll remember soon enough. And I'll see he thanks me for it."

Shianan could not help himself, and he ignored Ande to search Luca's face. But Luca did not see him. Shianan was not sure he would see anything, even if his eyes opened fully.

Heat flared in Shianan, a brilliant red flame burning large to cover the fear that screamed beneath. He was helpless—he had nothing to barter with Ande for Luca, he did not know what to do for Mage Parma, and did they also have Ariana?

Ande tugged Luca's chin higher, making the slave's throat work visibly, and moved the knife so that its point rested under the bend in Luca's jaw. Shianan tightened his muscles and did not move. Luca did not move, either, though Shianan was not sure if he saw or felt the blade.

"You asked what I wanted," Ande said, the words slick with

sick glee. "I want you to watch, and know, and beg, and surrender. I've found this slave useful in times past, but I will not hesitate to end his usefulness if you press me."

Shianan searched desperately for something to distract Ande. "And what about her? You said you would kill her, too."

Flamen Ande looked toward Mage Parma. "There will be a great fire, eventually, and she will die in it. This is fitting for the murderer of one of our own."

Shianan did not know what he meant, but it did not much matter. "You mean to open war with the Great Circle?"

"The Great Circle made war upon us! They sought to make me a criminal and traitor, and they refused our negotiations, and then at last they killed our emissary. He died by fire, and so will she."

"The Circle will come for you."

"The Circle will be dead."

Oh sweet all—they did have Ariana. Where?

Shianan had a sword a half dozen steps away and he stood in his own house, and he had rarely felt so helpless.

"But before she dies, I want your surrender," Flamen Ande said. "I want your obeisance. Beg me for their lives."

"You have already said it will do no good," Shianan answered, struggling to keep his voice steady.

"She will die, yes," Ande said. "But you want Luca alive."

"So do you," Shianan gambled. "You want him, or you'll have nothing to show for your supposed victory. How will you lord over your priests without a slave to bully and threaten?"

"Luca serves the order," Ande answered with a practiced tone, "and the high priest in particular only because the high priest is the greatest in the order."

"And—"

Ande tightened his hold on Luca's chin and snapped a sharp blow with his knife fist into Luca's face. Luca tried to cringe away but wavered on his knees as he was tugged back into Ande's side again. Shianan started forward but was checked by the short blade still in Ande's hand.

Ande grinned. "Argue further, commander."

"I will kill you," Shianan promised, hot fear blurring his words. "You think threatening him will protect you, but it only adds pia after pia to the debt you owe, more and more blood you must repay with your own. You believe you can kill the Silver Mage, as if the whole of

Chrenada will not rise against you for murdering their protectors."

"Who needs the Circle, now that you've placated the Ryuven?" asked Ande airily. "See what comes of failing to respect war as the crucible it is, proving the worthy and drawing out the dross? Mage Parma is the first to be skimmed, and then those who protest instead of growing strong."

"I will—"

"You will do nothing, bastard discard. With the fighting ended, you are useless, too. You will be mourned even less."

The words should have torn Shianan, but he had no time for them now, not while Luca trembled in Ande's grasp. He shoved them aside and fixed his fiercest glare on the high priest. "You think you can evade me forever?"

"You think you can evade us?" Ande replaced the point of the blade into Luca's neck, indenting the skin, and Luca flinched against him. "If I keep my knife here, and my priests surround you, would you fight them? Would you try to save yourself by killing this slave?"

The other men in blue started forward, spreading wide and raising short swords. Shianan hesitated. They closed on either side of him, not yet attacking. Ten, Shianan thought, without turning his head. He looked at Luca, kneeling with his head pressed to Ande's flank, needing to communicate somehow, and Luca did not look back.

Ande's head snapped forward and then back. Eyes to the ceiling, he slumped to the floor behind Luca.

Shianan seized the wine bottle from the table and swung it into the face of the nearest Gehrn. It did not break until his second blow. Shianan threw the jagged remnant past the staggering man toward another priest. Then he dove forward, snatching the sword and rolling upright an arm's length from where Luca wavered on his knees.

The priests stared in confusion, feinting forward but not working together, and Shianan cut one before he could decide how to react to the flamen's fall. Another made up his mind and rushed Shianan, and Shianan took a step and swept the sword across his chest. A third dropped in place, twitching, though Shianan had not touched him.

Shianan had seen men fall like that before. He did not spare time to look toward Mage Parma, but he wondered why she had waited so long to act. He thought of the blow to Luca's face, resented her delay, and blocked and thrust into a blue-clad priest who charged him with sword extended too high.

They had not practiced for such close combat and got in one another's way, giving him precious seconds to take them in turn. Shianan pursued the breaking priests as they retreated, taking refuge behind his chairs or table, rushing at him singly or in pairs with weapons they had practiced with, but never against a soldier who had grown up fighting Ryuven. Some he killed, and some fell convulsing before he reached them, or with lesser wounds that shouldn't have dropped them. He cut these as they fell, leaving no falsely wounded behind his back.

Shianan disabled a priest who had swung his weapon too wide and whirled on the last. But this one knelt low, head near the floor, hands outstretched. "No, please! Not me! I did none of it!"

Shianan checked the blade but snarled, "You are here."

The priest pushed himself up on his knees, and as he raised his face, Shianan's heart sank. He had been struck too, multiple times. And he held no weapon in his empty, wide-spread hands. "I didn't want to do this. I wanted none of this."

Shianan kept the point of the sword toward him as he glanced toward Mage Parma. "Is what he says—"

Mage Parma lay still against the wall, head drooping, hands limp on the floor. She had thrown no magic.

"I'm here," said another voice, and Mage Ewan Hazelrig came from the kitchen corridor. He crossed the room with rapid steps, hardly bothering with the bleeding bodies, and knelt beside Mage Parma. "Elysia? Can you hear me?"

Shianan, though interested in the mage's condition, was too accustomed to battlefields and enemies to permit distraction. He turned his eyes back to the beaten Gehrn. "They did not like your reluctance."

"This was wrong," he said in a broken voice. He was perhaps a couple of years younger than Ariana, younger than most of the priests around him. "They were going to—after her—I was going to have to prove, with the slave..."

"Go into that corner and shut up," Shianan snapped. "No—first tell me where Mage Ariana Hazelrig is."

"I don't know."

Shianan clenched a fist. "I'll not wait for an answer."

"I don't know!" protested the young Gehrn, shielding his swollen face behind an arm.

"Ariana is safe," Mage Hazelrig said from across the room.

"She's at the Wheel. She'd been given some of whatever Elysia's had, but they didn't take her."

The news ran like water through Shianan, and he gulped relief. He gestured the last Gehrn to the corner, and the priest crawled away, struggling with his robe as he tried to move clearly and deliberately. Shianan turned to Luca.

Luca had not moved. Mage Elysia Parma had been drugged somehow. But Luca looked different; it wasn't a drug that held him motionless and silent.

Shianan knelt beside him, taking Ande's knife from the priest's limp fingers and feeling for the cords binding Luca's cuffs. They were not as tight as they should have been, and Ande's arrogance in Luca's compliance inflamed Shianan all the more. "Luca. Luca!" He started on the cords. "Can you hear me?"

Luca blinked, focused on Shianan, widened his eyes. Shianan could hear the rasping of his breath. Had Ande damaged his throat?

No. No, it was no injury, at least not of a physical sort.

"Luca."

Luca's breath whistled, and he did not look at Shianan.

Flamen Ande choked and coughed—but of course, he used no real magic, and so magic would have struck him hard but not killed him. Shianan reversed the knife and pommeled the high priest hard in the temple, silencing the cough.

"Luca?"

His wrists came free, and Luca sagged as if the cord had been holding him in place. His head drooped. "I'm sorry," he whispered.

Shianan's heart convulsed and he embraced his friend, pulling him close. "You double-dyed idiot, only you would apologize for this." He pulled back and looked at Luca with quick assessment. "Hold on. Half a moment."

He turned Luca away to face the wall, away from the Gehrn all around him. "Wait here." Shianan then rolled the stunned high priest onto his face, furious at the necessary delay, and pulled his arms behind him with the cord from Luca's wrists. He had enough to draw up one of the priest's ankles too, immobilizing him. He wanted to strike the priest again—wanted to kill him—but the Circle might need to learn what other damage he had worked. The young priest behind Shianan had not known where Ariana was; he would not be useful if they needed more.

Luca made a low sound, but Shianan was not sure if it was

meant to be words. "It's all right. You don't have to say anything. King's oats, don't apologize again. Just get warm."

Luca was trembling now, but not for the temperature of the room. Shianan had seen it before; a body could believe itself suddenly chilled when it was no longer fighting for life. He cast about for a covering and started automatically for one of the fallen, to strip the blue cloak, but he stopped himself before he could make the mistake of bringing it to Luca.

The first thing was to get him away from Ande. Luca needed space, and air, and warmth, and more that Shianan could not give him.

"I'm sorry," Luca repeated hoarsely.

Too much demanded attention—Luca, Mage Hazelrig and Mage Parma, the cringing Gehrn in the far corner, Ariana at the Wheel, the surviving priests across the floor. He wanted captains and sergeants and soldiers to organize, enough hands to bear the many tasks, all urgent. But first, he could get Luca away from Ande.

"Come on," Shianan said, sliding his arms beneath Luca's. "Into the kitchen." He hoped the priests had not left any terrible surprises there. "Let's go."

CHAPTER 31

Luca's feet barely moved as Shianan carried him, one arm about Luca's waist and the other holding his arm across Shianan's shoulders. Shianan set him against the hearth, and then he added three pieces of split wood to the embers and blew up a flame.

Luca's face crumpled as he curled into himself against the wall. His breath choked in his throat.

Shianan swiveled to face him. "It's all right," he said in a low, urgent tone. "Do whatever you need to. It's all right."

Luca wrapped his arms about himself, shivering, and shook his head without looking at Shianan. "I'm so sorry," he repeated.

"King's oats, you carry on as if I've never seen a man lose himself before." Shianan put his hands on Luca's arms. "I'll be back. Just a moment, and then I'll be back."

He passed into the sitting room again, crossed the blood and bodies, and went upstairs to take woolen blankets from the bed. "How is she?" he asked Mage Hazelrig as he descended. He held out a heavy blanket.

Ewan Hazelrig extended a hand for it. "It's a cruel poison. She's aware—only she cannot move. She knew her danger but could not act. The monsters. Help me move her to a fire too, please."

"Dead monsters," Shianan growled. "Thanks to you. Half a moment, I want to bind this one."

Shianan tied the remaining Gehrn with a cord from the upstairs window curtains, fixing him to a heavy table's leg. The Gehrn did not protest, only leaned his head against the leg. It was far from ideal, but at least he would be hampered, trying to escape out the door and down the street with a piece of furniture, and it would have to do for now.

They lifted Mage Parma, who hardly shuffled with them toward the kitchen. "I ran over half the city, I thought," the White Mage explained in a hoarse, clipped voice. "Ariana made it to the Wheel, with a bystander's help, after he found her in the dye market. I started there, and then I went to Elysia's house, and I could not find them anywhere."

They lowered Mage Parma on the opposite side of the hearth from Luca, a blanket around her shoulders and in her loose fingers.

Shianan passed Ewan Hazelrig another blanket. “But Ariana is all right?”

Ewan nodded. “She’s fine. Confused, slow, but fine. I left her with Lydia and Katrina—that’s Scarlet and Forest—and Mage Callahan to monitor the drug’s progression.”

Part of Shianan heard that she was still under its effects, and they did not know what she had been given or how long it might last or what else it might do—and part of him heard that she was with three mages, and Mage Hazelrig had left her, which he surely would not have done if she were in grave danger, and Shianan must not take the time yet to worry about what he could do nothing for. His help was needed nearer.

Luca had drawn his legs to his chest, his arms tight against his torso. He looked up as Shianan squatted beside him, his wide eyes searching. Shianan felt a fresh stab of guilt for having left him. He laid the last blanket over Luca, wrapping him against the horror in the house, and then sat down beside him, his back to the stone and his arm over his friend. He pulled Luca close and breathed slow and deep, setting a marching pace for Luca to follow. “It’s all right,” he whispered. “Go ahead. It’s all right.”

Luca shook through the blanket, though his breathing was softer now. Shianan wanted to ask Mage Hazelrig more questions, but he hesitated to speak too much, afraid to speak at all of Flamen Ande.

Ariana is fine. She’s fine. She’s at the Wheel, with friends, skilled friends. She’s safe.

Mage Hazelrig was talking with Mage Parma, who was not answering aloud but was communicating in some way, perhaps by blinking or nodding. Shianan couldn’t see well past Luca, and he wouldn’t move.

“I’ll be back in a moment,” Ewan Hazelrig said, and he left the kitchen again. Shianan thought he wanted something with the dead Gehrn, but then he heard a piercing whistle, repeated, and then shouted instructions he couldn’t make out.

Ewan Hazelrig returned, and a moment later one of the message children came through the rear kitchen door.

“There will be quite a bit,” the White Mage said without preamble, as the girl looked in astonishment at the slumping Silver Mage and then at Shianan and Luca, “so try to remember it all. There will be ten pias if you can get everyone here within the hour.”

That was a veritable fortune in message currency, and the girl straightened with self-important urgency. "I'm ready."

"First, go to the Wheel, to bring Mage Taev Callahan here. That's the Indigo, if you've forgotten."

"We know the Indigo Mage."

"Tell him there's another with the same condition and he's wanted here to treat it. Give him this address. After he's on his way, go to my office, where you'll find the Scarlet and Forest and Black. Learn of my daughter's condition. And tell them I found Mage Parma, and she's here with me."

She nodded, resting two fingers on her opposite hand.

"Also, go to the city guard, to report several deaths in this house and prisoners who will need to be taken and kept secure. Then bring us word of Ariana."

She nodded, tapping another finger.

"Now, to repeat—"

"I have it, my lord mage," she said quickly. "Mage Callahan at the Wheel, to treat the same condition. Then word of both my lady mages. Then fetch the guard for the dead and prisoners, and then bring you the answer."

He nodded with a weak smile. "Well done. Now go."

"I will be like the wind." She went out the kitchen door again.

Mage Hazelrig watched her go. "I came though the kitchen," he said heavily. "I could not find Elysia anywhere, and I thought at last of the Gehrn's old townhouse."

"Thank you," Shianan said quietly. "If you had not come when you did..." He and Luca would be dead, with Mage Parma to follow.

Mage Hazelrig looked at the fire, dying again with neglect, and threw a ball of mage flame into the smoking remains. It roared with fresh energy and then settled into a steady burn. Then he settled into one of the kitchen chairs, dragged beside Mage Parma. "I'm sorry I did not come sooner."

The fire crackled in the silence, and its warmth bled into the kitchen. Luca gradually stilled, and Shianan resisted the urge to look at him. There would be enough to fight through without the scrutiny of his humiliation.

Shianan wished they could be alone, to let Luca spill whatever was necessary without the mages' eyes, but that was not to be at this time. He sat still, keeping his breathing steady. He could feel Luca growing heavier beside him, and that was a good sign.

"Filthy monsters," said Mage Parma at last, her words chewed and muddy. "Cheated me of my fight."

"You're speaking! Yes, they cheated," Mage Hazelrig agreed.

"You did," she protested slowly. "Got them before I could. Monsters."

"Hello?" Someone called from the front door, and Shianan stiffened despite himself.

"Callahan," the White Mage identified. He drew his feet under him to stand.

"Hello!" Mage Callahan's carried through the house. "I've come to—king's sweet oats, what a mess this is."

"Come through to the kitchen," Ewan Hazelrig called.

"I'll be—'soats, who are you? Don't answer, just hug your table. Kitchen, you say." The Indigo Mage came in, bearing a small case of worked leather, and frowned at all of them. "How many need treatment, then?"

"Mage Parma is affected by whatever was given to Ariana." Ewan Hazelrig gestured unhappily. "A larger dose, I'd guess. Have you identified it?"

"The Black Mage said it tasted ashy and bitter, or that the pie might have been burnt. That doesn't give me much to work with."

"You know its effects."

"I could bring about disorientation with any number of herbs or fungi." Mage Callahan set his case on the table and opened it. "The good news is, nearly all of them cause only temporary effects, and those that might be permanent are rarer and more expensive. Since they brought her here, we can assume they meant to do further harm, so it would be a waste to procure more troublesome and more effective materials."

"Your reasoning is clear and cold," Mage Parma said with effort.

Callahan grinned. "I would put meddleburr in a pie, because it would have the best chance of blending and producing a reliable effect. But Ariana said this had a strong taste, if indeed it wasn't burnt pastry."

"More than pastry," confirmed Mage Parma.

"Then it's more likely temptain, and they weren't clever enough to think of meddleburr. But I can give you a tea that will shorten the fog by an hour or three." He drew vials and sachets from his case, and then he glanced over at Shianan and Luca. "Not you too?"

Shianan shook his head. For a moment he wondered if he

should feel self-conscious before the Indigo Mage, holding a slave, but the thought faded almost immediately. He felt no shame cradling a wounded soldier, either.

Mage Callahan dipped water into a pot and set it on the fire to boil. Then he began dispensing materials into a cup, measuring some by eye and some by a tiny silver scale he took from the leather case. In a second cup, he crumbled a handful of leaves and added a dark powder.

"Mage Hazelrig?" came another voice from the other room. "Are you here?"

"That will be the city guard," Mage Hazelrig said. "I'll go and introduce them to the situation." He stepped over Shianan's outstretched legs and went out.

Mage Callahan aided the pot with a short burst of flame, and its steam increased. Luca's eyes were closed, as if he could not bear to watch the mage work. He was tense beneath the blanket, though still.

The mage rummaged through the kitchen until he found a cloth to fold about the pot, which he lifted free of the fire and poured into each cup, keeping his face clear of the steam. Then he stirred each in turn. "Just breathe this at first," he said to Mage Parma, folding her hands about the steaming cup. "There's a chance you won't be able to swallow well, and I don't want you choking it up. I'll be back in a moment."

Then he took the second cup and extended it toward Luca. "Drinking this will help."

Shianan looked at the cup in surprise, and then at the Indigo Mage, who looked impatient. Shianan took the cup, and Mage Callahan turned back to Mage Parma. "Do you have that steady?"

Shianan nudged Luca. "Come on, take this."

Luca's hand came slowly from beneath the blanket, and Shianan was relieved at this response. Luca accepted the cup and lifted it unsteadily to his mouth, flinching a little at the heat.

"Have you got that?" Shianan asked quietly, less for the question itself than for the invitation to answer. After a pause, Luca nodded.

Across the fireplace, Mage Callahan was watching Mage Parma drink, his scarred face set in a frown of concentration. Mage Hazelrig's voice carried from the other room, describing the short, fierce fight, in which the confident Gehrn had been disabled by a mage's battle spells and scattered by a soldier's attack.

Shianan wanted to keep Luca engaged. Desperately he asked, "How are you now?"

It was the wrong question. Luca jerked his head once, a short, tight movement.

Shianan pulled him closer, nearly sloshing the tea. "I'm sorry."

With the mage safe and medicated and the Gehrn turned over to the city guard, there was nothing left for Shianan to fight, and fighting was all he was good for. He would have faced Ande and his priests twice more before sitting here next to his silent, shocked friend with no help to offer.

"He's gone," he tried. "They're gone, all of them."

Luca did not answer.

Shianan concentrated on his own slow, steady breaths. He could not let his frustration take him now, or he would unsettle Luca further. Raw recruits needed calm guidance before and after their first battle, and they knew it was coming—they weren't caught unaware in what was supposed to be a safe townhouse, to be tied and held and displayed like a prize fish.

Shianan swallowed fresh fury and drew a long deliberate breath.

"I think it's helping," Mage Parma said, her words slightly clearer. "I can pick out a sentence now."

"That's good." Mage Callahan nodded in satisfaction.

"I'm so thirsty still."

"Yes, that's almost certainly temptain. Inelegant cretins."

Luca lowered the empty cup to his lap, as if it were too heavy for him. Shianan marked this, and the increased weight against his side and shoulder, with satisfaction. Exhaustion was brutal, but it was a milestone on Luca's bitter road. "It's all right," he repeated in a low voice. "It's ended. It's done."

"I stood," Luca whispered. "I just stood."

Shianan guessed this was his self-recrimination for how he'd failed to evade them or fight back when they entered. "It's all right. They came when you least expected."

"I just... I couldn't..."

Mage Callahan glanced at Shianan. "He may have some nausea or dizziness for a bit," he said in a quieter voice.

"From the medicine?"

Mage Callahan shook his head. "No, but the medicine will help." He latched his case. "I've left another dose for each here. The red dish is for Mage Parma. Don't mix them up." He indicated the counter behind him, and then he went out to join Mage Hazelrig.

"Commander?" called a voice. "Could you give us a hand with these?"

Shianan cursed. "I'll be back," he said to Luca. "Stay here, stay warm. I'll be back."

He went out.

CHAPTER 32

The pivotal moment had passed, and Shianan had been sorting living and dead Gehrn and explaining to the city guard instead of being there as he should have been. Luca had not even had a space to himself, to rock or weep or howl—though Shianan could not imagine him shouting his distress. Luca had learned to turn his fear inward just as Shianan had learned to turn his resentment.

But Luca's worst nightmare—and Shianan's—had come through the door and seized him, bound him, cradled his head to his hip. Luca had not had even the faint callus of living daily under Ande's dominion, expecting the worst. This had come without warning, while he was in Shianan's house, where he was supposed to be safe.

Shianan would not forgive himself. Or Luca. This could not have happened if Luca had not testified for the extractors and freed Flamen Ande to come for him.

Shianan had seen enough fresh recruits suffer after their first battle or, worse, their first visit to a freshly raided village. He had seen wives burying husbands, parents burying children. He had sat with soldiers too ashamed to shake before their fellows but too sick with horror and grief to carry water or clean equipment as if it were a normal day. He should have sat with Luca, more than he had. He owed Luca, even more than he owed the recruited farmers and shopkeepers.

And Ariana. He had not been with Ariana at all, and she had only just escaped abduction by the Gehrn. He needed to go to her. He was failing both of them.

Two guardsmen and Mage Hazelrig had brought Mage Parma into the sitting room to sip tea and give an initial account of what had happened. When Shianan returned to the kitchen, Luca was still by the fire, still under the blanket, but his posture had loosened and he slouched against the hearth. He looked paler than he should.

"How are you?" Shianan asked, feeling the inadequacy of the question.

Luca shook his head. "I want to be sick. It would feel better."

Shianan knew well the old bile of played-out terror, and he nodded. "Believe it or not, food can help."

Luca didn't answer.

Shianan waited. He did not ask if Luca wanted to talk about it; of course he did not want to talk about it. There was only to wait until what words could not be suppressed burst free, and then, with the boil drained, Luca could move on.

But Luca's next words weren't what he expected. "I'm sorry." Luca closed his eyes, as if he could not face Shianan. "I'm sorry. I'm so sorry."

Shianan shook his head. "King's oats, what could you apologize for?"

"I stood there." Luca's voice came quiet, almost too quiet to hear. "I just stood there, in the doorway. I didn't even—I should have slammed the door. I should have pushed against them. But I just..."

Even a second or two of surprise would have been enough for Flamen Ande to shove inside with the other Gehrn.

"I didn't even..."

Shianan turned and sat, facing the opposite wall but near enough that Luca's blanket brushed his arm. "You did not invite them in."

"I..."

"You did not welcome them. You did not bring them in."

"No."

"You were not expecting them. They counted on that. They relied on their effect upon you."

Luca sniffed. "And I obliged them."

"You were not in the arena."

Shianan had taken him to the training rings to teach him to hold a staff, to swing it in defense. Luca had taken Shianan to a training ring to be able to accuse and demand, where he was not a slave.

Luca needed a moment to work that out, and then he made a small jerk of his head, whether a nod or a dismissal Shianan could not tell. "I cannot live in a training ring."

In a way, Shianan was glad. If Luca could recriminate and be angry at himself, he had come out of that first helpless phase. Self-loathing was bitter, but it was better.

If Luca could speak, Shianan could go to Ariana.

"I'm sorry," Luca said softly.

"Don't you—"

"They were going to kill you. They were going to make me watch them kill you." Luca spoke toward the fire, so that Shianan strained to listen. "I knew they were going to kill you, and I heard you at the door, and I couldn't... I didn't say anything."

Shianan couldn't form an answer. They had held Luca by the face, bound on his knees, and he blamed himself for not warning Shianan. "You—they—that wasn't your fault. He was waiting for me, he had you—"

"I should have stopped you. I should have shouted for you to run. But I was—I just wanted—I hoped..."

Realization pinched Shianan's chest. Luca had hoped Shianan would somehow save him. Even in the worst of positions, he had counted on Shianan.

Warmth flared at his friend's blind faith and choked beneath the weighty responsibility it brought. Shianan looked across the room, his arms resting on his knees. "If you had shouted for me to leave, do you think I would have?"

For a moment Luca stared at the floor, and Shianan wondered if he would answer. Finally he whispered, "I suppose not."

"I would have come in with sword drawn, and they would have killed you immediately, and they would have set on me before the White Mage could arrive, and then they would have killed Mage Parma. What happened instead was terrifying, but it bought the most time. You didn't fail."

Luca shook his head. "You didn't know—"

"Luca." Shianan put an arm around him once more. "Don't worry over what did not happen. In the end, we all came through, and that tread-crust scut is gone."

Luca turned his head, but not enough to make eye contact. "Did you—did you..."

Shianan shook his head. "I didn't kill him. More's the pity, I think. But he's in the city guard's custody, and for crimes he cannot argue he did not commit—and this time, no one will testify for him."

Luca closed his eyes. "This time, he did all he will be accused of."

Shianan let himself dream of Flamen Ande's coming conviction. Sentenced to death? No, better sentenced to slavery, sold in the market to someone like himself. He could imagine.

"I'm sorry," Luca repeated dully. "I'm sorry I let them in. I'm sorry I let them use me against you. I'm sorry you had to stay with me when you wanted to go to Lady Ariana."

The final words lanced Shianan, who could not deny them. He could not think of a response that was not also a lie.

"I heard Mage Hazelrig. She's at the Wheel, and you're here."

"And it was good that I was," Shianan said.

"Go," Luca said simply. "Go see that she's all right."

Shianan couldn't reply, desperate to do as told.

"Go on. I'll—I'll be all right."

Shianan faced him, took him by the arms and squeezed. "Stay warm. Eat if you can. I'll be back."

Luca nodded, and Shianan went out the kitchen door.

CHAPTER 33

Shianan ran through the streets, weaving through the afternoon traffic. He did not sprint all the way; he did not want to alarm anyone, or invite questions from the guards at the Naziar gate. But they did not question his steady quick jog, and he passed into the wide yard. As he neared the Wheel, though, his stride lengthened, until he tore through the curving outer corridor to the White Mage's office.

The door was unlocked, but the mages inside were startled by his abrupt entrance, and the Scarlet and Forest Mages together half-rose, their hands already forming magic against an intruder. Shianan checked his advance and held up his hands in mute apology.

Between them, Ariana sat in a chair, not quite upright. Her eyes brightened for Shianan, though. "You've come."

He nodded, half-looking to the other mages for permission as he approached. They would be touchy after two of their Circle had been attacked, but Ariana's welcome might ease their concern. They watched him, faintly suspicious and more than a little surprised, as he slid into the chair the Forest Mage had left and leaned into Ariana. "Are you all right?" he asked foolishly, as if he was not looking at her.

She smiled, a little lopsidedly. "I'm better now."

He did not know if that meant she was recovering or if that meant she was glad he had come. Fresh guilt pricked at him again; he should have come sooner, the moment he'd heard she had been poisoned, no matter how urgent other demands might have been.

She saw something in his face. "I'm fine. I was safe here."

There was so much he wanted to say, wanted to ask, and he could not while the two mages watched him. "I'll stay with her," he said, hoping that statement was somehow enough to dismiss them from the White Mage's charge.

"It's all right," Ariana said, looking from one to the other. "You can go now."

"And what if the Gehrn come for you after we've gone?" the Forest asked.

Shianan shook his head. "Mage Ewan Hazelrig and I left most of the city's Gehrn in a townhouse sitting room. The city guard have those who are still living. If there are others yet remaining in Alham, they will not try the Wheel tonight."

Ariana's fingers tightened on his arm.

"Your father's fine," he told her. "And Mage Parma, she's unhurt, and she's recovering with whatever the Indigo Mage brought her."

Faint sighs came from all three mages, grateful for good news of their colleague. Shianan should have led with that.

"It's all right," Ariana repeated, her voice more settled. "You can leave us. It's all right."

Whatever secrecy they might have maintained would be shattered now; if any in the Circle hadn't known of the bastard's bid for the White Mage's daughter, that was ended. But they would not know of the marriage, and that was what had to be kept from the world. The king already knew of their affection, and Shianan no longer cared who else.

The two mages left without argument or warning, closing the office door behind them. Shianan had to restrain himself from springing up to lock it behind them. Instead, he bolted from his chair and into Ariana's, gathering her into his arms and pulling her against him. "Are you all right?" he asked again, for lack of any other way to vent his spent fears.

She nodded against his cheek. "The effects are fading. I'm just tired, and so thirsty."

"I'll get you some water."

She laughed. "I have drunk two pitchers already and been to the privy three times. Mage Callahan says it will pass eventually."

He held her close, probably too tightly.

"Tell me what happened," she said quietly.

"I'm sorry—I should have come sooner..."

Her free hand tapped his shoulder. "I was safe, and there was nothing you could have done here. It seems you were needed elsewhere. Tell me what happened."

He did, haltingly. It felt strange to put the events into words—his military reports could be difficult, especially when he had suffered more losses than usual, but they were not so raw as this, in what was supposed to be Shianan's own house, with his best friend humiliated and threatened explicitly for him.

Ariana's body tightened as he spoke, and he did not know if it was in anger for the violation of what might someday be her home or the insult of the Gehrn's bravado in taking the townhouse. But when he paused, she growled, "Flamen Ande is free only because of Luca's testimony. How dare he even stay in Alham, much less come for Luca again?"

Shianan braced against the heat which flared through him. "I thought the same."

"And threatening Luca, to keep you from him?"

Shianan had glossed over Ande's handling of Luca. It felt too near to betrayal, somehow, and Ariana did not need to know exactly how it had been done to be outraged. "They used him. Ande enjoyed using him, a tool and a toy."

"Now we have to stay there," Ariana said, softly but fiercely.

"What?"

"If we leave the house empty after the Gehrn have tried to use it against us, then it will always be that to us, and it will be difficult to ever go back to it. But if we overcome their intent with our own, then it will be our house in more than name only." She looked at him, and it did not matter that her eyelids still drooped. "It should be our home."

The words tugged at him, an aching longing for a memory he'd never had. "Even if—even if we are hiding?"

"The house is legally yours. You could stay any time without much question. I could sneak in by the kitchen, just as you've done at my house. We can stay a night or two, enough to reclaim it."

He understood her point, and he was impressed that she had seized on the idea so quickly. He might have flinched away from the townhouse, not wanting to think of Luca tugged to Ande's flank or the flamen's smug chuckle. But Ariana, who had not watched Ande press a knife to Luca's neck, knew the necessity of retaking the townhouse quickly.

Abandoned ground was lost ground. She would make a good commander.

He nodded. "Soon."

CHAPTER 34

"Hello, Rand."

The boy at the pie cart looked up, blanched, and glanced from side to side, as if for help or an escape route.

"Oh, no," Elysia Parma said. "You won't go, not yet."

Rand sucked air through his open mouth, a rabbit trapped against a corner. "I—I'm—"

"Don't say you're sorry," Elysia cut him off. "Words will not speak louder than your actions. So if you wish to make yourself anything other than what you've already made yourself, speak with your actions, and that means answering our questions."

Behind her stood Mage Ewan Hazelrig, his face impassively stony, and three of the city guard. Rand scanned all of them, then the market crowd fading back from the pie cart, finding today's lunch elsewhere.

Rand pressed his lips together and swallowed. "The Gehrn, the ones in blue. They came and told me they knew you liked our pies."

Elysia did not offer to complete the story for him, making him relate his treachery aloud.

"They wanted me to keep back special pies for you. They said it wouldn't kill you! Just make you sleepy. They said I didn't have to feel bad about making you sleepy."

"And you agreed."

"Not for—they offered..." Rand looked down, his voice falling. "Money's tight, and they offered me two hundred pias."

Elysia snorted. "You were shorted in that deal."

"I know. I didn't—"

"I don't mean now that you have been caught. I mean they would have paid you far more to have a chance at me. You were cheated, even before they left you to bear your part in this." She eyed him, but he did not look up. "And you do have a part in this. Why didn't you say something?"

"They told me not to tell anyone." But it was obvious that even he was embarrassed by the words as he said them.

"Not where they could hear you, of course. But when you passed me the pie? When you could have told me what was intended, and I could have played along as they expected, and then been myself when they came for me?"

Rand said nothing.

"And Ariana too?"

He shook his head. "They'd said anyone with you."

Of course; they wouldn't want their scheme ruined if she'd taken lunch with friends. They needed any companions to be unable to stop her abduction, and without her black robes Ariana had been unrecognized.

If Ariana had not self-consciously left her robes behind...

Ewan coughed. "Did they pay you yet?"

Rand didn't respond.

"Well?"

Rand directed his answer to the wooden counter. "Fifty pias."

"What?"

"They gave me fifty pias, not two hundred. They said I couldn't go to anyone to complain without saying what I'd done."

Elysia barked a laugh. "Didn't I say you'd been cheated?"

Rand stared downward.

"Well, that's enough," said the city guard. "Come on, boy. You can explain all this again to an adjudicator, and good luck dodging a conspiracy to murder charge too, what with taking down a Mage of the Circle."

Elysia held up a hand. "One more question, please." She looked at Rand, stiff and unmoving. "How's your mother?"

Rand looked up despite himself. His face was blotchy red and white, and when he spoke his voice was hoarse. "I—she's still abed. Breathing a little easier, though."

"That's good to hear." Elysia drew out a coin and dropped it into his box.

Rand sucked a quick breath and looked from it to her.

Elysia looked toward the guards. "If he testifies against the Gehrn, could he be a witness in their trial, instead of an accomplice?"

Rand tensed beside her, but she did not look at him, waiting instead for the guard's slow reply.

He was not anxious to commit to an answer. "There's a chance of it, sure. I can't say if the court will want to see it that way. We can't have people incapacitating our mages, not with the raids, and especially not with the intent to kill one of our best."

"I didn't mean to kill..." Rand began, and then wisely halted.

"But he can offer to testify, and see what comes of it."

Rand nodded, anxious to show his willingness.

The guard sighed. "You're a child; we'll need an adult to stand with you."

"Oh, no!" His eyes widened. "Does she—do we have to tell them? Do they...?"

"You can hardly go on trial without your mother and grandmother learning of it," Elysia said tiredly.

"Does your mother know what you agreed to?" the guard asked.

Rand shook his head. "Of course not. We're not to upset her, and..."

"And you believed poisoning the Silver Mage would upset her," Ewan supplied pointedly.

Rand said nothing.

Elysia sighed. "All right, then. Take him, and see what you can do for him. For my part, I would rather see him charged as a child misled than a co-assassin, if you can."

"I'll pass that along," promised the guard.

Rand left with the guards, and one of the women from the nearby fried dough booth came toward the abandoned cart. "I'll take care of their things," she promised. "I'll see Mother Ellie gets it all safely."

"Thank you." Elysia looked at Ewan. She felt drained, weary, and not only from the lingering effects of the temptain.

"Will you still go out to train with Edeiya'rika?" he asked.

"There is nothing I want more," she answered. "To practice new magics in the wild, away from markets and politics and Gehrn? If I cannot have safety in my own city, then let me have a safe target, tremendously powerful magic, and a chance of doing some good."

He nodded. "Be sure I can reach you. Just in case."

"Of course."

He moved to embrace her, and he held her just a second or two longer than usual, sharing his bedrock stability. "Take care."

Ariana squeezed her fists in slow repetition, trying to press down the fountain of emotions bubbling within her. If Mage Parma could sit in her seat, self-possessed and stern, after she had been far more vulnerable to the Gehrn's attack, then Ariana could sit without fidgeting in her own chair.

She wanted to burn it.

The temptain, as Mage Callahan surmised, had deadened her thoughts and buffered Ariana from her natural flow of emotions. She had still been with Shianan when the enormity of the incident finally struck her, and she not only understood but at last perceived the nearness of danger. She had been in his lap, with his arms around her, when she realized the thin whisper of grace that the strange Gehrn had not known her without her black robes.

She hoped someone knew where to find the kind young man who had helped her to the Wheel. She owed him a debt, and Mage Parma likely owed him her life. But someone had his name, surely, for the investigation already underway. They would want his account. He might even now be waiting his turn while Mage Callahan gave his opinion on what had been added to the pies.

But the next witness was a Gehrn priest in dirty blue robes. His face was swollen and mottled brown and blue.

"Flamen Giune," confirmed the interrogator.

"Just Giune, my lord."

Captain Sterne looked up from his notes and quirked his mouth. "It looks like you didn't come along reasonably."

Giune shook his head in a small, tight movement. "No, my lord, I have done all that the guard has asked. This was—this came from my priests."

Ariana stared. They had done this to one of their own?

"Explain," prompted Captain Sterne.

Giune looked at the table on which his shackled hands rested, his fingers laced. "I had been growing uncomfortable," he said, his voice low. "I suppose they must have realized that."

"Growing uncomfortable?"

Giune made a thin line of his lips. "I joined the Gehrn because I believed in their ideals. Protecting those important to me, protecting the nation, preserving order and security despite the ignorance and depravity of those around us—all of these made sense. I wanted to be a part of that. And it all made so much sense at first, and I felt... But then I started to wonder at things. I started—I thought I might want out."

"All that is very interesting," said Captain Sterne in a voice that made it a lie, "but we're here to talk about the abduction of Mage Parma."

"I didn't like it." Giune's voice was rough. "It was wrong, and—and it did not hold up against the precepts. There is no glory in killing a poisoned woman, especially one poisoned by a hired child."

"So you didn't like it, but you went along with it just the same."

Giune's head sank lower. "I didn't know how to—I couldn't stop it. I did as I was told. Right up until..."

"Go on."

"Flamen Ande said I was nearly ready for promotion to full priesthood, I only had to prove myself. On—with the mage, and then with the slave."

"Care to explain this proof?"

Giune's eyes flicked to Mage Parma and then back to his hands. "No, my lord, I don't."

"And did you agree to this demand of your loyalty?"

Giune shook his head. "I said it was not in alignment with the precepts they themselves had taught me. I said I would gladly fight any opponent they set me, but these were not opponents, only fish in a tub."

Sterne gestured to encompass Giune's face. "And that's when..."

Giune nodded.

"How many to your one?"

Giune thought. "Eight."

"Seems you were another fish in a tub." Captain Sterne looked at Mage Parma, sitting silent and upright in her wooden chair. "Can you comment on his report, my lady mage?"

"I cannot say I was quite clear on all the details, captain. But I can vouch that I saw a disagreement become a beating."

Ariana dug her fingernails into her palms until her flesh tore. She did not know how Mage Parma was speaking so flatly. Her own heart surged with both pity for the young man who had been betrayed by those he followed and fury for his foolishness in following them.

A hand slid over Ariana's, and Shianan settled on a bench beside her. He barely glanced at her before fixing his eyes on the questioning, but his fingers tightened about hers.

Giune's voice cracked. "I want out. I want out more than anything. Ask me about them, tell me what you want from me. I want nothing of them. I want out."

"You should have made that realization before you were arrested with them," Captain Sterne said, but the words had little bite.

"But for now, you can give us a plain accounting of the plan to abduct Mage Parma and how it was done."

Giune did this, eagerly, describing how the Gehrn had left Alham at the Silver Mage's direction but had not returned to Davan, instead stopping at a town called Greenwell to plot their return and revenge. He named each of the priests and their individual tasks to recruit the pie boy, to follow and collect the drugged mage, to hold her. He described the priests pushing their way into the townhouse and Flamen Ande's insistence that they wait for Commander Becknam before beginning.

Ariana gripped Shianan's hand.

"I suppose we'll want the slave next," Captain Sterne said when the Gehrn had finished. "He can tell us what he saw of this disagree—"

Shianan rose from the bench. "I'm sorry, he's not here."

Eyes turned toward him. "What's that?"

"Luca, whom the Gehrn took as hostage, isn't here. But it was my townhouse, and I'm here, and I can tell what I saw."

"Were you there for the"—Sterne waved his hand toward Giune—"dispute and altercation?"

"Excuse me, captain." Mage Parma lifted a hand. "I think you have enough from me, and so I'll be going."

"Mage Parma, you are key to this investigation, as the target of—"

"And that is my point. The Gehrn made me their target, to attack me personally and to weaken the Circle with threat. Each time I listen to one more person detail all the ways I was incapacitated and humiliated, we continue the Gehrn's work for them. I understand the need to verify events under the law—but is there any remaining question whether this took place and who was behind it? Or could you finish wallowing in this carnage without me?"

Captain Sterne looked chagrined. "I hope we are only doing our duty, my lady mage."

"And I wish you complete success in it." She rose. "I have delayed my departure from Alham already for this questioning. I've given a full accounting, and I've listened to others' accounts of the same, and I'm finished. If you should need anything further, leave word at my office and I'll see to it when I return."

"Yes, my lady mage." Captain Sterne turned to Shianan as the Silver Mage left the room. "And you were saying I am to lose another witness?"

"I am here and happy to give my account," Shianan answered. "But the slave who saw all is not here."

Shianan gestured to the door at the rear of the room. "Captain, may I speak to you privately?"

Ariana clenched her fists again, further abusing her bruised hands. Shianan couldn't shield Luca from the necessary investigation. She knew there was more than he had told her—she would not ask for stories that were not hers, but she was no fool—and if Luca's testimony was necessary to convict Ande this time...

She folded her hands in her lap and squeezed.

The military commander and the captain of the city guard faced one another. Shianan spoke first. "What do you need Luca for?"

Captain Sterne turned up his palm as if the answer were in it. "He can say how the Gehrn entered the house, whether they brought Mage Parma into it, if—"

"You surely can take Mage Parma's own word that she was taken into that house. Additionally, you have one Mage Hazelrig's report that she saw the Gehrn take Mage Parma from the market and the other Mage Hazelrig's report that he found her there with the Gehrn. What do you expect to find different in the middle?"

Captain Sterne shook his head. "Not much. But it will give a more complete picture of their invasion of your townhouse, as some were already there when Mage Parma arrived."

"And Luca's word, if you do question him—will it be accepted?"

Captain Sterne gave a regretful frown. "On its own, no, of course not. You know a slave's testimony must be excavated. I'm sorry for the inconvenience to you, commander, but we can have it done as quickly as possible and—"

"No." Shianan bit off the word before he could add to it. He made himself take a breath before continuing over the captain's surprise. "Luca will not be interrogated as a slave."

"But, commander, as he is a slave, his word is otherwise—"

"He cannot be questioned as a slave." Shianan drew the heavy document from his belt pouch and unfolded it, letting Captain Sterne see the gaudy seal first. "He is no slave."

Sterne stared at the paper. "I don't understand. This is a

manumission. A royal manumission. How...?"

"Luca was not legally enslaved," Shianan said shortly, "and so was freed by recognition of that fact."

"But then why does he remain... He is listed in our notes as your slave."

Shianan tried to imagine what silver-tongued Luca would say. "The men who illegally enslaved him have not yet been apprehended," he ventured. "We have made no public announcements."

"Ah." Captain Sterne frowned.

Shianan folded the borrowed document to replace in his pouch. He would return it to the coffer when Luca wasn't looking.

"It is possible," Sterne said slowly, "that you might, as his master, forbid him from testifying. As we have Mage Hazelrig's report—the elder Mage Hazelrig—to corroborate Mage Parma's and your own, a slave's account would be less necessary and less reliable."

Shianan nodded. "Thank you, captain. Yes, I believe I will restrict him from speaking of the incident. You can get what you need from the mages, the Gehrn witness, and myself."

Captain Sterne nodded. "Very well. It's a pity he won't be available to us, but with slaves this happens sometimes, and we'll work around it." He gestured to the door.

Chapter 35

Luca folded his legs in the prayer alcove and faced the painted wall. Safe within the protected atmosphere of the temple, he folded forward and at last let his soul scream as his mouth could not.

Why? Why? King's runny oats, why? He had done everything he knew to do, had done all that he could to do right. And how had that come to him?

Everything Flamen Ande had done to Luca back in Davan, he did under the law. What Luca did out of his own good conscience, the law required to be punished. He had not wanted to testify to save that man, but because the truth mattered to him and he wanted to be just. And honoring the truth had brought disaster upon Luca, first by the extractors and then once again by the freed Ande.

They would have made him watch them kill Shianan.

He could not scream aloud, and he could not even give words to this fresh betrayal. He had tried to be just, and justice had set a monster to nearly kill him and the friend he loved.

Why?

It was not just Ande, it was all that enabled Ande, strengthened Ande, excused Ande, permitted Ande. Luca had meant to be just, but he had relied upon what was unjust.

A flame kindled within Luca, and his silent shriek of fury blew it into leaping fire.

He could not expect justice from the unjust. They must be called to account.

Luca sucked his breath at the thought. He could never—he was not the one to speak angry truth to adjudicators and princes. He was a slave, in soul if no longer in law, a weakling who had cowered in silence instead of shouting a warning to his friend. He had flinched back before Isen's sparring feint, he had stood in silence to be slapped in Shianan's own office, he could not close the door on a threatening intruder. He was useless to speak against the wrongs that permitted these things, and he could not hope to be more than he was.

While you yet breathe...

Luca huddled in the alcove, adrift in fury and hurt and self-loathing. He hugged his knees to his chest and pushed his face against his sleeve.

Know that while you breathe, he is yet elaborating his careful craftsmanship in you.

No, the idea was ridiculous. He was the youngest son of a failed merchant, beaten down by slavery until he had hardly resisted his own death. He was not the one to protest.

Know that while you breathe, he is yet elaborating his careful craftsmanship in you, and so you may hope.

Sweet Holy One, what was he thinking? He had changed, yes, but not so much—clearly not so much, or the Gehrn would not have been in the townhouse. He had permitted that with his inaction as much as he had permitted Ande's freedom with his action. Both had brought him harm.

While you yet breathe, there is hope.

Shut up, shut up! Luca clenched his fists and squeezed his eyes shut. He could not. He was not capable. It wasn't for him to do.

But the words sat patiently in his mind, waiting for him to spend his fury and, panting with grief and fatigue, listen.

He did not have the courage or the strength to speak, that was evident. But he did not need the courage to speak before he could listen.

Luca knew history, and Luca knew markets, and Luca knew how to write. He could gather his thoughts and his evidence, and one day he could try a letter. Just a letter. He could spend his resentment in words to denounce the wrongs done to him, and he was near enough to share it with power.

He opened his eyes and stared at the painted wall, grateful for the half-light of the secluded alcove.

Elysia Parma lay back on the grass, silver robe spread beneath her head, her eyes closed against the sun. Around her she heard birds calling, insects buzzing in the grass, frogs singing in the trees. There was a distant trickle from the stream down the hill, and far across it, a few goats called jokes to one another.

"It really is lovely," Edeiya'rika said from a little distance away.

"You can see why we prefer to keep it this way," Elysia said, opening an eye. "Not on fire, not spoiled with corpses."

She had chosen a route that would be lonely enough for a human and a Ryuven to work together without much remark, and the scenery of the plains descending to the sea was a pleasant benefit. They had spent the day walking toward the foothills, where Elysia hoped to find a gully or canyon that would prove an adequate studio for testing their theories with the Shard.

Edeiya sat down an arm's-reach away. "You should see our planting lands. Great tessellations of green and gold, stretching in the sunlight as far as a ground-eye might follow, waving in the breezes so that they resemble a verdant sea."

Elysia turned her head. "It sounds beautiful."

"It was." Edeiya looked across the gentle slope. "I burned them."

Elysia rolled onto her side to look at her. "Mage Callahan is a difficult person to like, but his work can be trusted. He does not give promises or hope lightly."

Edeiya'rika took a long breath. "So they tell me." She glanced toward Elysia. "So he tells me."

Elysia chuckled. "He is quite honest about his own accomplishments."

"Shall we continue? Or are you exhausted from walking so far with only your legs and your heavy, thick bones?"

"Oh, my bones are just fine, thank you. What do you think of those hills over there? Does that look like a promising gap?"

"I'll check," Edeiya'rika offered. "I'll be back before you've made it too far."

"Only because I'm carrying all the weight," Elysia countered, shouldering her pack.

Edeiya'rika sped away, flying low to avoid attention from any goatherds out looking for strays. She disappeared toward the hills in question, and Elysia hooked a thumb beneath a pack strap and smoothed a wrinkle beneath it. Flight, so much faster than walking, would be grand...

Edeiya had asked few questions about the Gehrn incident. She knew enough, and she had previously asked about the Gehrn themselves, and once if there might be a connection between the Gehrn's blue robes and Mage Callahan's indigo. Elysia thought Edeiya knew more than she had heard from Elysia herself; she might have spoken with Tamaryl'sho, who seemed more conversant with Mage Hazelrig.

It was good to be away from the city, from others' eyes, from well-intentioned questions. It was good to have new magics to think on, different paths to walk, none of the same sights to remind her how very vulnerable she had been. How vulnerable she had allowed herself to be.

A blur of motion drew her eye back to the distant hills, where Edeiya'rika was returning. The Ryuven pulled up and settled to earth a few paces ahead of Elysia's steady pace. "There's a beautiful little ravine, all stone and a tiny cascade. We can work away from the moss and flowers."

"Excellent."

"And a village not too far, where you can buy supplies if we need them. I did not explore too near, though."

Remote villages were not ready to see Ryuven. Alham barely tolerated the sight. Elysia was still uncertain how it could already, at moments, seem natural to her. "We'll stay in the ravine then."

It was nearing twilight, with the sun behind them, when Elysia reached the ravine. Edeiya had flown ahead near the end with their tent—not one of the proper military tents, but a fragile little thing, nearer a cheap temporary booth at the market. The Tsuraiya ni'Ai, who had never needed to pitch a tent and had been curious and amused at the idea of portable shelter, had attempted to set it for use, with limited success. The tent was technically upright, but it sagged badly with no promises of holding.

Elysia set down her pack and opened it, working a loaf of bread and block of cheese from alongside the wrapped Shard. She tore away part of the loaf and offered it to Edeiya'rika. "I think we might need to tighten one end a little," she said lightly, eying the drooping tent.

Edeiya took the bread. "Remember, if it collapses, it's just another blanket."

Elysia swallowed her bite. "I prefer my blankets not to smother me. Let me see what I can do."

She had just pulled a line tight, with Edeiya'rika looking over her shoulder, when movement beside the pack drew her attention. "Hey!"

The raven gulped the last of the cheese and looked back at them, dark eyes shining.

"What do you think you're doing? Get out of there!"

The raven bit at the Shard, uncovering one end and testing the end of the crystal.

"It's too big for you," Elysia told it. "Pretty, though, isn't it? You can watch tomorrow. From a safe distance, though."

The bird cocked its head at her, bit the Shard again, and then dipped its head into the pack. It came up with another cloth bundle, partially unwrapped to show a smaller piece of gleaming crystal.

Elysia's heart jumped at the sight of the communication piece. "Now put that down," she said sternly. "I'll give you some bread for it."

But the bird of course did not understand the offer. It set down the crystal but continued to probe and bite at it.

Elysia eased back toward the pack and bird. "Edeiya, we need that."

The Ryuven was already circling. "If we startle it, will it leave the stone?"

Elysia jumped forward and flapped her hands. "Go!"

The raven took off with the crystal in its mouth.

"King's oats!" Elysia pointed. "Edeiya!"

But the Ryuven was already in the air, pursuing the bird. In a moment they both disappeared over the hill.

Elysia turned back to the tent, disappointed that she could not watch the chase. At least she'd had a Ryuven handy, she thought, amused at the novelty of the thought.

When Edeiya'rika returned a quarter-hour later, she was picking burrs from her disheveled hair. "I'm sorry," she began. "He had the advantage. The far side of the hill is mostly brambles, the little sneak."

"You couldn't recover it?"

"Not unless you have a way to harmonize with it to locate it. It's deep within a thicket somewhere."

"I can't, not without an attuned matching piece."

"I'm sorry."

Elysia swore. "Remaking that will be a month of work, and that's not to mention the inconvenience of not being able to speak with Ewan." She blew out her breath and determinedly drew back the tent flap. "But we'll deal with that as necessary. Let's enjoy this tent, now tall enough to sit within."

CHAPTER 36

"You must know someone," Shianan said with faint desperation. "You have someone for your townhouse."

"Mother Harriet does some work for us, yes," said Mage Ewan Hazelrig, "but she cooks excellent pies and washes dishes and hires out laundry. She isn't in the habit of cleaning up a battlefield."

"Neither is Luca," Shianan said, "and especially not one that centered about him. I don't want him going back to scrub dung and blood in the place where they humiliated and hurt him."

Once, Luca had offered to testify for Shianan, at the Court of the High Star. But he had done it for Ande. That cut Shianan, too deeply to speak of it. Luca had done for Ande what he had once offered for Shianan, and it had cost him so much more.

Shianan wanted it purged, wanted it all purged, and he would not let Luca wash the floor where they had shamed him.

He blew out a breath. "Mother Harriet must know someone. A team of cleaners who need funds. I'll pay well. "

Mage Hazelrig nodded with sympathetic understanding. "I can ask her."

Luca squatted against the wall in the narrow alley, out of the way of the street's traffic. Few would trouble him here, assuming a loitering slave was someone else's problem. But the warmth of the spring sun after months of stuffy closed rooms meant the tavern windows were propped open, and if Luca cocked his head, he could hear nearly every word from the table of new acquaintances complaining together on the other side of the wall.

"So they bought together and married together and partnered together, and in the end it's one company of merchants who has title to the mountain—the whole mountain, all the mines west of the peak, every one. And then they've been bringing in slaves, one mine at a time, and dropping off all the miners. We've been there generations, my great-grandfather carried copper out of that mountain, and this spring some fine prancing tony marches in lines of slaves to replace us."

"Like you're nothing, like you have no dignity."

"No one can farm up there, it's not land for it. Can't run more than a few sheep, and if you go too far you risk running against the great mountain beasts. If you take away our mining, we've got nothing."

"But you grew up a miner. You should know more than some idiot bred to pull corn."

"Shouldn't I just? And it wasn't two weeks before they had a whole team die in bad air, and lost two more trying to find out what happened."

A wagon rolled by in the street, muffling the words, and when it was gone the table was accepting more food and drink. Luca flexed his fingers and crossed his arms against his torso, though it was not so cold this day.

He was still a slave and a coward, not the man to defy the weight of centuries, but he needed something to do, or he would think. And he did not want to remember, to think on what had happened, what had so nearly happened. And so here he was, listening at windows for fragments of other people's complaints.

A moment passed before the conversation he wanted resumed.

"So I went to the collective's manager—that's a pine who never came from our town, just came in and took over, left old Harv Tettleson standing in the tails—and I told him he would lose more labor if he didn't bring back some who knew what they were doing. He said there were always more criminals to be had, and if I cared to take a swing at him, I'd be one and get back into the mine."

A chorus of disapproving grunts answered this. "I hope you popped him, just for the point of it."

"I didn't, only because my mother's still there in town and she needs a reliable place to buy her goods. The store closed to Goodwife Mercy after she tangled with one of them. But that's how I came down to the plains and Alham. I have to find something if I want to keep my family fed—but there's not much work for a miner here in the city."

"Could've told you that," grumbled another voice.

"And I'm not proud, I'll take any work. But whatever doesn't need much training is already done by more thrice-dyed slaves. A man can't so much as carry a load or repair a wheel without some slave beating him to it, and Holy One help him if he wants to do his own trade."

"Luca!"

Luca jerked his head to the street, where Shianan squinted into the alley at him, one hand raised to shade his eyes from the setting sun. "I wondered where you'd gone."

Luca rose and jogged to join him. "Let me take that," he said, reaching for the sack Shianan held.

"It's hardly any weight," Shianan said, but he let Luca have it. It indeed weighed nearly nothing, and it smelled of herbs; probably it was a fresh stock of medicines. "Did someone give you trouble?" Shianan asked, his voice low, nodding toward the alley.

Luca shook his head. He had sought gossip, not shelter.

Shianan didn't ask further. They started back to Shianan's quarters.

"I should buy a mattress tomorrow," Shianan mused as they wound out of the market district. "A good one, better than what they destroyed."

"I could go for you, if you have work," Luca offered.

Shianan nodded absently. "I might ask you. Things are more than a little frantic just now."

When they reached the rooms, Luca paused in the office. "Could I have some paper? And pen and ink?"

Shianan, already in his desk chair, flapped a hand at him without looking up from the topmost report in his stack. "You don't need to ask. Have a letter to write?"

"Sort of."

Shianan, reading, shook his head. "Take whatever you need. No, no, no, we can't lose a sergeant right now. I don't have anyone else in that squad. 'Soats, how am I supposed to hold a line without someone who has at least seen a Ryuven before?"

"And a pigeonhole of my own? From the disused ones?"

Shianan waved his hand again.

Luca got ink and paper and went into the other room, where he sat and began to make notes.

Chapter 37

"Why is everyone so interested in slaves of a sudden?" The thin clerk's protruding eyes shifted rapidly over his desk. "We had the prince's agents here, and wasn't that an event, demanding records—as if we have the life story of every slave who comes through here. We're a market, that's all, it's not my job to ask if they're real slaves, not when they'd all lie anyway."

Jarrick pressed his lips together and did not interrupt, because the clerk was pulling out a ledger despite his running complaints. He had good cause to be nervous; he clearly knew Cascais had been trading in illegal slaves.

"You're the second to ask after this one," the clerk said, rubbing a hand over his mouth. "Got a letter a while back about the same thing. Stuck in my mind because we don't get as many overseers on the general market, you know, at least not here. Mostly private trade, that sort of thing."

So Luca had tried to find Cole. "But you didn't answer that letter?"

The clerk shook his head, thumbing pages. "I have enough to do here with my own work. No one pays me to hunt down transactions long done. Besides, what does a count in Alham want with a slave from the Wakari Coast? Doesn't even make sense. Just someone making us jump for his own amusement."

Jarrick needed a moment to remember that Shianan Becknam was a count, too. Luca must have used his master's name. "Do you think I'm also making you jump?"

"Nah, you came here yourself, you—" The clerk froze. "You're a Wakari merchant, though."

Jarrick nodded. "On my way back from Alham."

"Then you—king's oats, you're not coming from that count yourself?"

Jarrick gave a tight, non-committal smile.

"Double-dyed oats. Look, you see I already got the ledger down for you, right? I was already looking it up for you. We're not doing so much wrong here, we're just busy. Look, if the prince comes down on this place, you'll remember I helped you, right? I'm here doing the helpful thing."

Jarrick tapped the desk. "Just tell me what you've found."

The clerk looked back at the logbook. "You've only got the sale to within a week, so that's a few dozen transactions. But there was one listed as an overseer, sold in a lot to Abbott."

"Where do I find this Abbott?"

The clerk leaned back from the ledger. "Hard to say. No reason for merchants to tell me where they're going."

But there was a tone in the words which Jarrick recognized. He sighed inwardly. "But in a crossroads town like this, you see the same merchants regularly."

The clerk tipped his head as if considering. "Sometimes, yes. Sometimes I recognize them, get to know their routes."

Jarrick shook out a handful of coins. "I don't suppose you might remember Abbott's route?"

The clerk leaned forward again. "He runs cheap lots, mostly, does a fair business in the mountain trades. Mines, Salfield. But if I wanted to trace his path out of here, I'd start at Salfield."

Jarrick put the coins on the desk. "Thank you for your help."

Luca glanced through the window of The Salted Seabird, and even a quick look confirmed it was the kind of place he wanted, not too reputable or too choosy about their customers.

Despite the name, it was not a house that catered to sailors; most of the customers gathered at tables appeared to be farmers and tradespeople from outside of Alham, enjoying food and drink after a day of haggling and selling before setting off in the morning for home. There were slaves in the room, too, sitting apart from the others.

Luca walked down the shoulder-width alley beside The Salted Seabird and found the side door. This was the side of the room where the slaves had been seated, so this was the entrance he should use. He took a bracing breath and walked into the public house.

Luca nodded at the serving man who glanced toward him and then found a seat near the wall, along the imaginary line separating the tradespeople and the slaves. He had dressed carefully for this, borrowing some of Shianan's own civilian clothing, so that he could pass as an educated servant to a noble, stopping for a drink at a public house that accommodated slaves such as himself. That would allow him to spread a few papers on his table to review and annotate, and give him a small measure of protection. Some did not like slaves who flaunted an education, especially if they had little themselves, but attachment to someone with power could slow their attentions.

A woman came for his order, and he asked for soup and ale.

"We have the first of the spring vegetables in today," she offered, "if you'd like some."

"I would," Luca answered. It was early, and they might not be good yet, but it was worth the gamble.

He propped his chin on his hand and fanned three sheets before him. They were loose copies of figures from Shianan's reports for troops and supplies, with changed labels and differing numbers, wholly meaningless now but authentic in structure to fool the casual eye. Over the inked lines, Luca now made a couple of penciled marks, as if to question or correct a figure, and then he let his eyes drift closed, the pencil still in his hand, resting on the topmost sheet.

He listened.

The slaves at the next table were arguing over a private debt. The family behind him was worrying about the Ryuven attacks and whether they were really over, or whether this new treaty could be trusted when it had been broken—"No, Mama, they said that was another tribe, I told you" and "You're too young to remember when our town was raided, and I tell you, they cannot be trusted, they're not capable of trust"—and across the narrow aisle a smith was grumbling with his friends over the price of metal. "You're cutting the profit right out of me, Ned, you know that."

"I'd like to give you a bargain, you know that, but I just can't. It's gone up again since the Falkes rebellion. Turns out when you set a whole mining town afire, supply goes down. And that means we down here pay for their poor management."

Luca turned slightly to better focus on the conversation, anxious to augment his notes.

"I wouldn't blame poor management," another said. "It's the slaves who revolted. Happens too often."

"True enough, they started it," the smith said. "But there's conflicting stories on how the town got burned, whether the revolting slaves set the fires or whether the mine owners did it trying to drive them out. But if it wasn't poor management, they wouldn't have had the revolt in the first place, right? Who oversees the overseers?"

Luca moved his pencil with lazy attention. *Destabilized price of commodities.*

"My grandfather was a miner," the man called Ned said. "A freeman miner, back in the day. He said they were proud of their work, and it was dangerous enough, but nothing like now. They'd have a few funerals a year, but it was their own sons and daughters they were training and sending in, so they were careful. Now they lose how many a month? And then the stops to clear collapsed tunnels, and rougher ore coming out not so clean. There's no pride in the work anymore."

"Sounds like you should bring your grandfather back out to work," the smith jested.

"Naw, he's gone this past autumn. But they won't take anyone now slave labor is their preference. They can buy slaves no one wants for what, two hundred pias, maybe three, and get weeks of work out of them. You couldn't pay my grandfather that for such kind of work; he'd slap you with your own shovel."

"Yeah, but he wouldn't have you stopping every few weeks to clear a collapse or rebuild your top-town, either. That's got to cost something."

"Don't know that anyone's counting that cost when they can't hire miners anyway. I sell ore and ingots, that's my work, but my father, he's still got nothing. He's a midden-grade farmer, just terrible at it, and those hills aren't for farming anyway. Learned to read the rocks as a boy and that's what he's good at, before labor got cheap. But burn the top-town, they still can't hire him—he's a freeman, and he's got naught to his name but a hide of hill dirt and his pride. He wouldn't hire on to do slaves' work."

Luca made another note. *Cheap labor costs more. Exclusion of skills.*

"Here's your soup," announced the serving woman to Luca. "Spring vegetables all through, too. And an ale."

"Thanks." Luca took a drink and looked about the room. Near the window, two women seemed to be trying to negotiate a deal on wool. He tried the soup—the beets were too young, as he'd expected, but the peas were all right.

"Look, he needs something," a woman's voice urged from the other side. "He's not been himself since Jer died, and I'm worried he's—he needs something, as I say. Just give him a try. He's a good worker, when he's got something to do, and—"

"A good worker, you say, but not in any of the trades I need. If he was a wheelwright, maybe, but I don't—"

"I know you've got the spring lettuces coming in. They'll need picking."

"I can get a lettuce picker for nothing. He's going to want wages, freeman wages, and I can't justify that."

Luca looked down at his soup. He had been a lettuce picker briefly, after Furmelle, bought in a lot of half-starved rebels. The grower was right; slaves for picking were cheap and plentiful.

He made another note.

He worked slowly through the soup, so that he had reason to peer at his papers and track the conversations around him. He asked for another ale and pretended to mark up the columns of figures between annotations about lost work and open fighting when a party of freemen had attacked a camp of field pickers.

At last he signaled to the serving woman. "Could you wrap a large lamb pie for me to carry on?" he asked. "And I'd like to settle." He put coins on the table, a little more than the bill.

She saw the amount, saw that he knew it was too much, and smiled at him. "I'll have the pie for you in a wiggle of a lamb's tail, then."

He folded his papers and put them into his shirt, wishing he had a proper document case to complete his look. But it had worked well enough; no one had paid any mind to the sleepy accountant working lazily over his meal.

The idea came from Fedstone, from the public house where Demario had humiliated Marla, where Luca had overheard freemen complaining of stolen livelihoods. He couldn't change things, not with his weak skills and weaker courage, but he needed fewer skills and less courage to listen and record. There was little peace or time, not with the Ientu raids and Shianan going to battle, but he could do a bit here and there, and maybe someday...

Moral arguments were often blunted against those callused by years of familiarity. The way things were was the way things should be; disruption was the real evil. But Luca came from a merchant family, and he knew money had the key to most barred gates. The costs were all around to be counted; they just were not included in the accounting. As long as only one column was shown, nothing would change. But if all costs were accounted and the bill presented...

The lamb pie would make a good supper, and it would give him an excuse if Shianan questioned his visit. He accepted the pie, still warm, and started home.

"Where did you go today?" Shianan asked.

Luca never hesitated as he straightened Shianan's boots against the wall, but Shianan thought there was a heartbeat of reluctance to answer. "I went to a public house."

"To meet someone?"

Luca shook his head. "To have a drink. To...listen."

"You can drink here, and for cheaper," Shianan said practically. "And I don't know what you were listening to, but I hope the musician cared for your efforts."

Luca gave him a questioning look.

Shianan nodded toward him. "Is that my shirt?"

Luca looked down. "It is."

Shianan leaned backward, bracing his hands on the bed. "Why? I don't mind, but that's...not like you."

Luca chewed his lip and looked across the room. Shianan, newly concerned, waited. Luca picked up Shianan's belt, letting it fall across the floor, and rolled it again about his hand.

"Leave that," Shianan said. "King's oats, I was raised in a barracks. I hardly need someone to fuss over how my clothing's folded."

Luca put down the belt. "It wasn't music." He looked at his empty hands.

Shianan waited.

Luca shook his head. "I haven't said this to anyone, not even properly to myself. And I don't know whether, when I do say it, I want you to talk me out of it or into it."

Shianan folded his legs and waited further.

"I thought—I don't know how to say this—I've been collecting examples of the economic and accounting costs of slavery. I thought I could collate the numbers, maybe illustrate the price of rebellions and of tradesmen unable to find work and of unskilled labor replacing skilled labor. And then I thought... Maybe I could argue them to someone. Maybe I could find someone to listen."

"The council?" Shianan asked.

Luca shook his head sharply. "Not me, not to the council. But if I could explain to someone, maybe someone who could reach the council... I could at least make a coherent argument for the financial view." His voice was tight. He slid his eyes at last at Shianan, his fingers locked together, looking as if he braced for mocking incredulity at the ridiculous idea of a slave changing the kingdom's laws.

A whirl of thoughts blazed through Shianan's mind, from the impracticality of a freed slave attempting to press such an enormous change before the most powerful men of the kingdom to the futility of convincing skeptical minds to look at less visible costs to the entire kingdom instead of the fat figure on their own balance sheet. He recalled how Chrenada had responded to the slave revolts with more draconian laws, and he thought of Furmelle and how quickly his own revulsion at fighting humans instead of marauding Ryuven had turned to justifying fury at those who would disrupt order—and how the council would do the same.

Luca saw it all in his expression, and the hope in his eyes began to fade.

But aloud Shianan said, "I wish I had half your courage."

A small smile kindled on Luca's face and slowly, cautiously, grew. He looked back at Shianan. "I know it won't be easy. But none of it has been easy, and that's the point. I only hope I am up to it."

Shianan nodded. "You went to testify for Flamen Ande—which I am still not sure I have accepted—and so there's no doubt you can face this, if you choose."

Luca straightened on the bench. "It's terrifying to say it aloud," he admitted. "It feels like commitment to something I am not at all sure I can do."

Shianan nodded.

"And if I try and fail, I may make it more difficult for the next person who tries."

Shianan had not thought of that, but he nodded again.

Luca tightened his jaw. "But at the least, I can do what I can do."

"You're braver than most," Shianan answered. "Most wouldn't do what little they could."

Deep within him, a fresh fear stirred, fear that Luca would ask him to take his complaint to the council. Perhaps Luca thought Shianan would have access where Luca did not, and when that request came, Shianan would need the courage he now envied in Luca. He was no one to press the council on such things.

But could he refuse Luca, when the time came?

CHAPTER 38

Ewan Hazelrig was sitting at his worktable, writing up notes, when he felt the first tremor. It was not a physical sensation, not really, but that was the nearest way to describe it. It was one every mage learned early, usually by unforgettable experience, and never missed.

"King's bollocks," he exhaled.

A moment later, the board of crystals began their humming as the other mages contacted him. He rose and flicked them in quick succession to silence, an acknowledgment. They would need to meet and plan.

The darkest crystal had not buzzed with the others. Either Ariana had not been in her own workroom, near to her crystal board, or else—

She pushed through the door, her tense eyes finding his. His heart broke at the worry there. She was a mage, and a capable one, but she was still his daughter.

"I know," he said before she spoke.

She closed the door behind her. "So many of them," she said. "So soon. Another Arakadamia."

He nodded.

"Could we raise the shield? Before they arrive?"

"We can't," Ewan corrected gently. "They have already leapt, as you sensed. The shield is a barrier when they pass into the between-worlds. Raising it now would be closing the gate once the goats have escaped. Or rather, once the wild dogs have already entered." He shook his head. "They are coming. And if it is the Ientu—"

"It is," she said breathlessly. "Tamaryl wouldn't lie to us."

"It would not be a lie if he believed he spoke the truth," Ewan said gently. "But yes, I think you're right. It is not the Ai who are coming."

"And we're not yet prepared for the Ientu magic," Ariana said.

"We are not helpless," he reminded. "Don't believe the rumors in the streets. You know better."

"I do know. I was there. It was my magic that failed. And if we go out against this onslaught, and if I cast a shield over Shianan, and if it fails like the last—"

"That is quite a lot of *if* all in a row." He sat down, hoping to lead by example.

"You know he will be sent out. You know we will. And if you mean to comfort me in saying I might not be in the particular place to watch him die, then I do not find your comfort anything of the kind."

Ewan raised his hands in surrender. "Shianan Becknam is a formidable man. He will not die so easily."

Her lips thinned. "Weren't the two of you nearly killed together, struck down in nearly the same moment? And I believed you were both dead."

She had him there. "And yet, neither of us died."

Her expression suggested she was unconvinced.

"What do you want me to say?" He turned up his palms. "That it's true we are unprepared for this enemy even in smaller battles, and we have no plan to meet such a large contingent, and this invasion will likely roll over our initial defenses with brutal effect?"

She looked down, gnawing her lip, and finally said in a small voice, "I want you to tell me it will be all right in the end."

Her words cut him. She was still, and ever would be, his daughter. But he had lied to her before, to protect her and her happiness, and it was not so difficult to do so once more. "Oh, my darling. It will be all right in the end."

She came and sat beside him, leaning her head against his shoulder. "What can we do to prepare?"

"Well, if you could capture an Ientu, or at the least manage to observe one practicing so that we could know better how to counter their magic, that would be a great assistance."

She smiled, if only to acknowledge the ridiculousness of his request, and that was a relief. "Well, I'll be sure to keep my eyes open in the streets."

"And I should begin on our response."

Twenty hours later, the sensation of many Ryuven entering the between-worlds at once rolled through the Wheel once more. Ewan Hazelrig snapped orders, sent reports and plans and recommendations, and dispatched three more messengers to search for Elysia Parma, still somewhere in the countryside.

Elysia would have felt the leaping as well. She should have rushed back to Alham and the Wheel to prepare for what she would have recognized as a massive invasion. She had not come. If he had lost Elysia in all this—lost her as the Silver Mage and as Elysia herself, his rock in a tossing river...

There was no time to lose himself in those thoughts. He could read them plainly enough in the others' expressions, as Ariana or Mage Odderman met his eyes and carefully said nothing. They were all afraid. Therefore, he could not be.

Until he was behind a locked door, when the certain knowledge rose high enough to numb his fingers and weaken his joints, and he felt all the useless hesitation that could not yet be turned into determination and rage.

But with or without fear, with or without Elysia, he had a duty, and he gathered his forces and arranged his resources and collaborated with the generals and prepared for another Luenda, another Arakadamia, but this one with magic that rendered his mages ineffective.

Shianan stared at the Wheel's report and then through it, as if not seeing it might deny it.

The Ientu were massing for battle somewhere in the east, and massing on the scale of another Luenda or Arakadamia. Such huge clashes were irregularly cyclical and necessarily spaced by years, because of the crushing cost of resources and lives. But the Ientu had lost nothing in Arakadamia.

Shianan's soldiers could not face it. He knew that for a certainty. It was too soon after Arakadamia, too soon after the morale-devouring defeats and the discovery that their defensive magic was insufficient. They had hardly replaced the officers they'd lost; they were not prepared for another such conflict.

But he had no choice. The Ientu were coming, and they could be opposed by a losing force, or they could advance unopposed across the countryside and, in a thought not entertained for two generations, upon the capital.

Shianan blew out a breath to steady his tingling fingers and began work on his command.

An hour later, he took his plans to General Septime's office.

"Ah, you're here," the general said as he entered. "I've just gotten an updated report from the Wheel. Sit down and let's have a look, see what we'll be bracing for."

Shianan tucked his papers aside as Septime untied a roll and spread it across the desk for Shianan to hold flat. "Along with this, the White Mage sent word to expect aid from the Ryuven—the Pairvyn. Seems he might fight with us again, though I don't know if that will be properly. We've seen enough of his work to know he held back when he was with us before."

"What about the other one? Edeiya'rika?"

"I don't know anything about that. Ah, see, they've pinned down where the Ryuven will arrive," Septime observed. Together they stared down at the slanting lines sketched over the map's features, indicating direction of travel upon arrival and probable numbers of Ryuven. "Look at these monsters. That's a lot of them. Going to be hard on that village, I'd say, but at least there's this estate house nearby—we can set up a field office there, have a solid roof over our heads as we plan and command. I shouldn't think the family would begrudge us the place."

"No, sir," Shianan said dully. "That's my own house. That's Fhure."

Chapter 39

Shianan decided to leave his cloak—the spring afternoon lingered into the evening, cooling but not chilly. After his meeting with the prince, the walk in the dark would be brisk, but the Hazelrigs' house would be warm.

"I'd like to go with you," Luca said behind him.

Shianan was caught off-guard—not that Luca was unwelcome, but that he so rarely put a request so plainly. "Of course," he said without thinking. Luca had accompanied him to the prince's rooms several times, even by the prince's own request. Perhaps he wanted now to thank Prince Soren for arranging the manumission, since he had not said much the night Soren had presented it.

They walked to the Naziar and were admitted, this time not to the prince's office and more general rooms, but to his quarters upstairs in the royal wing, the innermost circle.

Ethan admitted them, and though he gave Luca a lingering glance, he said nothing.

"I'm glad you're here." Soren embraced Shianan. "'Soats, I hated every word that came of the incident at your townhouse."

Shianan nodded and drew a breath against the memory. He was still angry, still belatedly and uselessly afraid for Ariana and for Luca, still furious as his initial ignorance and helplessness. He did not look toward Luca, but he wondered how he had taken the mention of the affair.

"I had an updated report only this afternoon. Five of the Gehrn are stable and expected to recover; two will likely not survive to trial. Flamen Ande—"

Now Shianan raised a hand and looked to Luca, who had gone still.

But Soren was moving to a leather chair and did not see either of them. "—will face trial soon, where, given the evidence against him, he will almost certainly be sentenced to execution."

"Not enslavement?" Shianan wondered viciously. "There are places I would see him go. Salfield always needs more hands, I hear."

"Justice is not vindictive," Soren said soothingly, "or it is not justice. And most would consider death the greater punishment."

It would be, if Shianan's bitter rage were not given rein, but Soren was right—as much as Shianan hated to admit it.

He glanced again at Luca, wondering if the news had brought him cheer or at least relief. But it was hard to read Luca's body, hunched slightly as if he once again thought himself best unnoticed in the palace.

Luca put himself beside and behind Shianan's chair, and then it was impossible to see him without twisting. Shianan took the hint.

Ethan put a tray on the table, a pitcher and two cups, and began to pour.

"Luca, I did not expect to see you here again." Soren's tone was surprised but friendly. "I have it on good authority that you are not a slave."

Ethan produced a third cup from a hidden location.

"I asked to come," Luca said quickly, his voice tight.

Soren nodded in vague acquiescence. "I suppose you might. I only did not expect it."

"Do you mean that as a slave I had more privilege to approach a prince than as a freeman?"

Soren hesitated, caught in the question. Shianan stared at Luca, uncertain of what he meant and what he meant to do.

Luca sucked a breath. "I must speak with you, my lord, and this is the only place or time where I might do it."

Soren glanced at Shianan, who gave a little shake of his head. He did not know what Luca meant, either. Eyebrows drawn, Soren gestured for Luca to speak.

Luca straightened and began as if reciting a memorized speech. "The institution of slavery is damaging your kingdom."

Soren held up a hand. "I wondered if you meant to say something like this—but we have already looked at reformations. You yourself bear a manumission that came of investigation and a new system to better register those enslaved, and reform—"

"That's not enough!" Luca caught himself. "My lord."

Soren blew out his breath and kept his eyes away from Shianan, not blaming him in this chaos. "Our economy rests on slave labor. While I understand your experience will have—"

"They are not telling you the truth of it." Luca's words tumbled over one another, anxious and disorganized. "That's what you've been told, again and again, but it's not true. Maybe they're not lying, but they're not telling the truth. Chrenada is succeeding despite slave labor, not because of it."

"I think our council of eminent—"

"Please, my lord, let me explain!"

Soren stiffened at the interruption.

Shianan held up a hand. "He might—let him try. The fraud in the military accounts, what the officers had missed for so long, he found it in a night."

Soren frowned. He took a drink and blew out a breath. Then he did look at Shianan. "All right. But be concise, if you please. I did not invite my friend here tonight to hear policy arguments."

Luca opened his mouth, closed it, bit his lip. Then he began counting along his fingers. "Slave labor is cheaper than hiring skilled freemen, which is why many prefer it. It is true these people profit more by purchasing laborers rather than labor. But that is the profit of the individual, not of Chrenada as a whole kingdom."

"Aren't those slave owners a part of the kingdom?" Soren asked dryly.

"They are—but so are the tradesmen they displace. Instead of forty families mining, you have one. That one gathers more wealth, certainly, but that leaves thirty-nine struggling without a livelihood."

Soren looked skeptical. "The numbers are not so clear-cut—"

"Please, my lord, let me put all before you first." Luca ticked off a second finger. "The slaves in that mine—or field, or workshop, or whatever we might discuss—are not paid for their labor. They do not spend in the market. Their master may spend more with his greater profits than he might have otherwise, but that is not as beneficial to the kingdom. You know that it is not merely the amount of money exchanged, but the number of exchanges that drive an economy."

Shianan understood only the vaguest idea of what Luca was saying, but he hoped Soren followed it. Luca would not have dared to use Shianan for cover and confront the prince unless he felt certain of his message, but still he was a former slave from the Wakari Coast challenging the prince-heir to overturn what his kingdom had known for centuries.

Was it possible? Shianan had seen the need for reforms—but was Luca asking for more?

Luca counted on his third finger. "Because fewer people are spending in the markets, and buying from fewer sellers, money is consolidated in the hands of fewer people. However, those fewer people are those you see most often, my lord. Those are the people on your council, who insist that the current practice is vital to wealth—because it is vital to theirs. But not to Chrenada's, which is a prince's interest and duty."

"Don't school me on my duty," warned Soren, but the words were not as harsh as they might have been.

Luca, nevertheless chastened, hurried on. "A slave does not profit by his efforts. There is no benefit in greater work; he will do the minimum to stay alive and well, and by necessity he will minimize the dangerous risk of experimentation or innovation. Slave workers are not artisans. Their product is cheaper but inferior. This harms Chrenada as well. Think, my lord: where does one find the best—"

"Enough." Soren held up a hand. "I asked you to be brief, and this is my private sitting room, not a ministry meeting. Give me your core argument in a sentence or two, and I'll decide if I'll return to it when I have not already started my drinking."

Shianan looked between the two of them. Soren was irritated, but he was giving Luca a chance to speak, which was beyond what might be expected. Luca was pale, and when he spoke his voice was tight, but he spoke in one tumbling stream.

"In short, my lord, consider this: If you look, you will see countless smaller tradesmen losing work and market to slave labor, and they resent it. The man who returns to them their dignity and their livelihoods would be a hero to them. The argument against slavery in Chrenada is not merely one of moral kindness or a wish to avoid unpleasantness, but an economic argument as well."

Luca gulped air and closed his mouth firmly, his eyes showing a hair more white than usual. He stared across the room, not looking to see how Soren or Shianan had received his words.

Soren blew out a long breath. "All right. Can you write up what you want to say further?"

Luca blinked and jerked his eyes to the prince. "Yes, yes, my lord."

"I won't see it before this coming battle with the Ryuven. I don't know how soon I'll see it after, especially if... I don't know how soon. But if you write it up neatly for me, I'll at least read it over."

Luca went loose all at once. "Thank you, my lord. I'll send it soon—but for when you have the time. Thank you."

Soren nodded. "And with that agreed, may we get on with—"

Luca bowed quick and low. "I will take my leave of my lords, so that you may enjoy your evening as planned. Thank you for your time.

I am very grateful." He rose and backed for the door, and then he escaped.

Soren shook his head and took a drink. "I suppose you didn't know that was coming."

"I had no idea." Shianan wondered if he should have guessed. Luca had clearly planned it. Why hadn't he told Shianan what he intended?

"I'll admit, I did not expect that." Soren gestured vaguely. "I don't mean I didn't think he would present a political argument here in my room, though of course I didn't. But when he started, I thought he would argue about humanitarian concerns and the need to give up profit in the name of kindness, the sort of thing that sounds splendid in speeches to those who expect to keep their own profits. He surprised me by making it a monetary pitch." He sat back and looked at Shianan. "You don't suppose he's right about that, the more and the fewer and the kingdom as a whole?"

Shianan shook his head and shrugged. "It's beyond me. I know how to stab those who are trying to stab me, and I let Luca do the numbers. But he did a merchant house's accounting before he was enslaved; he's no fool."

"I never thought he was." Soren took another drink.

They sat for a moment in silence. Shianan's thoughts raced. What was Luca doing now? What did Soren think of Luca's petition? Was what he asked even possible? And how could anyone focus on breaking apart the bones of Chrenadan society to reset them while another Ryuven onslaught was already on its way?

Soren blew out another breath. "I haven't much to say, after that. Or before that, really. Only that I am sorry for everything with the Gehrn, and I pray for the best in the coming battle."

Shianan nodded. There was little answer to be made, either.

CHAPTER 40

When his guest had gone, Soren remained in his chair, holding his drink without tasting it. Ethan worked silently around him, picking up glasses, fussing with cushions.

At last Soren looked at him. "I suppose you heard all that?"

Ethan did not play coyly innocent. "Most of it."

"It's not—look at this place, for one case. We could not run a palace without servants."

"No, of course not," Ethan agreed mildly. "And, if you will pardon my observation, he did not suggest it could or should be done."

"But we don't... I've seen what he came out of—some of it, anyway, enough of it—and it was horrific. There's no doubt we can do better, and I don't argue that. But you've been here all your life, Ethan, and I always..." Soren hesitated. He'd rarely put this into words. "I think much more of you than as a tool, and maybe it was presumptuous of me, but I believed you thought more of me than as a constant danger to be placated."

"That's so, my lord," Ethan answered succinctly.

"I can't be sure yet of what he says about the labor and the economy; I'll have to talk that through with more experienced heads. There may be something to it, and he's right enough when he says only the wealthiest advise the throne. But as for the whole..." He shook his head. "I know there are abuses, and I've already asked for reforms. I have a minister working out a registration system, all because I believed that man was taken unjustly. Surely we haven't been party to—do you know what I'm saying? If we have been reducing our citizens and choking our markets and enabling grievous abuses all in the name of a greater good, while in fact we were slowing that good... How could we face that? How could I go to my father and the council and tell them they've been wrong all their lives, we've all been wrong for hundreds of years? How could anyone admit that magnitude of failure?" He waved a hand. "But it cannot be that magnitude of failure. We would have rectified it before now. That it is still the way of things suggests that it is successful."

Ethan continued working, arranging and rearranging used dishes on a tray.

Soren gave him a sidelong glance. "All right, then, Ethan, tell me what you think."

"May I speak freely?"

"You know by now you needn't ask. Please do. Those on the other side of the matter certainly will."

Ethan set down the dishes and considered his words. "If we consider purely from an economic perspective, then we must ask what gains we certainly forfeit by barring so many working minds from entrepreneurial thought."

"You mean that slaves might be great men and women if not for their circumstances."

Ethan shrugged, a jerky, unusual gesture. Soren couldn't remember seeing it before.

"We make criminals and enemy combatants our slaves," Soren said, as he'd been taught. "We don't expect honor from such people."

"And their children, born into slavery?"

Soren shook his head. "It is unfortunate for them, but they are the natural children of criminals and a lower class of person. We know what to expect of them, just as we expect mages from a line of mages."

"Just as every son is a mirror of his father."

It was a sharp line, and dangerous, and entirely a surprise out of Ethan's circumspect mouth. Soren blinked, uncertain if he'd heard correctly. But Ethan's expression was mild as he resumed wiping a table of imaginary crumbs or spilled droplets.

Soren wondered, for the first time, if Ethan believed Soren thought ill of him, thought him a natural criminal or rebel. Soren had just said as much, and of course he hadn't meant it of Ethan himself, only as a general statement, but...

If Ethan might think Soren thought poorly of him...

The question glimmered, buried deep in the muck of politics and economics and unknowing endorsement, and Soren was both too honest to pretend he did not recognize it and too afraid to ask it.

Ethan had said he knew the security of his position, had even once said he would not trade his place. He had said these things to Soren, and Soren could cling to them and not ask the further question.

But Ethan saw it in his eyes, and his expression softened. He looked down, and after a moment he asked, "May I speak absolutely freely?"

Soren's throat closed, and for the first time he wanted to refuse. But he forced a jerk of his chin.

Ethan glanced up, not hearing the nod, and Soren had to repeat the gesture.

Ethan drew a slow breath. "Master, I have been with you all our lives. I have served you since we were both young. The royal family, if I may say so without appearing to advance myself, is my family. You, master, are all the family I have, and—while many servants do what they must for masters they must serve, I do not resent my service. I am glad to be in the household of the prince-heir, *this* prince-heir. If I woke tomorrow morning a free man, with the choice to go my way in Alham or to remain as your servant, I would choose to stay with you."

Soren swallowed hard, choking on relief and gratitude. Ethan did not secretly hate him; he was the close companion Soren had thought him.

"Now, master, imagine the service I could have given, had I ever been able to choose to serve you—and how you would never have needed to wonder if I would."

Icy shock splashed through Soren with the horror of steely truth, and he could say nothing as Ethan lifted the tray, made a small bow, and left the room.

Shianan found Luca leaning over pages with two candles to light them, making notes on the backs of used sheets. He sat up as Shianan entered the office, his expression caught between welcoming, hopeful, and chagrined, and then pushed himself to a stand. "I'm sorry," he said before Shianan could speak. "I hope I did not bring trouble on you."

"Not really, though you surprised us both." Shianan sat on the edge of the desk. "Sit down. I didn't mean to interrupt you." He bit down his irritation at the lingering habits from Ande's tutelage.

Luca sat, and he toyed with the pen but did not write.

"Why didn't you say anything to me?" Shianan asked. "I might have helped you to see him, you know. In a way that didn't have you leaping at him over his wine."

Luca's eyes widened. "Did I—"

"No, no, you were polite enough when you wedged in. Polite enough that you used a slave's language all the way through, instead of calling him His Highness."

Luca's shoulders fell.

"I don't think that was a crippling error." Shianan leaned on one hand. “But why didn’t you tell me?”

Luca looked down at the sheets. “I was afraid you would try to talk me out of it.”

Shianan bit down his first response to consider this.

“It’s the same reason I did not tell you that I would go to testify for Ande.”

Shianan clenched his fingers. “Now there, I would have tried to stop you.”

Luca nodded. “I know. And it was already hard enough, I was just barely clinging to the edge, nails breaking, and I knew I could not stand up to the both of us.”

“Good. If you hadn’t gone—”

“Please.” Luca’s voice was suddenly raw. “I’m not strong enough yet, either.”

Shianan clenched his jaw but said nothing.

“And I nearly wasn’t able to speak tonight, and I couldn’t risk seeing you hesitate if I asked.”

Shianan shook his head. “So you decided instead not to ask.” He smiled. “You were very bold tonight. You surprised him. And me.”

“Surprised...”

“Not in a bad way. I don’t think he was pleased to sit down to a drink and find himself hip-deep in politics and ethics, but you made a good impression with your market argument instead of accusing him of being heartless.”

“Did I?” Luca’s shoulders loosened slightly. He shook his head. “I was not bold. I was terrified.”

“Can’t be courageous without being afraid,” Shianan said lightly. “That’s one secret heroes don’t tell. But there’s no honor in doing what’s comfortable.”

Luca huffed the skeleton of a laugh. “Well, I was not comfortable.” He took a deep breath, held it, blew it out slowly. “But I was not on my knees with Flamen Ande’s hands about my throat. And I told myself that Prince Soren had already seen me naked and beaten—what humiliation could be left to fear? If he ordered me out of a room to which I had not been invited, what was that, after the extractors or Ande?” He gave a grim smile.

Shianan regarded him with appreciation. “That is...profoundly bold.”

Luca shook his head again, and his eyes glinted in the candlelight. “Flamen Ande did not know how he equipped me.”

Ande had broken Luca as a spoiled child breaks a toy. He had nearly shattered Luca beyond repair—believed he had. Made Luca believe he had.

Shianan turned and leaned over the table, looking between the candles. "Miners draw ore from the protected earth, where it has ever been, and they crush it with hammers. Then it's put into a furnace and melted and strained and boiled, and then it is beaten again. And in the end"—he reached to the sword he'd left on his desk before going to the prince and slid the blade from the scabbard to gleam between them—"in the end, it becomes a sword, fit to make a path through opposition."

Luca pressed his lips together, and for a moment he looked hopeful. "I'm going to write the best treatise that's ever crossed the prince's desk, and then I'm going to debate with his council, and then I am going to change everything." He laughed, high-pitched and nervous, at his audacity.

Shianan felt his mouth pull into a smile, and his chest burned with warmth. "I wish I had half your bravery," he said again, and he meant it.

Luca dipped his face, embarrassed, and he righted the pen in his hand. "Talk means nothing," he said, and he took more ink.

CHAPTER 41

Nathi's schoolroom was quiet. Even a mere dozen students could make plenty of noise during the morning arrival and afternoon departure, but just now there was only the sound of pens against paper, scratching out today's transcription and then recopying it in scribe's shorthand.

Then the door opened sharply, with only the barest of a knock preceding. "Good afternoon," said a woman in silver robes as she swept into the building. "I beg your pardon for interrupting."

Nathi knew her at once. She had never seen a Mage of the Circle, not in person, but she had seen images and read descriptions. It was almost unthinkable that one should appear in this outlying town, without a military attachment or grey mages in tow, but the woman carried herself like a mage and a veteran, and doubts stumbled back before her bold entrance.

"Who is your fastest scribe?" the woman asked. "Able to take accurate dictation without repetition?"

All eyes shifted from the mage to Aida in the second row.

Nathi looked from Aida to the Silver Mage. "Do you need a scribe?" she asked, feeling the stupidity of the question as it hung in the air.

The mage looked at Aida. "I am Elysia Parma, Silver Mage of the Great Circle, and I require rapid notes on urgent research I am carrying out. We have no time to write our own reports between efforts; we need someone to take down our impressions as fast as we can speak."

Aida nodded once. "I, er, I don't understand anything about magic, my lady mage. I can't say I'll understand what you're talking about."

"That is no impediment in this case," Mage Parma replied. "In fact, it's something of a boon, which is to say that along with speed, discretion is another necessity I am willing to purchase at a fair market price. Do you understand?"

Aida blinked and nodded. "I do. And I am fast, ask anyone."

"I don't need to. Everyone in the room already spoke for you." She turned to Nathi, standing at the front of the schoolroom. "Would you say forty pias a day for a student scribe is fair?"

Nathi's breath caught in her throat. It was the price of a lent apprentice in a city like Alham, but in such a town as this, it was a week's wages for a beginning scribe. And Mage Parma, holding her eyes, appeared to know that. "It is very fair, my lady mage."

"Then please be so good as to write a contract between Aida and the Great Circle, and I will sign it and leave the first day's wages, with the rest available upon requisition from any military post. I'm sure that's not ideal, but I did not know I would find myself in such need, and I did not bring sufficient coin with me."

Nathi seated herself and began the contract.

Mage Parma turned to Aida. "Go and pack for a week's stay in the fields; we're making camp away from villages, so bring blankets and what else you may need. You may be back sooner, but I can't be sure at this point. Meet me at the west end of town in thirty minutes, if you please. There's a little girl in slave cuffs at the last wall, eating a lamb pie; if you find her, you're in the right place."

"Of course, my lady mage." Aida blotted her pen and stuffed it into its case—she would have to clean that later, or at these wages, she could buy herself a new set.

Then Mage Parma addressed the rest of the room. "Is there a grey mage in this town?"

The students shook their heads.

"Then you won't have heard of the approaching battle. Expect the arrival of a major Ryuven force about forty miles to the southeast, the morning after tomorrow. Our own forces will be coming to oppose them. It might be good to share the word with neighboring villages, so that all know to be cautious and to keep clear."

They nodded, eyes wide.

Mage Parma reviewed Nathi's hasty contract, nodded, and signed it with efficient strokes. She poured out a small bag of coins, counted most of them into four stacks, and said, "I can trust you to get these to Aida's family?"

"Of course."

"And do you know if anyone will be traveling south? I have an urgent message which needs to be carried."

Nathi considered. "I believe Mother Eri takes honey and candles to sell every week or so. You might find her and ask about your intended destination."

"Thank you." The mage swept out the door as she had entered, leaving an unsettled calm after the storm.

Nathi looked about the schoolroom, watching the remaining students gape between the door and Nathi and each other.

"Well, I always tell you to train so that you're prepared for opportunity," she said at last. "Sometimes opportunity does not knock; sometimes it kicks in the door and orders you to pack."

They chuckled, and the awed tension broke.

"I'll still want your transcriptions at the end of the hour," Nathi said. "And let's all wish Aida well in her new position."

Tamaryl arrived first, giving himself just a few precious seconds to check if their arrival site was secure or a trap waiting to spring. He was dismayed by the relief which flooded him when he saw only Shianan Becknam standing on the dead grass threaded with new green; relief meant he had worried more about what they might find waiting than he'd admitted even to himself. It meant he did not trust this alliance—and if he, who had spent so many years living with humans and learning to love his friends here, could not trust in it, then how could he expect such faith from others?

Shianan Becknam's expression was taut as Ryuven burst into the sky behind Tamaryl, settling to the ground as they looked around. Tamaryl wondered what it must be like for the soldier to watch Ryuven warriors arrive into his world and to merely stand and watch.

He gave the first greeting. "Good morning, commander."

"Tamaryl'sho." Becknam's voice was gruff, and his nod stiff.

Tamaryl drew a breath. "I know this is...unusual."

"And useless." Becknam's eyes swept the gathering Ryuven. "You have brought, what, three dozen fighters? To assist us against a thousand?"

Tamaryl had feared this moment. "You know we could not have brought more, not if we were to arrive before the Ientu forces."

Becknam shook his head. "Mage Hazelrig said something about massing in the between-worlds."

"I can travel in a moment, by myself. But if a number of us travel together, and if we—"

Becknam raised a hand. "Don't bother; it's not my expertise and I don't want to have to judge if the White Mage told me right or wrong. I accept that his explanation is an explanation, and that is good enough for me. But what we are to do with three dozen Ryuven—that is a question I do not have an answer to."

"Perhaps we can discuss strategies together," Tamaryl attempted. He turned to face his warriors. "We've brought only weapons and the armor on our backs. Additional goods would have cost more time in the leap."

Becknam nodded, relaxing into a topic he knew. "We've established a camp for you just up the road. You can see Alham from the crest of the hill, which we hoped would be a point of amiability rather than contention. I have soldiers there to keep a secure perimeter, so that no curious tinker or resentful farmer can make their way into your camp."

"And to keep the tinkers and farmers at ease about us?" Tamaryl suggested gently.

"I'm not quite the fool," Becknam said tersely. "I know you could simply fly out if you wanted."

"We're not quite the fools to risk your arrows and mages."

"Well, then, I suppose we can rely upon one another." But Becknam's eyes moved again to the Ryuven warriors, too few to stop the approaching Ientu.

The camp had tents, cots, and blankets, and most importantly, generous food stores. Ronal'sho, who had volunteered so publicly that Oniwe'aru had not been able to refuse him, moved close to Tamaryl and muttered, "We'll have to watch that no one gathers up sacks and leaps home, to plunder without fighting."

"There will be no plundering here," Tamaryl snapped. "And these are good sho and che. They will not falter." There had been no time to bring nim, not if they meant to arrive before the Ientu. He had only a few, with enough power to cross quickly, to lend weight to Oniwe's assurances of friendship.

It was a fool's errand. The Chrenadan army, hunted and haunted for generations, would not distinguish between Ryuven divisions they had not even guessed at only weeks before. When the battle went ill, the simplest answer would be the most accepted—that all Ryuven were the enemy.

And King Jerome had made that clear in their final meeting: If the Ryuven raids were not stopped, then there was no advantage in a peace treaty meant to end Ryuven raids. If the raids continued, there would not be another generous gift to the Ai warehouses, and their fields were already scorched black. Tamaryl had to accomplish the impossible with these few.

"Will you walk back with me to Alham?" Becknam asked. "Or will you stay here in the camp?"

"I should present myself at the Naziar, and I had wanted to see Mage Hazelrig," Tamaryl answered. "And the younger Mage Hazelrig." And, as flying to the Alham city gates would undoubtedly prompt chaos, "I would be glad to walk with you."

CHAPTER 42

Ariana caught up to Shianan in the courtyard. "You'll come to supper tonight, won't you?"

"I hope to," Shianan said.

"We'll have guests. Well, one guest."

Shianan's stomach sank. "Tamaryl."

"Don't say it like that," Ariana chided gently. "He was with us most of my life."

That did not make Shianan feel better.

"We thought it would be good to visit—you know, before..." Before their peoples clashed and killed each other by the thousands.

Shianan looked ahead, avoiding Ariana's eyes. "You know that he and I are—"

"Fighting on the same side now?" she interrupted. "Working together against a common enemy to preserve our peace? And two of my own dearest people?"

He scowled. "That is an unfair tactic."

She laughed and bumped his arm, an expression of affection they hoped was less obvious in the street. "Any tactic that wins."

"I can see I will have to adapt my rules of engagement."

"Just not before the supper. Please. I want my family to get along."

Shianan's chest tightened. It was the first time he had been called *family*, and the word struck him more fiercely than he would have imagined.

If only he did not have to share it with the Ryuven.

He looked ahead, afraid Ariana would see the unreasonable emotion in his face.

When the time came, he did not cross the courtyard to the gate and go directly to the Hazelrigs' townhouse. Instead, he went to Tamaryl's quarters in the Naziar. "As your assigned aide, I am here to escort you to the Mages Hazelrigs' home."

"I believe I know the way," Tamaryl said with a smile, "but I thank you, Commander Becknam."

They did not speak on the way, walking a little apart. They did not comment on the eyes turned on them as they passed in the streets.

At least, Shianan mused, no one noting this visit would think it anything other than official.

"Come in, come in!" Ariana greeted them. "We have pork loin from the Spirit's Oven, one of my favorites. And I talked Mother Harriet into a pie with the plum preserves."

"That must be nearly the last of them," Tamaryl said. "You've been worrying those away for years."

Shianan set his jaw against this renewed reminder of Tamaryl's intimate place here and brushed imaginary dust from his leg.

There were four at the table, and if anyone had agonized over the settings, putting Tamaryl and Ewan Hazelrig on one side and Ariana and Shianan on the other, there was no hint of it in either Hazelrig. On the table was an enormous earthenware dish, painted with a wishing spirit who appeared to be gesturing to the edge of the lid with a self-congratulatory smirk. Ariana lifted the lid to reveal pork, cheese, vegetables, and a little bundle of spices at one end. The scent drew them all forward in their chairs. Shianan found the food, as Ariana had indicated, delicious.

There was nothing to resent; Shianan was not a part of this house as young Tam had been, but he had married into it, and now he visited it at will, and he had never been a slave here even in name. He should not be jealous of Tamaryl's easy familiarity with the room, the colorful hand cloths, his chair's irritating squeak and the best choice for a replacement. Both Ewan and Ariana kept the conversation balanced and inclusive.

There was nothing to resent, and Shianan knew it, and yet in a lull the words slipped from his mouth. "It must be quite different for you, Tamaryl'sho, coming back to this house. I can't imagine what it must have been like, a powerful Ryuven warlord pretending to be a child for so long."

Tamaryl suppressed a smile.

"What?" Shianan pressed, irritated first with himself and then Tamaryl's mild response.

Tamaryl took a drink, stalling, and then when he spoke, it was in falsetto. "Okay, Tam, now let's play mage and Ryuven. I'll be the mage, and you be the Ryuven."

Ariana's mouth dropped open. "Oh, no."

"No, Tam, that's not right! You have to die right!"

Ariana covered her face.

"I blasted you, Tam! You have to die like a Ryuven dies! No, no, healing isn't fair! Papa!"

Ariana buried her face in her arms and slid down her chair, sinking beneath the table.

"Sit properly, Tam!"

"Stop!" she shrieked. "Please stop. Oh, sweet all, I'm so sorry."

Tamaryl had mercy and stopped, grinning.

Ariana kept her hands over her eyes. "Oh, sweet all, I never—I won't be able to hold my head up now. Sweet—I can't believe I—oh, why didn't either of you stop me?"

"And lose this precious opportunity to later bring it up over supper?" Tamaryl rejoined. He looked across at Shianan. "It is different, now. And I am so grateful."

"We're grateful that we had you here," Ewan said. "It's what has made this treaty possible."

Shianan was also grateful, guiltily so, that Ariana was too embarrassed by her childhood ignorance to note his shame at baiting Tamaryl and at the Ryuven's gentle self-deprecation in return. Tamaryl was a Ryuven and the Pairvyn ni'Ai. He was also isolated, distrusted, and cut off from his place, and Shianan should have known better.

He should apologize, but he was not even sure how. He did not have the words, or the courage.

"I have to be honest, it was quite an adjustment," Tamaryl admitted. "And not an easy one."

"I tried to be careful of you," Ewan said.

"Oh, I know. But I was still living among humans. The enemy." Tamaryl's eyes flicked to Shianan and as quickly away. "Acting as a child was actually easier because of that."

Showing your belly so they wouldn't hurt you, Shianan thought, but he did not say it aloud. He knelt before the king and queen even beyond protocol's demands.

"At Luenda," Tamaryl continued, "I came into the military camp. My first day as a human, and I was to be just a child, so small. It had been only a few hours that I had known the White Mage as anything more than a title to fear, and I had just given up my magic, and I was afraid. I was afraid I had betrayed myself, my people, everything. And I was afraid of all the soldiers and mages around me, who would gladly kill me if they knew me, and all the faster for my infantile defenses.

"The White Mage had much to do, and of course it would have

been odd to keep a toddling child with him through it all—and I have never asked, but I wonder if perhaps he did not yet trust me fully, either." Tamaryl looked to Ewan, who smiled and took a bite of pork.

"So it came time to break camp, and everyone was busy, and I didn't know where to go, or how to stay out of the way, or even how to appear like a child to these strange people who looked nothing like me. I did not have to pretend too much to be frightened and displaced." Tamaryl smiled wryly. "And then—and then, as I was between two wagons, then she came. The Silver Mage herself, Mage Parma, sweeping around the tail of the wagon and directly toward me.

"I froze. I knew the Silver Mage as I knew the White Mage, a fierce and deadly opponent, and I was helpless and small. She stopped and looked down at me, and I reached for magic but of course there was none. I thought I would choke on my own terror."

All were still, hanging on Tamaryl's tale.

"And she bent down for me, and she picked me up with two hands, and she placed me on a wagon bed. She patted my hair and told me to stay out of the way of the wheels. And then she walked away."

Ariana laughed loud and long, her shoulders shaking.

"And there I sat, practically trembling in my ragged new clothes, and I couldn't have moved if I wanted to. And that's when I realized, having just been saved and soothed by the notorious Silver Mage, that being a slave child was indeed the most effective place for me to hide."

Shianan busied himself tearing more bread as the others laughed. Tamaryl's stories, gently mocking himself, were just another signal that he was no threat. And Shianan was foolish—and brutish—to press the fight.

"I doubt that is how you imagined meeting the mages of the Circle," Ariana laughed. "But—was Mage Callahan there? Because I don't think it could have been so different with him, either way. I don't think he's ever smiled, not really, not even for a child." She frowned. "He was at Luenda, wasn't he?"

"He wasn't in the Circle yet," Ewan said.

"Maybe not in the Circle, not yet, but I'm sure he was at Luenda. Isn't that where the tapper story started?"

"What tapper story?" Shianan prompted, anxious for the subject to shift.

"Oh, the usual bedtime story monsters." Ariana's eyes widened and she quickly modified, "But it may be tapper stories are told more often in mage households. A tapper is a mage who can take energy—magic, or life, or something—from someone else and use it for himself. They're not real, of course, but after Mage Callahan survived Luenda, I heard there was talk about him."

Ewan raised an eyebrow. "You heard that there was talk. How distantly said."

"I was a child for Luenda," Ariana defended herself. "I only heard about it later, from other apprentices, and it only came up because we were all afraid of him, because he was so grumpy all the time."

"Which, I'm sure, had nothing to do with the fact that people talked about him as a mythical bedtime story monster."

"Wait," Tamaryl said. "He survived Luenda and then he was suspected of illicit magic?"

"Not really suspected," Ewan said. "Tappers aren't real. It can't be done."

"But there was talk," Ariana insisted. "No one knows how he did it, so of course there was speculation."

Tamaryl looked down at his plate. "People disliked him for having survived?"

"It wasn't quite like that." Ewan sighed. "But Luenda was hard. Many died. And for a grey mage of his young age to have survived such an injury—there were questions, and he never gave satisfactory answers. I cannot say that it hasn't colored his reputation."

Tamaryl put his spoon down, picked it up again, turned it in his fingers. "I had no idea."

"How could you not know?" Ariana asked. "You worked in the Wheel! You knew him!"

"He never discussed it with another mage's servant," Tamaryl said pointedly. "And I wasn't invited to the apprentices' gatherings. How was I to know? I knew he wasn't well liked, but that wasn't unexpected; we've all met him. But I never guessed he might be the way he was because of how he was treated after Luenda."

Ariana squinted at him. "Why are you upset about this?"

"I think... I think he may have survived at Luenda because of me. I think I healed him."

They all stared at him.

"Before I found the White Mage. I was walking the battlefield, because I couldn't return, and I found a youth dying of a bolt to his face. It couldn't hurt to try to help him; if my efforts failed, he was dying anyway. So I tried to funnel my own healing into his body." He looked at Ewan. "Healing him is how I knew I could save you."

"Save you?" Ariana repeated, an edge to her voice. She looked at her father. "You never told me you were injured at Luenda."

"Because I couldn't have explained my recovery, either." Ewan sucked a long breath. "Yes, I was dying, but 'the Pairvyn ni'Ai healed me and then came home with me as a servant' was not a possibility. I couldn't tell anyone." He looked at Tamaryl. "But I didn't know you had also helped Mage Callahan."

"I think it must have been him. I didn't see him in the Wheel until a few years later, when I was plausibly old enough to go with you, and of course I couldn't recognize him as the boy swollen and dying on the field. I knew he'd been injured at Luenda, but that was true of many mages. I never put together that he was the one I had helped, but now that seems likely." He shook his head. "I didn't mean to create ill-will toward him."

"If you can help heal people," Shianan asked, "why not do it more? How many soldiers could you save?"

"As a human slave boy?" Tamaryl asked, smiling wryly.

"But he did," Ewan put in. "There's no reason you should have followed the research on our amulets, but they became much more effective in the years following Luenda. We cannot work in the way that the Ryuven do, but their technique helped to improve ours. And when you and I were...injured, in the cellar of the Wheel—"

When Oniwe had tried to kill Ewan Hazelrig and Tamaryl had tried to kill Shianan.

"—it was Tamaryl's technique, performed by a team of our best mages, which saved you."

This new knowledge made Shianan's guts slide over one another. Tamaryl looked at his plate.

Shianan set down his spoon, carefully so that it would not clink on the plate. "That night in the ravine—could you have helped the prince?"

The table went quiet. Tamaryl lifted his head to meet Shianan's eyes. "No. I can help my own hurts from physical weapons, but not in others. I could help Mage Callahan and Mage Hazelrig because they had been wounded with magic."

Shianan released his breath slowly and nodded. "But if I'd had an amulet with me..."

Ariana covered his hand with hers. "You couldn't have

activated it. Not without a mage."

"Well, next time I leap over a cliff, I'll be sure to bring a mage with me." Shianan forced a smile.

"I am sorry I left Mage Callahan to such suspicion," Tamaryl said. "Not that I wish I'd left him to die, but I had no idea the position it put him in."

"There are many things we might have done differently if we could have foreseen all the possible outcomes," Ewan said. "But you did your best in the moment for a dying youth in a horrific battle, and I don't think anyone could blame you for that." He smiled gently.

"Speaking of battles," Shianan said. "I hate to bring it up, but the coming confrontation with the Ientu..."

"Oh, I saw." Ariana sobered. "I didn't realize at first; I'd never looked for Fhure on a map."

"Fhure," repeated Tamaryl. "As in—is that your land?"

Shianan nodded. "I've never really felt myself a count, and I've visited the place barely a handful of times—but those are my people, after all, and I don't want to see them in danger."

"We will do our best," Ewan said, and Shianan's stomach felt a little hollow despite the pork when he realized that was the most the White Mage could promise.

"We will stop them," Tamaryl said, only slightly more confident. "In the first alliance between human and Ryuven."

Shianan made himself nod. "Right." And to keep himself from speaking his fear, he hurried to continue, "Now, I hear we have a fruit pie from Mother Harriet."

"I'll bring it," Ariana said as quickly.

When the evening had concluded, Shianan said, "I will need to escort Tamaryl'sho back to his quarters."

Ariana nodded. "Of course. I'll see you both tomorrow."

"Good night." It felt wrong not to kiss her, but he couldn't bring himself to do it in front of Tamaryl.

They went out into the dark, walking a little distance apart on the nearly deserted streets. For a long while they walked in silence, and Shianan's thoughts whirled, recalling bits of the night's conversation, doggedly reliving moments he regretted.

"I want to apologize," he said at last, too quickly. He sucked a breath and tried again as the Ryuven looked at him. "For what I said tonight. I'm not used to—I shouldn't have been defensive."

Tamaryl nodded and kept walking. "I am an emissary to a court that does not trust me. I am about to go to war alongside soldiers I have fought against. I am barely sure of my position in my own land. I have no interest in fighting one more battle, and one I've already lost."

Shianan looked down. Tamaryl already knew his most dangerous secrets; there was no point to preserving one more. "I—we're married."

"Ah." Tamaryl's voice was mild. "I had not known, but that does not surprise me. But it's not generally acknowledged."

"No."

"Of course." Tamaryl straightened and looked ahead. "Then I repeat what I once told you; I am happy for her happiness."

"Thank you."

"And don't ever hurt her."

Shianan looked down. "I try my best."

They walked on in silence, until they came to Tamaryl's door. Shianan gave him a truncated bow, Tamaryl nodded, and they exchanged carefully neutral farewells.

Shianan did not return to the Hazelrig house. He would barely sleep in his own bed this night. They had much to do in the early morning.

CHAPTER 43

An army cannot travel so swiftly as a single person, so it was late in the second day of travel when Shianan finally led General Septime to the oversized oaken doors of Fhure House. Thanks to Luca's service as a harbinger, the doors opened and released a bevy of servants to light their final steps and welcome them in. Shianan mused that they had done less for the prince on his visit, though his had been less expected.

"General Septime will be staying here, with some aides," he told Kraden, though of course the majordomo already knew. "Please see he has everything he needs."

General Kannan was still in Alham. Though no Ryuven raid had attempted Alham in a century, the possibility that this unfamiliar clan with unfamiliar tactics might try such an assault was great enough that they could not risk leaving the city undefended. The division of their leadership and troops was unfortunate, though.

Kraden nodded, his expression tight. That was only to be expected when a Ryuven battle came to one's doorstep. "And yourself, master?"

Shianan shook his head. "Put him in my room. I'll be at the camp."

"You're sure of that?" asked General Septime.

Shianan preferred that his soldiers thought of him as a soldier rather than as a noble. "I was raised on a post, sir. I have been a soldier all this life, but a count for two years. I would feel disconnected, away from the camp." General Septime could benefit from a more secure location from which to command; Shianan could do more good by staying close to enact those orders.

Septime nodded. "I understand. You'll let me know if there's anything unexpected."

Luca was not alone when he found Shianan in a storeroom, taking a wedge of cheese to carry back to camp. Marla stood beside him, holding a basket of oils, towels, and two short wooden rods. Shianan flicked his eyes between them. "I'm fine."

Luca said nothing in words, but his expression stopped only barely short of an eye roll. Shianan tightened his jaw, irritated that

Luca had brought an aelipto but even more that he had noticed. And he knew how foolish his response was, which irritated him further. "I'm fine."

Marla frowned and extended her hand to just above the level of his shoulder. "Can you raise your arm to mine?"

Shianan knew that he could, slowly and with a wince, and he did not care to demonstrate either. "I said I am fine."

"Yes, master," she answered, her tone obedient but unconvinced.

He sighed. What did it hurt to let her do as she offered, and what fool did not avail himself of an aelipto's skills when one stood before him? Especially while the fool was in pain? "Yes, my shoulder is off. Be good enough to examine it, please."

Luca's face relaxed, and he took the cheese to tie into a carrying cloth. "I'll go ahead to the camp, then."

Shianan started toward a kitchen table to sit, but she waved him toward her. "No, master, I've had a proper treatment bench made. Come this way, if you please."

He followed her to a larger storage room, lined with jars and sacks but with an odd bench in the center, not quite shaped for traditional comfort. She set down the basket and lifted his arm. "I can start with this, but I will need beneath your tunic."

"Fine." He shrugged out of it, and she helped before he would have needed to raise his arm. "But I can't stay long. I have to get back to the camp."

"Sit, please, and let me get at you." She took a light hold of his arm and manipulated it through several growing circles, slowing where his shoulder caught or where he resisted.

At last she spoke. "It seems your reach is limited, or at least it won't go smoothly past a certain point."

Shianan nodded tightly, admitting it for the first time. "And weaker. I have trouble lifting my sword if it's straight to the side—which fortunately isn't a likely angle."

"Hmm." Marla probed the shoulder and upper arm, at last placing a thumb and applying pressure. For a moment there was dull pain, and then she adjusted the thumb and fire lanced Shianan like a blade. He swore and jerked from her.

She pulled back. "How long has it been like this?"

"Two weeks or so."

"Was there a specific injury?"

He had pitched forward over a falling horse into a rocky stream and then fought for his life. "There might have been."

"I can help, but you'll need to rest the arm while it heals."

Shianan shook his head curtly. "We are in the midst of a war, with a battle in the morning. I can't simply stop using my sword arm."

"This will get worse, and not better."

"So will the raids."

"Could you give it rest outside the next battle, at least? Until you absolutely must?"

How long would that be? Tomorrow's combat. A day or three more until the next Ryuven attack. Whenever the king discovered his clandestine marriage.

"Just keep it still. A sling, maybe, to—"

"Absolutely not," he snapped. His soldiers were already frightened, mourning, dreading. He could not be seen in a sling.

She sighed. "As still as you can, then, master, to give it a chance."

Shianan did not answer.

Marla frowned. "Put your hand on your hip, please." She tugged at his elbow in minutely different angles, seeming to feel for resistance, and pain spiked through his shoulder.

"Can't you just, well, press it back into place?" Shianan asked her, frustrated with his weakness and so with the both of them.

She shook her head as if he were a child. "You've torn muscle and ligaments, and they've started to heal in the wrong way, like a poorly set bone. Someone should have seen to this right away."

"There were a few hundred other patients in greater need."

She did not pursue that. "It will take a couple of weeks to work it out of where it's started to stick. You have to fight, so we must be cautious about weakening it further to allow for proper healing."

"King's oats, don't make it worse."

"But I can loosen these muscles locked up around it. That will give you more range of motion for a day or so, at least. But you won't like it."

Shianan set his jaw. "I can take it."

She did not immediately respond, and after a moment he looked more closely at her. He recalled that she was an aelipto but also a slave, and that she had not always lived at Fhure, and that many might vent pain on someone they could blame for it.

He blew out his breath. "You won't mind if I swear copiously, will you? Maybe kick an onion bin when you've finished?"

Her expression softened, nearly a smile. "You can shout all you like."

He nodded once and turned his head forward. "Then do what you must."

He expected her to wrench his shoulder into a new place. Instead, she placed her thumbs precisely at the top of his arm, notching them in below the cap of his shoulder, and squeezed. He yelped despite himself and flinched away.

She moved with him. "I can't relieve anything while your muscles are clenched like this," she explained, maintaining pressure. "Relax them, please."

"Easy to say," Shianan grunted. Fire and ice ran down his arm, and he clenched his good left fist.

Then his arm seemed to surrender, releasing a tension he'd long forgotten he'd been holding, and his shoulder drooped beneath her talons. She lessened the pressure, and he was embarrassed at the relief.

She replaced his hand on his hip and tugged again at the elbow. "Better."

"If you say so."

She smiled. "You may now kick the onions if you like."

He shook his head. "Just now, it feels like too much effort."

"That's fine. You'll have another chance after the next one." She replaced her thumbs.

The massing clouds in the darkening sky urged Shianan to reconsider his decision to give up his stone house for a tent, but he steeled himself and went on to his place in the military camp.

Luca had everything ready in Shianan's field tent. "Good work," Shianan observed, sinking onto a field stool and accepting the warm cup of soup with a slice of cheese melting into it. "Thank you. Now get on your way."

"My way?"

"Back to Fhure House. You can make it before the rain catches you."

"But I can—"

"I'm not going to argue again about this," Shianan said wearily. "I have enough worrying over the soldiers I've drilled endlessly just for this situation. I cannot be distracted with someone who isn't prepared." He shook his head. "King's oats, look at what happened when I had to go after a prince who did not stay safely out of the way. I can't do that again."

Luca's mouth turned down, but at last he nodded curtly.

"Don't be sullen," Shianan sighed. "Go back to Marla, maybe let her reshape you like so much bread dough. You can take the opportunity to write more on that treatise for the prince-heir, if your arm will still work at the end of it."

Luca gave a single nod.

Shianan rolled his sore shoulder and stretched out his arm, grateful that it extended more smoothly now. He wanted to say something to Luca, something that would be appropriate if this was the last time they spoke—but the hour was dark enough without bringing a farewell between them. Still, it felt wrong to say nothing. "At least this time you won't need my death-will to secure your freedom," he said wryly.

Luca scowled at him. "You promised me employment in Alham. You'd better keep your word."

"I'll do my best," Shianan promised.

Luca gathered his own few items, gave Shianan a quick look, and then went out. Shianan sat in the tent alone and sipped his cooling soup as thunder rolled on the horizon.

CHAPTER 44

Tamaryl left his tent and the flanking rows of tents, separately housing Ryuven and humans, and went out into the night. Lightning flashed on the low horizon, with rumbles of thunder, but the storm was at a distance yet. He had time for a short walk to clear his mind.

Years ago, he had been the Pairvyn in every sense of the title, respected and obeyed and entrusted with the welfare of his people. Countless times he had come to the human world to lead first raids, then battles.

Tonight, he was a shadow of the Pairvyn. He had his crimson sash, but for the first time he hesitated to wear it. Ronal'sho made no secret of his skepticism and disdain for this plan—Tamaryl wondered why he had even come—and there was a general air of doubt among the others. That was no wonder; Tamaryl had been imprisoned not so long ago, and missing in exile before that. The burning of the crops had led many to wonder if their aru who had reinstated Tamaryl's authority was cruel or mad. Tamaryl had led enough warriors into enough fights to know when he had their faith, and tonight he did not.

He wondered if it was possible to win it back before they closed with the Ientu.

Dead grass rustled behind him, and he turned back to scan the dark. Ronal'sho stood facing him, his wings thrown wide as if braced for a rush.

Tamaryl stopped where he was and chose his words. "Good evening, Ronal'sho. I had not anticipated meeting you here."

He could not antagonize the sho, could not risk agitation in their fragile Ryuven ranks before they fought with humans against Ryuven. Ronal'sho craved division, and any division could be fatal. At the same time, however, Tamaryl could not sacrifice any authority. Ronal'sho would continue to press, searching for weakness, and undermine him in front of those they had brought to fight. It was a delicate dance Tamaryl did not want.

Ronal's voice came low. "I thought I would come to you at night, give you a chance to do it with less embarrassment."

That was not a promising opening. "What did you think to ask, that you thought might be embarrassing?" Tamaryl let ambiguity hang in the air, hoping to suggest it was the question itself that might be delicate.

But Ronal did not appear to catch the implication. "I have two propositions for you. The first is that we rouse the others, wait for the deep of night, and sweep through the human officers and mages as they sleep. We have never had such access, and it is not an opportunity to be wasted."

Tamaryl stared at him. "You would betray our treaty and our alliance?"

"What alliance? Does it look as if they trust us? Does it look as if we can trust them? They are as dangerous as ever, and they have contrived to weaken us where we are most vulnerable, convincing Oniwe'aru and Edeiya'rika to burn our crops. You would see it, if you had not become one of them and abandoned your people."

"I abandoned no one," Tamaryl said firmly. "I gave a full explanation of why I could not remain."

"And yet you are Pairvyn still."

Tamaryl could hardly explain that Oniwe had done that to limit the reach of Ronal's own house. "Oniwe'aru trusts that my desire is still to see the best for our people."

Ronal rolled his head in exasperated disbelief. "Oniwe'aru does not want to admit that his half-brother is destroying us."

Tamaryl sucked air over the fresh wound. What if none of this worked, and if the Ai found themselves at fresh war? "Oniwe'aru wants the best for the Ai, not the best for me. That should be obvious from the results of our disagreements."

"Ah, yes. You have been imprisoned, you have been sentenced to death. And again, yet you are Pairvyn." Ronal took a step forward. "You know you should not be the Pairvyn. That brings us to my second proposal: Step down and let me take your place. If you do not have the strength to lead this attack tonight, I will not shrink away."

Shock rippled through Tamaryl, stealing his words. He had doubted Ronal'sho; he had not considered insurrection. "You cannot become the Pairvyn without an aru or silth conferring the role upon you."

Ronal'sho shrugged one shoulder. "If I lead where you cannot, the formalities will be completed upon our victorious return."

Tamaryl's chest clenched. If Ronal might simply take the sash here, providing the other sho did not object too loudly, then he did not feel himself bound by law or tradition or his aru's will. He would take this band of warriors through the human camp, killing Ariana and others almost as they slept, and then on through the countryside, returning home with looted goods and the Pairvyn's crimson sash to defy Oniwe'aru and Edeiya'rika's decisions and to destroy what remained of the treaty.

"I am here to protect our people," Ronal'sho continued. "Unlike you, I will put them first and do what must be done. Because unlike you, I care about them."

Tamaryl had given up everything—everything—for the sake of his people. This jealous sho was angry that he had not been given the power and prestige he had not earned. He had undoubtedly been rehearsing this heroic complaint for his performance before first Tamaryl and then the warriors who had come with them.

Tamaryl wanted to drop him where he stood. But that would solve little and damage much, and Tamaryl had more concerns than a tantrum for recognition and power. "I will not step aside for you," he said as evenly as he could manage. "And there will be no attack upon our allies. We came here to help defend this land, not to raid it, and that is what you pledged to do when you volunteered. Whatever your complaint with me, you may bring it before Oniwe'aru when we return—but we will not waste our time here in argument over rank."

Thunder rolled, closer now, and large drops of rain began to splatter over them.

"Consider what will come, Tamaryl'sho! This is your only chance to redeem yourself—a traitor to your own people!"

"I have said I will not, and that is the end of it." Tamaryl flexed his wings behind him, resisting the urge to shield himself from the increasing rain. "In the morning, we will do what we came to do, which is to protect the treaty that feeds our people and to obey the orders of our aru who sent us here."

"It was you who brought us here," Ronal'sho shot. "You deceived Oniwe'aru, just as you've always influenced him for your own end."

Tamaryl had said what he could, and there was no point to continuing past the end. He turned and started back to the neat rows of tents, leaving Ronal'sho in the rain.

Lightning flashed overhead, making the tents leap into daylight before dropping back into darkness, impenetrable to his flash-seared eyes. He hoped he would not stumble where Ronal could see, and then he remembered Ronal was likely blinded by the same flash. After a moment his vision cleared, and he blinked beneath the wing he pulled over his head.

Energy struck him like a battering ram, lancing between his shoulder blades and running through his torso and limbs, and he convulsed. For an instant he stupidly wondered if he had been struck by lightning, and then he recognized the bolt. He struggled to catch his balance, to distribute the raw power rushing through him, to recover before Ronal'sho's next attack.

There wasn't time. He had only just turned, half-facing the angry sho, when Ronal struck him again.

Tamaryl called up an incomplete magical shield, enough to deflect the worst of the blow. Before he could form a counter-attack, with all his actions slowed by the devastating first blow, Ronal struck again.

Tamaryl grasped for energy, abandoning any attempt at countering. He could strike back at Ronal once he could think clearly; hampered as he was, he only made himself more of a target. He drew a shield about himself, throwing nothing back at Ronal, and the next magical blow wrapped around him instead of passing through, delivering only a sharp sting.

Ronal'sho roared and drew the mace from his belt. Lightning flashed over them, lighting him like a vengeful ghost.

Tamaryl rushed to adjust the shield to resist physical attack instead of magic, but Ronal was coming fast. Tamaryl skipped backward and threw up his arms to blunt the blow.

Something cracked in his left forearm. Tamaryl cried out and shot a bolt of offensive energy from his right hand, making Ronal grunt and fold. But he came on, swinging his mace once more. Tamaryl stepped out of its reach, threw magic, and tripped over something. He stumbled backward and Ronal rushed him, knocking him to the wet ground and jamming the weapon's shaft against his neck.

Tamaryl shoved against the mace, but Ronal crushed it against Tamaryl's throat. Tamaryl's left arm collapsed with a white-hot flare of pain, so that Ronal's clenching fist drove down beside his neck, the wood pinching him against the mud. Rain pelted them, blurring Tamaryl's vision. He grunted and braced his right arm against the shaft, choking and wavering. He threw magic, but Ronal was already pushing energy through the mace, burning his resisting hands.

Tamaryl summoned his strength for one mighty desperate attack that would not be enough—

Ronal grunted, his eyes widening, and the pressure on the mace weakened. Tamaryl drove magic into him, pushing him up and backward. Ronal reached for balance and magic, extending an arm again toward Tamaryl, and then he jerked crazily to one side, folding at the waist like a dancer as he cried out.

Shianan Becknam pulled his sword free and struck again, and Ronal stumbled and dropped limply to the ground.

Thunder rolled over them, and Tamaryl flinched from the stinging drops in his eyes. He pulled himself upright, using only his right arm, and stared at the commander.

Shianan pointed his sword, keeping Tamaryl in place. "Tell me," he said, his voice low in the storm, "that I have just saved the peace."

Tamaryl looked at Ronal, staring unblinking into the rain. "He wanted to attack the humans instead of fighting alongside them. Kill the officers and mages." The pain in his arm broke through at last, rolling over him like the thunder. "I did not realize he would kill me for that opportunity, though I should have guessed."

Shianan lowered the sword. "I saw him attack you from behind. How many others in your command do you think would do the same?"

Tamaryl bristled, but it was a fair question. "I think none, without Ronal'sho." He hoped that was correct. "His political grudge was partly personal."

Shianan shook wet hair back from his face. "King's oats. What if he had killed you? We would have been sitting prey for our supposed allies. In this storm he could have killed us, tent by tent, and we might not have heard a thing."

Tamaryl didn't have an answer for that. For a moment he wondered why Ronal'sho had not simply done it—but perhaps he had not wanted to try it while Tamaryl was not yet committed. Maybe he had not wanted to fight the Pairvyn, and that was why he had at last attacked only from behind.

Maybe.

Shianan took his left hand from the sword and extended it to Tamaryl—an aid to stand, while keeping his weapon ready. Tamaryl wanted to believe it was only the habit of a soldier often offering a hand during battle.

Tamaryl pulled his left arm close and concentrated. It began to throb, the bone drawing together again.

Shianan looked down and then looked away, his face twisting.

"That's unnatural."

Tamaryl did not answer. Cold rain sluiced the heat of healing from his flesh, leaving the rest of him chilled. "What do we do with him?"

Shianan looked down at the body. "What will it do for the rest of your warriors if we show them?"

Tamaryl was surprised by the question. He supposed it made sense, displaying the cold consequence of mutiny, but it might also inspire outrage, especially if they had been partial to Ronal'sho.

"Will his death make them more likely to distrust the both of us, or more likely to fall into line?"

Tamaryl wasn't sure. "I think most are in agreement with our task. We don't need to intimidate them. But they will be more likely to distrust a human officer who killed one of their own."

Shianan nodded. "I was afraid of that."

"The truth is, he attacked me. No one will be surprised that ended in death."

"Do you mean to hide my involvement? He's obviously cut with a sword. And there's a chance someone has seen us, just as I saw you."

"We won't lie. We'll start with the truth, that it was a matter between Ronal'sho and myself, and you came to a fight already in progress."

"I hate to wait until morning, but I cannot believe calling everyone out into the rain to look at a body obscured by the dark and to hear half a story through thunder will help anything."

"I'm afraid I agree with you. We'll do it in the morning, then." Tamaryl paused; neither of them would enjoy this next part. "Thank you."

Shianan looked away. "I'm your assigned escort. Allowing a diplomatic visitor to be murdered would be just the failure the king needs." He sheathed his sword. "I suppose moving the body falls to the one with more physical strength and two working arms."

Tamaryl watched him bend for the corpse. "How did you see us? It's hardly inviting weather for a stroll."

"I saw." Shianan heaved the body onto his shoulders, and Ronal's wings draped the ground behind like an obscene cape. "I don't rest well when it rains. Fortunately for you, I decided to look through the camp, check with the sentries."

Tamaryl nodded. "Will you take him to his own tent?"

"Oh, no. We can't risk someone else finding him before we

announce it ourselves." Shianan adjusted the body with a slight bounce. "I have room for him."

Tamaryl stared.

Shianan snorted. "It's hardly the first dead Ryuven I've handled."

"Yes, but I didn't expect you to invite one into your home."

"My tent, in the field. A much lower standard for hospitality."

Tamaryl chuckled despite everything. "I'll come in the morning, then. Early."

"And we'll address the combined forces. I'll pass the word to the officers and sergeants to expect some unrest and to be prepared to maintain order."

"Of course."

They looked at each other, rain sliding over faces and hair, and then turned to go their separate ways.

CHAPTER 45

"Shianan?" Ariana pushed through the tent flap. "It's—"

"Oh." He was standing in the narrow tent and he looked startled, which was perhaps fair at this time of night. "It's so late."

"You're awake." She frowned at him. "And you've been out. Your hair is wet."

He pushed back the dripping strands. "I was walking the sentries."

"So you couldn't sleep, either."

"Something like that."

She tugged the flap secure behind her and picked her way forward. There was a pile of wet laundry near the door, lumpy and indistinct in the low light of the single candle. That was unlike Shianan, and she regarded him more closely. "Are you all right?"

"Come over here," he answered without answering.

"If you need help with this mess—"

"King's oats, don't touch that. Come here."

She did, and he guided them both to the cot, sitting close beside one another. She leaned against him. "I just wanted to see you again before—before." She swallowed.

He nodded. "I understand."

She wanted so badly to be brave, to be strong, but she had felt her magic fail in combat. "I don't know how tomorrow will end."

"It will end," he said softly. "All days, no matter how horrific, come to an end."

"And the second front of Ientu?"

"We know what to expect of their tactics now."

He wanted to be brave too, she realized, brave despite the odds. She pulled him close, his throat warm against her cheek, wishing she had something to offer. "I love you."

His arms tightened about her, almost too tightly, and they clung to one another in the storm.

"A Ryuven died tonight," he said at last.

She jerked in his embrace. "What?"

"One of Tamaryl'sho's warriors attacked him. From behind. It seems he wanted to turn on us, kill the officers and mages in the night under the cover of the storm."

Horror pulsed through Ariana.

"Tamaryl'sho is well; he took injury to an arm, but he is Ryuven, that's merely an inconvenience." Shianan's voice was gruff. "I saved his life."

Ariana stared at him, trying to penetrate his long gaze across the narrow tent, trying to weigh what she thought she heard in those few terse words. She tightened her fingers, holding him close. "I'm glad."

He heaved a sigh and jerked his head toward the door. "That's the one."

"What?" She looked toward the tent door and the wet laundry. Not laundry. "...Oh." She had no words.

"We couldn't risk someone finding him before we addressed the troops. We have to somehow convince them to fight together tomorrow." He sucked another breath. "Knowing he's there...can you stay?"

"Can I..." Ariana looked from the corpse to Shianan. "Oh, no, I don't think I... I don't..."

Shianan looked slightly disappointed, but not surprised.

"Why do you... Why is he here?" Ariana managed.

"Couldn't leave him in the mud and storm," Shianan answered. "Tamaryl and I will show him in the morning when we explain what happened."

"What happened?" Ariana asked. "And—why here?"

"We don't want anyone to find him before we can explain the situation. Things are tenuous enough without rumor unbalancing it all."

Ariana looked at the sodden corpse, mostly concealed in its wet clothing, and made herself ask, "Won't the morning be—won't he be more...?"

"If your question is whether I like any of it, it's a simple no." Shianan blew out his breath.

"There are three mages in my tent, but maybe I could find a reason they should stay with others?" Ariana had no idea what that reason might be, but she would have a few minutes to think.

"And risk someone finding a Ryuven corpse hidden in my tent? Absolutely not. Much as I hate the idea, much as I'd prefer to be with you, I have to stay with him, for the sake of the battle." Shianan squeezed her. "I'm afraid I must send you back."

Ariana hugged him, shivering with the patchwork of warm skin and cold wet clothing. "I'm sorry," she said, and she meant for everything, for the dead Ryuven and the Ientu and their hidden marriage and the rain and all of it.

Shianan cupped her neck and jaw with two hands, and when he spoke his breath was warm on her face. "When this is done," he whispered, "when this fight is over, I will bring you into Fhure House, and I will make you its mistress, and no dead Ryuven will keep us apart."

Ariana leaned forward just enough to find his lips, and for a moment she hung on them, warm and reassuring and strangely alluring despite the coming invasion and overhanging doom. But there was the body opposite them, and she drew back. "Sorry, I..."

He stopped her with the gentlest of kisses, sealing her lips. "It's all right. I don't like it, either." He stood. "Until Fhure, then."

"Until Fhure." She rose and went with him to the opening. "I suppose that means I'll be a countess?" It had not yet occurred to her, not until she thought of going to Fhure House.

"Are a countess," he corrected. "My wife." He kissed her once more, briefly, and then pulled away from her and gestured her through the door.

She went, not daring to linger and uncomfortable beside the wet bundle inside the opening. She went back to her tent of mages and tried not to imagine Shianan passing the night with it, tried not to wonder if he would sleep.

She wondered if she would.

Tamaryl wanted nothing more than to let Shianan Becknam dispose of Ronal'sho's body and to pretend the confrontation had never happened. But at the slightest hint of duplicity, of secrets, of hidden agendas, the tenuous alliance would crumble. Neither Shianan's human soldiers nor Tamaryl's Ryuven warriors would stay if they sensed something was being concealed.

So he stood in the watery dawn, with slanting rays falling on the stiffened body of Ronal'sho, and waited for the sho to gather.

One by one, they emerged from the provided tents, and he could see the instant when each of them noticed him and the corpse in the little open space of wet grass. They looked around at each other and started toward him, silent and expectant.

Tamaryl crossed his arms against the cold—the human world had unreasonable weather—and looked to the side where Shianan waited, shrouded in his cloak. He had brought out the stiff body, awkward to move the short distance from his own tent, and then retreated to a moderate distance, letting the sho see the dispute as a Ryuven affair before they perceived it as an attack by a human soldier. But he was ready to step forward when necessary.

Tamaryl resented how responsible Shianan was being.

The sho and che gathered in a loose semi-circle, looking from Ronal'sho to Tamaryl. Questions were plain in their expressions, but they waited.

"We don't have everyone," a tall sho with dark red hair observed at last. "Who isn't here?"

"I'll go," volunteered another. "I know which tents to find."

Tamaryl estimated there were four or five who had not yet come out to join them. He took a measured breath and told himself they were merely slow to rise, that nothing was wrong, that neither Ronal'sho nor similarly bloody-minded humans had killed them in the night.

But here they came, prompted by the volunteer, hastily falling into the loose line and looking with mixed suspicion and outrage at the body.

They had left Ronal'sho face-down, but his bright hair made him easily identified. Tamaryl observed that they had all recognized him. He saw the calculation in their eyes; it could not have been a secret that Ronal had sought to displace Tamaryl.

"Ronal'sho came to me last night," he began without preamble. "He suggested we turn on our human allies and kill them in the night."

He scanned the group, hoping he might see signs of recognition or agreement and terrified that he would. He saw wings shift, small movements of feet or arms, a few frowns and tight expressions, but nothing conclusive.

"I refused. We came for a purpose, and betraying our word would irreparably end the essential trade we need to survive."

"That's a strong refusal," muttered someone.

Tamaryl was not quick enough to catch the speaker. "My refusal was with words. When I walked away, Ronal'sho attacked me."

These words fell uncomfortably, as the listeners inferred the obvious attack from behind. Tamaryl could only pray they found the truth credible.

"That's not a Ryuven blow," the one with dark red hair said. "And he was struck from behind. Have you taken to carrying a human sword while you work alongside them?"

Tamaryl opened his mouth, but Shianan answered first. "The sword was mine," he offered from his place at the side. "I saw the attack. I saw the fight."

"Did you hear the argument?"

Shianan came toward the group, moving with deliberate slowness, his hands both away from his weapons and loose at his sides, equally important to those who directed magic. "I would have, had there been an argument. What I saw was an unprovoked attack, from behind, mutiny against the Pairvyn ni'Ai and my co-commander."

He had laid it out plainly, and now they had to choose—did they protest the killing and thereby support open revolt against their command? Or did they agree to continue in the role they'd been sent to perform, fighting alongside the humans?

Tamaryl forced air through his throat and felt for the thin magic about him, bracing himself for a rush.

But the next words came tenuous and testing, as a sho with chestnut braids said, "What did Ronal'sho know, that he wanted to fight the humans instead of fighting with them?"

"A good question," Tamaryl answered, "but a better one would be, what did he want? Ronal'sho had no evidence or suspicion of treachery, if that is what you ask. No, his intent was to violate our sworn word in the night and carry back spoils as a raiding party. He hoped for acclaim, though it would mean the shield was raised and our trade here ended."

He did not spell it out for them; he hoped they would think it through, for it would mean more if they saw it for themselves.

"The fields are already burning," said the sho with dark red hair. "To close off trade at this point would be madness. He could not have meant to violate the treaty."

"He would have," someone else contributed reluctantly. "He said as much—that we had no business serving humans to protect what we could take for ourselves."

"The greater offense was not his revolt against the Pairvyn," Tamaryl said, as evenly as he could. "That should have been settled in a duel, not an assault from behind, but such disputes do happen. But he betrayed the Ai, forsaking the welfare of the clan for his own glory."

Exactly what Tamaryl had protested so long ago. They would all have heard of it, would hear the echo of his exile. He hoped they would think of his consistency.

"He meant to use us to elevate himself." The chestnut-braided sho lifted his chin to look around at the others. "He meant to make us liars so that he could seize a higher position." He turned to Tamaryl. "You won't remember me, Tamaryl'sho, but I fought with you back then, before your—before you were gone. I remember how you raged when a che let a command die while he personally fought where he would be observed—well, it's a long story, but you did not care that he won while he let others fall for him." He gestured to the half-circle of sho. "I don't know what others have heard or what they have believed, but I once saw the Pairvyn charge into a line of human mages to shield a group of nim, and I have always known he acted to a conscience I wished others had." He straightened. "I believe you refused to turn on the humans. I can't say I'm glad to be defending what we used to take for ourselves"—he looked at Shianan with a faintly uncomfortable lift of an eyebrow, and Shianan nodded in acknowledgment—"but I never want to be a traitor, and I never want a traitor to choose my action for me."

It was a bold speech; he was not the eldest or the strongest, and Tamaryl guessed he risked his standing in his declaration. But it was enough to tip the balance, and the others began to nod in slow agreement.

"Then we will hold to our agreed purpose here," Tamaryl said. "And if there is any who came like Ronal'sho, with another intent in his heart, he should return now. I will make no accusations regarding actions which were never taken; just leap back now and leave us to do our work."

No one moved.

"Good." Tamaryl drew a full breath, and relief tasted sweet. "Now, we have only hours before we meet the enemy, and we are not yet accustomed to fighting alongside humans. Let's organize."

CHAPTER 46

"King's runny oats," snapped General Septime.

"There's enough of them, but they're not so large an army," Mage Ewan Hazelrig said. "They'll come through yet today."

"Where?"

"Close enough. It's safe to assume they mean to flank us on the field, catching us off guard."

"They must assume we can't predict their coming," Marshal Vanguilder suggested.

Or they don't think it matters if we do, Shianan thought, but he did not venture it aloud. It was little advantage to know a superior force's position if it was still a superior force.

"Commander," General Septime said, "I'll ask you to take that defense. Protect our flank."

"Yes, sir," Shianan said, and his heart sank. His soldiers would fall under concentrated Ientu magic, and he could not shield them.

"And there's a message from the Ientu," Septime continued. He slapped a note onto the camp table. "Came by runner last night. They want to meet before we close battle. To hear our surrender, no doubt, now that we know they intend to pinch us."

"Came by runner?" repeated Mage Hazelrig. "That's odd."

"Do we treat with them?" Vanguilder asked quietly. "Is it an honest offer? And if..."

And if so, what should we trade for the lives of our army?

"It cannot hurt to open negotiations," Mage Hazelrig said. "At the worst, we refuse all, and it only delays the inevitable. At best, we find some point of trade we could leverage, or perhaps even a weakness."

No one believed this last bit, but neither did anyone protest it. Shianan knew the sound of silently agreeing upon hopelessness.

Let Ariana be away from there. Let her be safe.

There was a girl passing among the busy soldiers, markedly out of place as she looked from side to side. Shianan waved her to him, and she looked grateful for the attention.

"Excuse me, I'm looking for Commander Becknam," said the girl.

She was in her early teens, Shianan guessed, with serviceable clothing which had not seen a washtub lately. Not that he could afford to be too judgmental while in his field gear. "I'm Commander Becknam."

"Oh! They told me you'd be over this way. That is, I'm glad to find you. That is, I have something for you." She pawed through the bag she wore over one shoulder. "I was to give this to you, or to a general, or to Mage Hazelrig of the Great Circle."

That was a curious set of potential recipients. "Who sent the message?"

"Mage Parma," she answered, drawing out a folded letter. "You can see she's signed it across the seal here, showing it's hers and unopened."

Shianan took the letter and peered at the signature, though he did not know Mage Parma's hand. "She sent you as a runner?"

"I had this directly from her scribe. She said there would be payment?"

Shianan did not think it was common for the Circle mages to keep personal scribes, since they were all more than literate and doggedly academic, but there was less time to doubt as they faced the imminent arrival of the Ientu. He dug out three coins for the girl. "Where is the Silver Mage now?"

"I met her scribe to the northwest, but I think she will be coming this way. She said it's all in the letter." The girl nodded to the folded packet in Shianan's hand.

"Thank you. If you go that way and follow to the right, you'll find a tent that smells of fresh bread. Go inside and get something to eat."

"Thank you, my lord." She bobbed awkwardly and went off in the direction he'd indicated.

Shianan opened the letter and read down. Mage Parma had explained little, writing only that she would be joining them soon.

"As is her duty," Shianan muttered, frustrated. While it would be good to have the Silver Mage join in their defense, the letter offered little in the way of additional intelligence or hope. Where was the Silver Mage, and what was she doing, and why was she taking so long?

He would send it along to Mage Hazelrig, in case there was some meaning that had eluded him.

CHAPTER 47

The Ientu had arrived first.

They were arrayed in deep ranks and dressed in gaudy colors, too bright for what Ariana remembered of the Ai. She drew long, slow breaths, willing her heart to slow, flexing her fingers as they numbed from restless magic and fear.

She had dedicated her life to training for this moment. She would not back down.

A little distance ahead of the bulk of the Ientu forces stood a separate group. They had a banner of orange and white, held aloft by a tall, lean Ryuven in the rear, and a row of proud warriors waited at the front.

A small, frantic voice in Ariana's head screamed to shoot them. But they were certainly prepared for arrows and would shield themselves—just before ordering the opening assault. No, they had arranged themselves to meet with the human forces. They wanted to talk.

Maybe there was a chance they could negotiate away from battle.

Ariana moved toward where the generals and her father were in hasty, terse consultation. The chief question was whether to send those with authority to negotiate, avoiding the delay and awkwardness of sending back and forth for negotiations, or to keep them behind, avoiding the risk of a trap by those who had already ambushed them.

Ariana put herself next to her father. "I'm going," she said firmly. "I'm the only human who has been to their world. I don't know if I'll see anything useful, anything that can help, but I am more likely to than any other."

He only nodded, instead of arguing with her, and that frightened her more.

In the end they were a group of broad positions: the White Mage and the Black, General Septime, Tamaryl, Shianan with him, and a small honor guard.

Ariana walked beside Shianan. If things went poorly, she would shield him with whatever magic she had and pray it was enough.

The central Ientu had the clan scarring on his arm, prominently visible beneath his light armor, and a red-orange sash across his torso. He was tall and looked down at their party as they approached. "Let us not waste time," he said without preamble. "I am Demus, Pairvyn ni'Ientu, and I have come to take spoils from this land. But I will hear your pleas before we begin, as surrender and tribute may be efficient."

Ariana clenched her jaw. The arrogance! But he was not entirely without footing; his warriors had carried their battles so far. If only they'd had more time to study the Ientu magic...

"I am General Septime, and this is Ewan Hazelrig, White Mage of the Great Circle. We have not come to offer surrender or tribute."

"But perhaps there may be other negotiations open to us," Ariana's father said. "Trade is more efficient yet than fighting and dying."

"For those who do not anticipate a victory," Demus'sho agreed with a smirk. He turned toward Tamaryl. "Do you speak for these people?"

"I am here in alliance with them," Tamaryl answered. "I am—"

"I know who you are," Demus'sho interrupted. "And I know you bring a force with which you intend to flank us. But we do not fear warriors who struggled with and conceded to this army."

Ariana did not know how Demus thought he knew their strategy—though Tamaryl had not brought enough warriors to be an effective flanking force, so the information was incorrect—but his disdain chafed. The Ai warriors had not conceded to Chrenada's soldiers, and the humans who fell before the Ientu simply had not had the generations of studied practice against this new enemy. They would learn and adapt, if only they had the chance.

But they had to survive for that chance.

"Likewise, we know of your coming reinforcements," General Septime said, "and we are prepared to meet them."

Demus scowled. "Reinforcements? I need no additional help to take this day."

"We are not ignorant fools," Septime answered, adding a hint of disdain to his own tone. "We have observed their coming."

Ariana glanced at Shianan. What good could Demus see in lying about the coming Ryuven, when it would be more useful to further intimidate them?

Demus narrowed his eyes. "If you mean to play games of

disingenuity to buy time, then our purpose will be better served setting our lines against one another. It seems your request to meet was purely to insult us."

"Our request to meet?" repeated Septime.

"We received your message that you wished to speak before commencing battle," the White Mage said. "That is why we came."

They stared at each other. "Who carried this message?" asked Demus at last.

"We have a letter, delivered by a paid runner."

Demus shook his head. "We would never entrust the word of the Ientu to a human carrier," he said succinctly. "And I am to understand that the messenger waiting for us with your request for truce did not also carry your authority?"

"He carried mine."

They all turned at once, caught almost laughably off guard by the unexpected voice. Mage Parma advanced across the open field to join them, her silver robes drawn tight over her torso. Behind her a child followed, slipping a little on the wet grass and struggling to match her pace.

Demus looked back at the Chrenadan party with an expression of strained impatience. Then he looked back at Mage Parma and grinned in disdainful amusement.

But Tamaryl was smiling—not so broadly as the Ientu's grin, but Ariana could recognize it even in its quietness. He watched the figures approach.

Mage Parma, slightly winded, spoke first. "I apologize for this tardiness. We'd hoped to reach this location in time, but the roads were slow with mud and people avoiding the battle." She flipped back her silver hood, and Ariana could see that a knapsack stretched the silver robes. "I am Mage Parma, Silver Mage of the Great Circle."

"And you've brought your daughter to watch your surrender?" Demus suggested.

The child, a dark-haired girl of perhaps seven, stood close to Mage Parma, peering out from beneath her hood.

"There seems to have been some confusion regarding the requests for truce and negotiation," Mage Hazelrig said as diplomatically as possible. "What do you know of this?"

"I sent both messages ahead," Mage Parma answered evenly. "I hoped to resolve this peacefully before we set our forces against one another."

Demus shook his head. "And yet you have brought nothing with which to purchase our good will."

"I do not come to the market to buy." Mage Parma fixed her eyes on him. "I offer you the chance to withdraw."

Demus began to laugh, and the Ryuven behind him followed suit. A short distance away, the remaining Ientu could not hear the conversation but could see their Pairvyn's amusement, and they echoed it in sound and posture. Ariana felt the weight of hundreds of mockeries, and no matter how she knew they should not matter, her heart fluttered like a quail.

Demus ended with a snort. "I see the forces you have brought against me, human fighters I have already bested and a handful of Ai warriors led by one who still holds his position only because his half-brother is too timid to kill traitors. I do not fear you, human mage, and I do not fear the Ai warriors this failed Pairvyn has brought with his poor strategy to flank me."

"They are not my warriors," Tamaryl repeated levelly.

Demus glanced at him and huffed a little breath of disbelief.

"They are mine," said the child.

All eyes shifted to the little girl beside Mage Parma. She brought her arms from beneath her own cloak, and Mage Parma stretched a hand to touch the dull grey cuffs on her wrists. The girl twisted off the cuffs, letting them fall to the ground as she straightened to adult height and unfurled enormous wings.

Mage Parma gestured. "This is—"

"He knows me," Edeiya'rika said, her eyes on Demus. "I am the scythe to which he has brought his briars."

CHAPTER 48

"Good morning, Edeiya'rika," Tamaryl said mildly. "It's good to see you."

Ariana gaped. She should have known! But she had never imagined the Tsuraiya as a child.

Edeiya'rika nodded once to Tamaryl, keeping her attention on the Ientu. "It is Demus'sho, isn't it? We've never spoken, but I believe you brought a raiding party once." Her expression was poised, unruffled by her transition from unassuming slave child to Tsuraiya ni'Ai.

For the first time, there was a slight hesitation in Demus'sho's speech. "That's right."

As inexperienced warrior initiates, we go to battle another clan's defending host, where we are thoroughly blooded by their females. It leaves an indelible impression.

Understanding blossomed within Ariana, and she fought to suppress a smile of her own.

Demus'sho had not looked away from Edeiya'rika. "This is not an affair to concern you. We do not make war upon the Ai."

"To the contrary," she answered, "we have negotiated treaty and alliance with Chrenada to our mutual benefit. Your war upon Chrenada works direct harm upon the Ai, and so we find it appropriate to defend our interests, even when those interests are beneath Chrenadan skies."

"You do not defend the humans," he repeated, incredulous, as if insisting would make it true.

"We defend our resources," she answered. "Chrenada is, as I have heard it called, the breadbasket for the Ai—as you well know, as for this reason you have avoided Chrenada all this time. I would be a poor Tsuraiya to allow it to be plundered by another clan."

Ariana's breath came in short, shallow sips, and she caught herself and engaged the slow, deeper breaths she was trained to use, better for control of her mind and her magic. If Edeiya'rika could present a stronger resistance, if the Ientu were not willing to open a war with the Ai as well as with Chrenada...

Demus'sho stood a moment, his lips thinning. No one spoke.

The mass of Ientu warriors behind the delegation shifted in place.

Demus would be thinking of those warriors, thinking of how he had expected a short, victorious battle to win their acclaim and now faced a different fight, now faced leading them home without a victory or spoils.

But however feared as Tsuraiya, Edeiya'rika was only one Ryuven against a thousand.

His jaw firmed, and Ariana knew he had made his decision. "We will not be deterred by a Tsuraiya who does not know where her duty lies," he said. "If one thing has been made clear this day, it is that the Ai are degenerate and their roles of honor are honorable no longer. Your Pairvyn stands in defense, your Tsuraiya fights for another people. You did not even come to us honorably, but hid yourself as a human. We will not treat with such degenerates, and we do not fear those who fear to show themselves."

Edeiya'rika's eyes narrowed. "I concealed my nature from the humans in this area who would have thought me one of your raiders. If you doubt my honor, Demus'sho, I am prepared to stand on it."

Demus gave a little push of his chin. "You can prove your honor in open battle, as all warriors should."

"Of course he won't face her directly," Tamaryl observed to Shianan, almost—but not quite—too low to hear. Shianan, looking mildly startled to receive this comradely insight, recovered immediately and gave a single nod, one corner of his mouth raised in an expression that could not properly be called amusement.

Demus'sho had heard the soft words and their sting, and he turned on Tamaryl. "I did not come to duel," he snapped. "I came to carry home victory and goods, and I will not deprive my fighters of their opportunity to win honor and spoils. If the Tsuraiya ni'Ai chooses to debase herself by joining this pathetic force and—"

"Be careful of your words," Mage Parma said. "You may not want to hear them turned against you, shaming you further in reports of your ignoble defeat by a pathetic force."

Demus looked at her and then laughed aloud. "This negotiation is over. We will—"

Mage Parma extended her hands, palms to the ground, and pushed away from her torso. On either side of her, in straight lines between the two opposing parties, the ground boiled and liquefied.

The earth *boiled.*

They all moved back in a single action, gaining distance from the boiling ground and each other. Demus'sho stared at Mage Parma. "What...?"

"We have a custom here, in which one belligerent may draw a line on the ground and dare the other to cross it. That is your line." She brought her hands back to her torso, though she did not cross her arms or otherwise compromise her casting.

Brilliant magic danced in Ariana's vision, distracting again for the first time in years, and she blinked to clear her eyes. It was like when they had used the Shard in the quarry—

The knapsack. Mage Parma had the Shard with her and was using it to enhance her own workings. But how was she managing the surge of power so adroitly?

Mage Parma continued speaking to Demus'sho, her eyes and her voice level. "You have fought a few small deployments sent against small raiding parties. But you have never gone to battle against an alliance of the Great Circle and the Tsuraiya."

Demus tore his gaze from the scorched ground and looked at Mage Parma and Edeiya'rika. "You can't—"

Mage Parma blasted the ground again, drawing longer lines that arced around the end of the negotiation party and curved toward his assembled warriors. The magic did not approach them, but they shifted uneasily in place.

The Shard-enhanced magic glittered in the air, and Ariana blinked it away. How was Edeiya'rika feeding power to the Shard without touching it? How was Elysia Parma using the Shard's power with such accuracy?

A crackling pressure tore her mind from these thoughts, and she looked up with her father, Tamaryl, the others who knew magic. Shianan followed her gaze as Ryuven began to enter the sky.

They appeared and kept coming—a dozen, three dozen, a hundred, two hundred, more. They entered the human world, a sight that should have horrified and galvanized any Mage of the Circle and yet was pure joy to Ariana. The newly-arrived Ryuven split into two neat wings over the Ientu forces. They were all female—the Ai host for defense.

"These are my warriors," Edeiya'rika said. "I will say again: if you open battle here, you open battle with the Ai. We are prepared."

Demus'sho looked at the Ryuven overhead, poised for battle. He looked at Elysia Parma, standing at the center of twin streaks of steaming mud. He set his jaw. "We fight."

"So be it, then," Edeiya'rika said, and her tone somehow managed to simultaneously convey both disappointment and savage glee.

Demus'sho turned without a word or gesture and started back to his warriors. Ariana moved with the others back to their own troops.

"It didn't work," she said softly. "Edeiya'rika brought her warriors, but it didn't work."

"But we are less vulnerable now," Tamaryl answered. "We have more fighters in the air, and better capability against the Ientu magic. No offense, my lord and lady mages."

"None taken," Ariana's father said. "It's no secret they've been giving us trouble. Like my own Silver Mage. King's sweet oats, Elysia, you could have at least taken a harmonizing crystal so I'd have known what you were planning. That you were alive."

"It was lost," Mage Parma answered. "Though I never thought you might worry when you didn't hear from me. I'm sorry for that."

"Of course I would worry when my Silver Mage went missing!" He shook his head. "There's no time for that now; we'll take that up when this battle is won. Edeiya'rika, I must first thank you for your generous aid, and second ask how we can best deploy your fighters alongside our own."

"Indeed," General Septime said gruffly. "I thought it best to stay quietly out of the way for the moment, since I seem to be both the highest rank and the least informed, but would someone care to explain what has happened here?"

Mage Hazelrig gave him a succinct explanation while Tamaryl and Edeiya briefly conferred. "I'll set my warriors to protect the human general and rear," Tamaryl said. "If they won't find that too...uncomfortable."

Shianan looked between them. "But—why waste your fighters? Put them on the lines to help us!"

Tamaryl smiled and shook his head. "Oh, no—mine cannot fight alongside Edeiya'rika's. This is a battle of defense."

Shianan shook his head. "I don't understand. This is our hour of need. If you—"

"There's no time," Ariana said. "They're ready."

But they had prepared for this battle, and it was quick work to add the Ryuven defense. "Keep them out of the way," Mage Parma warned.

Edeiya'rika nodded. "They will be low and far to the flanks."

"But we can use them to harry—" began General Septime.

"Keep them clear," Mage Parma repeated. "I'm sorry to contradict you, general, but our capabilities have changed today. I'll need a clear path to our opponents."

"So I've seen," General Septime said with a nod. "Good enough, my lady mage. Now, everyone to places."

Shianan caught Ariana's wrist, pulled her close, kissed her hard. She tasted the salt and the urgency on his lips. Then he pulled back and, wordlessly, let her go. She felt she should say something, but there was nothing that needed to be said.

Then, by whatever impossible, invisible, inexorable means by which two armies communicate across a declared battlefield, they began to move toward one another.

CHAPTER 49

Ariana had not been present when the fighting began at Arakadamia, and this was not quite so massive a clash, but the swell of sweat and fear and excitement and rage had to be alike. She braced in her position behind the first soldiers and prepared the shields she knew would not be enough.

But Elysia Parma with the Shard would be enough, wouldn't she? And Edeiya'rika?

The Ientu rushed forward, sweeping upward to take clear aim at the first charge of Chrenadan soldiers. Ariana set her shields over the soldiers before her, bracing for the impact she feared.

The first bolt hit her shield and she could not route all the energy away. It burned through her—but not more than she could take. She sucked air, momentarily stunned, and then pulled her watery limbs together. As the enemy Ryuven rose to reset their position, she placed new shields in their path, walls for them to fly into and falter against. One fell, and soldiers rushed to make sure he did not rise.

"Get clear!"

Ariana dropped her shields and instinctively ducked her head.

The sizzle of Elysia Parma's energy blast reverberated through the air, and Ariana squinted against its perceived brilliance. Six Ryuven tumbled from the sky.

Ahead of Ariana, soldiers swore and slowed, and she saw them struggling through the deeper mud of the Silver Mage's boiled earth. The ground no longer steamed, but the terrain was newly treacherous and the Ientu, flying above, were not troubled by it.

Ariana swung both her arms in an upward arc, forming a shield as she went so that it coalesced just in time to meet an incoming Ryuven. He snapped backward, flapped in an attempt to recover, and fell into the entrapping mud. The soldiers stabbed him to stillness.

She formed her next shield too early, and it was already fading by the time the enemy Ryuven struck it. He was thrown back in the air but righted himself and continued on, directing a crackling bolt at a group of soldiers.

Ariana diverted the bolt with an inversion well, bracing herself against the brutal energies. She went down to one knee, pushing the magic into the ground, and for a moment she imagined the earth beneath her boiling as with Mage Parma's strikes.

She wavered as she stood, and she wasn't sure if she saw Shianan's face in the chaos. No, he mustn't see her staggered—he would want to come to her, he would be distracted, and distraction could be fatal—

Shouts and screams blurred around her as she shook off the magic's effects and renewed her fight. She had come for this.

The battle spread across field and sky, and for a moment it seemed there was nothing different, no advantage in the Ai's aid or the Shard's presence.

"Clear the way!"

Elysia Parma and Edeiya'rika pushed through to the front, working together. Ientu Ryuven fell back before their advance and then, rallied by their commanders, converged on that flaring point. They had to put those two down if they meant to keep momentum on the field.

Elysia turned in place, blasting energy in a semi-circle about her as Edeiya'rika, one hand on Elysia's back, moved with her, her other hand raised to guard their rear. The Ientu nearest them could not advance or attack, braced behind their magical shields which glowed in Ariana's sight with the impact.

Then Elysia changed magics, and Ariana recognized the same concussive bolt she had used at Arakadamia, which had flattened much of the field. Though she was behind them, she braced herself and threw a shield over her soldiers. Where was Shianan? There! He was finishing a Ryuven on the ground. She shielded him.

Elysia released a wave of crushing energy just as Ariana had done at Arakadamia, but without the time Ariana had needed to build and compress the blow. Energy rolled outward. The Ientu, not caught unprepared like the Arakadamia troops, staggered backward, braced with shields and knees but unable to withstand its full force. Ariana squinted against the light that was not really there.

And then the Shard-flavored energy snapped, leaving Ariana blinking against nothing.

Some Ientu pulled themselves upright. Others did not. Edeiya'rika swayed, one hand against Elysia's cloaked knapsack, her free hand hovering near her torso.

Mage Parma glared around at the Ientu. "Will you come again?"

A fighter near the end of her semicircular attack roared and charged. He sent two quick bolts ahead of his rush. Elysia Parma deflected hers, but Edeiya'rika was too slow, her gestures muddled, and she folded about the energy's impact and went down.

He roared his victory and went in with his mace, ready to destroy the Tsuraiya ni'Ai with a physical blow, assuring his prestige and place in lore.

Elysia Parma hooked a hemispherical shield about him and slammed him to the ground. She bent and poured two hands' worth of fire into his chest, so that he smoked as he writhed and went still.

Shianan was already running, spear ready, taking a position to the side of the Silver Mage, giving space for each of them to maneuver but remaining near enough to cover from physical attack. Ariana stretched to reach him with a shield.

Tamaryl swooped low, nearly brushing Ariana's hair, and plunged to earth beside Edeiya'rika. He braced beside her like Shianan, the two of them flanking the two Shard-wielders.

Demus'sho shouted something and pushed his way forward through the circle of hesitating fighters. "Why do you stand?" he demanded. "Can't you see she is—"

Elysia hit him with a concentrated stream of white-hot magic. He shielded himself and kept moving, ready to strike back when her attack faltered. She brought her right hand in from the side, drawing a shield like a battering ram. He stumbled and lost control of his own shield for just an instant, and that was enough. She burned through him as she had burned the Ryuven on the ground. Demus'sho died before his watching warriors, and it was not a glorious death.

Elysia Parma glared around at the Ientu, on the ground and in the air. "Who comes next?" she snarled, her eyes blazing.

"Which of you is now in command?" Edeiya'rika's voice was weaker, but Elysia repeated it.

The Ientu looked at one another, and then one raised his chin. "I am Duram'sho."

"There is your sash of office, a bit scorched." Elysia Parma jerked her head toward Demus'sho's corpse. "Do you wish to try your fortune? I am ready for you."

Duram'sho was not ready to command, and he had just seen his Pairvyn fall. Around them, at a little distance, the battle raged, Ientu against Chrenada and Ai, but in this small pocket all eyes were on this pivotal confrontation. Duram'sho scowled. "It would be poor honor to fight when the Pairvyn ni'Ai is on the field—or do the Ai concede their desperation in bringing their males to their battle of defense?"

Tamaryl's wings flexed behind him, arcing over Edeiya'rika and spreading slightly. "Make no mistake, Duram'sho," he said in a low voice that nonetheless carried over the half circle. "When I strike my first blow, this becomes a battle of conquest."

Duram'sho opened his mouth slightly, but he did not answer. Ariana, creeping closer to observe and to be better able to shield Shianan, strained to listen over the clash surrounding them.

But Duram had not been meant to face such a decision for such weighty stakes. He had followed on a simple raid against an easy opponent, and now he was responsible for deciding whether to war against another clan for greater stakes.

There was a buzz of arcane energy about them all, not penetrating Ariana's training but persistent.

Edeiya'rika braced upon one knee and got to her feet. She spread her wings and pushed into the air. Duram'sho followed, his expression growing alarmed.

"This is your final opportunity to end this," Edeiya'rika said clearly. "Retreat, or we continue the battle—and the Pairvyn will pursue you into your own lands, and you will explain to your silth why you have brought war upon your clan."

For a moment they faced one another, wings beating as they circled each other. Below, Elysia Parma raised her hands in preparation to release another stunning blast about her. In the air, the Ai defenders hemmed and corralled the Ientu for Chrenadan archers to target.

Elysia Parma cupped her hands toward him. "Will you fight?"

Ariana held her breath and prayed, implored without words as hard as she had ever prayed in her life.

"No," Duram said, as if the word had barbs which caught in his throat. "No, I cannot invite general war with the Ai without conferring with my silth."

Edeiya'rika nodded and lowered her arm. "Be sure to convey clearly, when you confer, how any further incursions here will be viewed, and how Elysia'rika and I will be waiting for your decision."

Duram'sho turned in place and shouted. One of the Ientu below bent to retrieve the damaged crimson sash from Demus's corpse and held it up for Duram to raise and display with his orders. Edeiya'rika gave her signals, and Ariana watched the fighting ripple into stillness as word was passed in either direction.

Duram'sho drew close with a handful of Ientu sho, conferring, and then he gave Edeiya'rika a curt nod and leapt away from the human world.

The other Ientu followed, leaving little snapping hollows in the air. Ariana's ears ached with the number of them. The rest of the Ientu began to disappear, leaving them alone on the plain with female Ryuven above them and an army behind them.

Edeiya'rika came to earth and her wings sagged. "Essence and flames," she breathed. "That was nearer than I had wanted."

The soldiers behind them began to cheer. Elysia Parma hurried to Edeiya'rika. "How bad is it?"

"What happened?" Ariana asked, rushing forward.

Shianan, ever the commander, was ordering troops into a protective phalanx about the Tsuraiya and Silver Mage, though the enemy was already departing across the between-worlds.

Tamaryl offered his hand to Edeiya. "Take mine, if you have need."

"The Shard," Ariana said breathlessly. "You were using the Shard. But how? How did you have so much control?"

"Clearly not enough," Mage Parma said tersely. "I felt it fail."

"I did too," Ariana realized. "I did not understand it."

"Time enough to sort that later," the Silver Mage said. "Edeiya'rika, how are you?"

But she was already drawing energy from Tamaryl, holding his hand to her forehead, just as Ariana had once seen Maru offer energy to an unconscious Tamaryl. The Tsuraiya ni'Ai closed her eyes and breathed deep, as if pulling the power through her breath, and her shoulders relaxed as Ariana watched.

"I'll be just a moment," she said aloud. Tamaryl put his free hand on her shoulder.

Ariana turned to Shianan, who was directing a soldier into position. She hurried to him. "Shianan!"

He looked at her, his face tight and conflicted, and gave another order to a sergeant, pointing across the field. He turned, checked something behind them, and then at last looked at Ariana. "Is it safe?"

She threw herself at him and embraced him, pulling him tightly to her, closing her arms on stiff armor rather than on his dense strength, but that did not matter, not when she could feel his breath on her hair and know that he was alive and the fighting was ended.

Ewan Hazelrig pushed his way through Shianan's defensive formation. "What's happened? What did you do?"

Elysia Parma looked at him, and her face broke into a creased smile. "I've done what you always wanted."

CHAPTER 50

Fhure House was the reasonable place to gather, with room enough for the officers and mages to assemble with their two remaining Ryuven commanders. Luca met Shianan at the door with the others, and though they said nothing in the flurry of arrangements and helping in some wounded, his relieved expression spoke volumes.

Kraden and his staff were more than a little surprised when Tamaryl and Edeiya entered with Shianan and the officers, but they followed orders, bringing bread and drink and promising a hot meal shortly.

They gathered about a large, long table near a low-burning fireplace which the elder Mage Hazelrig prompted into a blaze, and they tore into the loaves with the hunger of the physically and mentally exhausted. Shianan poured half a pitcher of the sweet spring water down his throat before he even joined the conversation.

"Well," Ewan Hazelrig said, looking across at Edeiya'rika on her bench, "I think we've done it. This is the start of a new alliance, and it's left to us now how to explain this to our king and council. There can be no doubt that we owe Edeiya'rika and the Ai a debt of gratitude, and we should formalize this fledgling friendship."

"Indeed," agreed General Septime. "I hate to think of how today might have gone without our two late arrivals." He looked down the table to Mage Parma. "Although I have to say, I would have preferred to know you were coming, and how."

"That was an unfortunate accident," Mage Parma said, raising her hand to forestall the White Mage's renewed complaints. "I did take a harmonizing crystal—I borrowed one from your office, Ewan, in the expectation that you would notice and carry its mate with you, and I would be able to reach you."

"I did. I even kept it in my hand as often as possible, when time continued to pass, just in case. I wrote half a battle plan with one hand while holding the crystal in the other. But you never contacted me."

She shook her head. "As I said, an accident. The crystal was stolen. By a raven with an expensive eye."

"A bird carried it off?"

"And dumped it into a thicket. I'm sorry, but it's lost. And on that subject..." Mage Parma picked up the knapsack from beside her feet and placed it on the table. She sucked a breath and looked down at the buckle. "I don't know how this will be."

Edeiya'rika nodded. "I know. I felt it too."

Ewan gestured with a resolute expression. "Well, let's see it."

Mage Parma undid the buckle and pulled the knapsack down around the crystalline Shard. At first glance, it looked the same as ever, the length of a man's forearm and faintly purple in its facets. But on closer examination, Shianan saw the fine webbing over its surface, like a poorly glazed crock.

Ewan let out a long sigh. "Well."

"It's not completely destroyed," she observed, only slightly relieved. "But it cannot be used like that again."

The pronouncement did not strike Shianan as brutally as he thought it should have. Yes, the Shard of Elan, their tool for shielding away the Ryuven, was broken, and that left them vulnerable and without a shield. But they had not had a shield for most of his life; that was a luxury of not even a year's time. And more, there was perhaps less need of a shield now than in previous years.

Or perhaps he was just too tired to be able to care yet. They had fought with it only today, after all.

"You broke the Shard of Elan." General Septime was better able to process the significance than Shianan, judging by the controlled horror in his expression. "The Shard..."

"It's not in pieces," the White Mage said, "and we have more than benefited from it."

"I felt it break," Ariana said. "I didn't know exactly what had happened, but I felt when it did."

Mage Parma and Edeiya'rika nodded.

"And—that was when you were challenging the Ientu." Ariana stared at her. "You knew it had failed, you knew you did not have the magic any longer to defend yourself, and you stayed steady."

"I didn't dare to give them the opportunity to recover." Mage Parma smiled. "I may be finally ready to join those bluffing strategy games they play at the public houses. If they'll allow a mage to join."

"Tamaryl'sho? Did you know Edeiya'rika would bring her host?"

Tamaryl shook his head. "I hoped. But I did not know."

"Did none of you receive my messages?" demanded Mage Parma.

"We had one," Mage Ewan Hazelrig answered. "It said you were coming, and that was all."

"Well, I could hardly put in writing that the Tsuraiya ni'Ai was bringing a defensive force," Mage Parma answered practically. "But the rest?"

They all looked at her blankly.

"After the harmonization crystal was shattered, I stopped a passing tinker and asked him to deliver word. Edeiya'rika and I were in the wilds when we sensed the Ientu crossing, and we compressed as much experimentation with the Shard and ourselves as we could fit into our days and nights. I found a scribe so we could save the time of writing out our findings, and I sent as many messages as I could: several to assure you we were coming and some to warn villages about the coming battle. Edeiya'rika returned to call her defensive force, and I sent to both sides to request negotiations, hoping we would be in time."

"I'm afraid my less alarming form is also less efficient for travel," Edeiya'rika said with a wry smile. "And essence, how it itches."

"So we have learned quite a lot about human and Ryuven magic," Mage Parma continued, "and how it can work together with an accommodating medium. But clearly the medium cannot take such a strain repeatedly and continuously."

"If we had not used it today," Mage Ewan Hazelrig said, "if the Shard had remained in Alham, we would have unnecessarily sacrificed many lives and given hope to our opponents to lure them here again. That firm opposition today will keep them out of Chrenada for longer."

Edeiya'rika grinned. "Indeed." She turned, her eyebrows lifted. "A war of conquest, Tamaryl'sho?"

He shrugged. "I could not dishonor either of us by openly participating in a battle of defense."

Shianan's brain was muddled with fatigue. "So you came to defend Chrenada as if it were an Ai territory?"

"An Ai interest," she corrected mildly but firmly. "We have laid no claim to Chrenada—and of course I as Tsuraiya could not claim land anyway."

Shianan caught himself reaching for his aching shoulder and stopped his hand. Ariana gave him a quick worried glance, and he shook his head. No need to worry her over common post-fighting hurts.

"Hot food, as I'm sure you're wanting," announced Marta, appearing with a number of servants, all bearing trays and steaming bowls. "We've got squash soup, and roasted root vegetables, and warm rolls full of cheese, and more, so tuck in."

It wasn't at all the formal service of the capital, but Marta had likely never seen a town larger than the village outside the oaken doors, and the general and mages and Ryuven did not appear to mind in the least. They set upon the food with glee and delight.

Marla was there, too, watching from a little distance away. Shianan wondered if she watched for Luca, who was pouring water and wine for the guests. For a single heartbeat Shianan remembered his faint envy of the slaves, and how foolish that was, and how good it was now that he had his own wife under his own roof.

Then he remembered that he had given his room to General Septime. He could hardly ask the general to return his room so he could bed the woman he had been ordered to keep at a distance.

The others would also be given rooms; the two Mages Hazelrig, Mage Parma, Tamaryl'sho, Edeiya'rika... He could not recall how many rooms the house boasted, but it was not enough. And the hall would be filled with wounded and their caretakers. He hoped Ariana at least had been given her own room, rather than sharing.

"There is much to do," General Septime said, "but much of it can wait until the morning. We have set scouts and sentries, and a watch for the night, so sleep well."

Shianan rose from the bench with the others and paused to warm his hands at the fire, watching them move toward the stairs. Ariana and Mage Parma stayed near one another as they walked, and he could not guess if that meant they were going to the same room or just to the same corridor. He would have to invent a question to knock and ask, or set Luca to learn from the servants.

"Will you sit, master?"

He jumped and turned to find Marla standing an arm's length from him. She had her basket of oils and wooden implements.

He shook his head. "I'm fine."

"With respect, master, you are not," she answered. "I had my hands on your shoulder only yesterday. You haven't sat up straight all night, and you keep your right arm close and low. If you reach for something at a distance, you do it with your left hand, though the right is your usual preference."

King's oats, he was the only man he knew whose slaves spoke

to him as if he were an unruly child. He blew out his breath. "Of course I'm sore. Battle fatigue." And staying awake in the hateful rain to fret over the consequences of killing one of the Ryuven who'd come to fight with them.

She gave him a flat look. "And would it not be splendid if you had someone especially trained to address fatigue and soreness after a battle."

'Soats, no wonder she and Luca got on well. "All right. But just for a short while; I have other business." Though it would not do to knock on Ariana's door so quickly.

If Marla guessed what that business was—but no, she had no reason to suspect. He followed her to the storeroom. She gestured him face-down onto the bench and he obeyed, shrugging out of his tunic and shirt as he went. She poured oil onto her hands and began rubbing them together to warm it. "I'll start with general work, for all of today, and then I'll look again at your shoulder."

He did not answer. He was wondering if Ariana was thinking of him. He almost wished he had put Marla off. How many times he had longed for something like this after a battle, and yet now he could hardly convince himself to stay as he wanted something else.

He had not realized how taut his muscles remained after the day's exertion and fears until she touched him, and then it ran out of him in a rush. He drew a breath, and it felt odd to inhale so deeply. The relief was almost dizzying, though he was lying down.

"Tell me if something hurts more particularly. I don't want to aggravate any muscle tears." Marla began to press and pull his tired muscles. He should have asked for her help before now—he should have asked after Arakadamia, when his efforts to save Prince Soren had left him shaking and aching for days.

Her hands, moving in ceaseless tempo which lulled him into compliance even when he wanted to shield a sore place, slid gradually to his shoulder, questing. He flinched as her fingers probed. "With the battle finished," she said softly, "let me work on this impingement here." The pressure of her fingers hurt, but in a way that promised relief rather than just pain. The soft tissue over the top of his shoulder yielded to her work. "Why didn't you have this seen to?"

"You were here at Fhure. I was in Alham."

"You could have found an aelipto in Alham, and I can tell that none has touched you. Adhesions take time to form."

"I did not want it," Shianan said defensively, and then he

wondered why. Then he wondered when Ariana's questioning gaze had taken root in his mind for when she was not present herself.

"Stubborn," Marla sighed, wriggling her thumb into a tender place along his shoulder blade.

But Shianan had another reason, drawn out by the questions he would not answer aloud. He could not afford to acknowledge lasting injury, not as a demon commander and not as a man who had known no other life, no other worth. If he could be injured, he would be less valiant to the soldiers he led, and if he could be injured, he would be less valuable to the king and country he had ever served as a soldier.

Anger flashed, for once again selling himself for a price he had not set, and he clenched his fists.

"Ah," observed Marla, and she squeezed something in his neck that screamed in answer. He tried to pull away, but he was already flat against the bench.

She released immediately. "I'm sorry—I didn't realize how tender that would be. I think I've found another cause of your shoulder pain."

"That's my neck," he said irritably.

"Which is connected to your shoulder." She added another oil to her fingers, and it burned a little when she touched the place again. "You took quite the blow, master. A kick to the head, or falling hard into a wall."

Or flipping over the shoulder of a stumbling horse. "I am a soldier."

"And I am an aelipto," she repeatedly gently. "Do your work, but then let us do ours."

"Hrmph," he grunted, because he did not have another answer to give.

"It will take more than one session to help this," she said, lifting and stretching his neck. He instinctively braced, but the expected flash of pain did not come—and he realized he had expected pain, though he had not admitted it even to himself. He admired and resented her keen observation.

"You have tonight," he said. "Then I'm back to Alham."

"As I said, there are aelipto in Alham. Or, I am your servant, and I could travel with you to do my work in Alham."

He grunted again. But her work did feel good, and he was breathing more easily than he had in a long, long time.

She left his neck and worked down the length of his spine, gradually convincing the tense muscles to relax and lengthen, and at last she withdrew her hands and began to towel the oil from him. "That's finished, then."

He was surprised by his disappointment. "Ah."

"Well, you took off only your shirt. I'll start with your legs the next time."

Shianan did not complain. He pushed himself up, surprised at how heavy his body felt, and how his legs ached by comparison now. But he also felt relieved.

He dressed. "Where is Luca?"

CHAPTER 51

Shianan felt self-conscious and foolish, tip-toeing through his own house and guessing at rooms. The east-facing dragon room, Kraden had said, but Shianan would not be able to see through closed doors which room was decorated with mythical beasts or which faced the rising sun. The third door on the right, Luca had said, but now that Shianan was in the wing itself, he was not sure if that included the door to the little storeroom behind the stairs.

If he knocked at the wrong door...

He paused and chewed the inside of his cheek until an excuse came to him. He would ask if they needed water or blankets. That would be reasonable as a good host, right?

In a corner, two doors nearly adjoined, and Shianan stopped at the right-hand one. This was the door. Unless it wasn't. He imagined the elder Mage Hazelrig coming to the door, and that was humiliating—but at least Mage Hazelrig would know the reason and would not suppose anything he was not to know.

King's oats, what if he knocked at Tamaryl's door?

Or Mage Parma's?

Hesitation would win nothing. He lifted his hand and rapped at the door, almost too softly to be heard.

For a moment there was nothing, and he could not tell whether he was disappointed or relieved, and then he heard Ariana call, "Just a moment!" He drew a great breath, glad he had guessed correctly, and set his hand on the doorframe so that he could lean close to her when she opened.

Her face broke into a smile as she saw him, and that warmed him more than any warmed blanket on an icy night. "Shh," she warned, though he'd said nothing. She gestured to the other door. "This is Mage Parma."

"I'm glad I chose correctly."

She snorted. "I don't think you would have been left in error for long. Now, come inside."

There was so much to discuss and to plan—with the successful alliance against the Ientu, the treaty with the Ai had been reinforced and forged stronger, and the chance of real peace was more secure than ever. The new treaty would change their defensive roles in small or large ways. And most importantly, their clandestine marriage would no longer be sheltered in the frantic bustle of impending war, and they should form a plan for when the king discovered it.

There was so much to discuss and so much to plan, but there was so much to celebrate, and Ariana flung her arms about him and whispered through the kisses on his neck, "I'm so glad you're all right," and then against his jaw, "I love you," and then she moved to the hollow under his ear and there was no more space for words.

When they had time and breath again, they drew the blankets high and lay close, basking in the nearness of each other. Shianan hugged Ariana close, blowing away her hair which tickled his nose and caught on his stubble, pressing her warm back against his bare chest, catching her feet with his. He closed his eyes and drifted, happy. He could not stay, not with so many people in the house and Mage Parma just next door, but he could remain for just a few minutes to soak in the joy of marriage.

Shianan woke to pounding on the door. He thought first of Ryuven attack, and then of discovery of his visit to Ariana, warm against his side, and he fought the blankets to push free and reach for his clothing or a weapon against the incoming royal guards.

But it was Luca's voice coming through the door. "Lady Ariana! Master Shianan!"

Shianan reached for his clothing instead of his knife. But it could still be either Ryuven or discovery. "We're coming. What is it?"

"The village is on fire."

Shianan swore and pulled his shirt over his head. Behind him Ariana slid into her field trousers and nodded for Shianan to open the door.

He did, just enough for Luca to slide through the gap. Luca saw Ariana adjusting her blouse and turned slightly, more for the assuring appearance than for the necessity, as his eyes were fixed on Shianan. "They say it was Ryuven."

"Of course it was," Shianan muttered. "Wasn't it too simple? They would not give up such a basket of spoils with such a humiliating concession." He jerked his belt tight. "Someone's gone to General Septime?"

"One of his aides. And someone to Mage Hazelrig."

Shianan's heart lurched. "And to Mage Parma, no doubt, so I'll need to be elsewhere."

"Go now," Ariana said, pulling her black robe over her shoulders. "Luca can knock at her door next as you go."

Shianan nodded, paused just long enough to kiss her, and let Luca open the door and nod that the corridor was clear. Shianan left at a run, his boots in his hand.

Ryuven attack on the village. His village. His village, at Fhure, which he had neglected and left to itself and now had left undefended while he slept within sturdy stone walls. His village.

His hands knew how to arm for battle at speed, even while his mind was occupied with anger and strategy. The village was not far from the main house; he had passed through it a dozen times during his last stay. The army camp was three miles away, though, to keep a buffer between soldiers and villagers, and even if sentries had seen the flames, they would need time to organize and to march.

What if it was another ambush? What if the village was burned to draw the soldiers out in disarray and to flank them in the dark?

He had to trust his officers. Captain Torg was a solid man and wise; he would not let the soldiers rush out unprepared. Shianan could not reach them in time; he had to trust his officers and do what he could at the village.

How had so many Ryuven returned so quickly?

General Septime was nearly as fast as Shianan. "What are our best approaches?" he asked without preamble, lacing his tunic. Two aides followed with weapons, cloak, and a box for writing and distributing orders.

Shianan cursed himself for not knowing the village as well as he should. "There are hills to the north and east, and it's wooded nearly all around. The road from the west is the widest flat space, and that's opposite this house. If it's an ambush, they'll have plenty of cover but little maneuverability."

Septime nodded. "Let's see what we have."

The mages were descending, joining them in the hall, and Shianan felt a moment of conflict when Tamaryl and Edeiya came in, their faces drawn in worry. But no, they had not wanted this, and he pushed down his suspicion to focus on practical action. The group went out into the night.

Even at a distance, it was clear the village was not merely burning, but was destroyed. It could not be only a building or two, not with the conflagration they saw before them. Shianan's gut twisted.

They ran.

Tamaryl and Edeiya took to the sky, soaring ahead. Shianan had covered half the distance when they returned and swept low to land running. Edeiya had her hand to her upper arm, slowing the flow of blood as a wound began to close. "It was assuredly a Ryuven attack," she reported dryly, "and the villagers are afraid."

Shianan groaned inwardly.

Edeiya's arm had sealed by the time Shianan sighted the group huddling at the side of the road, where an oak tree offered dense shelter from above. "I'm Commander Becknam," he announced himself, "with friends and aid coming behind me. What's happened?"

A man raised a bow and released toward the Ryuven well behind Shianan. Edeiya'rika gestured a shield about herself as he released. The arrow glanced off into the road, and Shianan pushed forward. "Stop! They have come with me."

Some people were on the ground, cradling crushed arms or bleeding heads. "Ryuven attacked," a woman said, coming toward Shianan and watching Tamaryl and Edeiya warily. "They fired the houses and struck us as we ran for water. We couldn't fight so many fires, and not with Ryuven swooping down with maces and axes. We had to flee into the trees. Some of us gathered here."

"The soldiers are coming," Shianan said, secure in the belief they would have seen the leaping flames.

"The raiders have already gone," a man protested. "The Ryuven set the fires, drove us out, and burgled our stores. Some of us tried to defend our homes, but you can see how that ended." He had a bloody arm in a sling. "Then they left, like they do. A fire raid."

"There was a battle today, and then they came here," someone called from the rear. "And then they came here! What did the soldiers do? Anything at all?"

The others were catching up, breathing hard. Shianan held up a hand. "We can discuss how this came about after we've taken care of the wounded. How many of the village are here?"

"Don't you know your own people?" growled a voice, barely audible, and the words stung.

"Help!" A man limped hurriedly up the road from the burning village, a shadow against the fires. "Is there any water? A ladder?"

"What is it?" the woman who had spoken first asked him. "Reg, where are your children?"

"They're in the loft," he gasped, pausing and stooping. Others gathered around him to support him and press for answers. "They're in the loft, Holy One help them, and the whole stairs aflame."

"The mill," the woman interpreted for Shianan. "Sweet Holy One, those children."

"Show me," Shianan said. He turned and shouted. "Tamaryl'sho! This way."

CHAPTER 52

The mill was not on the primary road but down a slope, extending over the stream which powered it. Of course, the mill would have been a primary target for a Ryuven raid, with so much grain gathered in one location—and burning it sent a clear message to their human opponents.

Shianan slowed and stared at the burning building. The waterwheel, still turning, was nearly intact, along with the axle it splashed with every rotation. But the walls and floors were burning about the stone base, and the fire would be eating into the central trunk-pillars that supported the upper floors.

The limping miller could not keep up, but his shouts were clear enough, and anyway Shianan could see them—two children in an open window on the topmost floor, a narrow room over the wide lower levels. They clung to one another but did not wave—overwhelmed by terror or smoke.

The group gathered, winded with their fresh sprints. "Dear Holy One," Ariana gasped, sighting them.

"Tamaryl'sho," Shianan said, "can you reach them?"

"No."

"What?" Shianan turned on the Pairvyn. "Fly up for them!"

"I cannot," Tamaryl answered heavily. "I can get to the window, yes, but I cannot carry them out, not from a still start. Even a child is too much weight to lift from a standstill. We would plunge straight into the fire."

Edeiya'rika nodded slowly. "Not even two together, not with having to crouch and squeeze our wings through that window. Maybe if they had a proper landing platform—but no, not to carry them off again."

"Wool blankets, wool cloaks!" a village woman shouted. "Bring all that's wool! Soak it in the stream!"

"What about the waterwheel?" Ariana asked. "Is that a way in?"

But the fire had claimed all that was not the wheel, hissing its fury with each splash. Shianan guessed the stairs and ladders were already impassible, and the floor going. There was no way to guess how long the pillars would last.

Despair crawled over Shianan, sickening him. He had seen losses, many losses, but not children of the village under his protection, not on the very day they were supposed to have turned away the enemy...

Mage Ewan Hazelrig put out a hand. "Elysia, you're the best with shields. Could you catch them? Break their fall above the flames?"

The Silver Mage pursed her lips, considering. "Yes...yes. But even if I maintained the shield, they would be hanging over the fire. We could try another moving shield to knock them away from the mill and into the stream, but it could merely shove them into the fire, or if I threw them far enough to be clear, that impact would likely break them. And if I was at all wrong, they would burn."

"But you could make a platform for them to land on?" Shianan asked.

Mage Parma pressed her mouth into a line. "If you could convince two terrified children to step out of a burning window onto an invisible plane hanging over a pool of flames, and without being able to speak with them, then yes, I could."

She was right; the fire was too loud to shout anything to them, much less to coax them into anything so counter-intuitive as jumping from a building into the flames.

Someone would have to go.

A terrifying idea came to him. "The shield—you can make it like a platform?"

Mage Parma nodded. "Yes, I can spread it about—oh." Her eyes widened, and for a moment she only stared at him. Then she began to calculate. "I can make it about five or six feet wide if I concentrate, but reliably about two feet if I'm working very quickly."

"Do something!" someone cried, as if it were only lack of prompting that kept them still.

"The supports are going to burn through," someone else said. "When those millstones break free, they'll take down the whole building."

Shianan's tongue stuck to the roof of his mouth, but he made himself say, "There's no other way I can see to make it."

"I can't cast fast enough," Mage Parma said. "Ewan, Ariana, I'll need you. Edeiya'rika, you too, please. Tamaryl'sho, if you could." She looked around at them. "We'll have to cast shields in sequence, very fast."

"But even if we're casting in succession, he'll still have to move from one shield to another, and he can't pass through—" Edeiya'rika stopped. "Oh, by the Essence. I see."

"Bring me those woolens!" Shianan wrapped two sodden blankets around himself and jigged in place. "We have to do it now. There's no time to debate."

"Give us one chance to rehearse," Mage Parma said. "In order, myself, Ewan, Edeiya'rika, Tamaryl'sho, Ariana, myself again. What's your stride, commander?"

Shianan had no reason to know, so he made a short dash and turned back to them. "About so?"

"We'll layer as closely as possible, and very fast. On my lead."

She gestured, and in rapid sequence the other magic-workers mimicked the movement, their attention trailing away together as they examined something Shianan could not perceive.

"That wasn't clean," Ariana said worriedly.

"We don't have time to practice further," Mage Parma said. "Get it right. Commander, keep your eyes on the window, and king's sweet oats, keep your pace steady."

He jerked a nod, threw a quick agonized look at Ariana—*I love you*—and ran toward the burning mill.

He fixed his eyes on the window, and his feet drummed the ground. A steady pace, steady pace. This was madness. He squinted against the heat as he neared the mill. Steady pace.

The next step came short, his foot striking just before reaching the ground, and he nearly stumbled. *Steady pace!* He kept his eyes forward, not looking down at the ground he ran over without touching, not allowing himself to feel how the invisible stepping stones gave slightly with each stride, as if he ran on dough or half-dried mud, sucking energy with each step but *steady pace!*

The sequence of rapid shields climbed through the surrounding fire. Flames licked the underside of his invisible path and coiled about the sides, so that sometimes he could see the way by where they curved. *Keep your eyes on the window.* There was not time to think about all the ways this should fail. If even one step was a heartbeat late or a hand-span away...

The window! He grasped for it, pulled himself into it, burning his fingers against the smoldering frame. He tried to pant after his sprint and his fear, but the air was hot and thick and he coughed until he remembered to pull his wet cloak up over his mouth and nose. It slowed the smoke, but the hungry fire devoured the air, leaving little for him.

A boy and a girl gaped at him, their hair singed, streaks showing where tears dried on their faces, choking as they stared. Shianan reached for them. "Hurry!" He drew them in and half-knelt, shouting over the roar of the flames. "You, on my back, under the cloak and blanket. You, here on my chest. You must hold tight. You must hold very, very tight, and keep your eyes closed. Do you understand?"

There was no time to wait for understanding. He rose, balancing their weight, and crossed one arm over the child in front, grasping the arm of the other so that it could not throttle him as the child gripped tighter. He tugged the woolen blankets over them and went to the window. "Eyes closed, now!"

He looked down through the smoke to the hungry orange flames. There was nothing to suggest a shield, no hint of the magic that had miraculously carried him here. He had to plunge from the window into wild conflagration, trusting to the mages and the Ryuven.

The children squeezed him, their fists balled into his shirt and their fingers clawing his torso. He would kill all three of them if the shield was not there, or if he missed it. He tried to look to the mages for reassurance, but the smoke from below was too thick. Could they see him? Could they even see well enough to place the magic?

The floor crackled like whips as flames pierced between the boards. Shianan breathed, "Sweet Holy One, save us," and swung out the window.

His feet landed on a surface, unseen but real and slightly mushy. It gave beneath him, and he rushed forward to the next, nearly tripping on the gap between them. The stumble frightened him, and he dared not run despite the sinking support. He kept moving, one arm on each child, gritting his teeth and sucking air through his cloak and praying with each step that the next would be there.

He was about six feet from the window when the millstones groaned free. A whirling storm of sparks and flame rushed up to Shianan's left, and he flinched. A child writhed in fear at the movement, Shianan over-corrected, and his next foot met only hot air.

He had no breath to scream. He flung an arm out in a futile effort to catch himself against nothing, and his palm struck something solid, something that should not have been there in the empty air. He shoved against it and got himself upright. *Forward! Steady pace!* He pressed on, eyes squinted against the scorching heat, feeling for the way with each step but moving too fast to stop himself if he fell again.

Holy One, he could see the end. He could see the bank, ground without flames, the crowd of villagers, the magic-wielders pressed close together. He made a final rush forward.

Too fast! He outran the next shield and his boot slid off the forward edge. He rotated, again cast for something to save him, fell. He clamped hard about the children, as if he could do anything for them as they rolled into flames.

Something caught him, cradled him in a gentle curve, as if he fell into an enormous mixing bowl. He choked on savage relief and rocked upright, feeling for an invisible bridge that should be near, found it. He hugged the children close and stumbled down the last stretch, falling to his knees upon the dark ground, seeing nothing with his fire-dazzled eyes.

Hands fell on him, many hands, pulling aside the steaming woolen blankets to draw away the children, and he wanted to tell them to move aside, that they were blocking the air, even though he knew it was the smoke in his lungs and not the crowding villagers. Someone put a cup to his mouth and he tried to gulp water and air at once, coughing harder.

And then Ariana had him, and though he could not see her through his smoke-burned eyes and coughing he knew it was her, and she pressed her teary face to his and said words he could not understand.

CHAPTER 53

Everything hurt.

Shianan was in his own bed in Fhure House, and the sun slanted through the narrow window and threw a bright rectangle across the foot of his bed and the floor toward the door. His whole body ached; that was typical after a battle. His ribs and gut felt as if he'd been kicked repeatedly, and instinctively he tried to suppress the coughing that came upon him—but he wanted air, and so he coughed, and the effort knifed through him.

He was curled on his side, coughing shallowly and trying not to vomit, when the door opened and Ariana came in. She muttered something and rushed to the side of the bed. "Breathe slowly! I know, it's easy for me to say, but try to slow down. Here, let me get another cloth." She splashed a moment at a table and turned back to him, pressing a wet rag over his mouth. "Moist air will help. You had a lot of smoke last night."

Shianan could smell it, could taste it. He was still in his smoky clothes, he realized, half-dressed beneath his blankets. His hair, loose in its tangled tail, reeked of smoke. His lips were singed, he thought, dry and crackling. "Ugh," he managed.

"I'm sure. Do you want a drink?"

She helped him up, more than he needed but her touch felt good, and gave him a cup of the spring water. He gulped it and immediately began coughing, spraying droplets. "How are the children?" he croaked. They had been in the smoke longer than he had.

Ariana looked serious. "The physicker said their windpipes were singed and swelling. To be honest, we're worried for them. But they're better than they would have been, if you had not gone for them."

Shianan closed his eyes, too tired to feel joy or relief or frustration or hope. He wanted sleep, and clean air.

"It's just like you to wake during the two minutes I haven't been by your side," Ariana said with mock sternness, taking the chair already beside the bed.

"Perhaps the door woke me as you left," Shianan guessed. "You were here all night?"

"And I did not even have to conceal it. Caring for a wounded hero is an acceptable reason to visit a man's room. Even if he's only singed a little."

"Luca?"

"The servants have been running all night, putting up the villagers and treating injuries and preparing meals and medicines. There's the others, too—General Septime is ordering the defense and recovery from here. The soldiers got most of the fires out. My father and Mage Parma are sweeping for Ientu who might still be nearby, and Tamaryl'sho and Edeiya'rika went back to report to Oniwe'aru. The whole house is a beehive."

Shianan understood, but still he wished Luca were near.

"I'll bring Luca back with me. I have to go down for your medicine; they've been scavenging in the surviving houses and the woods for the right ingredients, since the herbalist's shed burned, and I was to ask again when you were awake. I'll see what they've put together."

She left him lying against the pillow, staring upward into the worry that if the Ryuven had been able to return so quickly once, they might again. The mages had given days' warning of the Ientu's invasion, but no one had warned of this; had this raid been a smaller, separate group, traveling at the same time?

When would they come again, and would Shianan know?

At the edge of the hall, where servants and patients and villagers crowded for space, Mage Parma caught Ariana's arm and held her back a moment. "A word, Mage Hazelrig, if you please."

The warning tone made Ariana's stomach leap as if she were an apprentice caught substituting powders to prank a friend. "Yes?"

Mage Parma must have read her expression. "I have no interest in chiding you; I only offer a word of caution. Tending an injured soldier is one thing, but if I notice you kissing Commander Becknam during an unguarded moment of celebration or opening your room to him at night, then others may notice as well." She tipped her head. "I offer no comment on either. Strange things can happen in the desperate times when one believes one is about to die or suddenly finds that one has lived, only—"

"We're married."

Mage Parma stopped, considered, and at last smiled. "Good."

"Not just—not just now, but we have registered the marriage in Alham and all."

"Well, good for you." Mage Parma gave her a hug. "I'm glad you found your way."

"We're still finding it," Ariana admitted. "You're the first I've told other than my father."

"I have so much confidence in you." She regarded Ariana fondly. "So much. Now, let's turn back to our work."

Ariana's return interrupted Shianan's fretting. "Here's lobelia, and marsh mallow, and a sort of mushroom I don't know. They tell me it will help to clear your lungs and soothe the irritation."

"At least it will distract me. What must all that taste like?"

"Better than smoke, I'm sure. Drink this," Ariana directed. "And don't argue, or I'll turn you into a newt and dunk you in it."

Shianan blinked. "You're quite the wyvern when I'm injured and helpless."

"I prefer you uninjured, and you'll heal faster if you're bullied into taking your medicine." Ariana took back the empty cup. "Here is a sachet of lavender. Hold it close to your nose."

Shianan scowled. "Do I look like a lady's maid needing something to simper behind?"

"Don't be contrary. I have more air than you and can argue longer." Ariana folded his fingers about the sachet and rested his hand near his chin. The scent reached him almost immediately, and he wrinkled his nose. But it wasn't unpleasant, just strong. After a moment he sniffed, testing the scent, and noted that he had not coughed with the attempt.

Ariana eased herself onto the bed beside him, careful not to jostle him. "And now, take this and hold it over your chest." She presented a mage healing amulet and began to activate it.

"'Soats, why didn't you give me that to start?" Shianan pressed it against his heart, bracing against the swell of heat.

"I only just found one that wasn't spoken for. We had a battle yesterday, you know. And if I'd given you that first, you would have refused the mushrooms, and don't deny it."

Shianan flinched with the uncomfortable healing and thought of something worrisome. "If there weren't many amulets—what about the children? You said they weren't doing well..."

Ariana shook her head and pressed her hand over the amulet, pushing it back where he'd unconsciously pulled it from his chest. "Oh, no, they each have one. We carried them into the hall and injured soldiers all around offered their own amulets. We had to turn them all down, some repeatedly. You have good troops." She smiled. "They follow their leader."

Shianan shifted, embarrassed, and disguised it with another flinch from the amulet. "Can't you mages make these so that getting well doesn't feel like getting hurt?"

Ariana made a face. "If it didn't sting a little, you soldiers would grow careless and get yourselves in trouble all the time and we'd never keep up."

But he could not focus on banter, not even with her leaning comfortably close. "What does this mean?" Shianan asked, his voice catching hoarsely. "If the Ientu agree to withdraw and then come back to raid, what then? Or was this even the Ientu?"

Ariana shook her head. "I don't think it was an Ai raid under the cover of the Ientu invasion," she said. "It might have been a second Ientu group, I suppose. That would be a good tactic."

"Very good," agreed Shianan resentfully. "Deceitful and effective."

"It's possible they didn't know of the withdrawal at the battle," Ariana said, but she did not sound convinced.

She looked suddenly upward, as if something had moved on the ceiling. Shianan followed her eyes and saw nothing. "What?"

"They've returned. Ryuven just arrived, only two."

"Double-dyed mages," Shianan muttered. "Is there anything to wear that doesn't smell of smoke and singed wool? I want to go down to see them."

"But—"

"I drank the mushroom broth, and now it's my turn to insist." Shianan paused. "This is my land, my village, my people. I should have done better for them. The least I can do now is to be present to ask what happened to them."

Every movement seemed to need more air than it should, but his breathing was growing easier, and he was soon dressed in fresher clothing. He hung the amulet about his neck, letting it rest burning against his chest to continue the healing. Ariana kept a concerned eye on him as he made his way down the corridor, but he felt stable enough. He descended the stairs toward the growing voices marking the Ryuven arrival.

Shianan did not allow himself to wonder if Mage Parma looked too long at them. Did she know? Heat prickled at his neck and his stomach churned. What would it be, just to be what he was, hiding nothing, never holding his breath for the second boot to fall?

Shianan stepped into the hall, gingerly, and a ripple went through the crowd as he was recognized. Shianan saw them turning, felt their eyes, and he set his jaw as he always did.

They began to cheer.

For just a heartbeat he stared, amazed, and then warmth flooded his chest in a way that had nothing to do with his inflamed lungs. The servants, the soldiers, the villagers sheltering in Fhure House after their homes were destroyed—they cheered him.

Shianan swallowed against the nut in his throat. Ariana stopped to one side and gave him a shy, proud smile.

"Commander." Mage Ewan Hazelrig raised a hand to beckon him toward the hall's front. "Tamaryl'sho and Edeiya'rika have returned, and I think you'll want to hear the news."

But it wasn't the Ryuven whom Mage Hazelrig turned to when Shianan reached them, but a spotty youth with wild hair that stood up like sheaves of grain. "Say again what you saw."

"Dead Ryuven," the boy answered promptly. "Lots of them. A whole field of them."

Shianan didn't understand. "They left their dead after the battle, of—"

"No, my lord, this isn't there. This is a field of them, at the grazing." The boy looked around eagerly. "I can show you. I can take you there."

"That would be best," agreed Mage Hazelrig.

Chapter 54

Shianan walked out with them, feeling an uncomfortable pull in his chest even with the easy pace but able to keep up without the struggle being too evident. He put a hand to the amulet beneath his shirt to press it against his chest as he walked.

Luca appeared beside him. “How are you?”

Shianan was glad to see him. “Recovering.”

“You’re holding in your lungs.”

“That’s the amulet.”

That was not enough for Luca, whose expression worked between relief and anger. “I wasn’t—you could have died.”

Shianan, surprised at his intensity, tried to make a lighter response. “I was on a battlefield yesterday. I could have died there, too.”

“You’re trained to fight, at least. No one is trained to walk through fire.”

“I ran.”

Luca’s jaw bulged. “That’s not what I mean.”

Shianan began to understand. “Do you mean that I did something bold and yet foolish, putting myself at risk, and it was only for two innocent children, not a worthless Gehrn priest who deserved prison at the least?”

Luca gave him a sidelong glance. “That’s unfair.”

“Is it?”

“I never shouted at you.”

Shianan flinched. “I—I’m sorry. I was worried.”

Luca looked ahead. “And how do you think I felt when they dragged you in, wheezing and tripping on an empty floor? And I couldn’t even sit with you, because there were three dozen more people who needed patching and care?”

“I’m sorry.” Shianan put a hand on Luca’s shoulder. “I’m glad you helped them.”

Luca blew out his breath. “Of course I did.”

“Of course you did.”

The youth led them to the south of the village, where the geese and ducks were taken to forage. The green was marked with dead

Ryuven, scattered mostly separately but occasionally near one another, facing each other with cold, unseeing eyes.

"Flame and essence," breathed Tamaryl. "They did it."

"What?" Shianan asked.

"They pulled a slingshot."

The words meant nothing to Shianan, and he looked toward Ariana, but she only shook her head, her eyebrows raised to share her confusion. Mage Ewan Hazelrig's and Mage Parma's expressions showed no understanding, either, but Mage Hazelrig was quick to ask. "What do you mean, pulled a slingshot?"

"I thought it was primarily hypothetical," Edeiya'rika murmured, looking about the green. "No one actually tries it." She approached the nearest corpse and knelt an arm's reach away from it.

"It is a method of traveling in the—what you would call the between-worlds," Tamaryl answered. "It is a way of traveling without committing to crossing." He glanced from the mages to Shianan and Marshal Vanguilder. "In the between-worlds there are lanes, of sorts, places where travel is easier."

"The Leaping Plain," Ariana volunteered. "You said it is easier to travel from there to our world."

"Yes, exactly. There are places where it is easier to cross into the between-worlds, and paths in the between-worlds itself that are easier to travel. These are easier still for a sho than a nim, through both can make the journey."

They nodded, listening.

"If one wishes to enter the between-worlds and immediately exit again, without losing time in actual travel across to the other—that is what we lightly call a slingshot. One leaps along a path, but uses the natural resistance of the between-worlds to check energy and then... I suppose it might be something like running down a street and then grasping a column at a corner to help turn, only then you turn and sprint directly through the column."

Shianan shook his head. "I understood none of that."

"The technique does not matter. The practice is leaping in but immediately circling and leaping out again. It does not cross the between-worlds. One enters, skims along the void, and then attempts to re-emerge. It is not easy."

"And it is not safe," Mage Parma observed dryly, looking over the range of bodies.

Tamaryl shook his head. "No, it is not safe. For all the dead we see here, there were probably twice again left within the between-worlds itself, lost entirely."

Shianan looked about them at the Ryuven abandoned on the grass by their own.

"Why?" Ariana asked. "Did they sacrifice their own warriors just to return before we could expect them?"

Tamaryl nodded. "That is exactly it." He turned to Shianan. "It is much the same as force-marching your soldiers through a desert to reach a battlefield—and then, upon coming out of the desert, setting immediately upon the enemy without rest or recovery, lest you lose the advantage of surprise. It is a strong move, if your target does not have time to prepare their own advantage of strength, but it has a high price." He looked out at the dead. "They did not want to submit to Ai warriors on Chrenadan ground, so they slingshotted back to attack those who believed the battle over. They wanted to claim a victory and to carry home spoils."

Shianan looked over the field. He expected to lose soldiers in battle; that was the nature of battle. But he could not imagine killing so many—and more, if what Tamaryl said was true—just for the opportunity to make war. "Not for defense," he murmured, "nor to bring home supplies for a starving populace, but for pride." They had killed their own to burn Shianan's village, all to avoid admitting defeat.

Heat rose in him like the flames he had walked through, and he swallowed down his rage at this deadly, deceitful, unworthy enemy.

"What do we do?" Ariana asked, her voice hollow. She, too, understood the enormity of it. "What do we do against an enemy who will throw away their own lives for so little reason?"

"Not their own lives," Edeiya'rika corrected sourly. "The majority of the nim and che probably did not know what would happen. They often follow in the wake of the sho through the between-worlds, when traveling as a large group, and it's possible they did not know at all what would come. Almost certainly they did not choose to sacrifice themselves. The new Pairvyn—what was his name?—he gave orders to his sho, and they led the che and nim into the slingshot."

"And then the sho survived?" Mage Parma asked sourly.

"Most of them." Edeiya'rika nodded toward a body a few paces from her. "Not all. And some of the che likely would have made it." She stood and faced the mages. "But, to answer the question of what is to be done, you stay here and prepare a defense. When the Ientu return, you fight without quarter and give no mercy, because they have proved they cannot be trusted to retreat and abide by traditional exchange." She looked at Tamaryl, who nodded grimly.

The breath went out of Shianan, leaving him hollow and weary. They had been wrong; nothing had changed. It was the same as ever, endless warfare, always catching up to raiders who traveled just a little faster.

But Mage Hazelrig was looking suspiciously at the two Ryuven. "What does that mean?" he asked.

"I'm sorry?"

"You specified that we were to stay here and prepare a defense. That seems a rather needless distinction unless someone else will not stay here."

Tamaryl's mouth curved. "An astute observation, my lord mage. Indeed, Edeiya'rika and I will not be staying with you and your military."

Mage Parma grasped it first. Her eyes brightened. "They are traveling in a large group of mixed abilities; they will need more time to pass through the between-worlds."

Edeiya'rika nodded. "While Tamaryl'sho and I, being only two and being sho and rika, may make the journey in minutes."

Shianan was able to follow the idea once the magic had been worked out. "You will arrive before them."

"They attacked what they had been told was under Ai protection," Edeiya'rika said, biting off the words. "They have opened a war of defense and carried it back to their own land."

"And I promised a war of conquest," Tamaryl'sho continued, his tone hard. "Now I will lead my warriors to take spoils from the Ientu."

Shianan felt his face ease into a grin. This, at last, was what he understood. "You will arrive before them and take their unprotected city."

"The city is not unprotected," Edeiya'rika corrected, "but I will confer with the Ientu silth, and I will explain how her Pairvyn has brought upon her people the first combined action of a Pairvyn and a Tsuraiya in more than three centuries."

Tamaryl looked at her. "Are you certain? You speak as more than a Tsuraiya."

"I am the coming silth of the Ai, and that is precisely why I must go. I cannot permit an attack on the goodwill that aids our people during their crisis, and I will not suffer an attack from a force that had been allowed to retreat in good faith."

"That may...that likely will open war between our clans."

"And I would prefer to avoid that, of course, but not at the expense of our welfare."

Her expression was steely, and Shianan found himself glad that she was on the side of the Ai, so that he did not need to face her ferocity. Then the irony of that struck him, and he suppressed an inappropriate chuckle.

Tamaryl was solemn, watching the course of his clan change with Edeiya's decisions, but he did not argue. Shianan thought he understood. Tamaryl had fought for peace between the Ai and Chrenada, and he would not allow the Ientu to destroy that, and especially not in betraying their word with false retreats. But fresh war on another front was not what either of them wanted.

"That sounds like you lay some claim to Chrenada," Marshal Vanguilder said dubiously. "Is that what you mean to suggest?"

Shianan saw Tamaryl's shoulders and wings rise, as he was caught between opening a new war, offending his people's benefactors, and letting his clan starve. The Pairvyn's mouth drew into a tight line.

"Wait," came Ariana's voice, and Tamaryl wheeled to face her. All followed, and Ariana looked startled at the concerted attention. "I think the conflict is between the Ientu and Chrenada."

"But Chrenada cannot take the fight to the Ientu." Edeiya'rika's voice was growing tight. "So that must fall to us."

"What if we could?" She held up a hand to stave off questions. "You offered to duel the Ientu Pairvyn. Would that be binding? Or, more binding than their retreat?"

Tamaryl flexed his wings. "If we dueled formally before the Ientu silth, and if it were known, it would be binding. She cannot afford the loss of status such a betrayal would bring."

"Then can you arrange such a duel?"

"I intend to," Tamaryl said tersely.

"Not with the Pairvyn ni'Ai, but Chrenada. Direct combat with a champion of the land he despoiled. It would relieve any impression of the Ai laying claim to Chrenada."

Tamaryl's patience was wearing thin. "I doubt Duram'sho will come to Alham to stand against Chrenada's champion."

"But some of us can go to the Ientu."

Two quick heartbeats passed as they worked out what she meant, and then simultaneously Shianan and Mage Hazelrig snapped, "No."

"You can't go to fight him yourself," Mage Parma protested.

Ariana shook her head. "I didn't mean I'd go alone."

"Of course you'd have Tamaryl'sho with you, to bear you there—"

"I meant a champion of Chrenada."

They paused, confused, and she looked at Shianan. "Those who do not use magic are not affected by the Ryuven atmosphere. I should have asked you privately, but—"

Horror and fear and years of pent rage shifted inside Shianan all at once. "Take the war to the Ryuven? Instead of waiting and hoping to catch up?"

It was madness, and it was the opportunity they had always longed for. To strike directly, to challenge an enemy who at last could not simply slip into another world to return elsewhere...

Everyone was staring, suspended between shock at the suggestion and the struggle to judge its wisdom.

Shianan straightened. "This is my land, my village, and they attacked after their surrender. I want to do something, if I can. But no matter how willing, I cannot face Ryuven magic without protection." It would be suicide, and in a formal challenge, suicide for both him and Chrenada.

"Shianan does not carry magic," Ariana said, her words articulated carefully. "He is a soldier, a fighter, and he does not use magic, or carry any weapon with magical attributes or that could be a magical component."

Shianan did not understand, but he saw Tamaryl's startled reaction, his widening eyes and catch of breath.

Edeiya'rika opened her mouth, her eyebrows drawn close in protest, and then she stopped. With her mouth still open, she turned from Shianan to Mage Parma to Tamaryl and to Shianan again.

"Edeiya'rika," Tamaryl said, "may I speak to you a moment?"

Edeiya'rika turned back to Tamaryl. "I know what you mean to ask, and I remind you that it was your assurance that brought me here. You told me you trusted these humans. Do you trust him?"

"I trust these humans," Tamaryl agreed, with a subtle emphasis to limit the scope of his confidence. "That does not mean I trust all."

"Do you trust this one?"

Tamaryl looked across at the commander. "I don't know if I trust our friendship, but I know I trust his principles."

"And would his principles permit him to turn on us?'

Tamaryl stood a moment. "I don't think so." His expression relaxed. "Certainly not while in our own world, from which he cannot return without us. He will want to come home."

"I will come as well," Ariana declared. "I can help. This has to be a clean end, or it will not be an end."

Mage Ewan Hazelrig drew his eyebrows together, but when he spoke, he said only, "Be careful, and come home safely and quickly."

Mage Parma slid a hand around his forearm, and she nodded.

Chapter 55

Ariana had received a pair of slave cuffs from Edeiya'rika, and she slid them onto Shianan's wrists. "You'll need these."

"I don't understand," he said, but he did not resist.

"These were mine," Tamaryl said, and with that statement Shianan recognized the shape and the small rings, though they seemed entirely the wrong size for a human child. "They have enough of a magical foundation, somewhat similar to a Subduing, that we should be able to use them to armor you against Ryuven magic."

"What? How is it we've never used this before?"

"It can't be done in your human world," Tamaryl answered. "We're hoping it will work in ours." He stepped close and put his arms about Shianan. "Try to keep still, even if it feels strange or alarming."

"I'll be steady," Shianan said with more confidence than he felt.

Edeiya took hold of Ariana, and then the world fell away and blackness slammed into them.

Shianan sucked air, or tried to, but he could not tell if there *was* any air. They were not flying, for there was nothing below them—or above them, or around them. There was only void, and he could not sense Ariana, and all was cold blackness forever.

His hands tightened on Tamaryl's arms, though he could not see them.

And then there was light, and the coolness of a spring day, and they were in the air above grey-green grass, and they were falling. Tamaryl's wings snapped outward and he grunted with the strain, but Shianan weighed more than the Ryuven trying to carry him.

"Halt!" A Ryuven on the ground twenty feet below looked up at them, raised his hands in a casting gesture Shianan had seen too often—

Tamaryl's arms slipped away from Shianan, leaving him mid-air. He drew his knees upward and focused his aim. The strange Ryuven threw a bolt but it splashed against a magical shield at Shianan's legs, and then Shianan hurtled into him with the awful crackling of snapping bones. Shianan cut once, twice, not waiting to see if the falling blow had been fatal.

Tamaryl landed beside him. "Well done."

"You dropped me."

"You're heavy, and you could be more useful down here."

There was no time to argue further, for Edeiya and Ariana landed, and Ariana folded to the ground, hands to her chest and her eyes squeezed shut. Her breath came in little wheezing moans.

"Ariana!" Shianan dove for her.

But Tamaryl caught him back. "Don't touch her! Give her a moment. She has done this before."

Shianan stared as Ariana struggled, coiling her body first as if to shelter from blows and then as if she writhed from internal pain, and he hung in helpless agony. But the eternity of waiting lasted only a moment, and then she pushed herself upright and blinked at the three watching her. "All right," she said simply, breathless but clear-eyed.

Now Shianan knelt beside her. "Is that the magic? Are you injured?"

She shook her head. "There's no simpler way through that, I'm afraid. But I'm fine now." She put a hand on his shoulder and pushed herself up. "Let's go."

They had come to an open space outside a Ryuven city. Tamaryl and Edeiya led the way.

The city was all wrong, Shianan thought at first, and then he realized that of course it would need no walls; walls were useless against winged invaders. With that in mind, he began to note the tall window-doors on upper floors, landing platforms at all heights, and nets both plain and decorated to shield from above.

Ryuven were staring at them now in open shock. "A Pairvyn, a Tsuraiya, and two humans," Edeiya'rika said in a low voice. "They'll know we've come."

"We'd best hurry, then," Tamaryl replied.

Shianan recognized a training ground, not so unlike where he led troops at the Naziar. Tamaryl and Edeiya turned here, targeting a sparring ring like the one in which he had once taught Luca.

"We'll strip the fup here," Edeiya said to Ariana. "You'll need to handle it, as we don't have the usual tools, but we can talk you through it."

"I can put it in terms you'll know better," Tamaryl assured her. "Commander, the cuffs, if you please? And then if you could stand guard while we work, so that we're not interrupted for a few moments, that would be best. I have no doubt that you can present a menacing defense."

Shianan gave them the slave cuffs and then turned back to the thoroughfare, one hand on his sword hilt, glaring around them. The staring Ryuven stayed well back, not too far to cast but offering no first action.

Behind him was a hurried, complicated conversation about magical transfer and seating materials and woven spells. Ariana and Tamaryl agreed to fold a mineral within a hinge for easier manipulation, and Shianan dismissed the arcane discussion. He did not need to understand; he had his own tasks here, and he knew those well.

"A quick test," Edeiya said, and then a pleased, "Ooh!" from Ariana, and then the three of them rejoined Shianan.

"Put these on," Ariana directed, and she slid the cuffs over Shianan's hands. Then she put her fingers on the cuffs and closed her eyes. "I don't know what this will feel like for a human, but stay still if you can."

He was being told this too often today. But then the cuffs melded about his wrists, sealing in place, and he felt something pull at him—not at his arms or head or chest, but at *him*, his soul.

And then it was done, leaving him only with an impression of disorientation. Ariana opened her eyes. "Are you all right?"

"Shouldn't I be?"

"Excellent," she said. "Let's go."

"But walk a few paces away from us," Tamaryl suggested. "That damping effect should reach only just around you, but I prefer to be certain of my ability if needed."

"It should not be needed," Edeiya said firmly. "We come to discuss and negotiate first. And I expect we will have an escort any moment."

They had gone not even forty steps when a band of female Ryuven came to earth or circled above them, each with a sash across her breast, though narrower than the red and blue sashes Tamaryl and Edeiya wore. "Stand and state your business," one ordered, mace in hand.

"We come to speak with Ridya'silth," Edeiya said loudly. "Will you escort us to the Palace of Lilies?"

"Ridya'silth has not told us to expect guests," the Ryuven guard answered.

"There is more than our presence that was not expected,"

Tamaryl replied. "And if you choose to delay a Tsuraiya and a Pairvyn from delivering a warning, then what comes will be your doing."

The guard—a captain, perhaps?—considered this a moment, and then she gestured, and another flew away, presumably to carry word ahead. The captain lowered her mace. "Are we walking, then?" she asked with a contemptuous look at the humans.

Shianan had trained under contemptuous looks. He strode forward, unflinching.

The Palace of Lilies looked nothing like the Naziar, all graceful lines and open porches. One of the guards stepped in front of Shianan. "You cannot carry your weapon inside."

"Are you going to take their magic from them?" Shianan asked with a jerk of his head toward Tamaryl and Edeiya. When the Ryuven hesitated, glancing back and forth, Shianan stepped past her and kept pace with the others.

"What brings the Ai to my court?"

The speaker was seated in a courtyard between two sparkling fountains, shaded by a flowering vine which perfumed the air in the walled garden. They entered, guards flanking, and Shianan flicked his eyes to watch how the others greeted this Ryuven monarch.

But today's visit was not one for pleasantries, and Edeiya gave only a sharp nod before speaking. "Ridya'silth, have your raid leaders returned yet?"

Ridya'silth frowned. "Do you come to complain of a raid? Was this raid against the Ai?"

"Choose your answer carefully," Edeiya'rika challenged. "Did you authorize your Pairvyn to raid what was promised to the Ai, and did you tell him to practice whatever treachery he might require to bring back whatever stained accomplishment he could manage?"

Ridya'silth raised her chin. "Demus'sho has always led honorable battle."

"Demus'sho is dead. Duram'sho took his sash and agreed to withdraw by our grace." Edeiya made a gesture which included herself, Shianan, and Ariana, but only tangentially Tamaryl. "And then he returned to press attack. He used a slingshot to dishonor the word of the Ientu, killing your warriors and making your Pairvyn a liar."

Despite her poise, Ridya'silth was taken aback. "I hope you speak the truth, Edeiya'rika."

"We can wait for your dishonorable Pairvyn and you will hear it again from him. It shouldn't be long; he's returning with far fewer than you sent." Edeiya crossed her arms and held Ridya'silth's eyes.

The silth did not flinch. "And these humans in my court?"

In this place, he was not the bastard, only a commander. Shianan stepped forward. "I am Commander Shianan Becknam, count of Bailaha. It was my lands that were burned after we agreed to the retreat of your raiders. I am here to see your Pairvyn answer for his lies."

"Does it not seem somewhat petulant to you, to come so far to complain that you could not defend your land?"

Shianan bristled. "It is not petulant to recognize that your Pairvyn took advantage of a permitted retreat to re-attack."

"Had you agreed to a formal truce? If not, then he was bound to no peace." Ridya'silth turned to Tamaryl. "And what is your purpose here?"

Tamaryl shook his head. "It may be that I will have no purpose at all," he said levelly. "Or, Duram'sho may explain how he chose to bring the Pairvyn ni'Ai to the heart of the Ientu."

The threat was mild and clear. Ridya'silth's fingers tightened on the arms of her ornate seat. "Duram'sho did not speak for me."

"He claimed authority to act on your behalf. If you do not condone his words and actions, then cut him free, and we will deal with him alone—or leave him to the families of those he led to die in the void." Tamaryl tipped his head. "But if he spoke with your voice, then our quarrel is with more than him."

Ridya'silth drew a slow breath. "Tell me what you saw, and when he arrives, we will hear his account."

"Your Pairvyn Demus'sho died at the hand of the Silver Mage," Edeiya'rika delivered solemnly. "He fought bravely and the clan should regard him well."

"The clan gives him regard," agreed Ridya'silth formally.

Shianan did not like to hear the raider praised, but these were his own people, and he had at least died in open battle, fairly facing an opponent.

"Duram'sho then claimed the position of Pairvyn," Edeiya continued, "and he declined to face the Silver Mage in combat, claiming it would be dishonorable to fight before the watching Pairvyn ni'Ai."

She recounted the scene in sparse, pointed words, emphasizing Duram's reluctance to fight either in single combat or in battle.

Ridya'silth listened with a controlled expression, betraying nothing.

And then everyone at once hesitated, and Shianan looked around to see what they had noticed, his hand twitching toward his sword, but there was nothing. But Tamaryl said, "And here he is to defend his actions."

"Bring him," Ridya'silth said curtly, and two guards left.

Tamaryl gestured toward Shianan. "We have brought the Chrenadan champion to face him fairly, if at last he can be persuaded to stand and fight."

Ridya'silth's mouth tightened. "Let us hear him first."

Duram'sho strode into the garden court as if expecting welcome and acclaim, head high and the Pairvyn's sash still on his torso. His cultivated half-smile faded as he saw them waiting beside his silth, and his stride faltered. "What lies have they brought?" he began angrily.

"That is an odd greeting to your silth," Ridya'silth replied coolly. "And what is it they should have lied about?"

Duram'sho checked himself and knelt. "Ridya'silth, I bring spoils from the human world and honor for your reputation."

"Tell me about this honor in battle," she said. Her tone was neutral, but her eyes were cool.

"We have grain and medicines and—"

"I did not ask what spoils you bring." Her voice carried a note of impatience; she was growing suspicious of his evasions. "I am told you retreated rather than face a human mage in battle. Is this true?"

Duram'sho stood and flexed his wings close. "I ordered a strategic withdrawal from a defensive threat, and then we regrouped to press the attack."

"We allowed you to withdraw with your warriors," Edeiya'rika accused, "and you used our mercy to instead attack peasants."

The courtiers stiffened, and even Shianan could read the shift in standing. Duram'sho had risked his honor on a successful raid and his ability to report his own glory, and he was losing his gamble.

"I made you no promise," Duram'sho snapped. "What oath did I swear to you?"

This at last provoked Edeiya to fury. "That is the weakest of protests, a coward's refusal to stand by his actions." Her eyes burned with anger and disdain. "I offered you the choice to retreat, and you retreated—and then you continued the battle. And as promised, now you have brought the Pairvyn here."

Shianan clenched his jaw. They had come this far, and now it had fallen to accusations and protests, and Duram'sho would not admit his treachery, and there would be no resolution.

Duram'sho shook his head with arch defiance. "I never said I would not fight. I never said I would not return, you assumed that on your own. I never—"

Ariana slapped him. She did it properly, Shianan noted, feet wide and with her weight behind her hand, and Duram'sho did not see it coming. It rocked him, and he needed two steps to recover his balance.

The courtyard went icy-hot with tension, and Shianan put his hand on his sword's hilt.

Duram'sho turned back to Ariana, his face patchy pale and red but for the bright mark on his cheek. "Human mage, you do not—"

"I know exactly what I do," she snarled, in a tone Shianan had not heard. "And I will do it again, before all this court, for if you cannot stand by your own deeds then you have no honor to be respected. Did you flee before the foe who killed your predecessor, or did you sacrifice your own warriors to land a blow against a lesser opponent rather than fight a battle you knew was beyond you? Or was it both of these?"

Duram'sho fairly blazed with fury. "I owe you no explanation. I will destroy you."

"If it's a fight you want, then I am ready for you," Shianan growled, grateful at last for what he could contribute. "I will fight to avenge my lands and my people, and you may fight to demonstrate you do not always flee or hide."

The words were calculated to provoke, and Duram'sho was already livid. "A duel of champions? Between the Pairvyn ni'Ientu and whatever it is you are?"

Shianan lifted his chin. "I am the lord of Bailaha."

"A duel between Duram'sho and Bailaha," Ridya'silth said quickly, and the missing *Pairvyn* spoke nearly as loudly as her anxious tone. She was eager to separate herself from the presumptuous sho who had brought considerable trouble with a title she had not conferred upon him, and a duel between a sho and a single human would end the matter well, with honor regained through formal combat and the human champion dead.

Shianan took a measured breath, in and out, deep and steady. The human champion would not die this day.

"Between Duram'sho and the champion gentry of Bailaha?" echoed Ariana. "Is that what Duram'sho agrees to?"

"Yes, a duel! Done!"

"Yes, as you say," Ridya'silth confirmed irritably. "Now let's get on with it."

Chapter 56

Shianan looked up at Tamaryl and Edeiya with Ridya'silth on their raised platform to observe the training ring. Ariana, with the two Ai between her and the Ientu silth, swung her legs to sit atop the ring's tall fence.

The rings were larger than those at home, intended for ranged magic as well as close weapons combat. Duram'sho was about thirty feet away, wings slightly spread and a short axe hanging on his hip. Around them, Ryuven clustered about the walls or flew above the others for a higher vantage—but not over the ring itself, exposed to the fighting within or possibly within the accepted vertical range of combat.

Shianan should have brought a bow.

Range was a Ryuven advantage when facing a human soldier; magic could reach much further than even a pike. Shianan did not fully understand what Ariana and the others had done to the slave cuffs he wore, but he would have to trust them. They would supply some sort of shield, and if he could survive Duram'sho's first bolts and close the distance...

His breath was coming faster in anticipation, and already his incompletely healed lungs were tightening. He resisted the urge to roll his bad shoulder to loosen it. He could afford no weakness now.

"This duel between Bailaha and Duram'sho shall end when one yields or cannot yield," declared Ridya'silth, "and the outcome shall additionally settle any dispute between the Ientu and the Ai. Begin!"

Shianan sprinted, intent on reaching Duram as quickly as possible. As he had expected, Duram brought up his hands to cast at his easy target.

Please let these work.

The bolt struck him directly, and he felt it penetrate his skin, an unholy worm writhing through his torso at lightning speed. He stumbled, caught himself, ran—for the worm wriggled, but the explosion of pain and disorientation never came. Whatever they had done, the magic's effect was blunted.

What *was* this he wore?

Duram lost a precious moment in gaping at the human who

only flinched under his direct attack. Then, as Shianan closed and swung, he sprang into the air and flew out of reach.

Shianan cursed and wheeled, prepared for another magical attack from the air.

But Duram'sho soared about twenty feet up, angling for the far side of the ring, and then jolted midair as if he had struck an invisible wall. Wings askew, he fell, barely catching himself to land awkwardly on the ring's floor.

"Hold!" barked Ridya'silth. She turned her fury on Ariana, who had dropped into the ring itself. "How do you dare to interfere in this combat?"

"I do not interfere," Ariana declared, hands raised in innocence. "I take my own part in it."

"How do you call yourself a combatant?" demanded Duram'sho, straightening.

"You agreed to a fight between yourself and the gentry of Bailaha," Ariana said, mildly but loudly. "I am Commander Becknam's wife, thus I am the Countess of Bailaha, and your opponent by your own words." She turned toward Ridya'silth and made a small bow. "And by yours, as well."

"That was never what we agreed!" roared Duram'sho.

Ariana turned back with undisguised glee. "I never said I would not fight. I never said I was not attached to the estate of Bailaha, you assumed that on your own. I made you no promise." She gave him an arch glare. "If your words are good enough to permit one attack, they are good enough to permit another."

Duram'sho sputtered something that was probably a curse or epithet or both.

"Is this how you treated for the end of battle?" Ridya'silth demanded, eager to catch out bad faith and so end the embarrassing debacle.

"Of course not. But it is how he treated with us, on the field and then here before you," Edeiya'rika answered.

Ridya'silth could hardly deny his own words in her own court, and she did not reply.

Duram'sho looked from Shianan to Ariana to Ridya'silth and back. He had not expected the commander to resist his magic, and he had not expected to also fight a Mage of the Circle, and he was increasingly unlikely to receive aid from the silth he had embarrassed before the Ai and her own court. Still, he did not back down. "There is no dishonor in lying to those without honor," he growled. "I am not bound by words to humans."

"Then why do you waste time in words?" Shianan charged him.

Duram skipped back and raised a shield against Shianan's first cutting swing. He leapt into the air and gained a few feet of distance before Ariana's shield knocked him to a halt.

The next magical bolt wormed into Shianan and scorched through whatever strange shield had been on him, swelling in his chest and shoulder so that he lost one hand on his sword. He gasped and gave a little cry, staggering and catching himself.

Duram'sho closed on his success, throwing more bolts in quick succession as Shianan maneuvered backward. Ariana circled them at a run, shielding Shianan, and still each bolt pushed through her shield, weakened but effective.

Shianan gritted his teeth and pushed himself forward. Her magical protection was incomplete, but it was enough to keep him on his feet, and he was enough to protect Bailaha.

But Duram slid away from Shianan, leaping into the air and soaring out of reach. Ariana could not hold him in place while she shielded Shianan from his attacks. He could move at leisure, taking no blows and wearing Shianan down until his screaming shoulder gave out.

Shianan had taken magic before. He gritted his teeth and panted, "Hold him close," and he rushed the Ryuven.

It was a dance, a deadly dance more vicious than any king's ball. Ariana hemmed Duram with rapid shields on three sides and above, never letting him move more than two or three steps before encountering an invisible wall. The shields did not last more than a few heartbeats, but she blocked each new attempted direction. Duram could not turn on Ariana lest Shianan reach him, and Shianan edged nearer and nearer with each attack, reeling under the blunted magic and never able to draw enough air but coming ever on.

Then Duram leapt directly over Shianan, trying to escape above him, and Shianan raised his sword for a quick overhand swing. The Ryuven spiraled into the dirt and Shianan wheeled, bringing the sword around and down as his shoulder shrieked in protest.

But Duram threw up a shield against the cutting blow and swept his axe up for the first time. Shianan checked his rush and struck aside the clumsy swing, wincing as the next muted bolt burned through him. He stepped inside the weapon's reach—Duram had not practiced fighting from the ground and relied too much upon his magic—and took the next blow from the shaft instead of the axehead. He was too close for the sword as well, and he made several savage punches with the hilt against the invisible shield Duram raised.

Duram swung the axe shaft into Shianan's shin, abandoned it, threw a scorching bolt. Shianan retreated a step and brought the sword to full bear, trying to drive between the flashing shields. Ariana circled them, flanking Duram, and cast again and again.

Duram kicked himself back along the ground, hands raised against Shianan and Ariana. He roared his desperate rage, and visible flame licked out at Shianan as if spat. But Shianan had seen fire, and this was not enough to deter him. He drove in harder, beating the blade against the shields and keeping Duram on the ground.

"Stop!" Duram cried, frantic. "Stop!"

Fury erupted through Shianan. He was so near! He had his opponent down! But he could not kill a champion trying to yield, and so he pulled his next blow and drew back, panting as he let Duram'sho bring one knee under him and gulp several deep breaths. His shoulder howled in the sudden stillness, and his lungs burned. But it was over, and they had won—

Duram released a killing bolt.

It struck Shianan in the face, boiling though him, blacking out the ring and the Ryuven and the sky as he fell back. The cuffs squeezed tight on his wrists as his legs went slack, and he landed heavily on his back. He did not know where his sword was. He did not know if Duram closed on him.

He couldn't see. He couldn't hear. He couldn't breathe.

But the feeling swelled and then shrank, like a bubble failing to pop, and his vision lightened. The cuffs clung tight on his wrists. Gaping Ryuven hung in the sky over him, staring. Someone was screaming.

Ariana.

Shianan rolled gasping to his hands and knees. It wasn't a scream of pain. He pushed himself to his feet. He didn't see his sword.

Ariana had her fists in Duram'sho's hair, shrieking rage as she drove magic directly into him. His hands hovered at the level of his face, desperately shielding beneath the arcane onslaught.

Shianan seized one of his wings and hauled him backward from her grasp. Duram'sho reeled as his shield shifted and he twisted on his knees, eyes wide.

"If humans have no honor, then you should look more like a human," Shianan snarled, drawing his heavy knife. Grasping the bony upper ridge of Duram's wing, he found the joint and plunged the point in, twisting.

Duram screamed and writhed, but Shianan had a firm grip, and he braced his knee against the Ryuven's wing-shoulder. He twisted against tendons and ligaments, and with a crack the wing slid in his hand. He cut again, savagely, and it came away, dropping to the dust.

There was gasping horror all around them, but Shianan did not stop. Duram had reattacked twice already, and mere defeat was not enough. Shianan seized the other wing, braced his knee against the Ryuven's back, and cut.

Ariana shoved the screaming Ryuven to the ground, and she raised her head to the watching silth and others. "Does this end it?" she demanded, a razor edge to her voice.

Shianan put a foot on Duram to hold him in place, though the Ryuven seemed to have finally ceased to fight. Shianan found his sword on the ground and motioned toward it one-handed, and Ariana passed it to his left hand. He wasn't sure he could lift it again; his right arm trembled and his shoulder felt as if it hung wrong, and every movement grated.

Ridya'silth wore an expression of shock and horror, and for a moment she could not speak. Then she looked at Edeiya'rika and Tamaryl'sho. "This sho was not my Pairvyn," she said hoarsely, "and these humans were not your champions." There was a question under the statement, and Shianan understood; she feared for her clan and her rule.

Let her fear.

"They were human champions," Tamaryl answered, but his tone left room for more, should she press further. "And as you decreed, their duel settles our own dispute."

"Does this end it?" Ariana repeated, her voice rising. "Does this contest settle the Ientu raids on Chrenada? Or will your word be as unreliable as your Pairvyn's?"

"He was never my Pairvyn," Ridya'silth repeated, and her words were for Ariana, the watching Ryuven, and the bleeding, gasping sho who had shamed her and put her in this position. "And you said you came to avenge your village."

"Then must we fight again?" Shianan gestured with his good arm. "Send your next champion now. For all of Chrenada."

He gambled on their shock at a human resisting their magic and their horror at their severed sho. He had to act quickly, while they still reeled.

"Which of you will duel for the right to raid?" Ariana challenged.

Shianan leaned forward, making Duram squirm. Already his stumps had stopped bleeding—but they would never grow wings again.

"For the right to raid," Edeiya'rika added, "not the right to raid unchallenged. The Ai will not give up our trade goods so lightly."

"Who here will fight these two"—Tamaryl gestured toward Shianan and Ariana—"for the privilege of fighting them again on their homeland, along with Ai defense?"

Ridya'silth made a final effort. "The Pairvyn, serving as their defense, and the Tsuraiya, fighting for another people? Are the Ai not ashamed to be dragged into mercenary service to humans?"

Edeiya laughed. "Dragged into service? Do you think it was they who carried us here?"

Ridya'silth sniffed. "We should not quibble here in the sun. Let us retire to a more comfortable location with refreshment, to conclude our discussion."

That was it. Shianan's heart soared. A refusal would be public, a display for her watching court. A private conclusion meant a concession.

"One moment." Tamaryl turned and scanned the watching Ryuven. "Which of you is a recorder? I ask that a recorder swear for this fight."

Ridya'silth pressed her lips together, but she nodded, and a female Ryuven descended from her vantage point and faced the three of them. She pressed her palms together at chest height and bit her lower lip before tearing it away from her teeth with her hand. Shianan, his foot still on the gasping Duram'sho, nearly flinched at this self-mutilation and the subsequent smearing of blood across her forehead.

"I swear to bear faithful witness to what has passed here this day, a record of word and deed for all to know."

Ridya'silth tightened her jaw, and Shianan guessed that this act had just ended her hopes of quietly forgetting the defeat of an Ientu warrior in their own city by human hands. Tamaryl had ensured all the Ientu would hear of the fight and how it had ended—not with the acceptable death of their champion in combat, but with his disfigurement as he betrayed his honor.

Shianan withdrew his foot and stepped back from Duram'sho, sheathing his sword in what he hoped looked like disdain as he freed his good hand to hold out for Ariana's. Two Ryuven dropped into the ring and knelt beside the injured Ryuven, assisting him to his feet and supporting him as they left the ring.

Ariana, blood-spattered and disheveled, squeezed his hand, and they went out to follow Tamaryl and Edeiya as their peace was negotiated.

CHAPTER 57

Mage Elysia Parma did not often dabble in court affairs, but like any good public servant, she knew the value of having an ear to the ground, and therefore of having an ear ready at her call.

She went ahead of the returning soldiers, traveling alone for greater speed. Her charge was to present a report of the first battle at Fhure and then the night's re-attack. A military runner could have carried the news, but Elysia had suggested that it might be better to have a mage explain the curious features of the Ientu return. Ewan, aware she had known no more about it than he had until that morning, had given her a curious look and then agreed.

The first thing she did upon arriving in Alham was to flag one of the children patrolling for messages to carry. She paid well—she believed in maintaining a reputation that made her messages a priority—and then went on to the Wheel.

She had been in her office only fifteen minutes when the messenger returned, a testament to her generous payment and to the benefit of retaining an owed favor. She read over the reply, crumpled the note, and tossed it into the fire, newly restarted after her long days away.

She finished her outline of events and then walked to the Naziar and directly to the royal secretary. "I would like an audience with His Majesty, if you please."

The secretary nodded. "Of course. I have the Circle's report later at—"

"No, this is not only the official report from Mage Hazelrig. I have my own matter to discuss."

The secretary frowned at his notes. "For a personal matter, I will have to see when time may allow..."

Elysia shook her head. "This is somewhat urgent. Please tell His Majesty so." She gave him the smile she kept for overconfident grey mages. "He'll see me."

Elysia strode into the audience room with her back straight and her head high. She swept one leg behind her and curtsied with a practiced swish of silver robe, and then she straightened and waited for the king's acknowledgment.

He was curious. "Good morning, Mage Parma. I am anxious to hear your account of the battle."

"Indeed, Your Majesty, I have insight I hope you will find useful and much news to report. To begin, our encounter was initially successful. We killed their Pairvyn ni'Ientu and drove them back."

"Splendid!"

"The details of that battle will be significant, and I look forward to giving you a full account. I must also report the sad fact of a second Ientu attack, one that devastated a village with fire."

King Jerome sobered. "I am sorry to hear that. What happened?"

"I will explain all, Your Majesty. But first, let me ask if you have heard the quiet word about Commander Shianan Becknam."

The king's expression darkened in the space of a heartbeat. "If you have come to tell me that he has married against my will, I already know. He has been seen making regular visits by night to the Hazelrig home—shameless!—and one of my informants has worried free the official record of his marriage."

Elysia nodded somberly. "What will you do?"

"I have not decided yet." King Jerome began to pace. "If they had fasted hands in the street or on a campaign, there would be a possibility of denial. They were persistent enough to have it recorded, and that makes it more difficult. But not, after all, impossible; even recorded marriages can be annulled."

"So you intend to punish them?"

King Jerome turned to her. "I see the point of your concern, Mage Parma. But there will be few repercussions for the Circle in the end. I am prepared to accept that young Mage Hazelrig was overwhelmed and encouraged against her usual good sense to participate in this treason, and to that end I will be magnanimous in—"

"Treason?" repeated Elysia.

"Well, what else would one call it, when a man defies specific orders and encroaches upon the succession to the throne?" King Jerome resumed pacing. "A bastard's marriage is a threat not only to the princes, but to their own heirs."

"But you will spare Mage Ariana Hazelrig?"

"I can be merciful," he answered tersely. "I will make an

example of him, and so she may remain in the Circle."

"If she wishes to serve a kingdom that took her husband," Elysia said softly.

King Jerome looked sharply at her. "What?"

"They are both heroes of this conflict, which may have just been ended through their efforts," Elysia said. "Generations of war, brought to a conclusion. Commander Becknam—his lordship—has a long and distinguished service, and I need not remind you of Mage Hazelrig's contributions. It seems a poor reward to take their marriage from them."

"So you came not to inform me of their treachery, but to plead for them," the king realized aloud. "And as a woman and as a member of the Circle, you have taken her side."

"It is not only Mage Hazelrig I speak for."

"For the both of them, then."

"For more than the two of them." Elysia crossed her arms and regarded the king frankly. "Your Majesty, do you know how long a mage must suspend magic to have a child?"

"What?"

"You know that practicing mages cannot sire or bear children. Yet there must be children. Power does not breed true, but a child descended of mages is more likely to exhibit potential to become a mage."

"I know all this."

"You must have forgotten it. Grey mages request their absences six or twelve months in advance. Mages of the Circle, however, are subject to the needs of the kingdom and what unexpected or unpredicted demands those might be. If they break from their duties to recover their reproductive abilities, if they stay home for months and then a Luenda or Arakadamia comes, they must take up their magic again and lose all their time and hopes. They must wait for the world to settle and hope for another window of opportunity."

"Yes, of course. But the burdens of such a prestigious position are known when—"

"Your Majesty, you misunderstand me," Elysia interrupted, ignoring his indignation. "Indeed, all of us knew the price when we entered the Circle, and you have not heard complaints. But my point is, we know the cost of a child. We understand the value of a daughter or a son." Her voice hardened. "And how dare you forget that."

King Jerome drew back slightly. "What?"

"How dare you consider a child, no matter how inconvenient or how embarrassing, something to be discarded. What an insult to your most dedicated mages, that while they wait and hope, you flaunt your surfeit of sons by throwing away one you find unnecessary."

She had shocked him. "I do not—I have not..."

"You say you intend to make an example of him. Think for a moment what example you set for all the mages who serve this kingdom. If you demonstrate that you are willing to destroy what we spend months or years hoping to achieve, because you distrusted your ability to arrange a smooth succession and because you distrusted a Mage of the Circle's oaths and loyalty, you demonstrate both instability and a wanton disregard for your most valuable resources. It is not an example to inspire confidence, or love."

He stared at her. "You would... Do you mean to threaten me?"

"I have made no threats. I have told you what such an action would mean to those who have dedicated their lives, and sacrificed their hopes, to the service of this kingdom."

"But he is a threat. You know he is popular among the soldiers."

"He is admired by those he commands, yes, because they trust him. They believe he respects them and cares for them, and that he will, while making full use of their abilities toward the common good, use them as carefully as possible and with the greatest respect for their sacrifices."

King Jerome set his jaw. "And by that, you mean to say that I do not."

Elysia cocked her head. "Do you, my lord?"

"I am the king."

"Then you have little to fear from a loyal soldier who is already sworn to serve your sons and whose wife might never bear a child."

"It is your place to protect the kingdom from invaders, my lady mage. It is not your place to dictate the management of my court, nor to advise on the security of my heir's succession."

"I have dictated nothing, my lord. What you will do with this shared insight into your mages' minds is known only to you." Elysia dropped her arms to her side. "I have every confidence that a wise, noble, and generous king would consider the implications and do his best to honor those who served him well."

King Jerome scowled. "And is there anything else you wish to bring to my attention, Mage Parma?"

"I have prepared an initial written account of the negotiations and battle, of the surprise attack that night for which the Ientu sacrificed many warriors, and of the wondrous rescue of two children from certain death by a collaboration of Ai Ryuven, mages, and one of your most dedicated soldiers. It also explains that two Ryuven, the Black Mage, and the commander departed for the Ryuven world to pursue the guilty Ientu." She placed the sheaf of papers on his table. "This is a brief report, but it is entirely by my own eyewitness, and I am happy to answer any questions you may have upon its reading."

He looked at the papers, intrigued despite himself by her summary. "They—they went to the Ryuven world? Bailaha too?"

She nodded. "He was most anxious to take the fight to the cowardly Ientu." Was that concern on his face? "We had no word yet when I departed."

He stared at the papers.

"Tomorrow or the next day, Mage Ewan Hazelrig will bring his full report and, we hope, word of how the final pursuit ended. I look forward to witnessing your appreciation for his efforts, and the efforts of his family and of the Circle."

King Jerome jerked his attention from the report. "I reward those who serve me," he growled, and there was a new tone to his voice, a torn edge matching a quick shift of his eyes. "I reward well those who serve me."

He repeated as if he tried to convince himself, and Elysia said nothing, letting him face his own doubts without the benefit of an argument to brace against.

He blew out his breath and turned away dismissively. "I assume they have returned safely, or you would have told me."

"I have told you nothing because I know nothing. The four of them departed for the Ryuven world, and then I departed for Alham. I have had no word since."

He turned back sharply. "They are still there?"

She shook her head. "The distance was great, but I believe I sensed a Ryuven arrival. Even if I were but one room apart, though, I could not say if they arrived carrying humans with them."

King Jerome pressed his mouth into a line. "Thank you for bringing this report, my lady mage," he said curtly. "I will not keep you longer."

That was as much of an acknowledgment as it seemed likely she would receive. She made her curtsy. "Thank you, Your Majesty." And she withdrew.

Chapter 58

Ariana unmade the slave cuffs, or whatever they had been for Shianan. Edeiya and Tamaryl firmly refused to leap across the between-worlds with them otherwise.

"The merest of influences," Tamaryl warned, "and we could be lost in the void. I leapt through the shield, but I draw the line at some risks."

"But you cannot leave the fup lying unprotected," Edeiya added. "It might harm someone. We must replace it in the practice ring."

Shianan still understood little of it, but after all, none of them knew how to efficiently use a staff to entrap an arm and break a wrist. When they had finished returning the borrowed material, they walked out of the city, ignoring the awed or resentful stares, and leapt.

They arrived at a point along the road between Fhure and Alham, which they hoped was still ahead of the returning troops. Shianan looked up and down the empty road, lined with greening young grass and wildflowers, and with a sigh he stumbled and dropped heavily to the ground.

"What's wrong?" Ariana asked, crouching beside him. "Was it something in the crossing?"

It was not. He had only at last found himself out of Ientu eyes, and the pains and exhaustion he had suppressed now swept over him and carried him, and he succumbed to fatigue he'd dared not show before. "I'm fine."

"You're not fine."

He propped his arm across his knee and rested his forehead against it. "I'm not fine, but this is expected. I'll be fine." Mostly. Eventually. His shoulder screamed with every movement, and his legs burned with strain, and there was a bone-deep bruise on his shin from Duram's axe handle, and his lungs still felt too shallow, and he wanted to sleep for a day. But all this was much, much better than it might have been.

It had been worth it.

Shianan drowsed on his knee while Ariana walked to a nearby inn to bring back bread and cheese for all of them. Two and a half hours later, they spotted the marchers' rising dust.

A cheer went up when the soldiers sighted them waiting on the road. Shianan supposed their return from the Ryuven world was a success, regardless of any other outcome. Mage Hazelrig, General Septime, and Marshal Vanguilder were at the front and anxious to hear their report.

"The main point is, we have a concession to leave Chrenada untouched," Shianan said. "Ridya'silth swore to Edeiya'rika there would be no raids for two years."

"To Edeiya, and not to a representative from Alham."

"That does not matter," Ariana explained. "The oath is binding, no matter to whom it was made. We will have two years without raids. And in that time, we should have both better magic and more trade to counter."

General Septime exhaled. "That is good news, then. We should be back at Alham tomorrow evening, and if all has been well there, this will be one of my most pleasant reports to deliver."

"We could fly ahead and give word," Tamaryl'sho offered with a glance at Edeiya'rika, "but I'm not sure we would be welcomed without officers and mages."

"We should arrive together and present a united front," Ewan Hazelrig said. "The idea that the Ai and Chrenada are allied now is going to be unexpected, to say the least, and hard for many to believe. We need to give them every chance to see that we are working together, marching together, celebrating together."

It was indeed going to be hard to accept that the Ryuven—the Ai—were no longer enemies but allies. Shianan was not quite sure how to comprehend that shift himself, though he had just leapt the between-worlds in Ryuven hands.

There was little else to do before rejoining the train to the capital. Shianan went out and gave orders, but before anyone had the time to find him, Luca appeared. First he embraced Shianan, holding him close as if he could not quite trust releasing him again. But at last he stepped back and looked at Shianan. "You're injured?"

"I've been worse," Shianan assured him. "I'll ride back in a wagon, but I'll be fine. It was worth it."

"What do you need?"

"At this moment, water and rest. And a healing amulet if there's any to spare." He could dream of breathing deep again.

"I'll find two, and a mage to activate them."

"I think I can come by a mage," Shianan said with a smile. Then he sobered. "I should have thought to mention this in Fhure, but we didn't know how things would go... It's late to ask, but—but if Marla is willing to come to Alham, I could use her skills." He gestured to indicate the whole of the train. "I know we won't move so quickly as you can, so you could catch up again on the road or in Alham..."

Luca nodded, his expression mostly neutral. "I will go back and ask her."

Cole squatted in the meager shade of the wagon, resting his forehead on his arms. Sweat ran down his face and over his lips, tasting of salt, but here everything tasted of salt.

He hated this place. The sun's glare on the relentlessly white plain burned skin and eyes without mercy. The ground was treacherous, and straying from a tested path might break through the crust to thick mud which could mire wagon or man. The air reeked of rotten eggs, so that Cole could hardly smell anything else any longer. He was miserable, and his only relief lay in making others more miserable, and that worked only for a short while.

Not even unchecked dominion over the men who had sent him here could salve his salt-seared mind. He had taken solace in his revenge at first, driving them into the flat to harvest, but in the end, he was still sunburned and thirsty and here.

Cole had dreamed, long ago, of joining a rebellion and fighting. Then he had been made an overseer, turning his anger on safer targets, and he had put aside that hope of fighting back—and had, without noticing, grown so attached to his new advantages that he would sacrifice anything to keep them, even the possibility of freedom. Now that his cowardice had cost him his dream, he had nothing left but salt and self-loathing.

Four days ago, a slave had put down his tools and walked off the path, pitching himself face-first into a mud pit. He was unable to sink fast enough, and another overseer and three slaves had gotten him out. Cole was still thinking about it.

It would be time to water the workers soon. He straightened and went to the rear of the wagon to dip a ladle for himself, where he saw someone coming down the rutted wagon road, arm over his eyes against the sun.

"Didn't think you were out here today," Cole called. "Thought you were playing toady to the governor."

"He sent me out for you," Keng said. "Someone came in asking about you. Go on, I'm to keep an eye here."

That made no sense at all. Cole followed the trail back to the encampment. There was an unfamiliar wagon at the edge, with water barrels in the covered bed and slaves squatting underneath for shade. Not delivering supplies or slaves. Who else would come here?

Trav managed the labor camp and thought that made him grander than he was. The overseers called him "the governor" behind his back, but Cole wasn't sure that Trav would have recognized it for mockery even if he'd heard it. He had one of the few real buildings in the camp, with thin wooden walls instead of the tents which cost less to carry in, and Cole's shoulders sagged with his relief in its shadow.

The door was open for air, and a negotiation was going on inside. "Price what you will, but I have made my offer. Remember, I'm only on an errand to ask. If I don't like the price, I can always go back and say he wasn't here."

Cole knocked at the door.

"Come!" barked Trav.

Cole stepped inside the dusty office. There was a man in a chair, sitting back, wearing a mildly irritated expression. Cole needed a moment to recognize him: Garrett—Jarl—Jarrick. Jarrick, Luca's brother.

The brother of the man who had bought him out from under the whip and promised him a chance at freedom. The brother of the man Cole had let be beaten senseless and sold into slavery. The brother of the man Cole, refusing to risk his overseer position against the possibility of capture in escape, had abandoned.

"No one counts your laborers here. You can sell for what I offered and pocket it entirely for yourself, or you can get greedy and lose it all when I walk out." Jarrick finally turned to look at Cole, and his eyes ran up and down the overseer with appraisal and disdain. "And be glad I made my offer before I saw him."

A sardonic laugh tried to work through Cole's broken lips, but he managed to bite it down. Did Jarrick think to avenge Luca? His most effective punishment would be to leave Cole here, wait for his inevitable slide from overseer to salt picker, and let his death be slow and excruciating.

Trav lifted his chin, as he did when he thought he was saying something regal. "Fine. But you're getting a bargain, and I hope you know what you've cost me."

"I'm sure I do." Jarrick pushed himself up from the chair. He reached for his moneybag, and without looking at Cole he said, "If you have anything here beyond your skin and the ragpickers' discards you're wearing, get it now."

Cole had nothing, and so he waited outside the door as Jarrick paid the bargain price Cole had fallen to. When Jarrick came out, Cole followed him toward the wagon. "Master, I—"

Jarrick held up a hand. "This first," he said. "What happened to Luca?"

Cole's stomach fell. He had not imagined that Jarrick might not know, if he'd found Cole here. For a moment he considered lying—"he sold me down here"—but it would be too easy to be caught out, and Jarrick had already managed to trace Cole to Salfield. "We were attacked and taken," he said simply. "My master was struck in the head. We were sold at Cascais." There was no reason to say aloud that Luca had begged him to walk them out, or that Cole might have managed it but his own cowardice had condemned them both. That would do Jarrick no good to hear, nor Cole to say, and Cole had felt it every day in this salty torment.

Jarrick gave a curt nod. "And if you hadn't been taken and sold here? Would you have done well by him?"

Cole would have gladly stuck a spade in most of his masters, but Luca had been different—a soft brat with rich relatives to save him, but different anyway. Luca had offered him a clear path to both freedom and the sense to manage it, and Cole thought he'd even meant it. "I would," he said hoarsely. It was true, and more urgently, he had to convince Luca's brother, who undoubtedly regarded him the way Cole had regarded Garl and Esar. "Seeing him sold away was my greatest regret."

"Because you didn't protest that he wasn't a slave to be sold?"

The accusation struck Cole like a switch across his chest, biting deeper for the truth of it. He fumbled for an answer. "I was a slave there too, master."

"Don't call me master," Jarrick growled. "I don't want you. I still don't know what he sees in you, but he asked after you in the first minute I learned he was alive. So I'm taking you back to him."

Cole missed a step and slowed, staring after Jarrick. Luca—had survived, and maybe was free again. Luca had thought of him. And Cole would go to him.

As Jarrick neared the wagon, the slaves slid from beneath it and took their places in the traces, shrugging into harness and setting their hands to the crossbars. Cole hurried to catch up, going automatically to the rear wagon tongue to push with the team. Could he face Luca, now that he'd refused to help him and let him be sold? Dare he expect Luca to take him again?

But Jarrick believed Luca would want him. And even if Cole had a choice, even if there were any shame left to him, he could not stay in this salt-rimed hell.

"Where is he, m'lord?" he asked.

"Alham."

Luca had made it to Alham. He was where he had promised Cole he could hire out and keep his pay and earn his freedom. It was just as if Cole had never failed him—except he had, and he'd paid for that, and he would do better. Cole had once wanted to kill freemen; now he would become one.

He ducked his head against the sun and pushed the wagon, tasting salt.

Chapter 59

The streets looked like a festival day. Vendors hawked pies, sweets, breads, and more from carts smothered by crowds cheering and waving colored cloths. Shianan had seen eager receptions when soldiers had returned, but this was unexpected.

The Ryuven forces had been dismissed outside of Alham, as the treaty had made no provision for the entry of warriors, but Edeiya'rika and Tamaryl'sho walked side by side along with the Mages of the Circle, and Shianan's mind was boggled. Never had he imagined such a sight.

He was grateful that others had.

Ahead of them, General Septime and General Kannan rode horses, and Shianan's stomach did an unhappy twist whenever he let his guard down. His nerves were unsettled enough that it did not require much to jar them. No matter how he wanted to be glad—look at what they had done!—the feeling was too unfamiliar to hold for long.

"You don't seem quite as happy as I'd expect for the end of a war," Ariana said quietly to him, waving to the crowd.

Shianan looked past her. "I'm worried."

"About the Ryuven?"

"About us." He watched Ariana wave again, and he lifted his left hand self-consciously. "I married. I married a Mage of the Circle. I married in defiance of both tradition and royal prohibition. And if the war is ended, there's less distraction to screen us."

She leaned into him, avoiding his painful shoulder, as she smiled at the waving crowd. "It will be harder for the king to punish a war hero."

He had believed that himself, once. He shook his head.

"Come on. You protected the Ryuven emissary, thereby preserving our alliance, thereby enabling our joint victory over the Ientu. Then you went across the between-worlds to punish the raider who struck your village, and you returned with a pledge from the Ientu silth."

Shianan frowned at her irritating factualness. "Still."

"Do you think no one will talk of that?"

"That's just the point. Acclaim makes me dangerous to the prince-heir and the succession."

"That's ridiculous," Ariana protested, but he could see that she believed him—or believed his anxiety, anyway, even if she thought the king's speculation beyond redemption. "All right, then. It will be harder to punish the hero who saved the life of the Ryuven emissary, especially while celebrating alliance with that Ryuven emissary."

Shianan blew out his breath. "I don't know why I bother to argue with you."

"And don't you forget it." But she bumped him again. "I do understand. But I also think we have a better position to negotiate, given what you did for Tamaryl'sho and the victory over the Ientu."

General Kannan's horse reared and twisted, startled by something in the crowd, and the general clung to the saddle and mane as stable slaves rushed to settle the horse. Shianan thought of the training they had done with Kuolema, and he wondered for a moment if the bay colt would have been as alarmed, and he clenched his jaw and tried to swallow the fresh sorrow. It was foolish, wasn't it, to grieve an animal? When so many humans had died in the same war?

Ariana's fingers tightened on his wrist in quick sympathy.

The horse tossed its head and moved forward again with the stable slave, and the line that had hesitated again proceeded. Shianan reminded himself to take a breath and walked on. He wondered if his waves looked as wooden as they felt next to Ariana's natural enthusiasm.

Tamaryl'sho and Edeiya'rika waved at the crowd, careful smiles on their faces, and Shianan watched the crowd gape and occasionally shrink back when the Ryuven's eyes fell on them. They had seen Ryuven paraded in Alham before, but as prisoners, and these two with their bright sashes of office and bold waves were so clearly different. Shianan found himself hoping that they liked the idea of Ryuven walking beside the Circle, that they accepted the new-forged alliance between them.

The people were still cheering, even as they stared at the Ryuven. They feared the Ryuven, but what they really feared was war, death, deprivation. They could learn to see the Ryuven as people, not as threats. They could learn to see Tamaryl, not the Pairvyn.

They could learn to see Shianan as a married man, not as a bastard grasping after the throne.

Ariana bumped him again, and he made himself smile and

moved the tongue that had adhered to the roof of his mouth.

They would have to tell the king. It would be better if they told him before he learned, and surely that was only a matter of time. Ariana was right: Now was the time to tell him, in the flush of the good tidings of their surprising victory and new alliance, and when Shianan was partly shielded by his part in it all. And it would be best if he heard from Shianan rather than ferreting it out and believing himself further deceived.

Shianan would request an audience, and he would tell him.

By the time Shianan made it back to his office and quarters, Luca had unpacked his gear and brought a tray from the military kitchens. "I've already put all the reports and requests that can wait in this box," he said, "so there's no need to worry over sorting straightaway. And Marla's waiting for after you've finished. She said she saw your waving in the street, and you're protecting your shoulder."

Marla was right, but Shianan didn't like to hear it so plainly. "I'm fine."

"Of course."

Shianan threw a glare at Luca, who ignored it with the confidence of one who had already provided a hot supper and relieved his master of burdensome paperwork and thus wore an armor of immunity.

Shianan rubbed his chin through its short growth. "Will you go to the palace for me and put in a request with the king's secretary? I need to speak to him."

Luca sobered. He knew Shianan had not often gone uninvited to the king. Just once, in fact.

"I have to tell him before he learns about Ariana, and we think immediately after this victory is the best time. If you would ask for an audience—when he can see me... Just tell me when."

Luca nodded.

Shianan ate the meal, annoyed when he caught himself stretching his neck and shoulder and looking forward to Marla's treatment. It would have to be brief; he still had many tasks awaiting him, now that they had returned to Alham. He would have to go to the laying out of the dead, as well, a duty never made less difficult with victory.

Tomorrow, though—tomorrow he would face the king, and he would explain that Ariana and he were married, legally and irrevocably, and he would take what came of their decision.

How could he return from so complete a victory, and yet feel so small and unprepared?

"Master Shianan."

"One moment." Shianan finished his sentence directing the sergeant to keep the new recruits at their assembly camp for the time being, rather than bringing them to Alham, and then turned back to Luca. "When you have the time, please show Marla to the Hazelrigs' house. I'd rather she stay there, where she can be comfortable in her own room, than try to squeeze her underfoot here. And she'll no doubt be happier in a house than in this military arrangement."

Luca nodded. Neither of them mentioned Shianan's townhouse, standing empty.

But Marla, coming to the door between office and sleeping room, had not been there that day. "Don't you have a townhouse, master? I could stay there."

"You wouldn't want to be there alone."

"I sometimes kept my master's mountain house alone, when he sent me ahead. I wouldn't mind a bit of housework, if it's been empty."

Shianan shook his head, too preoccupied to explain his reluctance and too embarrassed to say that Ariana had promised to reclaim the house. "I don't have the time to argue it now. Go to the Hazelrigs'. You can tear my shoulder apart again when I come to visit."

She nodded. "I've brought you more willow bark and jackwort," she said, setting the cup on the desk. Then, with the air of one who has said it a dozen times and does not expect to be heeded with one more repetition, she added, "That should be in a sling."

"I cannot write with my arm in a sling." Shianan started to reach for the steaming cup, checked his motion as a twinge shot through his shoulder, and took it with his left hand, irritated at his body's treacherous support for her nagging. Then he looked at Luca. "Yes?"

"I made your request to the king's secretary."

Shianan's stomach sank. "Ah." Once it was scheduled, the confession was real and the consequences inevitable.

"You have an appointment for tomorrow afternoon." Luca's

words were a flat statement, but his eyes spoke empathy and concern.

Shianan made himself nod and say, "Thank you."

"And while I was there, I was intercepted by another royal servant."

Shianan looked back at Luca. "Who?"

"You're also called to present yourself before the queen. Tomorrow morning."

Did she know? Did she mean to talk him out of telling the king? Or into it?

Shianan sucked a long breath and then let it go. "I suppose I'll need to dress for court tomorrow, then. See that I have something appropriate, please?"

CHAPTER 60

Soren stared at the sheets in his hand, though he no longer needed to read them. He had read them through three times in completion, and some sections far more often. He had read them in his office, out of curiosity and obligation, and then again in a sitting room chair in amazed incredulity, and then once more in his private bedchamber in growing discomfort. Much of him wanted to put the sheets down, reject such damning knowledge, forget what he had read.

There was such comfort in ignorance.

And if he brought these arguments to the council... They would want to resist this realization as well, and more fiercely for their closer ties and greater disruption. He could more easily afford to consider change because his position was protected; he would need to tread carefully if he brought this to others.

But he had been wrong. He had been wrong, and he had helped to permit what should never had been permitted, and now he as prince-heir and future king had to acknowledge and act.

It would not be quick, not even in the best of imagined worlds with the council's full support and enthusiasm. Even a king without a council could not, with the stroke of a pen, change business transactions and livelihoods across a kingdom. But even a long, steep journey could be made in stages.

The army had returned, and Shianan would be back in Alham. But he would be more than occupied, settling the troops and dealing with the dead and wounded and the myriad demands of his position, and Soren did not want to face him until he had come to some faint idea of how he would respond to Luca's petition.

He put Luca's explanations and examples down and made a note to send several invitations. He would not start by approaching the council; that would be ambitious and futile. But he could ask a few opinions of those who would be flattered to be asked, and see if they arrived at similar conclusions if presented with similar scenarios, and then he might have a shared understanding from which to gradually ask for a shared conviction.

"Master, Her Highness is here."

Soren jumped in his seat and looked up. "Already? Er—what time is it?"

Calissa leaned into view behind Ethan. "Not so very long after you were to join me?" There was a smile in her voice.

Soren pushed himself up. "I'm sorry! Come in. Have a seat. I mean, I'm just coming." He gave up. "I lost track of the time."

"I supposed as much." She moved past Ethan, who bowed and retreated. "Something profitable, I hope?"

Soren blew out his breath. "Or hugely unprofitable, but clinging to hopes of a better future? Or is that too ominous to say?"

"It's certainly intriguing to say." She settled in a chair near Soren's desk, and he sat to face her. "It sounds like the opening to a bardic epic. You should say it over gently plucked chords."

He wanted her opinion, he realized. She was clever and anxious to improve the world by more than a politically expedient marriage; she would be able to sort through the stories and speculation as well as he would, and she might have better ideas on how to approach advisers when he was ready.

"How many will we have to sacrifice for this better future?" she continued, sitting back. "Or is that too literal for a jest?"

He shook his head. "No people to sacrifice. But you did not come tonight to sort my political tasks."

"Is that a polite way of telling me this is something for Chrenada alone, and not for Wakari eyes? Because I cannot see how something that does not sacrifice anyone and has hopes of a better future could be much of a question."

"It does not sacrifice anyone. It might even save some. But it is so significantly different from what we know."

"It might save people, but it's unfamiliar? I still fail to see the dispute." She grinned. "If you're trying to put me off, it's having the opposite effect. But I can take a hint."

He sat forward. "No—no, it's nothing you cannot see, I only did not want to let it take your evening."

She tipped her head and looked at him. "I am somewhat keen on Chrenadan politics."

He fought an uncomfortable flush—he did not know how successfully—and turned to the desk. "I really would like to hear your thoughts."

Ethan reappeared in the doorway, bearing a tray. He moved silently to the desk and set down two cups, a bottle of wine, a pitcher of water, and a bowl of nuts with a cracker ready beside it. Then he retreated.

Calissa gave the refreshments a significant glance. "Is it that he knows you very well, or is it that we are very predictable?"

"We are not so predictable," Soren said firmly. "He brought the drinks here, but we are going to read and talk in the sitting room, where there are comfortable chairs and couches." He picked up the cups and a pitcher. "My lady?"

She tucked the pages under her arm, collected the nuts and wine, and followed him into the sitting room.

"Well, this is a different view," Calissa said at last, not quite dismayed but definitely surprised. "Wouldn't this undermine nearly all material production?"

"The author argues it would not—perhaps even have the opposite effect."

"And what do you think?"

"I'd prefer you to form your own reaction, and then we can see where we agree and where we think the weaknesses are."

"Fair enough." She settled against the couch arm with the pages.

Soren tried to occupy himself with another paper while Calissa read, but he only fiddled with it as he surreptitiously watched for her reactions. She frowned, pursed her lips, raised an eyebrow, frowned again. She looked like a playactor rehearsing; she did not have his mother's cool expressions that hid what she wished. But her catalog of expressions fascinated him.

He watched her eyes, moving side to side and down a page, leaping higher to reread a passage. He watched her feet in embroidered slippers jerk to the side or slide on the rug, giving movement to some emotion raised by the words.

She was two-thirds through when she lowered the sheets to her lap. "Who wrote this?"

"I'll tell you when you've finished. Why?"

"He's not a practiced political writer, I'll wager that. But...I've never considered this. Most of me wants to laugh it off as so obviously misguided and ignorant. But if I pause and ask whether that's logic or avoidance of change... He raises intriguing questions." She shook her head. "Let me finish."

CHAPTER 61

"But it makes sense to do it soon. The Wakari emissaries are already here. The arrangements were canceled only a short time ago—they could be put in motion once more."

Soren's protest was cut short by their entrance, and Shianan guessed at what they interrupted. He felt a quick flash of empathy, though the prince-heir risked less in pressing for his marriage. But it was too late to withdraw, even if he could have explained to the generals and mages he followed. They were assembling before the king, and Shianan placed himself just behind Generals Kannan and Septime and bowed with them.

King Jerome turned from Prince Soren and ran his eyes over the group. "Welcome, my heroes. I am glad you have come safely to report a victory." His eyes rested on Shianan for several uncomfortable heartbeats, and then he gestured to the council table. "Please, be seated, and tell me how it happened."

He would not care exactly how it happened, of course; he had generals to manage strategy and tactics, and mages to understand the magics. But he would want to know that they had won a battle, and how they had allied with the Ai when the Ai had declared Chrenada an interest to be protected.

Shianan did not know how that would be received. The king could not be anything but pleased with their fewer than expected losses, but he would not like the surprise of their newly enhanced Ryuven alliance. Once Shianan had brought him the Shard of Elan, but with the Gehrn, and it had cost him a rib.

General Septime and Mage Ewan Hazelrig shared the recounting, trading off as they briefly reviewed the confrontation and Mage Parma's belated arrival. She began to speak then, too. "Edeiya'rika and I spent a week experimenting with the Shard, discovering how to channel power across the between-worlds and into a usable, manageable form."

"You—worked with the Ryuven? On magic?"

"It was incredible," Mage Parma answered, her eyes bright. "I've never made so much progress in research so quickly. And to have access to Ryuven magic to observe so closely—without, of course, trying to counter it—was a great help. I have mountains of notes for the Circle to review and discuss, and a scribe who needs a week's rest."

"But Mage Parma, if you made our military secrets available to the Ryuven..."

She shook her head. "The Ai have been fighting and observing us for generations, Your Majesty, and our magic is less agile than the Ryuven magics, as we saw with the Ientu. I gave away much less than I learned."

"And the Shard? Our greatest tool for defense?"

"We used it for defense," she answered evenly. "As you will hear."

They recounted the brief and unsuccessful negotiations and then the battle, and how their cooperation led to the death of the Ientu leader.

"Wait," King Jerome interrupted. "You killed their Pairvyn?"

Mage Parma grinned. "We did."

Shianan could appreciate the announcement and her justified pride. He had grown up listening to tales of the Pairvyn ni'Ai, a legend to unsettle recruits and veterans alike. That Mage Parma had killed another Pairvyn in their first encounter was a stunning victory to claim.

King Jerome, listening to her account, was growing visibly excited. "So the Shard is not merely a tool of defense, but a powerful weapon!"

"I'm afraid that's not as promising as it sounds. It cannot be used on its own, it—"

"But skilled mages could wield it?"

Mage Parma drew a breath and braced herself for the distressing admission. "The strain was great—we drew incalculable energy through it. Well, not incalculable, I do have the figures, but far more power than ever we placed upon it for erecting the shield. When I used it to full effect, not thinking about a careful test or demonstration but freely in combat, it was too great a strain. I regret to say, the Shard is damaged."

"What?"

"During the encounter, we felt it buckle and the channeled magic faltered. After the battle, when all was settled, we examined the Shard and found the crystal cracked and its overall structure compromised."

"What does that mean?"

She shook her head. "It means it cannot be used in that way again, at least not more than once, and I expect it would not survive a second incident."

There was a moment of quiet as the king tried to accept this information and the room waited to see how he would take it. Shianan risked a glance at Soren, who had been listening without interruption but who, at this revelation, had sat forward, his eyes staring and his shoulders stiff.

"We can reserve it for milder use," Mage Ewan Hazelrig said. "To generate a shield, though perhaps a smaller one than before, or similar purposes. While we have lost its ability as an amplifying weapon, we did not have that ability available to us until just before its loss, so practically speaking, we are nearly where we were."

King Jerome scratched his beard and considered this. Prince Soren asked, "And what was the conclusion with the Ientu?"

"We thought we had achieved a victory, but the one who stood in the fallen Pairvyn's place was not true to his word." Mage Hazelrig outlined the retreat, the happy rest, and then the dawn attack.

When the narrative reached their departure for the Ryuven world, Ariana and Shianan took up the story. "So we challenged their new Pairvyn to combat—though the Ientu leader was quick to emphasize she had not named him her Pairvyn," Shianan explained. "And so Mage Hazelrig and I fought him in a duel." He could not explain here how they had fought together as the married lord and lady of Bailaha. He did not want to break the news to the king in this crowded room. But he could perhaps use that in his defense later; Ariana and he had been successful only because they were married. "Mage Hazelrig and the Ai Ryuven provided me with an additional form of magical shielding that blunted the Ientu's attacks."

"What was this shielding? Do we have it here, if it is so effective?"

Ariana shook her head. "I saw it when I was in the Ryuven world, but it is some substance that does not exist here. And it cannot be brought across the between-worlds; it suppresses magic, and clearly that is a risk that cannot be taken in the leap."

"What can we do to get it here?"

Ariana's voice took a faint edge. "We have no mages who can leap the between-worlds, and the Ryuven cannot carry it across."

The king nodded. "Fine, fine, we'll consider that later. So you defeated this champion?"

"Commander Becknam and I did, together. And then Edeiya'rika reminded Ridya'silth that she had lost two Pairvyns in as many days, and she would suffer greater losses if she challenged our combined forces again, and they concluded negotiations and we came back to Chrenada." Ariana fairly beamed with their achievements.

"In the end, they do not wish to embark upon a war of conquest against the Tsuraiya and her fighters," Mage Ewan Hazelrig answered. "To their understanding, that is a very different enterprise than raiding our world, and they have no wish to enter a formal war with another Ryuven clan."

"But do they believe that we are a part of the Ai lands, then?"

"Not at all," Mage Hazelrig assured him. "They understand that the Ai depend on us and must fight with us to preserve their own welfare."

They continued to summarize and explain, until the king agreed to also receive the two Ryuven, Tamaryl and Edeiya, and thank them personally and individually for their efforts.

Shianan rolled his shoulders, gradually relaxing as the explanations continued without royal fury. His right shoulder twinged, making him think of Marla. Tentatively he stretched his neck, probing where she had pointed out his injury, and ah! Yes, there it was, and inflamed.

This audience was going well, and he was glad. But he had two more royal audiences today.

When the king dismissed them, Shianan bolted, backing out as fast as he reasonably could and then escaping into the corridor. He did not wait to chat with the others; there was nothing for him to accomplish here. He paced up and down the corridor and at last moved down the hall. He could not be still, not with the queen's summons hanging over him and then his own private audience with the king later that afternoon.

He did not want to think on that audience. He did not want to think on how he would react to the king's reaction. He did not want to give himself over to a—a common beating, he should say, because that was what it was. He did not want to submit to what he would not allow his slave to face. But he did not think he could refuse, or escape. He did not think he could resist.

It felt as if his heart pounded in his stomach, and he felt ill. Had he eaten? Would that help, or would he be sick?

It was bad enough to be afraid; he loathed his own worry over his fear.

But whatever came—it could not change that they had married. They were legally bound, recorded for all, no matter what the king said. He might separate them or humiliate them, but he could not change what they had done.

The queen's summons would be first. He did not know what she wanted, but he trusted—he trusted the queen—that it would be less dangerous. But he could not anticipate it with the king's audience so closely following.

He was thirsty, or at least his mouth was dry. He went in search of water.

Chapter 62

Shianan entered the queen's reception room and knelt. He might have bowed, but he had not come here since reporting Kuolema's death, and the heaviness of that meeting hung over this one. It cost him little to demonstrate his continued regret.

"Come and sit," Queen Azalie invited him, with a gesture to one of the padded couches facing her chair.

Shianan did, keeping his eyes averted. He had wept here, had cried in her arms for sorrow and relief, and surely she had not forgotten that. He did not want to see his shame pitied in her eyes.

The queen gestured, and her maid brought a tray to the low table within easy reach of both of them. She poured out two teas, precisely dispensing the queen's milk with practiced skill, and then paused to look questioningly at Shianan.

He cleared his throat. "Just tea, if you please."

She placed the two teas at their respective places, and the queen nodded. "Thank you, Eve. Will you see that we're not disturbed?"

"Of course, my lady."

As always, Shianan's stomach clenched, and he fought it down. A private audience with the queen had never been like one with the king—but still, he was vulnerable here, in a different way. He had not realized how precious the queen's regard had become, even seen so late, until Kuolema had died.

She had so much more power to hurt him now, far more than when she had been a faceless entity of fury in Kalifi.

Part of him wanted desperately to believe she had meant all the words she had said, that she did not loathe him, that she even liked him. But he had lived too long in the shadow of other words, and the habits grown in such shadows could not be overturned so quickly.

With the doors closed against intrusion, Queen Azalie sipped her tea and gazed into it. Shianan waited, holding his tea without drinking so that it could not run out.

She gave a little shake of her head. "They say some read tea leaves to know the future," she said. "I don't know much about that; there's nothing helpful in the bottom of my cup. I am only putting off what is difficult."

This did little to calm Shianan's apprehension. His fingers tightened and he feared suddenly he might break the delicate little cup. He shifted his hand to loosen his grip.

The queen put down her tea, and his heart raced.

"Did you want to come to Alham?" she asked abruptly. "From the outpost where you were raised?"

Shianan did not know how to answer. As a child, yes, he had wanted it. So often he had imagined the king galloping through the gate, calling for the missing son he had been searching the countryside to find, pulling Shianan upon his massive horse and apologizing for how long it had taken to locate him, for the error that had buried Shianan fatherless in the frontier.

By the time Shianan had become a sergeant, however, he had abandoned his childish fantasies. He had bent his head to his military career and done his duty, taking satisfaction in his rise through the ranks and the lives and property he saved.

When the order came to summon him to Alham, he had not known what to think. But it had not mattered what he thought; he had gathered his few belongings and obeyed.

"I had not expected to be given a title," he said, hoping it did not sound like an evasion. "I was glad to serve in this location, with the Naziar troops, if that is what you mean. There is some prestige to assignment here rather than a frontier outpost."

"But you were comfortable at the outpost?"

What a ridiculous question, one that could be asked only by a woman who had never been thrown from her mattress in the dark before dawn, or who had never scrubbed blood and feces from a tower walkway where Ryuven had attacked, or who had never worked twice as hard to prove she was more than a discarded bit of refuse cast out of sight. "It was all I knew."

"But you were given no choice in coming here to Alham," she pressed. "If you had wanted to stay—if you did want to stay—you had no choice in the matter."

Shianan shook his head, grateful for a simpler, if meaningless, question. "No, it was a military order to transfer my attachment. I came."

She nodded twice, her eyes moving back to her tea. "I see. That is my concern."

"Your Majesty?" Was she preparing to ask him to return?

Would she send him from Alham? Now that he had finally found his footing, found friends and purpose, would she send him back under the guise that he would have preferred to stay?

Oh, 'soats, he was a fool. She had been quite clear before that she would not step foot in Alham while the bastard was there. Now she had come home to her city, and she needed to remove him. It was simple and obvious, and he should have foreseen it. He had been mistaken—he had misunderstood before, blinded by his hopes, and—

"It is very important, then, that you understand me," she said, folding her hands together. "I am the queen, not an officer, and I am in no position to give you a military order. Nor is this a case where I bestow a gift that is no gift, like giving a horse to break a man."

Shianan hid a flinch. Her horse had broken him. He understood; this was no formal order, but she was the queen, and he could not refuse.

She was looking at her folded hands. "The prince-heir's wedding will be announced soon."

Shianan had not expected this lead.

She smiled tightly. "I'm going to break the news to him and his bride this afternoon, so please don't spoil the surprise. But I don't believe it will be such a surprise, given how they've been leveraging for it."

This would be about the succession, then. He had become too familiar with the prince-heir, and she needed to emphasize the gulf between them.

"The wedding will be next month; there is little reason to put it off, and Soren is right when he argues that we had already planned one." She drew a breath. "It is traditional for the queen to arrive with her Queen's Guard."

Shianan nodded automatically.

"Are you familiar with the Guard?"

"Not very familiar, Your Majesty." He had heard of the Queen's Guard, honor functionaries at the highest state ceremonies such as weddings and coronations, but royal tradition had never been a part of his education.

"The history of it is a bit convoluted, a tale about a contested queen who had been put aside for a new wife, and how the royal household was divided in whether she was to be recognized and who stood with her at the wedding of her daughter to an alliance prince, and how she was protected from those who would have forbidden her entrance to the wedding but who could not assault the prince-heir and his brothers. All very dramatic." She waved a hand. "What matters is, the Queen's Guard traditionally consists of the queen's sons, nephews, brothers, and occasionally other key members of her household she may wish to include."

Shianan again nodded where he should.

Queen Azalie drew a breath. "If you are amenable, I should like to include you in my Guard."

For a moment Shianan could not think. But he was not—that would be—

"It would be your choice," she said quickly. "Do not feel any obligation merely to please me. I do not want to pressure you into an uncomfortable public display; from what I've been able to learn, you have kept a low profile around the court. I only ask if you would."

Shianan stared at her. King's sweet oats, it seemed she was nervous. She really wondered whether he would, and it mattered to her.

Their last exchange in this room swept over him again, and this time it was not the soul-crushing guilt that stood tallest among the chaos, but the astonishing wonder of her pulling him close, quieting his apologies, asking if he was injured.

He did not dare to trust his interpretation. The risk for misunderstanding was too great. "Your Majesty—are you asking me if I will walk with you as one of your household?"

She nodded, as if speaking was difficult for her as well.

Something cracked within Shianan, deep and dangerous. The delicate tea cup trembled in his hand. He nodded. "If you would have me, I would be honored in every way, Your Majesty."

She released a pent breath, breaking into a smile. "Oh, I am so glad. Thank you."

How could she be thanking him? Shianan sat in shock.

"I will make the arrangements and have word sent to you. There will be details to be seen to, traditional bits and bobs to wear and such, but that will be easily done by those who manage such things. Oh, I am glad to hear that you will walk with me. Thank you, Bailaha." She hesitated, tried a word as if testing its flavor. "Shianan."

His name was strange and terrifying, and it shamed him with how he wanted it again, like a woolen blanket in the winter night. "It is I who thank you for such an unexpected honor."

"Stop that," she said. "Stop going so formal on me. It's what you say when you don't know what to say, and it makes it difficult for me to guess what you want to say but won't."

This was uncomfortably true, and Shianan closed his mouth sharply.

"Shianan," she said, and she watched him keenly. "May I call you that?"

He was embarrassed at how much he wanted her to do so. *I would very much like one person to call me by name—please.* His voice came out tight. "Please."

She nodded, and she pressed her lips together. "Shianan, if you will agree—and again, I must emphasize, this is not a royal dictate that must be obeyed. I would not act against your will in this, and I only—well, anyway, I suppose the key is to simply ask it."

Shianan's heart raced, and his lungs seemed frozen.

"Shianan, I would like you to serve in my Guard not merely as a member of my household, but as my son."

The words hung in the air, glistening and incomprehensible. He tried to speak. "But...."

"As an adopted son of the queen, you would stand behind the natural royals in rank, after the prince-heir and even the younger son. You would not bear the name of Laguna, because that is Jerome's name, not mine. But you would be my son, by law and by desire."

Tea dribbled over his lap, the cup forgotten in his hand. He stared, hardly daring to believe. "But...."

Her eyes hung on him, wide with anxiety and hope. "What do you think?"

What before had cracked within him now broke completely, and a torrent of emotion crashed free and swept through him, choking him and blurring his vision and roaring in his ears. Closing his eyes against the onslaught, he could only nod.

She was there in a heartbeat, close on the padded couch, and the last of the tea poured on the floor as the abandoned cup slid free. She embraced him close and for the second time he wept against her shoulder, embarrassed at what she had revealed and incapable of pulling away.

"Shianan, I am so sorry," she whispered, nonsensically. What had she to be sorry for?

He shook his head.

"I should have seen before. I should have been willing to see. But now..." She pulled them apart, so that they could face one another, equally teary. "You are the son of my husband. You are too valuable to leave unclaimed, and if no one else is sensible enough to lay claim to you, then I shall certainly do so. If he will not do his duty, I will do mine, and gladly. I would have you as my son, and I would own you before all the world."

Shianan choked, and he nodded, which was hardly the correct response but which seemed to delight her, and she hugged him close again.

At last they separated, and the queen sniffed and blotted her eye with a knuckle. She pointed to a little coffer behind him. "This time, I thought to be ready."

Shianan opened the coffer to find a collection of neatly folded handkerchiefs. He laughed aloud and took out two.

CHAPTER 63

Shianan's fingers were numbing as he paced in the corridor, the rich carpeting devouring the sound of his footsteps so that he moved as inconsequentially as a ghost. An hour ago he had literally wept with joy, and already that dizzying joy faded before the looming doom of facing the king over his marriage.

He did not know the way through this, but there could no longer be any other way but through.

"Your lordship?"

He turned and saw one of the court clerks, a man who often handled council paperwork. He couldn't recall his name. "Yes?"

The man gave him a friendly smile. "I wanted to be one of the first, I hope, to offer my good wishes to your lordship. I've had word from Her Majesty to continue with the documents, you see." He made a little bow.

"Thank you," Shianan said, more flatly than he felt he should. "It's—been a surprise to me. So sudden." That was a queen's power, to hear of his accomplishment at Fhure and order a prompt adoption.

"I'm sure. It was such a rush for us, too, getting her requests in order. Laws, precedents, open titles, the like."

Shianan arrested the motion of wiping his clammy palms on his tunic. "I can imagine. We only returned to Alham yesterday. You must have spent half a day looking up what was needed."

"What? Oh, your lordship, that would have been grand! We've been working on this for weeks. It's a lot of looking through dusty books, and that's once you find the right books." The man chuckled.

Shianan's stomach did a slow turn. She had not heard of his efforts in Fhure or the Ryuven world. She had begun this before he had won fresh acclaim.

"Your lordship?"

Something must have shown on his face. "It's nothing," he said quickly. "I had misunderstood. I'm sorry for my confusion, and thank you for your efforts."

"Of course, your lordship. And again, our best wishes to you." The clerk bowed and went on down the corridor.

She had chosen him before. After he had carried Soren, yes, but before he returned a champion against the Ientu. She had planned to ask him while the raids were continuing and when the king was furious.

His knees weakened, and that was ridiculous, for this was only good news, and he shook his head a little and walked to shake off the sensation.

She had chosen him *before*.

He pulled a deep breath and turned at the end of the corridor. He wanted time to consider this, and he did not dare take it while waiting for the king's audience. He could not afford to be weakened by feeling, not now.

But tonight, he might bring out this revelation and warm himself by it.

He turned again. For now, he must brace for the king's words. He must not be touched by what storms would come. He wished he could fade entirely and not have to face this audience.

Strange, how he could face a vertical sweep of charging Ryuven with steely determination, yet falter before a single unarmed man like a raw recruit.

The secretary opened the door as Shianan approached. Shianan pulled air through his tight throat and did not allow himself to hesitate at the entrance. He went inside and knelt directly. Best to start with the most conciliatory approach.

"Rise, Becknam."

Shianan did, but he did not go closer. The king was seated in his large chair, slouching on one arm. He did not look at Shianan.

Shianan waited.

"It's not often that you come to me of your own accord."

If that was meant to be a rebuke, Shianan would not take it as one. He did not reply.

"Well? What have you to say for yourself?"

This was the moment. This was when he cut himself free of the false security of obedience and plunged into the free-fall of royal fury. His voice rasped on the words. "Your Majesty, I came to inform you that I have, with Lady Ariana Hazelrig, the Black Mage of the Circle—"

"I know who she is," the king interrupted irritably. "I also know you married her."

Shianan stared, caught without words. But he should have known. He should have seen the embers in the king's eyes.

The king's voice was drawn taut. "I learned only lately, and it was confirmed through the registration you took the time to make. Which you meant, I suppose, to make your disobedience known and your marriage impossible to ignore." He scowled. "I debated while you were away facing the Ientu, and then all last night and this morning, how to respond. What could I do with a returning war hero who had so openly defied me?"

But perhaps Shianan's efforts had saved him? At least in part? Or the king would not have measured his anger against Shianan's renown...

"You're a rebel and a traitor, and you have turned them all against me." King Jerome heaved himself out of the chair, glowering down at Shianan. "The queen, my son, the mages—all against me! And all while we need stability and unity more than ever." He sliced the air with a savage gesture. "You're a threat to this kingdom!"

It felt as if smoke had filled Shianan's lungs again, and he couldn't get air.

The king advanced on him, his face reddening. "You have made me a laughingstock in my own court—as if I cannot control the least of my subjects, as if a soldier can defy my orders on a whim. Should I tolerate this defiance? Should I allow you to endanger my people?"

Was that so? Did Shianan's brazen defiance bring too much turbulence to the chaos of Ryuven allies and a new Ryuven enemy?

"I am the king! How could I lead a country if I let myself be trod upon by a common soldier? I cannot be humiliated by your mockery and defiance! You push so far, and what do you think must happen? What did you think would come when you provoke me so?"

But Shianan had seen the trick of it now, had tasted such false justification in his own mouth, and he would not accept it again.

"After all I have done for you? Ungrateful goat!"

Shianan saw his intent, knew the expression, sensed the blow coming. The king balled his hand and made a wide swing.

Without thinking, without daring, Shianan slid his right foot back, so that the king's fist brushed past his face with a caress of air.

For a heartbeat they stared at one another, equally shocked. Now Shianan had further baited the beast. Now the king's fury would flare white-hot—

"Look how bold," the king sneered, each word dripping with disdain. "How bold you are when you have a woman's skirts to hide behind. Do you think the queen will protect you from what you do? Or is it your little wife you hide behind?"

It was neither, for all Shianan could think of was how terrible this would be for both of them, entangled with him in the king's wrath, and how foolish he was to have moved a few inches instead of simply accepting what would come and letting it pass, as it always at last did.

"You are a coward, waiting to defy me until you had the queen's protection."

He had not. "I requested an audience before the queen called me."

King Jerome ignored this. "You never dared when you did not have the queen's name to shield you. You never dared."

Shianan's words were barely audible. "That's not true."

For another moment they stared, each remembering. For Shianan, it had been a moment of desperate terror, sliding in front of the prince to protect Soren from the blows meant for him. He wondered, for the first time, what it had been for King Jerome, and how he remembered it now.

You don't fight for yourself—but you are your strongest when you are protecting someone else.

He still fought for others. He had protected Soren then, and now he protected the queen and Ariana. The king would reach through Shianan to hurt them, and they should not be made vulnerable by Shianan's weakness. And now, to protect them, he must protect himself. He must be their shield.

He saw the rage flare, saw the fury rise, and for a moment he thought the king would lose all his faint inhibition. He saw the fist rise again.

A shift of weight, a scuff of his foot, and once more he was just beyond the range of the blow. He met the king's eyes, and he waited. He would not strike—but he would not be struck.

His heart raced. If the king ordered him to kneel, if he—

But then, somehow, the anger spilled out of King Jerome, like grain from a rent sack. For a long moment he stood, looking at Shianan, or through him, and then he turned away.

Shianan did not breathe.

King Jerome stared at the floor, as if fascinated by the pattern in the carpet. Shianan did not move; the king would speak when he was ready, and Shianan did not dare upset the fragile balance of the moment.

But the king waited a long time before he spoke again. At last he shifted his weight. "Why did you do it?" he asked softly. "Why did you marry her?"

A dozen answers crowded together, striving to air complaints, to strike back, to plead, to defend. But Shianan squared his shoulders and said, "Because I love her, and she deserves the honor of my commitment."

The king's shoulders stiffened, and too late Shianan realized that might be heard as criticism of the king's own dishonoring deeds. But the words were out, and he would not draw them back.

King Jerome stalked to his chair and turned, still standing, to face down Shianan once more. The bite was back in his words. "You could have taken her as a mistress. You could have had her and yet preserved the illusion, let everyone pretend that all was well, let us all go on as if no schism loomed in the line of inheritance. You could have bedded her, if army whores were not enough for you, without making a public record of your defiance and making a mockery of your king. That would have been enough, and I would have granted you that."

This was a lie, and at least one of them knew it. Perhaps the king could convince himself, now that the marriage had been done, that he would have forgiven a lesser infraction. He had not convinced Shianan.

But even if it were true—why should Ariana have been dishonored to preserve Jerome's comfort? Why should she have no marriage because he had sullied his?

But even in his anger, Shianan could not bait the king with such words. He walked a knife's edge in this moment, and so he merely said, "You would not have accepted a mistress."

The king's face darkened. "Do you call me a liar?"

"A king does not lie, Your Majesty, which is why I remembered your previous words so clearly." King's oats, he sounded like Luca.

"If you remembered my words so clearly, why did you ignore them to the point of marrying against my will and all tradition and the state's security?"

Shianan would not be lied to in this way. "I am sworn to the prince-heir, Your Majesty. I carried him out of Arakadamia where he could have been left for dead. I offer no threat to the throne."

The king gestured savagely. "And can you speak for your son, or who might use your son?"

"What son?" Shianan demanded, his voice rising. "I have sired no sons out of the royal line."

It was a bold statement, and a dangerous one. It went too far, accusing the king of the wrongs he predicted in Shianan.

"I wish I never had!" the king roared. "I wish I'd never been plagued with such an—ungrateful useless monster, who used his pitifulness to turn all against me with ill-gotten sympathies. I wish you'd been drowned at birth or ripped out of the womb. I wish you'd never happened!"

The words should not have cut Shianan. He knew them for anger, for defensive attack. He should have heard them for their worth, blunt rocks thrown wildly by a man afraid to face a blade.

Still, they were spoken by the man he knew was his father, and stones could bruise as well as a blade could cut.

But the king's words were selfish. If Shianan had not been born, things would have been different for Luca, for Ariana, for Fhure. The king should not wish away the good Shianan had done them to salve his own conscience. Shianan ground his jaw until his ears ached.

The king glared at him. "Have you nothing to say to that? No defiance for me?"

Shianan's rigid shoulders ached. "I am sorry to hear that my service has been so unsatisfactory that Your Majesty would have done better without it."

The king snorted and waved a hand as he turned away. But even he could not dismiss the ravine at Arakadamia, or the battle at Fhure and beyond into the Ryuven world.

Shianan had pulled the younger prince from a mud pit and the prince-heir from impalement. He was no threat to the succession—without him, there would be no succession. The words hovered on his tongue, anxious to fly free.

But this was uncharted territory, and he still knew the need for circumspect caution, and something was different today. They had never spoken like this, even in their greatest anger.

King Jerome dropped into the chair once more and stared at the carpet. Shianan could not guess what he thought, or what he meant to do.

Finally King Jerome lifted his head and looked at his chair, away from Shianan. "I wish you had asked me again."

Shianan bit down his surprise and indignation. Ask again? After what had followed his first attempt? After this outburst? There had been nothing left but to do it without regard for the king's permission.

But he said nothing. There still were limits. And it seemed, in this moment, the king was withholding his wrath, and Shianan did not dare to jeopardize that.

King Jerome raised his head to look at Shianan. "I know what the queen has asked you."

Queen Azalie had told Shianan to say nothing until she had dealt with the details, but of course she would have told the king. Giving her name to Shianan would change the court and Shianan's position in it.

King Jerome's expression was sullen, and his tone nearly petulant. "Yes, I know. And if you are her son, you can do as you please—even to marrying a mage of the Circle."

Shianan's heart caught, swelling against his chest. Was that belated permission?

"If the queen gives you her name, you are no bastard, and you can marry as you will." The king's mouth worked as if the words had a foul taste. "You would be no king's son—you choose to be her son, not mine. But you could do as you please."

The bittersweet pronouncement scalded Shianan. He thrilled to the tacit permission, but at the same time, the implied and unfair accusation galled him. He had once refused a legitimacy in name only, a title in exile. The king had never offered what the queen had. "I chose to accept what she offered," he answered as evenly as he could. "And I will be ever grateful for it."

The king's fingers tightened on the arm of the chair, and for a moment Shianan thought he had gone too far, had roused again the beast which had been somehow placated this day.

"So you have accepted her offer, then." King Jerome's mouth made a tight, flat line, an expression Shianan did not remember seeing before. His breath hummed. "I see."

Shianan did not see. He had the sense that he had disappointed, but he would not be made to feel guilt for accepting the queen's generosity. He had not asked for it—he would not have dreamed of the possibility. She had chosen him, and he would not be ashamed.

The king passed a hand over his face and lifted his head. "I would like to give you something as well," he said thickly. "To show my appreciation for your contributions and for keeping our soldiers safe on this last expedition. I had thought perhaps another title, to elevate your rank, or some other means of public commendation, but I will consider any reasonable boon you care to ask."

The words hung like gossamer in the air, glittering invisibly like the magic Ariana worked. Once, Shianan would have walked over coals for them. Once, he would have bent his head for insults and blows for them.

But he no longer traded in this market, and he had brought nothing to sell.

"I am proud of my service, Your Majesty, and it has been an honor. I am delighted in my marriage to a woman who will serve and defend Chrenada as I will. I ask nothing else."

The king's mouth tightened again, twin lines appearing at the outside corners. For a long moment he said nothing, and Shianan saw his throat move. Finally he nodded tightly, and he waved toward the door. "You may go."

Shianan bowed and retreated. The king passed the hand over his face again, and the secretary closed the door behind Shianan as he escaped into the corridor.

As the queen's son, he could openly acknowledge his marriage to Ariana. As the queen's son, he was no longer the bastard, and he had no need to limit himself to a bastard's place or achievements. He had not even considered this glorious new horizon that her offer opened to him.

He did not understand the king's seeming despondency, filling in where rage receded, but he was grateful for it. At the moment all he could feel was a bright ball of warmth, like a lit candle with hands cupped about it, burning within him. What he wanted more than anything in this moment was to find Ariana, wrap his arms about her, and bury himself in her hair, her scent, her joy.

Shianan's smile broke free and spread over his face, and he did not care if the royal secretary saw, or if the guards in the corridor saw, or if anyone in the Naziar saw. He displayed his smile and headed for the Wheel. Whatever Ariana was doing, this was news she deserved to hear directly.

Chapter 64

The Wheel was not far from the Naziar, but though Shianan felt he hardly touched the ground between the two, he could not arrive at the Wheel fast enough. He hurried along the curving corridor until he came to the black-painted door. "Ariana?"

"Hush," she cautioned in a low voice, hardly glancing at the door. She had a pair of crucible tongs in both hands, and she raised one to warn him back as she kept her eyes on her small vial of a dark powder. "Stay by the door a moment; this is very delicate. Did you knock? I didn't hear you."

"I didn't knock." Shianan chafed in place. "I have news."

"Just a moment, then. This is already hot and I have mere seconds." She maneuvered the powder from the athanor to a small pewter tray on her table. "All the way by the wall, please. In case this does not go well."

Shianan put his back to the wall, and Ariana inverted the powder so that it fell toward the tray. In the same moment she dropped the crucible tongs and brought her hands sharply together, cupping air.

The powder struck the pewter tray and exploded, throwing fire up and outward. But the flames struck an invisible wall and rolled back in on themselves, trapped by Ariana's shield. Though Shianan heard the rush of fire, the expected wave of heat did not reach him.

The flames lessened and Ariana released the spell, letting them fade into a low smolder on the tray. "Yes! Kinetic bursts as well!" She clapped her hands and came around the table to embrace Shianan. "Congratulate me, I'm going to contribute something really useful."

"Congratulations. What have you done?"

"This shield can contain an internal kinetic burst, instead of only shielding against one externally."

"I don't understand why, but congratulations," he said amiably and with genuine enthusiasm. "Well done."

"Thank you." She squeezed him again. "Now tell me your news."

He had never had such news to share. He would never have such news to share again. It seemed he should have another way to tell her, not in a room with smoke drifting over them and threatening to make him cough. At least the burning fireplace's updraft was already helping to clear the smoke.

"Oh, it looks like good news," she said, putting her hands on his forearms. "What is it?"

"I've been to see the queen," he began, "and the king. The queen called—I don't even know how to tell you this."

Ariana was watching him, her lips slightly parted, excitement and firelight shining in her eyes. Even without knowing what he would say, she was already breathless with joy for him, and that was a gift in itself.

"The queen asked me—asked me, for my permission—she has asked to adopt me. As her own son."

Ariana's hands flew to her mouth, and her bright eyes went round like twin moons. "Oh, Shianan!"

"I would be a member of the Queen's Guard for ceremonies, and I would be her son legally. And"—he tightened his grip on her arms, too excited to be still—"and the king knows about us, about our marriage, but with the queen's adoption, legally I'll no longer be a royal bastard. As the queen's son, I can marry, and I can marry whomever I like."

Ariana fairly quivered in his grasp. "I hope you like me."

Joy bubbled out of him in a laugh.

She seized him and pulled him close for a kiss and then embraced him, crushing him in her effusion of happiness. "I am so glad for you," she whispered, her voice tight. "So, so glad."

He held her close, sharing a giddy joy they had never expected.

"So, should I call you my prince?" she asked as she pulled back, grinning.

Shianan's heart went still. "What?"

"You'll be the queen's son. Will you be a prince?"

For a moment, he could not think. "I—surely not."

Her smile faltered as she saw how he was struggling. "I was more than half-joking. What will they call you?"

"The demon commander, I hope. Loyal to the prince-heir." Behind the surprise at her question, the old fears clawed to the surface, refusing to die quietly. "I cannot be a prince, or they will think I mean to rise..."

"They will think you are the adopted son of the queen," Ariana said firmly. "The son she chose to take for herself."

Shianan drew a breath and nodded. "Perhaps you might remind me of that, if the need arises."

"Oh, as often as required and more. You know how wives can nag." She grinned, and her joy was contagious, washing like small waves over him and, if not clearing away the lines of his worry, at least smoothing them.

"What about you?" he asked. "You're working on new experiments. For—there?"

"Eventually. Once I have a shield to reliably control non-physical kinetic impact, I might be able to do some controlled tests to explore exactly how our magical atmospheres are different, and why that might be. Though I doubt I'll have quite as much giddy enjoyment as Mage Parma and Edeiya'rika blasting out old quarries."

"They didn't. Did they?"

"Oh, they certainly did. Took me along once, and what an experience that was." She turned back to the table and started sweeping together the residue in the pewter tray. "You will come tonight, of course? And by the front door, now that we don't have to hide?"

His stomach gave a curious little flip at that fresh realization. "Yes, of course. And tomorrow, will you come to the townhouse?"

"Yours, you mean?"

It still felt awkward to say. "My townhouse. Our townhouse."

"If we feel no ghosts of the Gehrn have returned while you were away. We still need to reclaim it." She stacked her equipment together and turned back to him. "It's late enough, you've probably eaten."

He had not eaten before going before the king. "Not yet."

"I was too caught up in my little fire blasts, so I have not eaten, either." She gave him a sidelong glance. "You know you should not take a celebratory drink on an empty stomach. Have you had a celebratory drink yet?"

It felt so natural, and yet still so new and wondrous, to draw near her and slip a hand about her waist. "I hope I might buy you one."

Luca was thrilled, more excited than Shianan had seen him for his own manumission. "The queen's adopted son! You'll be a legitimate son, a noble and a courtier, and—a queen's son!"

"I am not sure yet if I believe it," Shianan confessed. "I mean, I don't doubt Her Majesty, that's not it at all. But I might need time to feel it."

Shianan and Ariana had stopped at his office on their way to the Hazelrigs' home, and she was folded into a chair beside the desk, beaming at the two of them. Now she sprang up. "I'm so happy for both of you." She embraced Shianan, kissing him, and then pulled back and turned to Luca, arms open.

He froze, and then he lifted his arms, and that was all the invitation she needed. She pulled them together, hugging him. "I'm so happy for you, too."

Luca flushed and drew back. "I'm still just a—"

"Part of this house," she finished, "and making me late for supper with your dawdling. Are you coming with us?"

Luca's expression faltered. "I have something to finish."

Ariana put on mock indignation. "Shianan, are you working him too hard? Can't he come to supper?"

"Leave it," Shianan told him. "Whatever it is, it can wait."

"But it can't." Luca shifted. "I had a message, and His Highness is willing to talk over what I sent. I have to be prepared. This is my one opportunity, and I cannot waste it."

"The prince?" Ariana asked. "What is it?"

But Shianan was caught in the glimpse of hope. "He'll hear you? He wants more?" He turned to Ariana. "Luca's put together a document or treatise or petition, something showing how slavery is not just hard for an individual but is damaging to the kingdom itself."

Luca hastened to explain. "I know it's not the conventional thinking, but if you look at the economic effects and how the common craftsmen are—"

"Oh, you don't have to argue it to me," she told him breathlessly. "My father argued it long ago. And you're going to present this to the prince?"

"He's seen my first arguments, yes, but as he has asked to discuss them, I will need more thorough examples and explanations."

"And if he's asking, then he's considering, and that means you may need to speak to councilors, or the king."

Luca blanched.

"You'll need practice," she said. "You'll want to rehearse all the protests and have your counter-arguments fluent."

"I hope to review them tomorrow night, if I can complete writing tonight—"

"Good, good. Sweet oats, it must feel like the Circle examination, only a thousand times worse. I will make sure we have crisped cheese and barrels of tea to sustain us during practice."

Luca looked a little lost. "You—you would go over them with me?"

"Of course! This is important, and I will help any way I can." She checked herself. "Do you really need tonight to finish putting your arguments together?"

He nodded. "I do, my lady mage."

"Then we'll talk over them tomorrow evening. That is, if his lordship can be persuaded to give you the time."

Shianan raised his hands in surrender. Then he nodded toward the desk. "You have everything you need?"

Luca nodded.

"Good. Then I'll see you in the morning."

CHAPTER 65

Azalie did not want to go to his rooms. It would have been a difficult day for him, and that would make him difficult. But she was his wife, and if nothing else, the servants might want a rest from him.

She did not wait for the servant who opened the door to announce her. "Her Majesty the Queen," he delivered, a little belatedly, and then at her nod he disappeared. A rat fleeing the ship that had been taking on water all afternoon.

No, not water. She saw two bottles on the table beside him, and the servants would have taken away others.

He turned red, bleary eyes on her. "Your Majesty," he drawled, "the queen of the land, the true ruler of Chrenada, the one who does what she will."

He couldn't even be properly insulting when he was drunk. She sat down to face him. "Good evening. I see you're taking it well."

He scowled at her. "You lied to me."

"I beg your pardon?"

"You lied to me. You said you would do—would do what I could not. I thought..." He picked up a cup to avoid finishing the sentence.

"You thought I meant I would do what you would do in my place." She shook her head. "I told you plainly, Jerome. I told you to cut him off cleanly or to bring him in, or you could leave him to me. You left him to me, to do with as I pleased."

"I thought...I thought you would sever him." He looked down into his mostly empty cup. "I warned him to stay away from you."

Well, that explained a few things. "You had your chance. More than a chance, and a second, and a third."

"I did what was necessary."

"You did what you wanted," she snapped, tired of his justification and self-pity. "You wouldn't let him live without you and you wouldn't be a father to him, and so you toyed with him. Even now you're behaving like a child who doesn't want a toy but wants no one else to have it, either. You had him to yourself for nearly thirty years, and in the end you squandered it, and you cannot complain to me now."

"I am the king," he said petulantly. "You cannot tell me what to do."

"You are the king, and you should have acted like one! You had responsibilities, and yet you took out your own weakness on him. How can you claim to govern a kingdom when you cannot even govern your own right arm?"

He looked away. She nearly regretted the words, but he was drunk and still well-armored with self-pity. Her words would not pierce him, not until he had passed to morose.

"You shouldn't have done it. Not without asking me."

"Are you the only one who can bring an extra son to this marriage?"

"You can't adopt him. It makes me look heartless."

"Really? Is that my doing?"

The king was silent a long moment, and when at last he spoke, his tone was less defensive. "This means he is yours, now."

This was a turning point, potentially volatile. "I did not take him from you. He was not yours. You never claimed him."

He did not look at her, and at last his voice held the tone no one else would ever hear. "I wanted to. I didn't want to, but I wanted to. I gave him a title, lands—"

"You gave him many things, but never what you both wanted."

He slouched back against the chair. "I did what was necessary. I did what I had to."

She did not answer. Arguing with him would solve nothing, and his repetitions would not make what he said true.

After a moment, he set down the cup. "Where's Fulton? I want to send for Becknam."

"What? Not now."

"I want to speak to my son."

"*My* son," Azalie corrected quickly. "Mine is the name on the documents. I am the one who claimed him." She set her jaw. "I asked you again. I said if you would not do what should be done, then I would. And I have. And now he is my son." She quirked her lips to the side and relented slightly. "But as my husband, you are kin to him."

"A little more than kin," he murmured. "I want him brought here."

"Do you want him to see you like this?"

That stopped him, and he fell quiet again. She blew out her breath and sat back in her chair, watching him.

"If he calls you 'mother,'" he said, petulant, "it won't mean anything. It won't be true."

"Won't it?"

King Jerome poured into his cup and did not answer.

When Shianan made his way back to his office, hurrying just ahead of the pink light breaking through the streets, Luca was still sitting at the desk. Candle stubs littered one corner and there was ink on his fingers and face, but he had a stack of neatly copied sheets and a satisfied expression.

"King's oats, Luca, you should get some sleep," Shianan said by way of greeting.

"You're not setting much of an example." Luca sat back and rubbed his eyes. "But it was a good night of work."

"You have your materials for Prince Soren?"

"Yes, yes. And I've also worked out the rest."

"The rest?" Shianan sat on the edge of the desk.

Luca laced his fingers together. "You'll be a royal son soon, and that will bring prestige and additional social responsibilities. You have a steward at Fhure, but I could be your secretary and majordomo, handling your affairs here and at your estates, so that you can continue living as a commander—as you will no doubt prefer."

Shianan smiled a little at the truth of it.

Luca squeezed his paling fingers. "I would continue doing just what I have so far, though with more responsibilities, and I would study on Chrenadan court procedures to be a good secretary."

"I'm sure you would."

"Then—that's all right?"

"Of course it's all right." Shianan looked at him, and belatedly he realized the weight of the question. "More than all right; I think it's an excellent proposal."

Luca's shoulders dropped, and he drew a breath. "I didn't know if I could assign myself such a position."

"I had not even thought that I would need such a position, so clearly you're more qualified to fill it."

"I will be a good secretary."

"I expect you'll bring the best out of Fhure as well."

"I don't know what I can promise there. I am a merchant's—I am from a trading family, and I don't have experience with managing estates."

"No. But I trust you to choose people who do."

Luca drew a full breath and nodded, his smile now a grin. "I will do my best."

Shianan rose from the desk. "I suppose that means the cuffs must come off."

Luca looked down at his wrists. "One more time over the table." He started to reach for a cuff and stopped himself. "I wonder how quickly the marks will fade. I don't want to address the council with my wrists..."

"Double-dyed lot of goats," Shianan said archly. "Don't mind what you look like. Speak your words in a way that they must listen." He shook his head. "Besides, you shouldn't think so highly of politics; it will only frustrate you. It will be weeks or months before the prince is ready to bring something so jarring to the council. You have plenty of time."

Luca nodded.

"So get some sleep, and then this evening we'll go into the market."

CHAPTER 66

When the cuffs came off, Luca simply sat on the ground beside the table. It was not the first time they had been removed, nor the second—but it was the first when he felt grounded in what would come next.

"Go on, get up," muttered the workman as he set down his tools. "Things to do."

"Here, tell me what I owe," Shianan said, distracting him so that Luca could have a moment.

But Luca did not need a moment. He had a life stretched out before him.

"Go ahead," Shianan told Luca as they walked. "I want to stop by a bakery."

"I can go," Luca offered.

Shianan shook his head. "It's fine." He wanted, irrationally, to be the one to pick up the garlicky rolls Ariana liked. And it might, nonsensically, feel as if he could overwrite that dark day. "Go on, and I'll meet you there."

Luca, absently rubbing one bare wrist, nodded and went on down the street.

Shianan turned toward the market, and a few minutes later he wondered belatedly if he had done the wrong thing. Luca had not been back to the townhouse since the Gehrn's invasion, and his offer to go for the bread might have been an effort to put off returning, or at least returning alone. Shianan would hurry.

Fresh trays of the dough knots had just come out, and Shianan bought too many. It was their first night in their new home, and he would short nothing. Then he jogged back, hoping to catch up with Luca.

He hadn't seen him yet by the time he reached the townhouse, and he panted a little—his lungs were nearly recovered—as he tried the front door. His stomach tensed for a heartbeat as the latch moved, unlocked, but then he pushed it open.

There were too many voices inside.

Shianan closed the door and went into the sitting room. Ariana was in one of the chairs, leaning forward as she faced Luca, who stood straight as if awaiting orders. Beside her, Princess Calissa sat on a short couch with her legs and arms crossed, nodding.

Shianan blinked. The Wakari princess was here?

Behind them, in the doorway that led to the kitchen, Ranne was laughing at something Lady Bethia said, holding a platter of cheese crisps. She turned and delivered them to the table between Ariana and Luca.

Bethia sighted him first. "Your lordship!"

Shianan extended the sack of bread numbly. "I have enough, I think."

Ariana leapt up to catch his hand and draw him further in. "Thank you for thinking of these! Calissa and I are probing Luca's arguments for weak points, but my father will be more use when he arrives. Mage Parma too, of course. If Luca can hold against her, he's ready for the council."

"How did we come to have so many people?" Shianan asked. He wasn't upset, he didn't think—only surprised. He'd rarely had guests, even counting the merchants courting military contracts. He had never imagined his sitting room full of visitors.

"It turns out Calissa has been reading Luca's dissertations as well, and so I asked her to come and help," Ariana answered. "And then my father, because he'll be a good adviser too. And then, well, it spread. Do you mind?"

He wasn't sure. It felt unfamiliar, even a little intrusive—but if he was honest, he wasn't sure if that was true irritation or only a shying away from the unexpected.

"If anything, it will help to purge the air of the Gehrn," Ariana said more quietly. "Like scraping inked parchment for reuse."

He gave a half-hearted chuckle. "Is that a sort of wishful magic?"

She laughed, a little embarrassed. "I suppose. But I don't want that day to be your chief memory of this place. I want it to be ours."

The door opened, and Tamaryl called, "Hello? May we enter?"

Shianan started for the entryway. Edeiya'rika was with him, and Shianan stepped back as they came inside. He glanced down at the floor with its tiled stretching cat, and then he looked at the two Ryuven. "You are welcome," he said, and he tried to give it gravity. "Welcome in my house."

Tamaryl'sho nodded formally. "Thank you, commander. Your hospitality is appreciated."

They went into the sitting room, and the Ryuven took the remaining seats, pressing their wings awkwardly against the rear wall. Shianan leaned against the mantel, watching the room.

This was where he had fought the Gehrn, where he had struck Ande, where he had dragged Luca away from his former master. But as Ariana had said, now it was full of conversation and smiles.

He had thought to reclaim this place by bringing Ariana and making sweet love to his wife here. But this—this was a more comprehensive claim. This was firelight and laughter and, where Calissa and Ariana tested Luca, shared purpose and higher cause, and it was nothing Shianan had ever expected in a—a home, and everything he discovered now that he wanted.

And at the end of the night, they would go home, leaving him with Ariana.

Across the room, Ranne was visibly uncertain as she offered refreshments to the two Ryuven, but they were all speaking pleasantly. Shianan took a moment to bathe in the wonder of that.

A knock came again at the door, and Shianan went to it. Mage Parma stood on the step, with Ewan Hazelrig close behind her. "Good evening," she said, "and look what we've found along the way." She gestured to Prince Soren, who grinned.

Shianan caught his breath. "Come in! Your Highness, I did not expect..."

The prince entered and waved a hand dismissively. "I sent no word and relied entirely upon your hospitable goodwill. My only defense is that I was called here by a beautiful woman."

"Ariana?" She'd asked the prince as well?

"An understandable interpretation, but in this case, a different beautiful woman, Princess Calissa." Soren beckoned behind him. "I have a couple of guards who would appreciate a drink in your kitchen."

"Of course," Shianan answered, a little numb. "Please go in with the others." Mages of the circle, the prince-heir... His poor garlic knots would never be enough.

"I beg your pardon, commander." Mage Parma caught his attention. "Ariana had mentioned there might be more guests than had been originally expected, and I took it upon myself to order some additional refreshment. I hope you don't mind?"

"Not at all."

"Thank you. I expect it will come within the half hour."

"That's fine, thank you. Please, come in."

In the sitting room, Ariana was challenging Luca. "But slaves have no honor; that's how they become slaves."

"My father sold me for his debt," Luca answered levelly, his spine straight. "That says more of his honor than of mine."

"But it was your debt too, belonging to your house." Then Ariana faltered, apparently unwilling to press a point so personal.

But Princess Calissa did not quibble with such sensibilities. "You worked in that house, you were educated in that house, you came out of that house, so why shouldn't one assume you would practice the same practices? You would not trade with an unreliable businessman; how is this caution so different? Oh, good evening, Your Highness."

Prince Soren slid onto the seat beside her, resting his hand atop hers, and fixed his eyes on Luca.

Luca bowed to the prince. "Your Highness."

Soren gestured. "I did not mean to interrupt."

"We were—that is, I was preparing for my discussion with Your Highness."

"So I have stepped behind the curtain to see the rehearsal?" Soren reached for a cheese crisp. "Please, answer her question."

Luca straightened and visibly braced himself before speaking to Calissa. "So you enslave the children of slaves, on the pretext that they will show the faults of their parents and so should be punished for them before they appear. Is it right—no, is it profitable to punish children for the sins of their fathers?"

"It is not so ridiculous to think children will take after their parents. We see it in appearance, we see it in behavior." Calissa turned a palm up, as if the point were evident.

Soren nodded. "We may be wise to be wary of those who descend from questionable lineage."

Luca turned toward him. "Like Ethan, Your Highness?"

Soren frowned. "What?"

"Ethan is one of the least questionable and most capable people I know. I am, to be perfectly honest, a little in awe of him, and I am certain you value him, Your Highness. Do you think that whatever his father, or grandfather, or great-grandfather may have done has tainted him today?"

"That's not—"

"They would do it to Ethan," Shianan said in a low voice, coming to stand beside Ariana. "When I crept into the palace to see you, because you were dying, and when Ethan saw me there—if they wanted witness of what I'd done, they would do to Ethan what they did to Luca. They would have to do it, by law. Do you say that would be justified by a crime or a debt from generations before?"

"King's oats, that's unfair," Soren said tartly, "and it's not helpful besides. I cannot make that sort of personal argument to the council."

"Is it the council we need to convince?" Luca asked.

"Of course. Even the king cannot merely snap his fingers and take our labor away from our industry and agriculture, and can you imagine if we simply turned thousands of slaves into the street to fend for themselves? What a nightmare, and we'd have them all enslaved again within a fortnight with more proof than ever of why it should be impossible and unthinkable to do otherwise."

Luca nodded. "Yes, of course, what you say is correct. But I meant to ask, Your Highness, whether it is the council who must be convinced now."

Now Soren understood the question. He sat back in his seat and looked down. No one spoke. Calissa tightened her fingers on his.

Ariana was tense beside Shianan. Luca held his breath.

Soren gave a great sigh. "I don't know how to do it. It's—this is so much larger than a trade embargo or a land dispute."

But that was enough to betray his standing, and Shianan felt his own breath slip out of him.

Calissa closed her hands on his. "It is so much larger," she agreed softly. "So much greater."

"So you're convinced, then?" he asked her directly.

"I've read his previous arguments, and I won't deny that they gave me much grief—not only in the abuses they related, but in what they required me to acknowledge." She gave a tight smile and shrugged. "But now as you see, I agreed to help him prepare to convince you."

Soren nodded, chewed his lip, nodded again. "King's oats, I need a drink. A large one."

"I'll bring it, Your Highness," Luca said quickly, his expression happy and strained.

Shianan squeezed Ariana's shoulder and followed Luca toward

the kitchen. But Luca stopped at the servants' room along the passageway, where he sank onto the narrow bed and dropped his face into his hands. Shianan pushed the door shut and sat beside him.

"King's double-dyed oats," Luca breathed raggedly. "Sweet Holy One. I thought it would be months to gain an audience, and so much longer to persuade... I never dared to dream..."

Shianan had not dared, either.

"Last year I was a slave to the Gehrn," Luca choked. "Tonight, I just talked with the prince-heir, and he has listened."

Shianan looked across the room. "Ande will go before the adjudicators next week."

Shianan would not attend. There was no chance, with the high priest taken in the commander's house, and with Ariana, Mage Parma, and the regretful Gehrn to testify to all, that he would be released again, and that was enough. If Luca wanted to see the end of it, that would be up to him; he was his own man.

Luca sobered. "I don't know if I want to see that. I might. It will be good to know that—that he's not coming again. But I don't know if I want to be there."

"There's time yet to decide."

Luca had not hesitated tonight when Ariana and Calissa had called up what had been done to him. His betrayal by his family, his beating at the hands of the extractors—he had made his shame a tool, and now he wielded it against royalty and the council. Shianan could not express his awe and pride.

Luca wiped his eyes. "I'd best get that drink for His Highness."

But when they reached the kitchen, Soren's guards were not relaxing at the table but helping Marla and a handful of strange servants with a train of covered dishes. "It's all here," a woman said cheerily to Shianan. "Someone will be by in the morning to collect the crockery."

"Mage Parma told me what to order," Marla explained, "and said to add anything else that sounded good. She said to feed a small army."

"'Soats," Shianan breathed, looking at the array. There were a dozen dishes, at least, from The Merry Spirit. "Luca, get that drink to His Highness, and we'll start shifting these into the dining room."

But Shianan's dining room boasted only six chairs, and with royalty, foreign dignitaries, and Mages of the Circle, he could not seat only some. "Maybe we can carry plates back into the sitting room. Like a midwinter meal, but in the spring." He lifted a lid, and a cloud of honeyed pork-scented steam rolled out. He replaced the lid and took hold of the heavy stoneware dish.

Marla placed a hand on the dish and pressed it gently to the table before he could lift it. "No, master," she corrected with an apologetic smile. "Here," she called to one of the prince's guards, gesturing to the pot, "you take this one." She picked up a basket of bread and placed it in Shianan's left hand.

He would have to take time to let his shoulder heal, he supposed. But for the first time, he thought he might have the time.

It was Mage Parma who set the example, filling two plates at the loaded dining room table and then handing one to the prince before returning to her place in the sitting room, and the others followed, to Shianan's embarrassed relief. Lacking sufficient seats for great guests had never been a problem he'd thought to solve.

Ariana squeezed beside him, making room for Ranne at the other end of the couch, and Shianan looked around at the people in his home, and he was grateful.

CHAPTER 67

Tamaryl pushed aside subtle guilt—his plate was so full, while the Ai warehouses were only just sufficient for the season—and took a bite of preserved carrots. He did no harm to those Ai who were hungry by eating here, and this meal honored those who aided his people.

He had so much to be grateful for, and so many friends and allies to honor.

Across from him, Mage Hazelrig and Mage Parma balanced plates in their hands and picked out bites. He would need to thank Mage Hazelrig—again—for all his part in their long efforts, and apologize—again—for when Tamaryl had wavered. But he could not speak before the Silver Mage; they still had secrets to keep.

Edeiya'rika, eating a spring shoot, glanced at Tamaryl and gestured to encompass the crowded room. "Did you think it would end this way?"

He chuckled and shook his head. "I only hoped it would end. I hardly dared to dream how."

"You had long enough to think about it." She rolled a shoulder. "Now that I've been in those cuffs, shaped as a human... However did you manage that for fifteen years, Tamaryl'sho?"

"The feeling numbs after the first year or two," he replied glibly.

"No wonder you were glad to return home." She arched an eyebrow. "You know, if you were not who you are, you could not have survived this experiment."

"If I were not who I am, I could not have tried it."

She gave a genteel snort. "And now I suppose you will want someone to continue spreading wings to shield your unconventional politics."

"That must be the reason I have indebted myself so deeply to the next ruler."

"Indeed." She selected a parsnip.

Mage Hazelrig joined the conversation before Tamaryl could fully parse her meaning. "I am told you will be the next silth of the Ai," he said to Edeiya'rika, tearing bread.

She gave a small smile and nod. "It is not settled yet."

"It's all but settled in formal proclamation," Tamaryl corrected. "Especially given what has just transpired with the Ientu and the Chrenadan pledge of trade and aid."

"I hope you might still find time to visit once in a while," Mage Parma said. "Or at the least, we can exchange letters, with Ariana to carry them."

"I wish Maru were here," Tamaryl said with real regret. "He would love this meal. I think he secretly likes human cooking. And this peace belongs to him as well."

"Maru... Oh, he also came here with you," Mage Parma remembered. "Yes, it's too bad he's not here. Is he not still in Alham?"

"He's working with the distribution of the food carried over before the battle."

"Good, good. And oh, that reminds me." Mage Parma adjusted in her chair to better face Mage Hazelrig. "Edeiya'rika had the most fantastic set of wrist cuffs with her, able to help her hold a different form and suppress her natural Ryuven essence. They were quite useful when we needed to travel through villages without raising alarm, and then of course while approaching the Ientu. I thought at the time they looked familiar."

Tamaryl's heart froze in his chest, and he fixed his eyes on his plate. He could not see Mage Hazelrig's reaction, but surely they shared the same alarm.

"But then, of course they looked familiar; they were of a slave cuff design, but for their impractically small rings. No reason for them in a magical artifact, of course, just a curiosity."

These words did not soothe his apprehension. Tamaryl slowly lifted his eyes. Mage Parma wore an indifferent expression, but Mage Hazelrig's lips were tight.

"And so I thought of slaves and magic, and that brought something else to mind." She ran her bread through a puddle of gravy. "I have not seen your famulus for quite a while."

Tamaryl's gut twisted.

"There has been more than enough distraction, what with the battles and Ariana's abductions and all, and it was easy enough to miss what was missing. But don't you think that was a great risk to take, Ewan?"

Mage Hazelrig did not move, pinned like a moth.

"Letting the boy run away like that?" Elysia waved a hand. "I should have expected it eventually, given your speeches on slavery years ago, but still it was illegal to simply release him. I hope you gave him enough coin to get him far from harm."

Mage Hazelrig drew a slow breath. "I sent him far, far away. He is well out of slavery."

Tamaryl's fingers loosened on his plate.

Mage Parma picked up a piece of fried dough. "What have you done, Ewan?" she asked quietly.

"I saved lives." He looked at the dough in her hand. "I saved thousands of lives. Just as you hoped I would, when you voted me into these white robes."

"I wanted someone who could do what I could not." She looked down at her plate and opened her mouth as if to speak further, but no words came. Finally she sat up again and nodded. "I'm glad you stood by your principles, however illegal, and I wish the best to that boy." Her eyes flicked lightly to Tamaryl. "He was a cute kid."

Edeiya'rika converted her laugh into a sneeze, but only a moderately convincing one.

It felt strange, putting his arm around Ariana's shoulders in the view of others, but it was one of many strange new aspects Shianan would not mind becoming accustomed to. Guests in his home—his own home—were another.

But as Ariana's head grew lower and she began to nod, jerking upright with an embarrassed smile, the guests began to fidget, and when the first roll of soft spring thunder came through the windows, they hurried to make their farewells. Shianan slid free of Ariana and rose to thank Mage Parma again for the generous meal, to bow to Prince Soren and Princess Calissa, escorted away by their guards, and then to help Ranne and Luca, who were already gathering the plates and leftover dishes.

He was carrying a large platter with a few pork scraps when Mage Ewan Hazelrig stopped him. "Thank you for your hospitality tonight," the White Mage said. "It was a pleasure to be invited to your home."

"Thank you for coming, my lord mage."

Mage Hazelrig gave a friendly roll of his head. "I think by now we can dispense with both formality and obfuscation. We're family now, and now we can be open about it. I wouldn't even mind if you called me Father."

Shianan's heart leapt and for a moment he couldn't answer. It shouldn't have been so startling or so disturbing a statement, but he'd been unready for it. He was still growing accustomed to a family—he had not thought yet on how to address his new father, was not even sure whether he wanted to use the word. And then he realized his hesitation might be a different insult. "I—I'm sorry, I did not mean to suggest... I only had not thought..."

"Cheese?" Tamaryl extended a plate of cheese crisps between them. "There are a few left."

Shianan looked down at it and then at Tamaryl. Irritation and relief vied for expression. Tamaryl smiled.

Mage Hazelrig took a crisp. "Thank you. I'll take these into the kitchen and dispose of the remainder."

Shianan followed and set down the greasy platter. "I'm sorry if I offended you," he said quietly to the White Mage, his back to the others working in the kitchen.

"Not at all, and I did not mean to discomfit you."

"I know I was never the obvious choice for your daughter, and I am—"

Mage Hazelrig put a hand on Shianan's shoulder, silencing him. "Shianan Becknam, do you undercut yourself before the soldiers you command?"

Shianan blinked. "No, my lord mage."

"Nor should you here." The mage looked at him evenly. "I said once I would be proud to call you my son. Now I am. I know you love my daughter; you have demonstrated that in every way. I could not hope for more, and I am pleased with her choice." He pulled Shianan close, wrapping him in an embrace. "You are my son now, and I am glad."

Shianan flushed hot and looked down. "Thank you."

The first drops of rain knocked at the window, and they separated. "We'd best hurry," Mage Hazelrig called to the others in the kitchen, "or we'll have to hire a boat for home. Good night, Shianan!" And he left the kitchen with Shianan's name echoing behind him.

CHAPTER 68

Three weeks later

The morning dawned, barely, though a grey layer of cloud with a firm promise of more rain in defiance of the first turn of summer. Despite the weak and watery light, Shianan woke early and completely.

He lay on his back, cushioned by the luxurious feather mattress, with Ariana's head pillowed on the hollow below his left shoulder. The enormity of the day hung over him, but he closed his eyes again and counted each of the coming wonders.

His adoption would be completed in a formal ceremony with the queen, who would then introduce him as her son. There had been a question of a larger court ceremony, with more courtiers attending and the whole affair more grand, but Shianan had asked for a private affair, and placing it on the morning of the royal wedding ensured it would not be the chief focus of the day. He did not care if others in the court thought his adoption a quiet event to be half-hidden behind the pageantry of the wedding. He did not want to sign his adoption writ and hear himself formally declared son of Queen Azalie as the king looked on.

He suspected the king was also glad of the minimized fuss, not forced to watch as his bastard was adopted by his queen.

Then would come the wedding itself. Prince Soren had urged it forward, and so it had been accomplished in the same time as originally planned, albeit with a different bride. There Shianan would march behind the queen, alongside Alasdair, as an escort of her Queen's Guard, confirming to all that the rumors were true.

He kissed Ariana's hair and then wriggled from under her. Cold air slapped his bare flesh where she had been, and the chilled cloth did not help as he dressed. There were losses with a new wife in his bed—but they were worth it.

She stirred, half-awakened by his departure, and he bent over the bed. "It's early yet. Go back to sleep."

"Mmwhat about the ceremony?"

"Plenty of time."

She believed him and drifted off again. He finished dressing—Luca had selected the new clothing, ordering it without Shianan's knowledge and arranging a fitting by listing it as a meeting—and went downstairs. He needed a way to work off nervous energy, but without performing drills in his new formal clothes.

But as he moved lightly toward the stairs, he heard movement from another room. "Luca?"

"I'm here!" Luca emerged a moment later, partly dressed. "What do you need?"

"Nothing. I was just surprised to hear that you were up already."

Luca nodded, a little embarrassed. "I had a hard time sleeping."

"You? Why?"

Luca looked down, to the side, back at Shianan. "This is my first day as the queen's son's secretary and majordomo. I have much to do, and I don't want to do it poorly."

Shianan tried not to laugh. "It may be your first official duty, but there's hardly so much that could go wrong. It's only—" He stopped, feeling Luca's incredulous gaze. "What is it?"

"You don't know how much paperwork there has been, because none of it reached your desk," Luca said, mostly patiently. "I found the deed to Fhure, for one thing, because I've gone over your office like a bee over a garden, and turned it over to be officially recorded with your new name. Or did you think you really had only to walk in a room and all would be done?"

Shianan stared at him, feeling stupid. "No," he admitted. "But I assumed someone would take care of that, knowing I was ignorant of court ways. And someone did."

"Every letter I write, every conversation I have, I feel the court secretaries spot me for an impostor, like they can look straight through me and see a slave chained to a tinker's cart. This is such an important event, and you should have a proper ceremony without anyone scorning you because your slave made a mistake in the—"

"My servant," Shianan said quickly. "My secretary. The man who thought to prepare for this ceremony when I did not."

Luca gave a tight smile. "And that is why I am nervous. Because I don't know what I might have forgotten."

"You've already taken care of more than you've forgotten," Shianan assured him. "Thank you." He paused. "I owe you."

Luca relaxed. "You do, Master Shianan."

"Go and dress. You're less likely to embarrass us if you're wearing all your clothes."

The sky was lightening outside. Shianan thought he could hear Marla in the kitchen. He paced between fireplace and window, peering out at nothing.

"Do you want breakfast?" Luca asked, coming down behind him. He was fully dressed now, and Shianan thought that while his clothes weren't so fine, he would not look out of place among the Naziar's royal secretaries—or moving through the Naziar, presenting his evidence and arguments, when he was ready.

Shianan shook his head. "I don't think so."

"All right. I'm sure no one will think anything of it if your stomach starts growling in the middle of the signing, much like General Septime noted at the Founding Festival."

"King's oats," growled Shianan. "Something small, then."

Time crawled until Ariana descended, dressed in court finery of deep red and midnight blue with the black scarf twisted into a perfect circle pinned above her left breast. She sat down at the table, thanked Marla for the fried eggs, and looked excitedly at Shianan. "I am so happy for you."

Her joy coaxed his into the open. "I'm glad."

"Do you want me to be decorous? Dignified and staid, not kissing the new prince?"

She was grinning, but her question was genuine. She would not put him in a position of discomfort. Once the adoption was formalized, their marriage was both legal and faultless, and they could carry on publicly like any couple. But it would be a long while before he felt he belonged in court—perhaps longer now, with the queen's own name on him. "I will be pleased and proud to have you beside me," he answered, hoping she read the gap in his words. He did not want to say his reluctance aloud.

She nodded without protest, and he felt a little rush of unexpected relief. He did not want to begin this day by disappointing her.

"And I will not be a prince."

"Perhaps not to the court." She could speak in gaps as well.

At last the three of them departed for the Naziar. The air had no bite to it despite the early hour, and a few flowers showed brave faces in front of the townhouses they passed. A hopeful butterfly hovered over one, mirroring its cousin in Shianan's stomach.

But this was a good royal audience. This was a day unlike any he'd ever dreamed of, even as a child.

As they reached the Naziar, Luca moved in front of them and spoke to the guards and secretaries, moving them smoothly through the stops and doors as if they were—

As if they were a celebrated Mage of the Circle and a count favored by the queen.

The queen awaited them in a small, formal audience chamber, richly decorated and crowded with officials Shianan did not know. Queen Azalie rose from her chair of deep green when they arrived. "Come in, come in. Good morning."

The ceremony was, as Shianan had hoped, mercifully brief and uncomplicated, saving the pomp for the royal wedding that afternoon. Duke Farlyle read out a formal announcement of the adoption, someone else proclaimed that Shianan would now be a marquess—wildly he thought he would have to ask Luca to find where the estate was—and then he was gestured toward the table where thick, creamy paper with elegant script waited for signatures.

Queen Azalie signed first, with a flourishing *I, the Queen*, and then passed the pen to Shianan. Luca had instructed him beforehand; he would not bear the queen's name and his new title until after he had signed, so he wrote, *Commander Shianan Becknam, Count of Bailaha.*

Then Farlyle and Stowmarries signed as witnesses, and the whole thing was done, a flick of a page to change Shianan's life.

There was polite applause and nodding around the room, and Shianan wondered how many might resent his new position and their obligation to cheer it. But then he saw Mage Ewan Hazelrig, beaming next to Ariana, and beside them Luca looked as happy as Shianan had ever seen him, and there was General Septime, unexpected but smiling and nodding, and Shianan realized that it did not matter if not all courtiers welcomed his rise. He did not need them all; he had enough.

Queen Azalie faced him, and he bowed as he had been instructed and in gratitude. She nodded to acknowledge his respect and then took him by the shoulders, pulling him near for a soft kiss on his forehead. "My son," she said quietly, a formal declaration and a private promise.

Shianan was pulled away by someone else who hugged him close almost before he could recognize Prince Soren. The prince crushed him in a happy embrace. "I'm so glad for you," he said softly, for Shianan's ear alone. "So glad for all of us."

The ceremony done, queen and prince had to leave first, and Shianan nearly forgot to go with them instead of bowing them out. Safe in a more private room, he took a shaky breath and tried to guess what he was feeling.

Soren passed him a drink from the set table. "Take this."

"Soren, it's a bit early for that, isn't it?" Queen Azalie chided gently.

"Not for a man who's just become a queen's son," Soren answered. "And not for a man about to submit to the royal dressing of the royal bridegroom." He looked at Shianan. "Unless you can figure a way to free me from their minute attentions."

"I am only a commander, my lord. I work no miracles."

Soren regarded him. "I don't know about that. You are the first Laguna bastard to marry. And to be adopted by another royal."

"I did nothing for that," Shianan said too quickly, betraying his anxiety. He knew Soren had not meant it in that way, but he could not bear the possibility of a rumor that he had sought out this adoption for his own advancement. But to soften his protest, he smiled and added, "That is one thing to be grateful for, I suppose. Not being a prince, I had no one to fuss so closely over my wedding."

"Quit your sneering."

"Your Majesty?" The servant's voice was quiet but insistent. "If I could interrupt, there is a question..."

"Of course there is," Queen Azalie answered with a soft sigh. "I'm coming." She embraced Soren, and then Shianan. "And I'll need to dress as well. I'll see both of you in a bit. Don't give Alasdair any of what you're having."

Soren laughed and they bowed as she went out, followed by the apologetic servant. Then the prince sobered and turned back. "Shianan...I don't jest. About the miracles, maybe, but...I lost a great opportunity in waiting so many years to know you."

Shianan shrugged, uncomfortably self-conscious. "Perhaps if we had spoken years before, we would not have become friends."

"That might be." Soren sighed. "But if there's anything I can do for you..."

"Promise me," Shianan said suddenly, surprising himself, "you will sire no bastards."

Soren blinked and then nodded.

Shianan looked away, embarrassed by his unthinking outburst. "I should let you return to your preparations. It won't be long now."

Soren nodded. "Come and see us. Princess Calissa and Lady Ariana are friends; I hope you'll like her as well."

"Not as well as you will," Shianan said with a grin, and he bowed his farewell.

CHAPTER 69

The task was so simple, and Shianan's heart raced as if he faced a battle.

He was already in place, standing behind Queen Azalie, erect in his formal clothing. Alasdair was beside him, looking as if he could not decide how to approach Shianan now. That was fair enough; Shianan was on unfamiliar ground as well.

Before them, Soren was pale and perspiring, but his eyes shone with the joy of a prince who would marry both for his state and for himself. Azalie whispered to him, kissed him, and then turned him by the shoulders to face forward, leading her way into the great hall. The horns blew, marking the queen's entrance, and they started forward.

Shianan had marched in many parades, but today he felt the weight of spectators' eyes as he never had marching in a unit of soldiers where he belonged. How many stared in confusion, wondering how he had come to walk with the queen and princes? How many whispers were hidden beneath the music?

Let them whisper. The queen had chosen him.

At last they reached her seat, and she gave a formal nod to Prince Soren, the nominal head of her Guard, who bowed in return. He stepped aside as she took her chair, spreading her skirts and robe with practiced carelessness, and Alasdair took a seat behind, and Shianan one beside him. Soren bowed again and went to his place for the marriage ceremony.

Shianan wanted to look at the king seated on the dais but also wanted to avoid him, probing and withdrawing as for a missing tooth.

Princess Calissa entered and made her graceful way to the dais where Prince Soren waited. She curtsied to the king, to the queen, to Prince Soren, who bowed in return.

The royal wedding was a state affair, sworn before the king as witness. The vows were longer and more complex, but it was fundamentally the same exchange that Ariana and Shianan had shared over Kuolema's warm shoulder. These vows committed countries as well. Soren and Calissa did not marry for duty only, though; their tender expressions betrayed that they married for love, and it warmed Shianan to be glad for them, that they also could have the ones they loved.

They swore to one another, standing before the king, and then turned away for ceremonial wine, first taken separately and then shared. King Jerome, his part in the ceremony finished for the moment, stood and watched them.

Shianan set his jaw. Luca had faced Ande, a court of adjudicators, torture. Shianan could look at a king. He rubbed his hands across his legs and shifted his eyes toward the high seat on the dais.

King Jerome looked away, his eyes flicking haltingly across the hall, to the wine, to the musicians, to the floor.

Shianan stared for just a moment, stunned at the king's avoidance, and then he withdrew his own gaze, focusing again on the back of Queen Azalie's head. There were pearls, black and white, worked through her braided hair.

The king had avoided his eyes.

Shianan thought back to their last meeting, how different that had been. Something had changed. Shianan had walked on from where he had been, and now King Jerome had to turn to meet him.

Alasdair drew his feet under him, and Shianan started. The ceremony had ended, and they were to escort the queen once more.

The Queen's Guard, now without the bridegroom, escorted her out in the same way. Once they were clear of the hall, she stopped and reached to remove the crown, rubbing at the deep red indentations on her forehead. "They never warn how uncomfortable the double-dyed thing is. Well, let's wait to greet the happy bride and groom, and then on to the feast, where there will be many sweets and no crowns."

Alasdair reached out for the crown. "It doesn't feel so heavy. And it's not as big as Father's."

"It feels much heavier when it's pressing on your skull, I assure you. And you're right, his is heavier, much heavier." She raised an eyebrow. "And he never takes his off, which goes some way to explain his disposition."

Alasdair laughed. "Yes, he does. He wears the crown only at formal court events."

"Well, then, you've caught out my mistake." Azalie gave him a quick smile.

Soren and Calissa burst through the door, their beaming smiles a perfect match. They checked their pace long enough to make a quick obeisance to the queen, and then the three flung themselves together, arms entangling. Calissa turned and engulfed Alasdair in a hug.

Then Soren embraced Shianan again, and Calissa kissed his cheek, and all was right.

"Now go on to the hall," Queen Azalie chided gently. "You know they'll want to fuss over you and practically re-dress you before you may enter, and some of us are hungry."

They laughed and ran on ahead down the corridor.

"You too, Alasdair," the queen instructed. "I'll go back and meet your father as he comes."

But though Alasdair nodded, he did not move away.

"Yes?" she prompted.

He looked from her to Shianan. "Well, this morning, Dunstan said...he said I would be embarrassed now that I had another brother—a brother older than me."

Queen Azalie's expression tightened. "Why would you repeat—"

"But I told him," Alasdair rushed, "I told him that he would be embarrassed, not me, because now I'd have the demon commander to tutor me and I'd whip him in sparring. So"—he looked at Shianan—"so can I? Have my sword training with you, like you said back when Soren was ill?"

The queen put a hand on Alasdair's shoulder. "The commander has many duties, and training is but one of them. And then, he must train our soldiers first." She looked at Shianan.

"I can make time for a prince." Shianan turned to Alasdair and risked a smile. "I think I said we'd have to see you better equipped than Soren."

It was such a small thing when considered beside the greater matters of the day, but Alasdair's request warmed Shianan. There was hope yet for the bastard and the little turd.

Alasdair grinned back, a little awkwardly—he was feeling his way, too—and nodded. "I can't wait." He made a quick bow. "My lady mother." Then he darted after the newlyweds.

"Alasdair!" The queen shook her head with a smile. "He's forgotten which way to go. Ah, well. Someone will find him."

"I'll take my leave as well." Shianan bowed. "Your Majesty."

Queen Azalie reached and caught his forearm, a gossamer hold he could not break. "Just once," she said softly, "and I know you may be too old to take up a new way of speaking. But once, please, for me."

The floor tiles seemed to soften beneath Shianan, but he could not deny her mild request. "Then—I'll take my leave, my lady mother." The word felt like wool in his mouth, but it tasted of honey.

She smiled, and it was a delighted smile, a younger cousin to the one she had given Soren. "Thank you for your service, Shianan."

He bowed again and retreated, and though he felt foolish, he could not shake the smile from his lips.

Chapter 70

Shianan's new status did not afford him a seat on the royal dais—officially, he was the son of the woman who had married the king, not a son of the royal line itself—and he found no disappointment in that. But as a marquess and count, he had a place at another high table, with the Black Mage beside him, and they weathered the glances and whispers with good spirits.

"You won't mind if I dance with Tamaryl, will you?" Ariana murmured. "I think that final act of daring might drop the few remaining jaws in the room."

Shianan braced for a flare of jealousy, but it did not come, and he was glad. "Go ahead. That will provide some entertainment for all of us, and I hear royal celebrations are interminable affairs."

But the food was delicious, and the opening dancing brief. The prince and princess were dispatched to perform their state duties in their new marriage of alliance, and then the wedding feast settled down to drinking, dancing, and socializing. Ariana did dance with the Pairvyn, and Shianan did regret it, because she set him to dance with a baroness at the same time and he was terrified of treading wrongly.

"Are you enjoying yourself?" Ariana asked as they met again at their dais seats.

"I'm not miserable," he admitted. But he had never felt comfortable at state events, not like Ariana sparkling at a royal ball.

"We can't leave too soon," Ariana cautioned, "or it will look as if we're ashamed to be here. But after the right number of dances and enough chatting, we can slip out."

"How does one know how much is enough?"

"I asked Bethia. Just stay with me, and be polite."

He followed her into the rows of dancers and among smiling, curious nobles, and he lost count of how many times he thanked them for their good wishes and insisted he was glad to do the military services for which they thanked him. At last Ariana's secret tally sheet was completed, and they escaped into the summer night.

"Rain's coming," Shianan observed. "Let's hurry."

They only just made it to their front door, wincing and laughing as the incoming downpour pelted them. Shianan fumbled with the key, hampered by trying to keep one arm over both Ariana and his face, and Ariana laughed even more and called for Luca.

Luca let them in just as the key finally slid into the lock. "I have dry clothes laid out," he promised, "and hot tea in the kitchen."

"You're a treasure," Ariana told him.

When they descended again, no longer in their formal court clothing, Marla came into the sitting room with a handful of short, dripping wands. "I've soaked them for toasting. Luca says he's never done it."

They propped a bag of barley before the kitchen hearth and softened a crate of turnips with a blanket, and then they settled before the fire to roast tidbits and stare into the dancing flames. Ariana leaned upon Shianan, her head on his chest, and he could have held her weight forever.

Luca set his pierced bread into the fire. "Is that a fresh wand, or has it already dried? You'll want to be quick," Marla admonished gently. "Or else it will—well, there it goes. Your bread will be well toasted."

"Try this side," Ariana suggested. "More ember, less flame."

But Luca kept an arm's length of distance from the reclining lady mage. "It's all right."

"There's room here," Shianan pointed out, indicating the cushioned turnips.

Luca hesitated. "I..."

Shianan, grinning, stretched to catch Luca by back of the neck and pull him nearer. "Come on."

Luca flinched, and too late Shianan realized what he had done, what he had clumsily recalled. Fool that he was—

But Luca relaxed and slid closer. "I'll make enough to share, if I can keep another wand from catching."

Rain pelted the kitchen window, and Marla pulled her shawl about her shoulders. With cheese melted over the toasted bread and shared out, Luca leaned against the turnips and pulled one knee to his chest. They sat in the quiet of falling rain and crackling wood. From time to time, thunder rolled distantly.

Shianan stretched his feet toward the low flames, his arm around Ariana and his shoulder against Luca, and drowsed in the firelight. Marla laid woolen blankets over each of them and then settled with her head on Luca's shoulder. Outside, the rain drummed all the night, and it bothered Shianan not at all.

THANKS FOR READING!

Please be sure to review the series at your favorite site. I read every review! and I'd love to hear from you.

If you haven't already, come visit **LauraVAB.com** and join us for side stories in the Shard of Elan, a prequel, and deleted scenes, as well as more books, sneak peeks of coming work, and special offers.

www.ingramcontent.com/pod-product-compliance
Lightning Source LLC
Chambersburg PA
CBHW022036120726
47899CB00004BA/1187
* 9 7 8 1 6 3 1 6 5 0 3 0 7 *